THE TITHE™

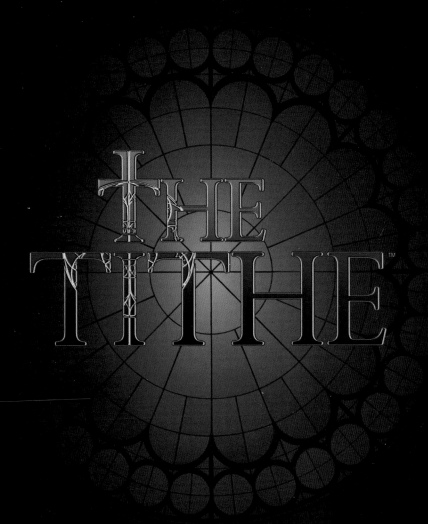

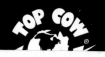

THE TITHE

MATT HAWKINS
CO-CREATOR & WRITER

RAHSAN EKEDAL
CO-CREATOR, LAYOUTS & COVERS

PHILLIP SEVY
ARTIST & VARIANT COVERS

JEREMY COLWELL
COLORIST

TROY PETERI
LETTERER

RAHSAN EKEDAL
COVER ART

RYAN CADY
EDITOR

LINDA SEJIC
THE TITHE LOGO DESIGN

TRICIA RAMOS
PRODUCTION

Want more info? Check out:
www.topcow.com
for news & exclusive Top Cow merchandise!

IMAGE COMICS, INC.
Robert Kirkman – Chief Operating Officer
Erik Larsen – Chief Financial Officer
Todd McFarlane – President
Marc Silvestri – Chief Executive Officer
Jim Valentino – Vice-President

Eric Stephenson – Publisher
Corey Murphy – Director of Sales
Jeff Boison – Director of Publishing Planning & Book Trade Sales
Jeremy Sullivan – Director of Digital Sales
Kat Salazar – Director of PR & Marketing
Emily Miller – Director of Operations
Branwyn Bigglestone – Senior Accounts Manager
Sarah Mello – Accounts Manager
Drew Gill – Art Director
Jonathan Chan – Production Manager
Meredith Wallace – Print Manager
Briah Skelly – Publicity Assistant
Sasha Head – Sales & Marketing Production Designer
Randy Okamura – Digital Production Designer
David Brothers – Branding Manager
Ally Power – Content Manager
Addison Duke – Production Artist
Vincent Kukua – Production Artist
Tricia Ramos – Production Artist
Jeff Stang – Direct Market Sales Representative
Emilio Bautista – Digital Sales Associate
Leanna Caunter – Accounting Assistant
Chloe Ramos-Peterson – Administrative Assistant
IMAGECOMICS.COM

For Top Cow Productions, Inc.:
Marc Silvestri - CEO
Matt Hawkins - President & COO
Bryan Hill - Story Editor
Ryan Cady - Editor
Elena Salcedo - Operations Manager
Vincent Valentine - Production Assistant

CAST OF CHARACTERS

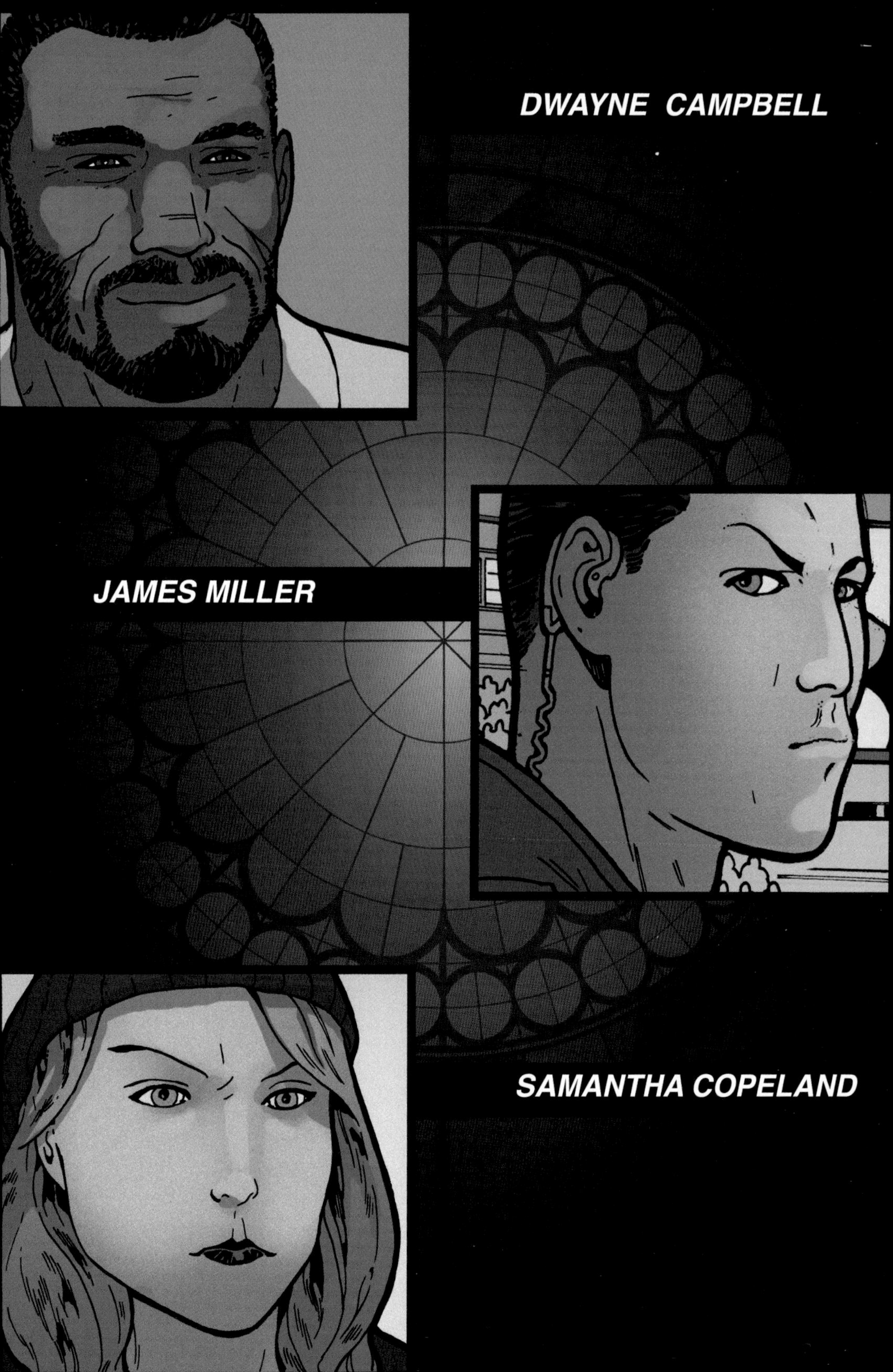
DWAYNE CAMPBELL
JAMES MILLER
SAMANTHA COPELAND

O BELIEVERS, TAKE NOT JEWS AND CHRISTIANS AS
FRIENDS; THEY ARE FRIENDS OF EACH OTHER. THOSE OF
YOU WHO MAKE THEM HIS FRIENDS IS ONE OF THEM.
GOD DOES NOT GUIDE AN UNJUST PEOPLE.
- SURAH 5:54 (KORAN)

Islamophobia: Chapter 1

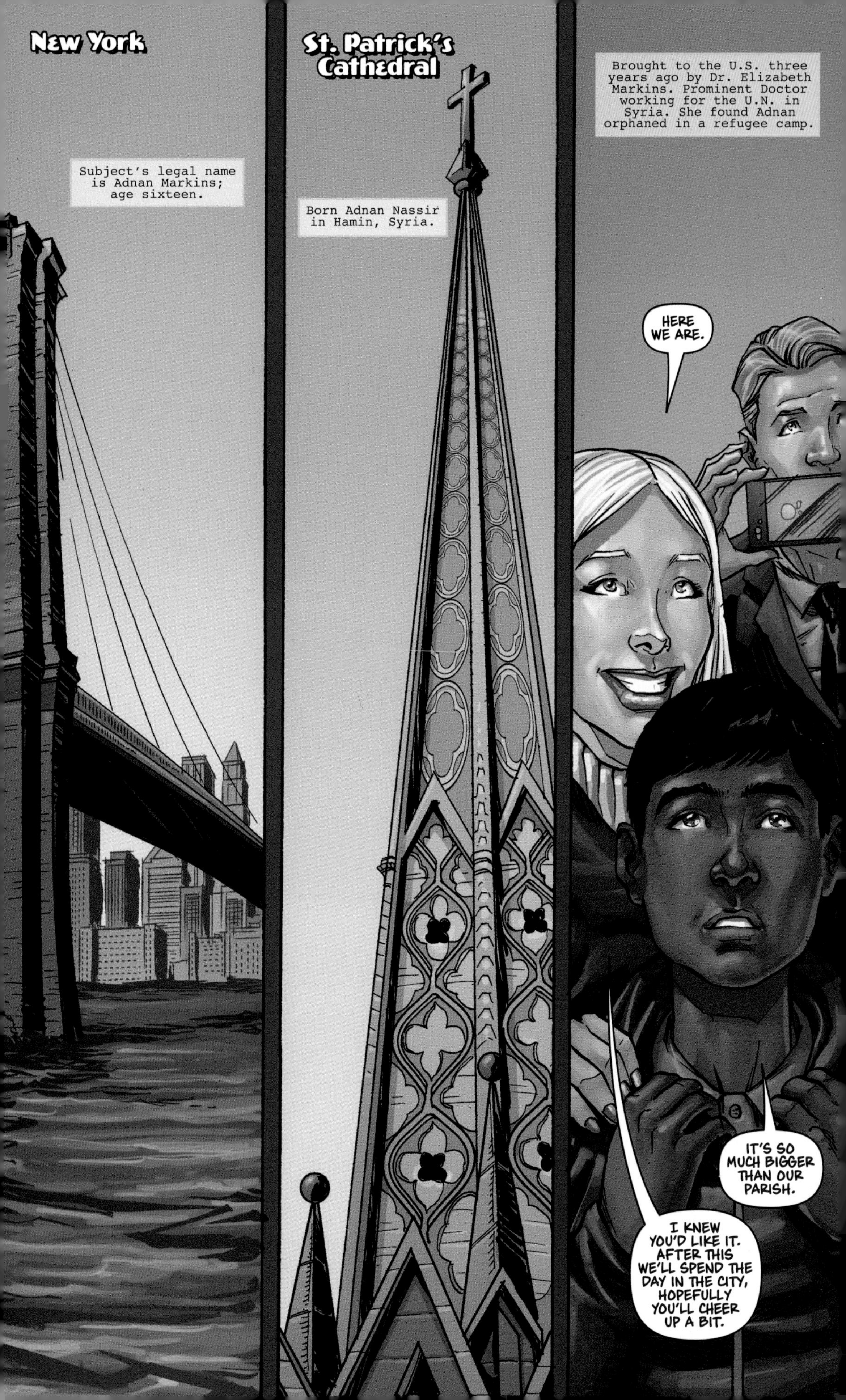
New York
Subject's legal name is Adnan Markins; age sixteen.
St. Patrick's Cathedral
Born Adnan Nassir in Hamin, Syria.
Brought to the U.S. three years ago by Dr. Elizabeth Markins. Prominent Doctor working for the U.N. in Syria. She found Adnan orphaned in a refugee camp.
HERE WE ARE.
IT'S SO MUCH BIGGER THAN OUR PARISH.
I KNEW YOU'D LIKE IT. AFTER THIS WE'LL SPEND THE DAY IN THE CITY, HOPEFULLY YOU'LL CHEER UP A BIT.

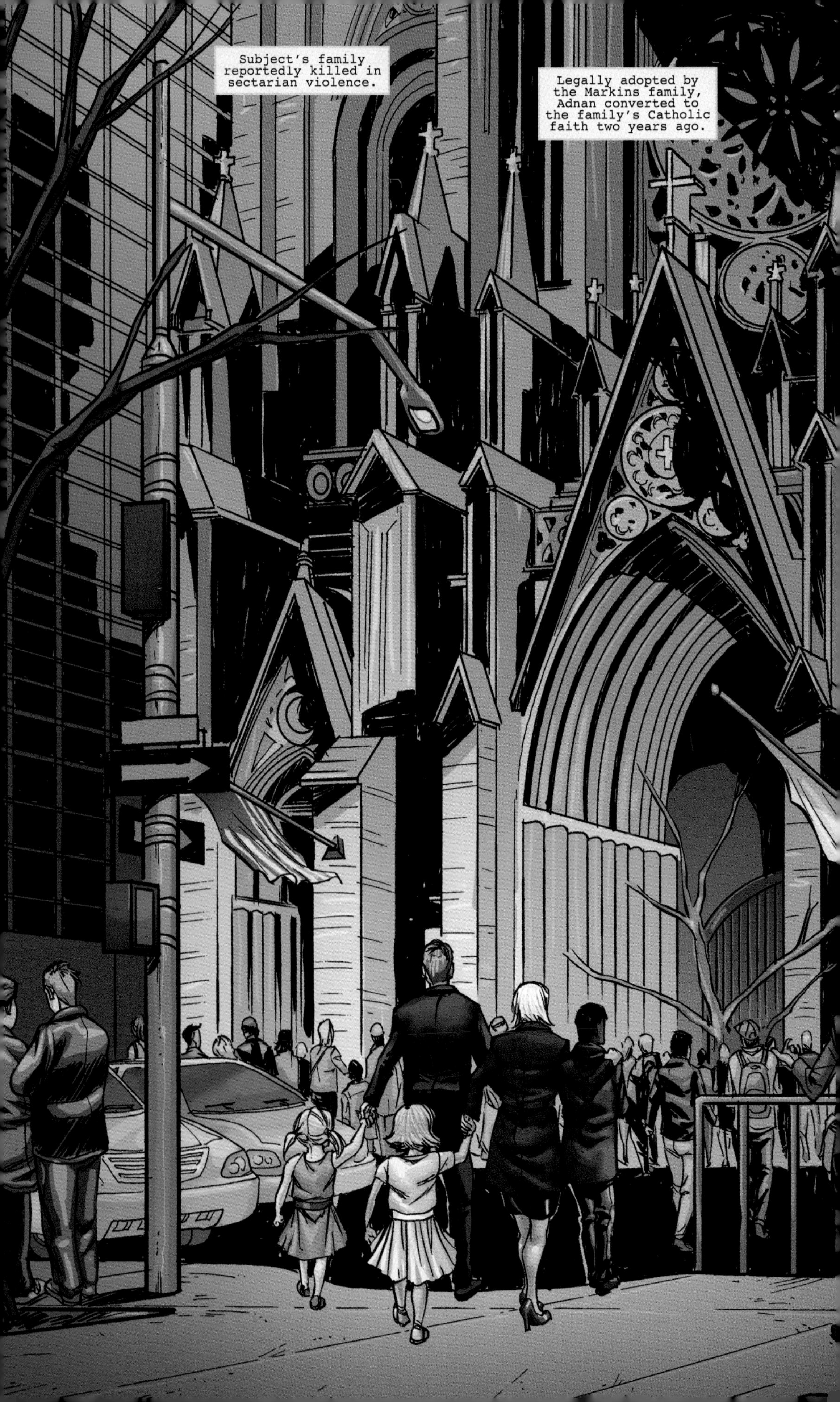
Subject's family reportedly killed in sectarian violence.
Legally adopted by the Markins family, Adnan converted to the family's Catholic faith two years ago.

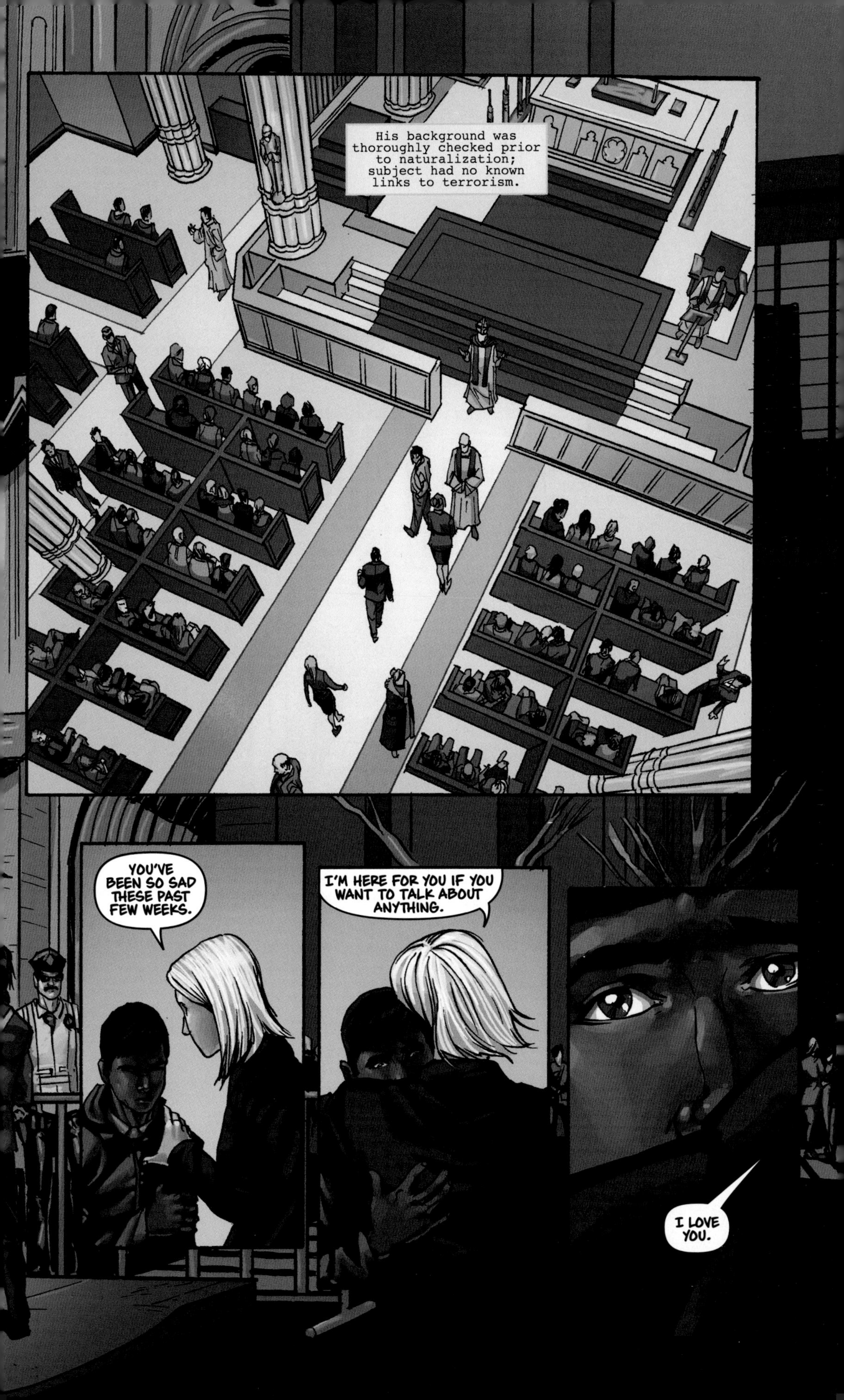
His background was thoroughly checked prior to naturalization; subject had no known links to terrorism.
YOU'VE BEEN SO SAD THESE PAST FEW WEEKS.
I'M HERE FOR YOU IF YOU WANT TO TALK ABOUT ANYTHING.
I LOVE YOU.

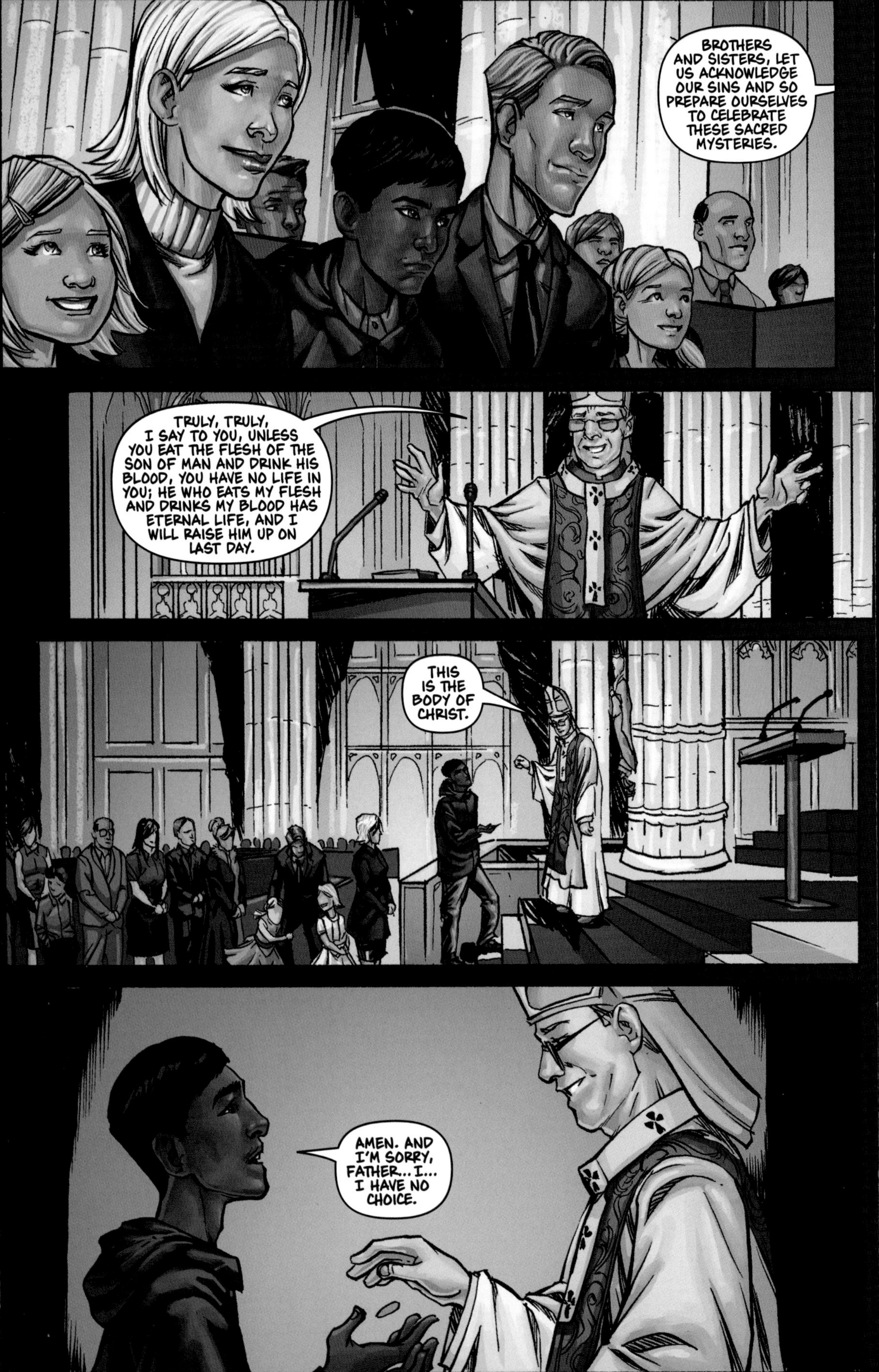
BROTHERS AND SISTERS, LET US ACKNOWLEDGE OUR SINS AND SO PREPARE OURSELVES TO CELEBRATE THESE SACRED MYSTERIES.
TRULY, TRULY, I SAY TO YOU, UNLESS YOU EAT THE FLESH OF THE SON OF MAN AND DRINK HIS BLOOD, YOU HAVE NO LIFE IN YOU; HE WHO EATS MY FLESH AND DRINKS MY BLOOD HAS ETERNAL LIFE, AND I WILL RAISE HIM UP ON LAST DAY.
THIS IS THE BODY OF CHRIST.
AMEN. AND I'M SORRY, FATHER... I... I HAVE NO CHOICE.

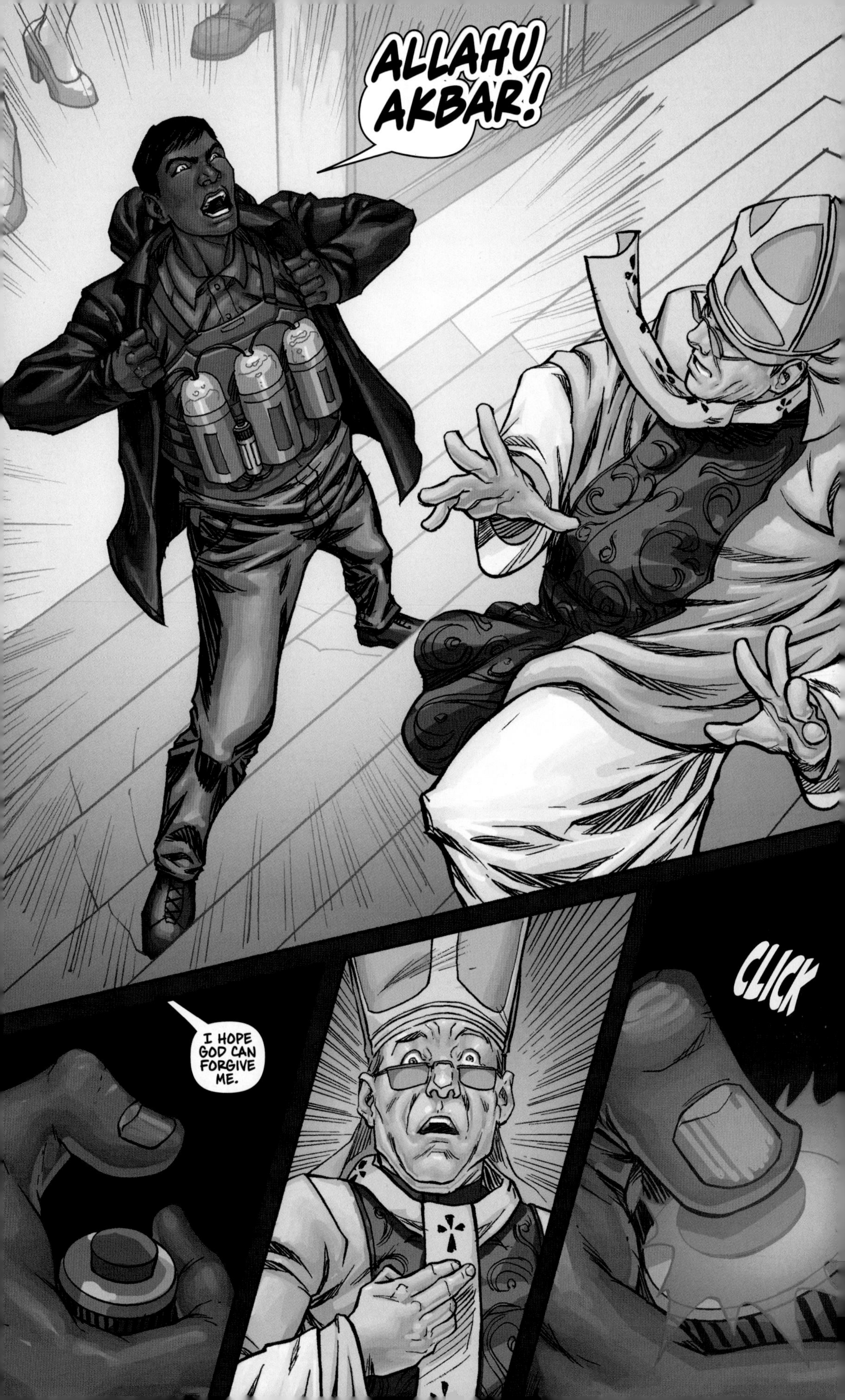
ALLAHU AKBAR!
I HOPE GOD CAN FORGIVE ME.
CLICK

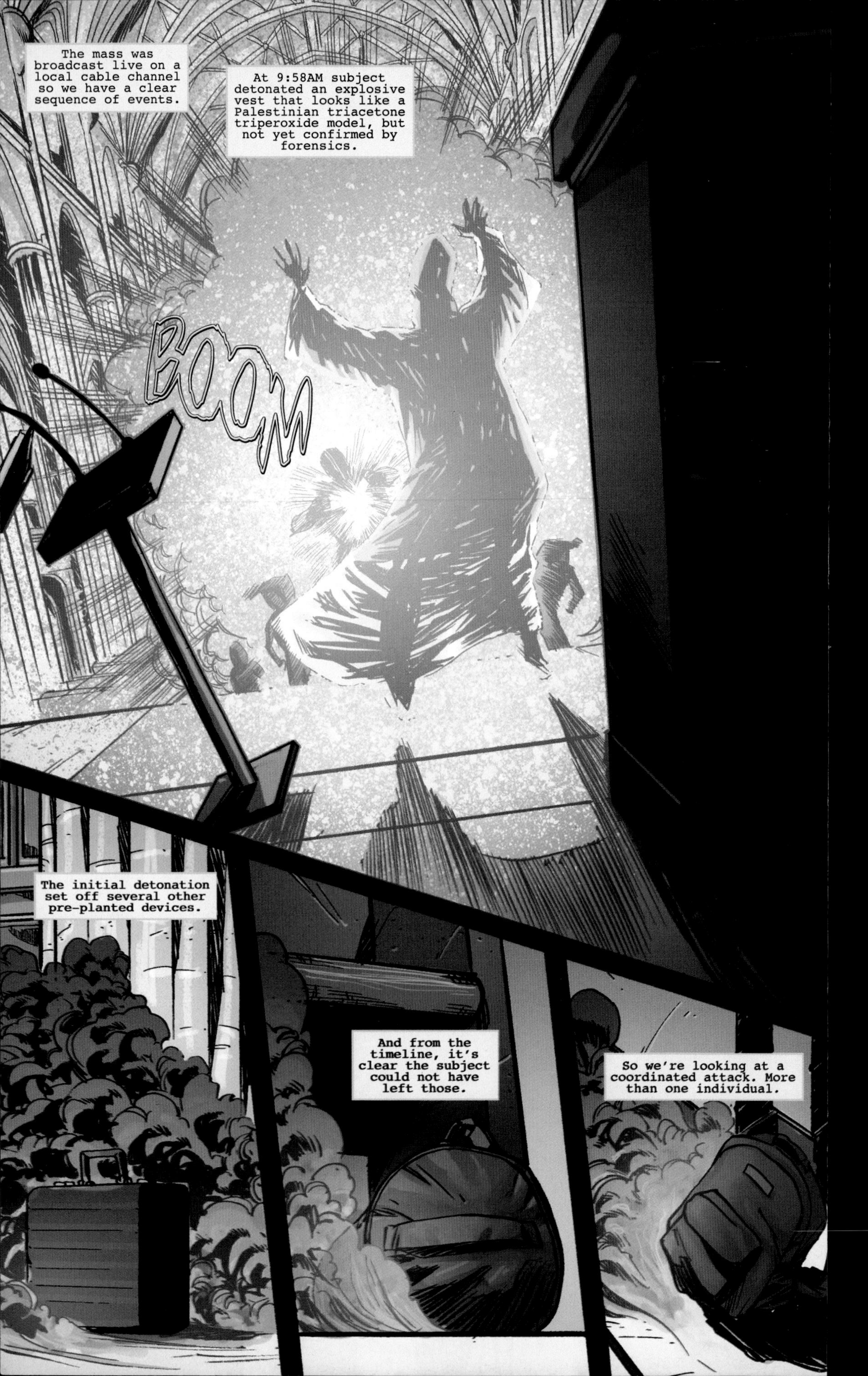
The mass was broadcast live on a local cable channel so we have a clear sequence of events.
At 9:58AM subject detonated an explosive vest that looks like a Palestinian triacetone triperoxide model, but not yet confirmed by forensics.
BOOM
The initial detonation set off several other pre-planted devices.
And from the timeline, it's clear the subject could not have left those.
So we're looking at a coordinated attack. More than one individual.

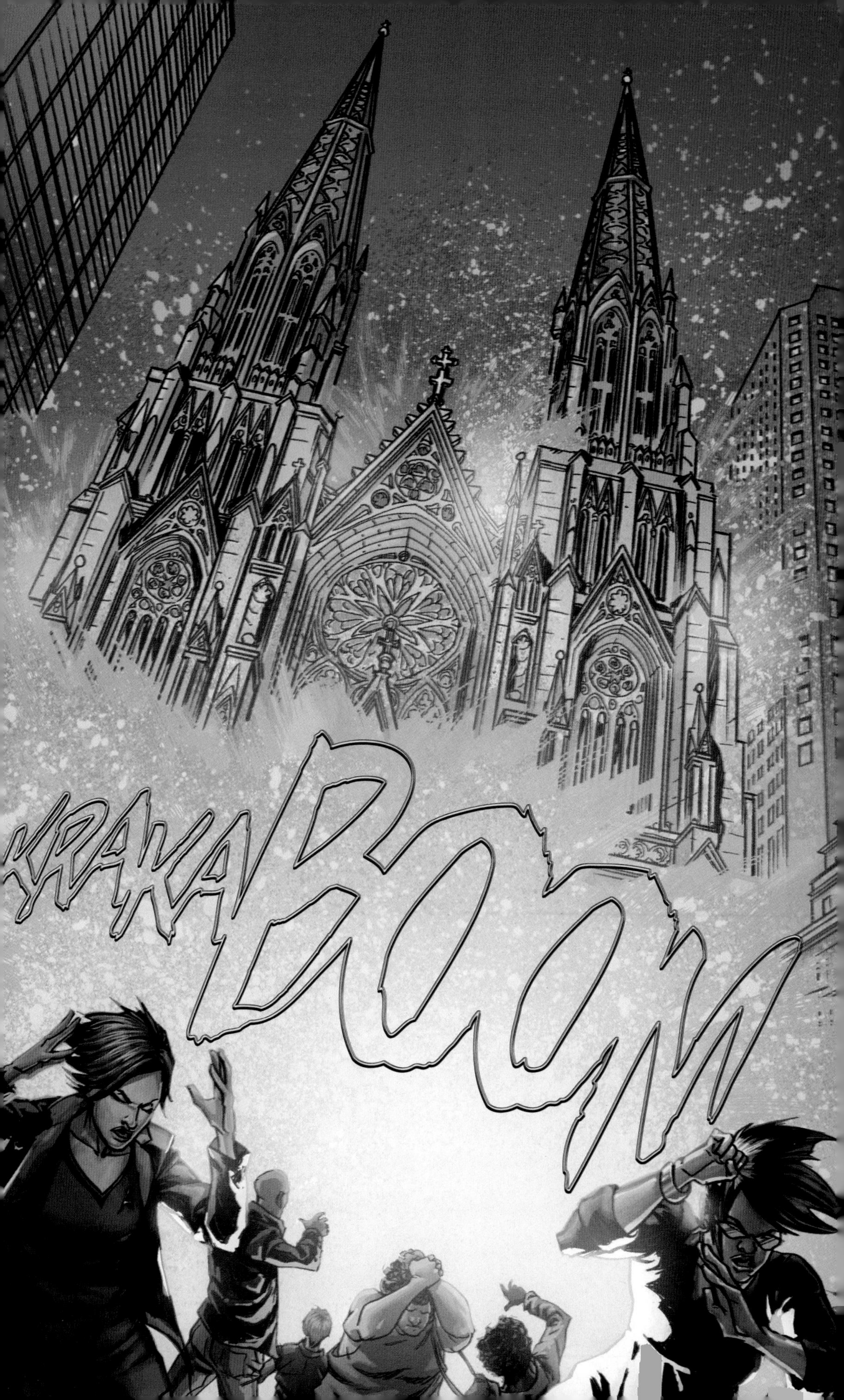
KRAKABOOM

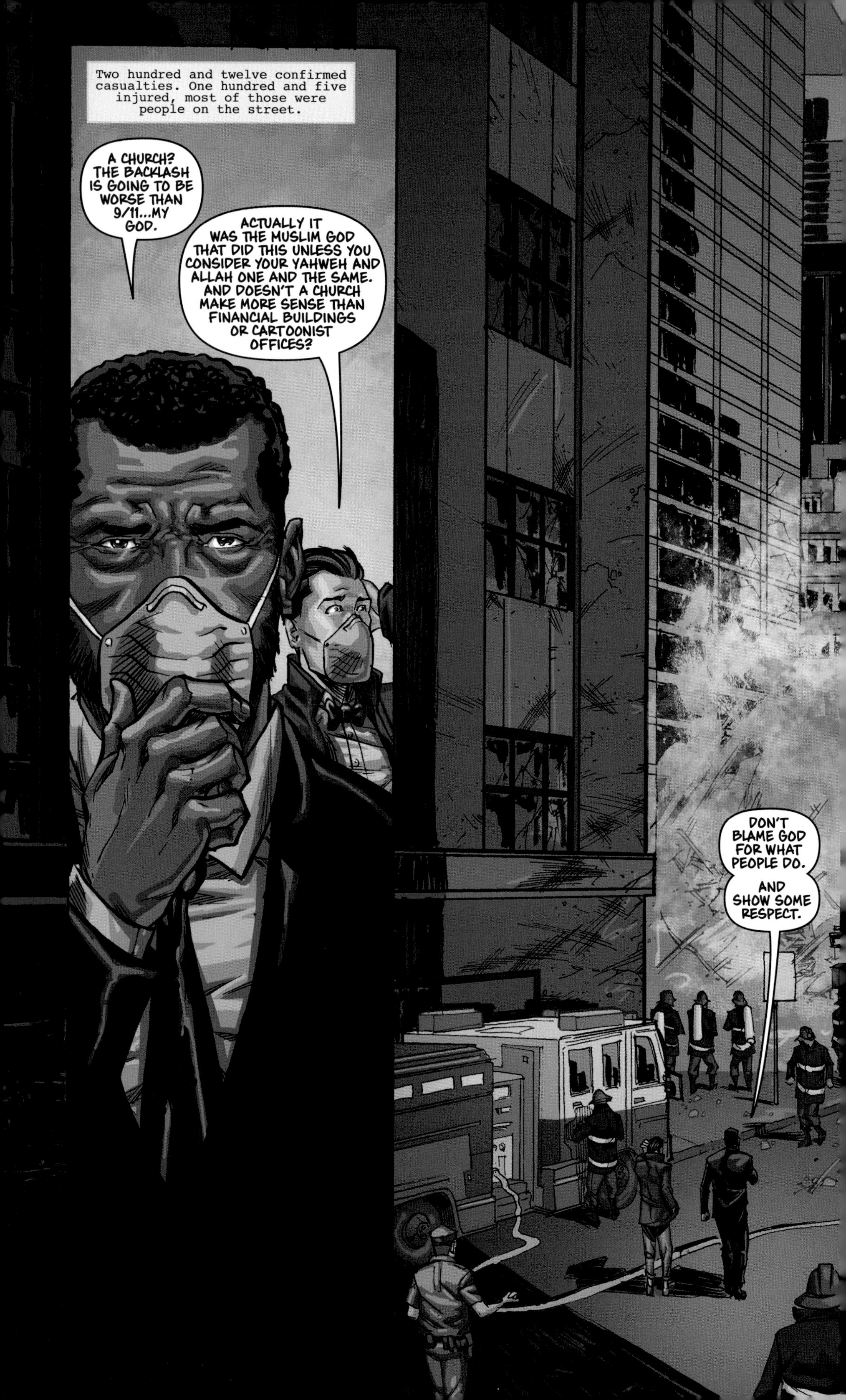

Two hundred and twelve confirmed casualties. One hundred and five injured, most of those were people on the street.
A CHURCH? THE BACKLASH IS GOING TO BE WORSE THAN 9/11...MY GOD.
ACTUALLY IT WAS THE MUSLIM GOD THAT DID THIS UNLESS YOU CONSIDER YOUR YAHWEH AND ALLAH ONE AND THE SAME. AND DOESN'T A CHURCH MAKE MORE SENSE THAN FINANCIAL BUILDINGS OR CARTOONIST OFFICES?
DON'T BLAME GOD FOR WHAT PEOPLE DO.
AND SHOW SOME RESPECT.

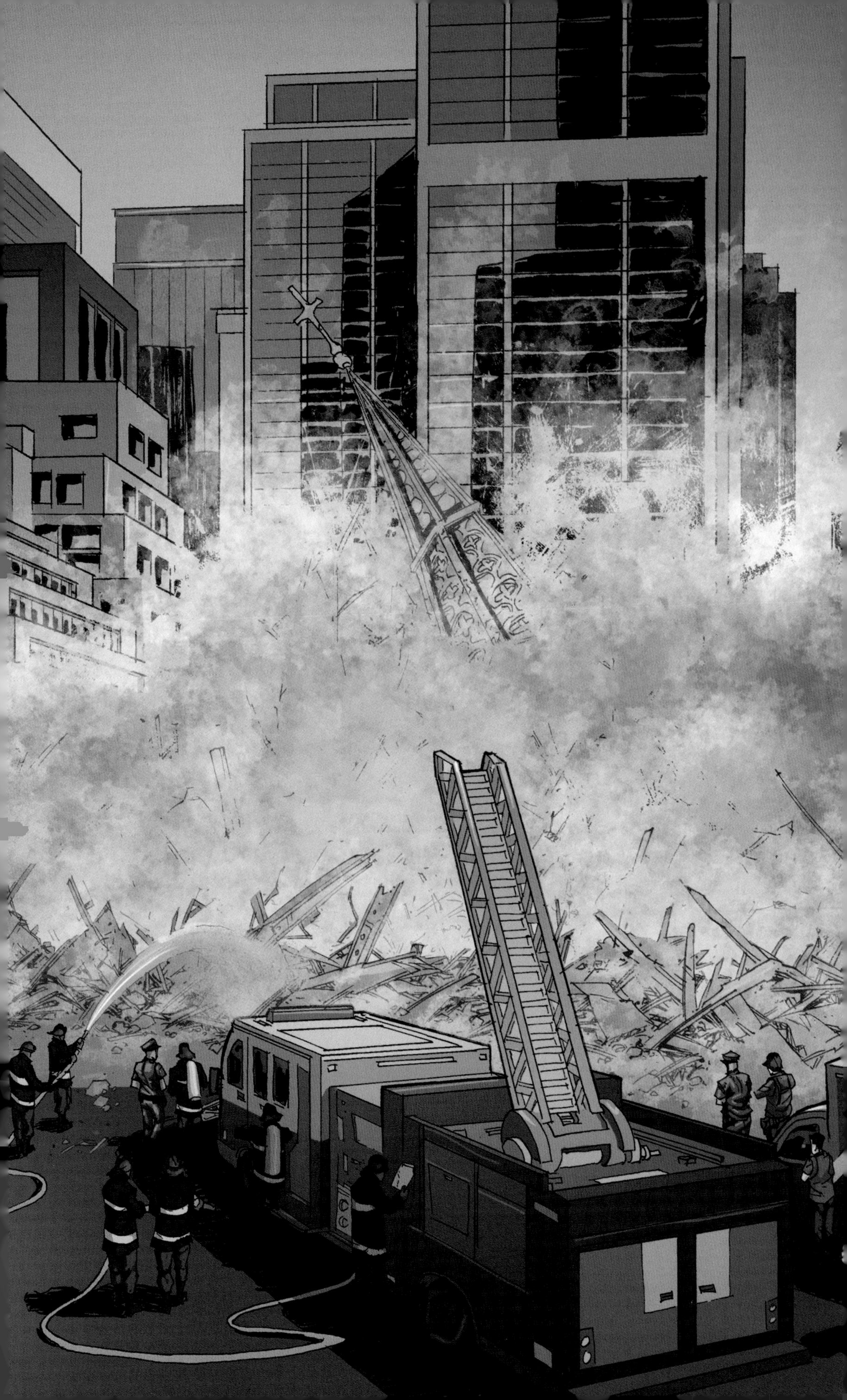

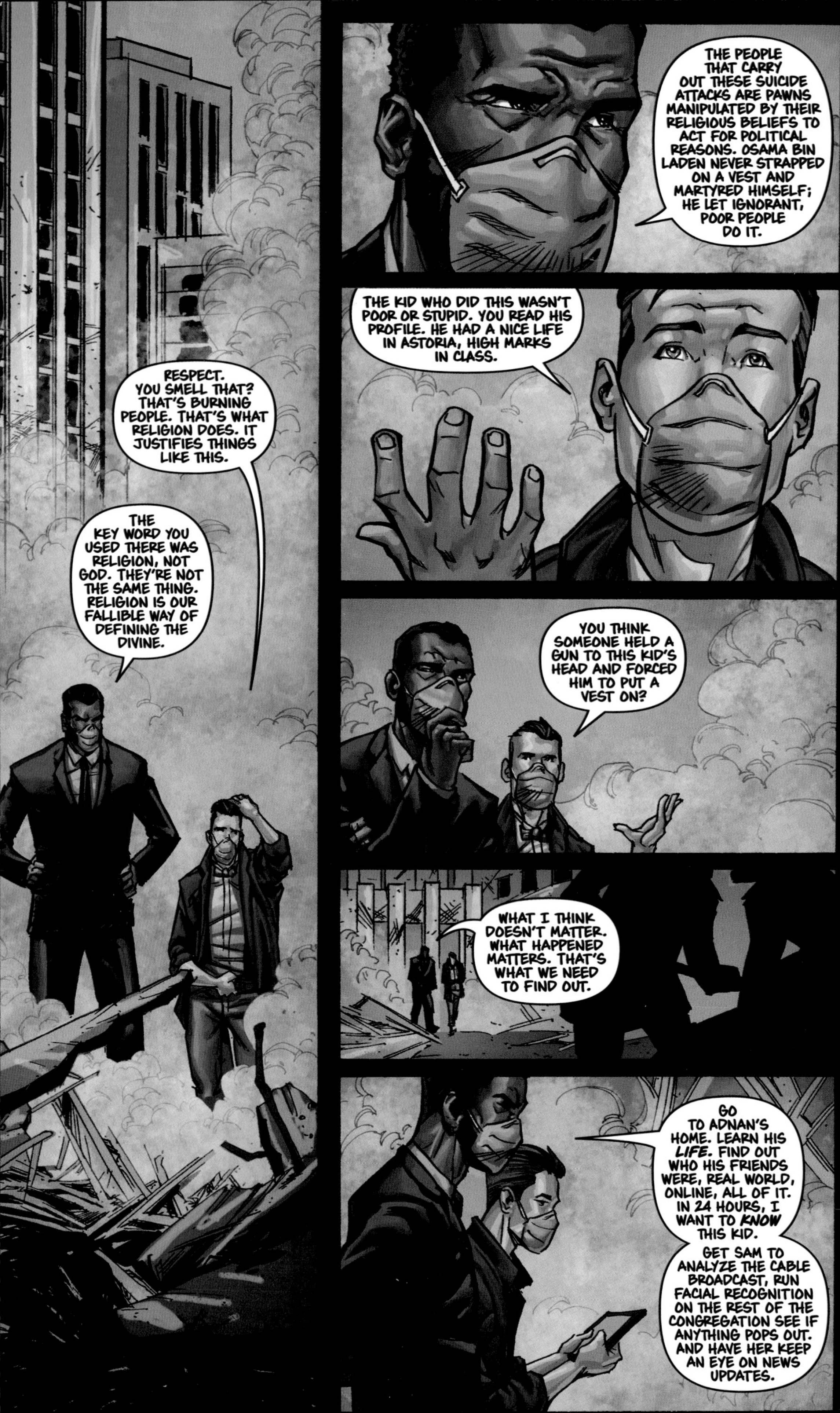
RESPECT. YOU SMELL THAT? THAT'S BURNING PEOPLE. THAT'S WHAT RELIGION DOES. IT JUSTIFIES THINGS LIKE THIS.
THE KEY WORD YOU USED THERE WAS RELIGION, NOT GOD. THEY'RE NOT THE SAME THING. RELIGION IS OUR FALLIBLE WAY OF DEFINING THE DIVINE.
THE PEOPLE THAT CARRY OUT THESE SUICIDE ATTACKS ARE PAWNS MANIPULATED BY THEIR RELIGIOUS BELIEFS TO ACT FOR POLITICAL REASONS. OSAMA BIN LADEN NEVER STRAPPED ON A VEST AND MARTYRED HIMSELF; HE LET IGNORANT, POOR PEOPLE DO IT.
THE KID WHO DID THIS WASN'T POOR OR STUPID. YOU READ HIS PROFILE. HE HAD A NICE LIFE IN ASTORIA, HIGH MARKS IN CLASS.
YOU THINK SOMEONE HELD A GUN TO THIS KID'S HEAD AND FORCED HIM TO PUT A VEST ON?
WHAT I THINK DOESN'T MATTER. WHAT HAPPENED MATTERS. THAT'S WHAT WE NEED TO FIND OUT.
GO TO ADNAN'S HOME. LEARN HIS *LIFE*. FIND OUT WHO HIS FRIENDS WERE, REAL WORLD, ONLINE, ALL OF IT. IN 24 HOURS, I WANT TO *KNOW* THIS KID.
GET SAM TO ANALYZE THE CABLE BROADCAST, RUN FACIAL RECOGNITION ON THE REST OF THE CONGREGATION SEE IF ANYTHING POPS OUT. AND HAVE HER KEEP AN EYE ON NEWS UPDATES.

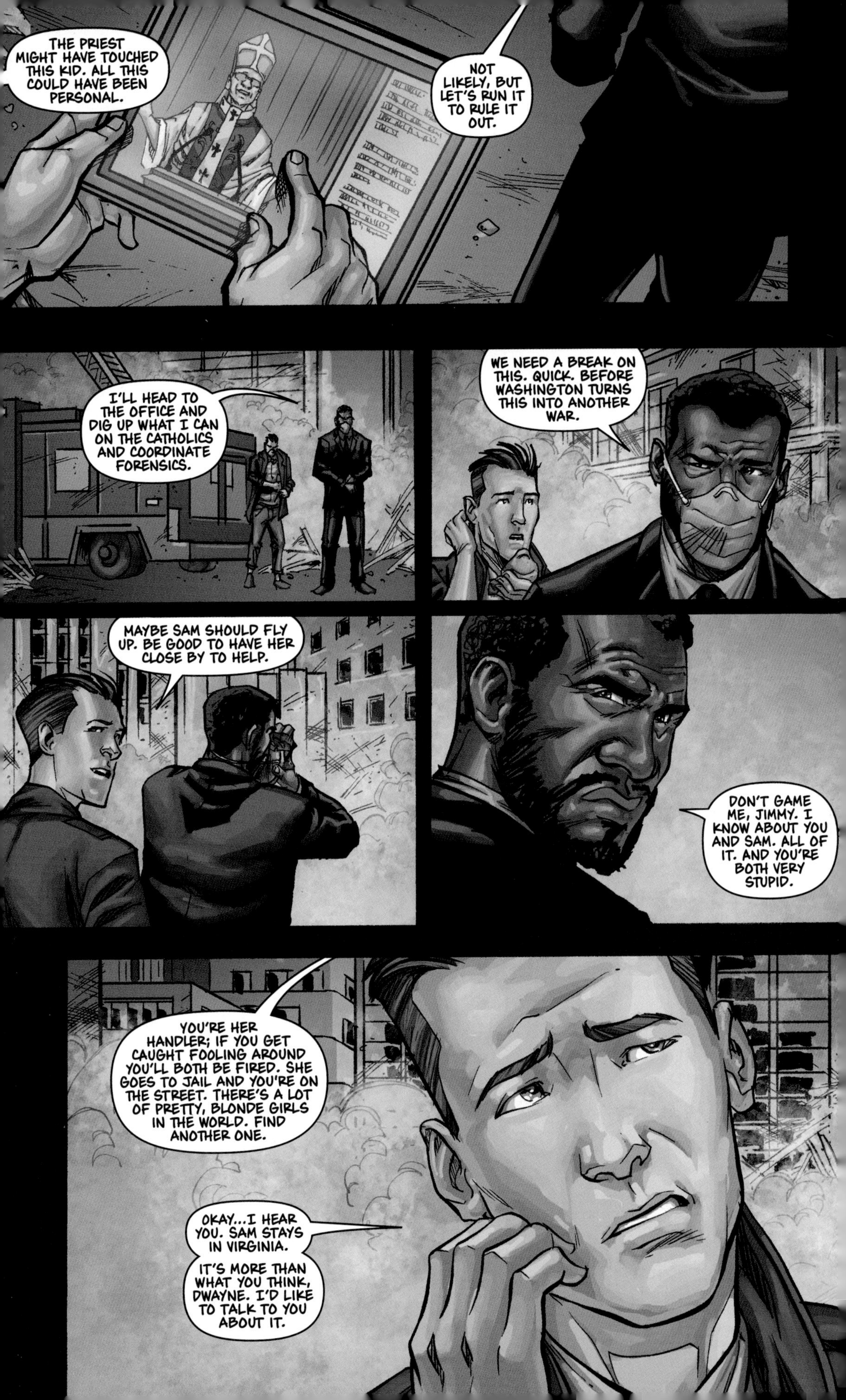
THE PRIEST MIGHT HAVE TOUCHED THIS KID. ALL THIS COULD HAVE BEEN PERSONAL.
NOT LIKELY, BUT LET'S RUN IT TO RULE IT OUT.
I'LL HEAD TO THE OFFICE AND DIG UP WHAT I CAN ON THE CATHOLICS AND COORDINATE FORENSICS.
WE NEED A BREAK ON THIS. QUICK. BEFORE WASHINGTON TURNS THIS INTO ANOTHER WAR.
MAYBE SAM SHOULD FLY UP. BE GOOD TO HAVE HER CLOSE BY TO HELP.
DON'T GAME ME, JIMMY. I KNOW ABOUT YOU AND SAM. ALL OF IT. AND YOU'RE BOTH VERY STUPID.
YOU'RE HER HANDLER; IF YOU GET CAUGHT FOOLING AROUND YOU'LL BOTH BE FIRED. SHE GOES TO JAIL AND YOU'RE ON THE STREET. THERE'S A LOT OF PRETTY, BLONDE GIRLS IN THE WORLD. FIND ANOTHER ONE.
OKAY...I HEAR YOU. SAM STAYS IN VIRGINIA.
IT'S MORE THAN WHAT YOU THINK, DWAYNE. I'D LIKE TO TALK TO YOU ABOUT IT.

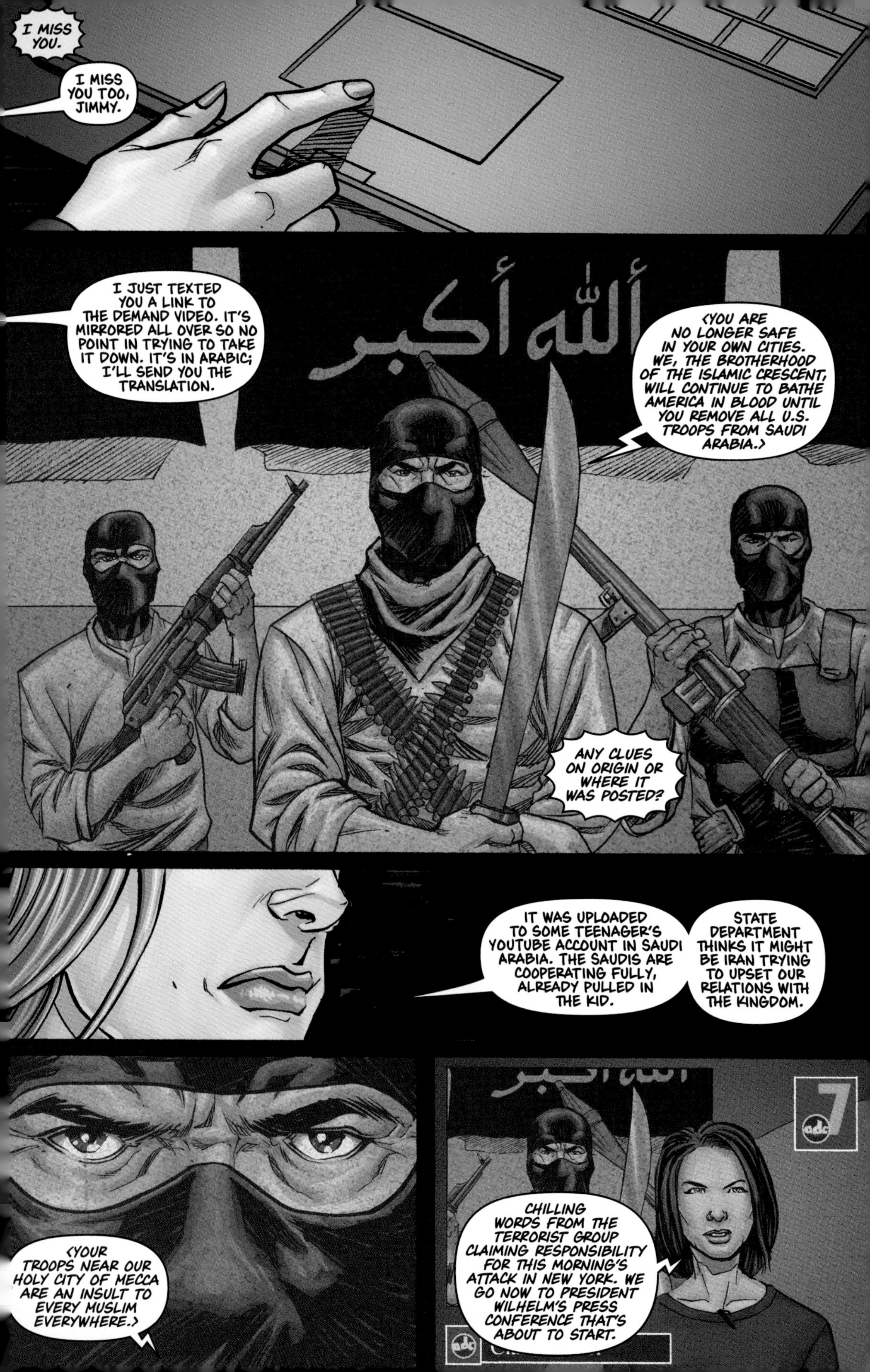
I MISS YOU.
I MISS YOU TOO, JIMMY.
I JUST TEXTED YOU A LINK TO THE DEMAND VIDEO. IT'S MIRRORED ALL OVER SO NO POINT IN TRYING TO TAKE IT DOWN. IT'S IN ARABIC; I'LL SEND YOU THE TRANSLATION.
الله أكبر
<YOU ARE NO LONGER SAFE IN YOUR OWN CITIES. WE, THE BROTHERHOOD OF THE ISLAMIC CRESCENT, WILL CONTINUE TO BATHE AMERICA IN BLOOD UNTIL YOU REMOVE ALL U.S. TROOPS FROM SAUDI ARABIA.>
ANY CLUES ON ORIGIN OR WHERE IT WAS POSTED?
IT WAS UPLOADED TO SOME TEENAGER'S YOUTUBE ACCOUNT IN SAUDI ARABIA. THE SAUDIS ARE COOPERATING FULLY, ALREADY PULLED IN THE KID.
STATE DEPARTMENT THINKS IT MIGHT BE IRAN TRYING TO UPSET OUR RELATIONS WITH THE KINGDOM.
<YOUR TROOPS NEAR OUR HOLY CITY OF MECCA ARE AN INSULT TO EVERY MUSLIM EVERYWHERE.>
7
CHILLING WORDS FROM THE TERRORIST GROUP CLAIMING RESPONSIBILITY FOR THIS MORNING'S ATTACK IN NEW YORK. WE GO NOW TO PRESIDENT WILHELM'S PRESS CONFERENCE THAT'S ABOUT TO START.

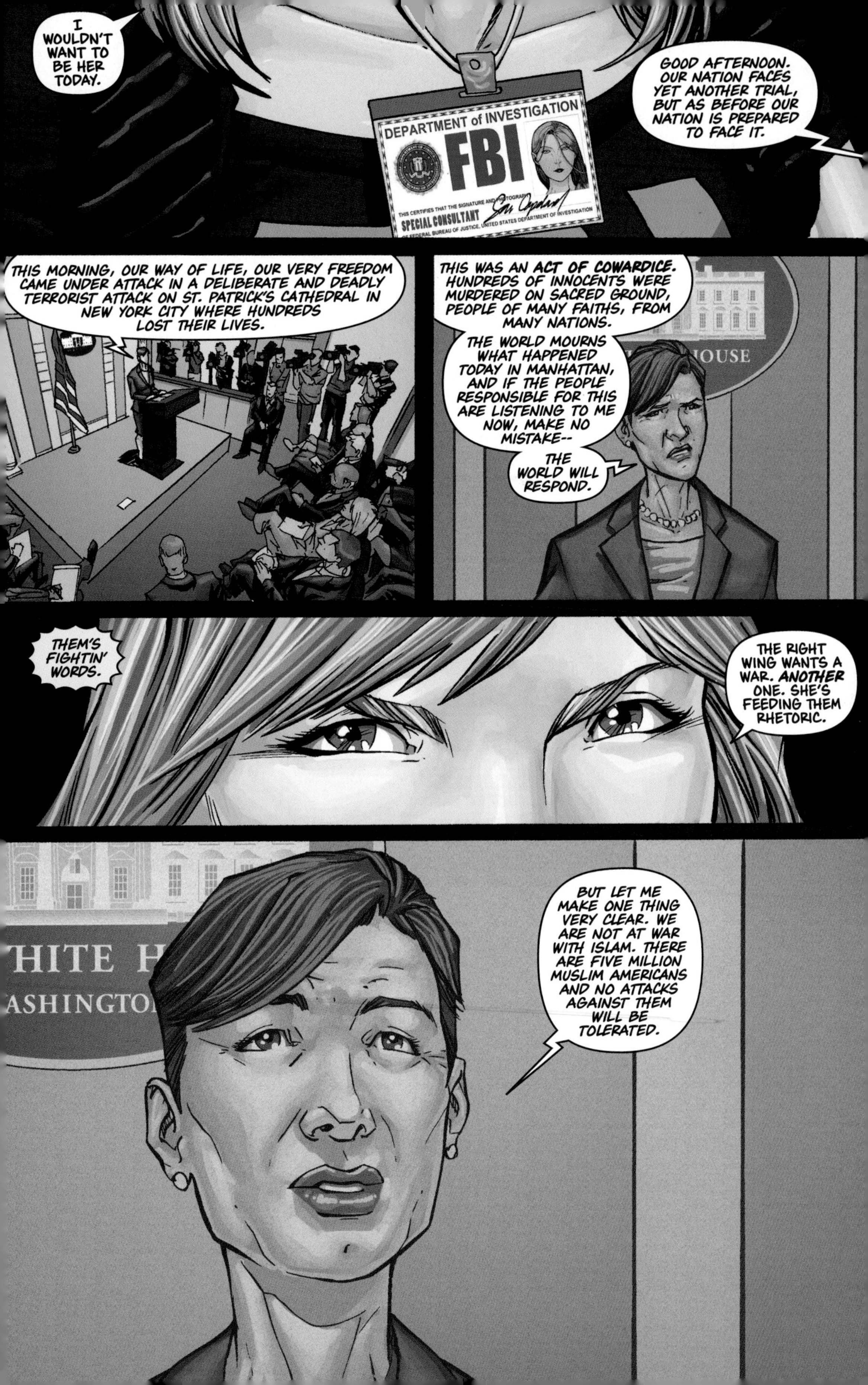
I WOULDN'T WANT TO BE HER TODAY.
DEPARTMENT of INVESTIGATION
FBI
SPECIAL CONSULTANT
GOOD AFTERNOON. OUR NATION FACES YET ANOTHER TRIAL, BUT AS BEFORE OUR NATION IS PREPARED TO FACE IT.
THIS MORNING, OUR WAY OF LIFE, OUR VERY FREEDOM CAME UNDER ATTACK IN A DELIBERATE AND DEADLY TERRORIST ATTACK ON ST. PATRICK'S CATHEDRAL IN NEW YORK CITY WHERE HUNDREDS LOST THEIR LIVES.
THIS WAS AN ACT OF COWARDICE. HUNDREDS OF INNOCENTS WERE MURDERED ON SACRED GROUND, PEOPLE OF MANY FAITHS, FROM MANY NATIONS.
THE WORLD MOURNS WHAT HAPPENED TODAY IN MANHATTAN, AND IF THE PEOPLE RESPONSIBLE FOR THIS ARE LISTENING TO ME NOW, MAKE NO MISTAKE--
THE WORLD WILL RESPOND.
THEM'S FIGHTIN' WORDS.
THE RIGHT WING WANTS A WAR. ANOTHER ONE. SHE'S FEEDING THEM RHETORIC.
BUT LET ME MAKE ONE THING VERY CLEAR. WE ARE NOT AT WAR WITH ISLAM. THERE ARE FIVE MILLION MUSLIM AMERICANS AND NO ATTACKS AGAINST THEM WILL BE TOLERATED.

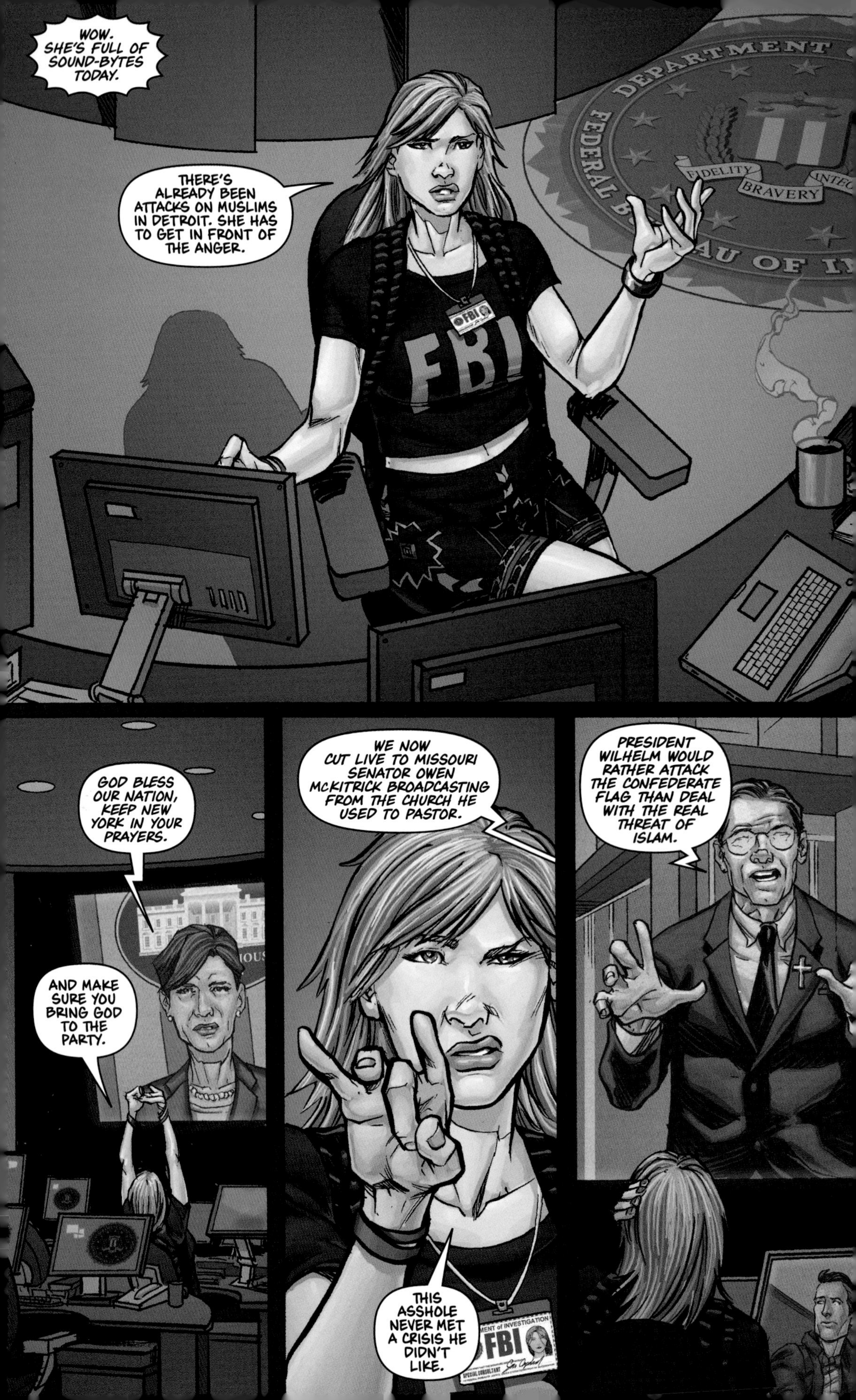
WOW. SHE'S FULL OF SOUND-BYTES TODAY.
THERE'S ALREADY BEEN ATTACKS ON MUSLIMS IN DETROIT. SHE HAS TO GET IN FRONT OF THE ANGER.
DEPARTMENT
FEDERAL B AU OF I
FIDELITY BRAVERY INTEG
FBI
GOD BLESS OUR NATION, KEEP NEW YORK IN YOUR PRAYERS.
AND MAKE SURE YOU BRING GOD TO THE PARTY.
WE NOW CUT LIVE TO MISSOURI SENATOR OWEN McKITRICK BROADCASTING FROM THE CHURCH HE USED TO PASTOR.
THIS ASSHOLE NEVER MET A CRISIS HE DIDN'T LIKE.
PRESIDENT WILHELM WOULD RATHER ATTACK THE CONFEDERATE FLAG THAN DEAL WITH THE REAL THREAT OF ISLAM.

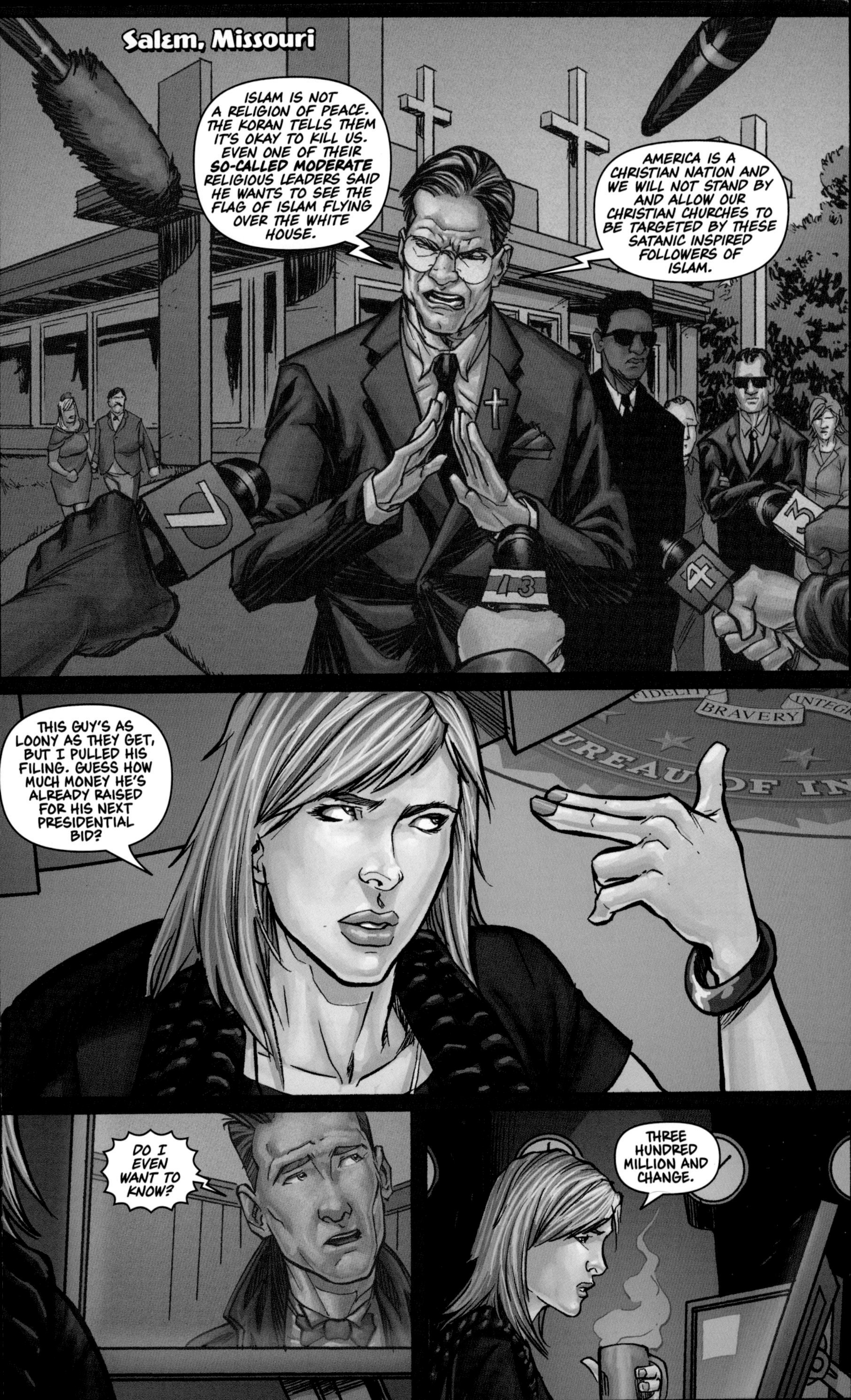
Salem, Missouri
ISLAM IS NOT A RELIGION OF PEACE. THE KORAN TELLS THEM IT'S OKAY TO KILL US. EVEN ONE OF THEIR SO-CALLED MODERATE RELIGIOUS LEADERS SAID HE WANTS TO SEE THE FLAG OF ISLAM FLYING OVER THE WHITE HOUSE.
AMERICA IS A CHRISTIAN NATION AND WE WILL NOT STAND BY AND ALLOW OUR CHRISTIAN CHURCHES TO BE TARGETED BY THESE SATANIC INSPIRED FOLLOWERS OF ISLAM.
THIS GUY'S AS LOONY AS THEY GET, BUT I PULLED HIS FILING. GUESS HOW MUCH MONEY HE'S ALREADY RAISED FOR HIS NEXT PRESIDENTIAL BID?
DO I EVEN WANT TO KNOW?
THREE HUNDRED MILLION AND CHANGE.

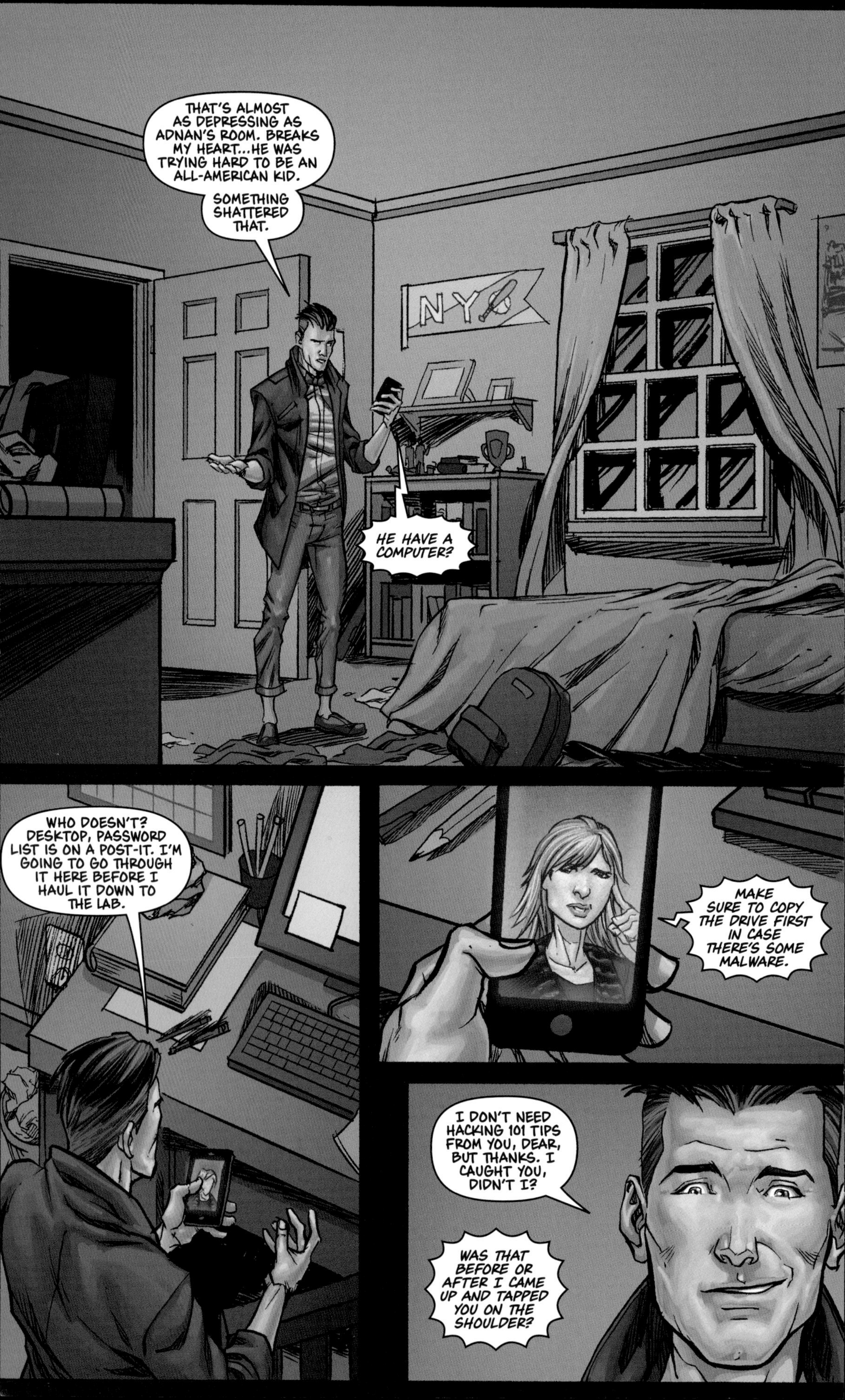
THAT'S ALMOST AS DEPRESSING AS ADNAN'S ROOM. BREAKS MY HEART...HE WAS TRYING HARD TO BE AN ALL-AMERICAN KID.
SOMETHING SHATTERED THAT.
HE HAVE A COMPUTER?
WHO DOESN'T? DESKTOP, PASSWORD LIST IS ON A POST-IT. I'M GOING TO GO THROUGH IT HERE BEFORE I HAUL IT DOWN TO THE LAB.
MAKE SURE TO COPY THE DRIVE FIRST IN CASE THERE'S SOME MALWARE.
I DON'T NEED HACKING 101 TIPS FROM YOU, DEAR, BUT THANKS. I CAUGHT YOU, DIDN'T I?
WAS THAT BEFORE OR AFTER I CAME UP AND TAPPED YOU ON THE SHOULDER?

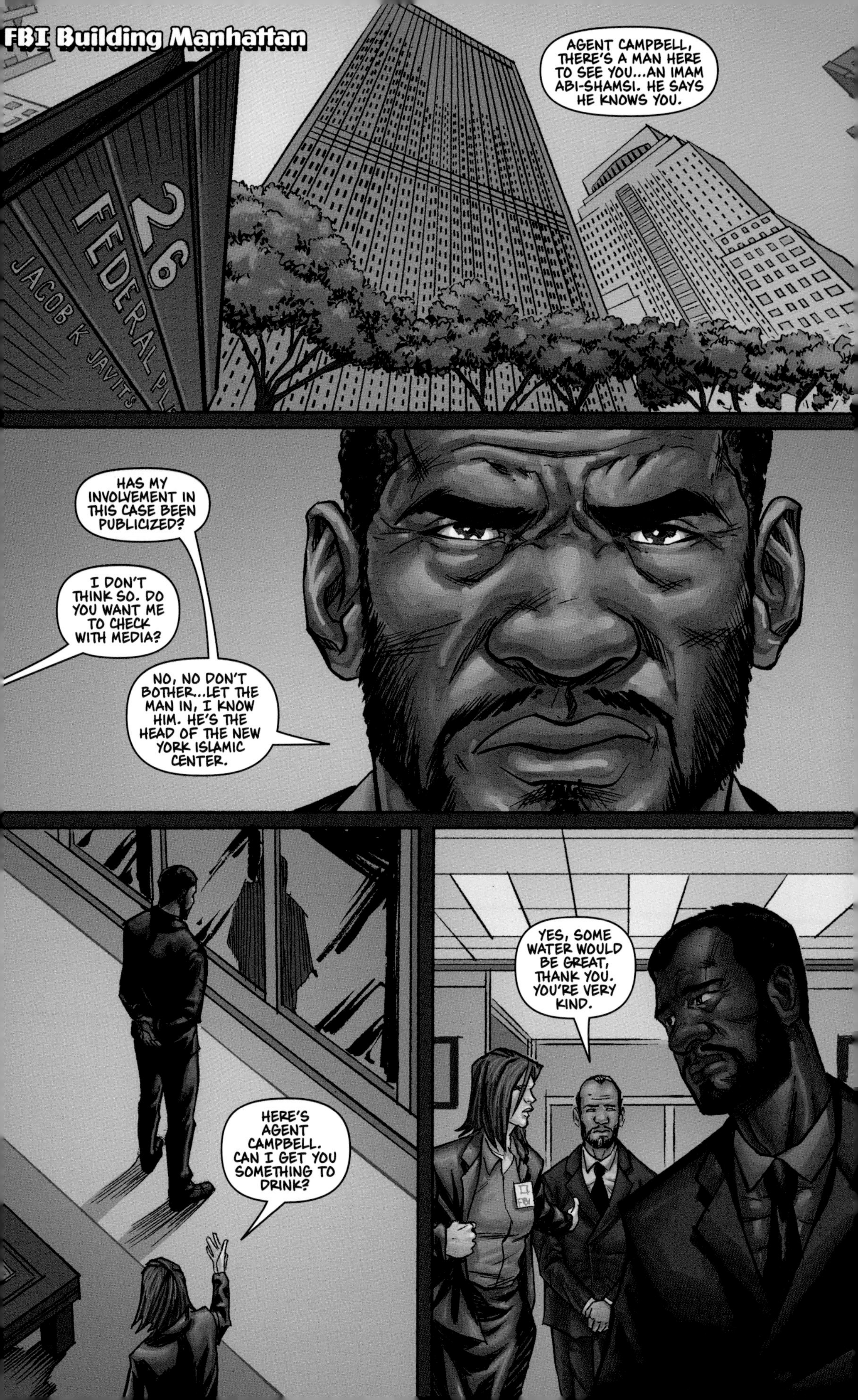
FBI Building Manhattan
26 FEDERAL PL
JACOB K JAVITS
AGENT CAMPBELL, THERE'S A MAN HERE TO SEE YOU...AN IMAM ABI-SHAMSI. HE SAYS HE KNOWS YOU.
HAS MY INVOLVEMENT IN THIS CASE BEEN PUBLICIZED?
I DON'T THINK SO. DO YOU WANT ME TO CHECK WITH MEDIA?
NO, NO DON'T BOTHER...LET THE MAN IN, I KNOW HIM. HE'S THE HEAD OF THE NEW YORK ISLAMIC CENTER.
HERE'S AGENT CAMPBELL. CAN I GET YOU SOMETHING TO DRINK?
YES, SOME WATER WOULD BE GREAT, THANK YOU. YOU'RE VERY KIND.
FBI

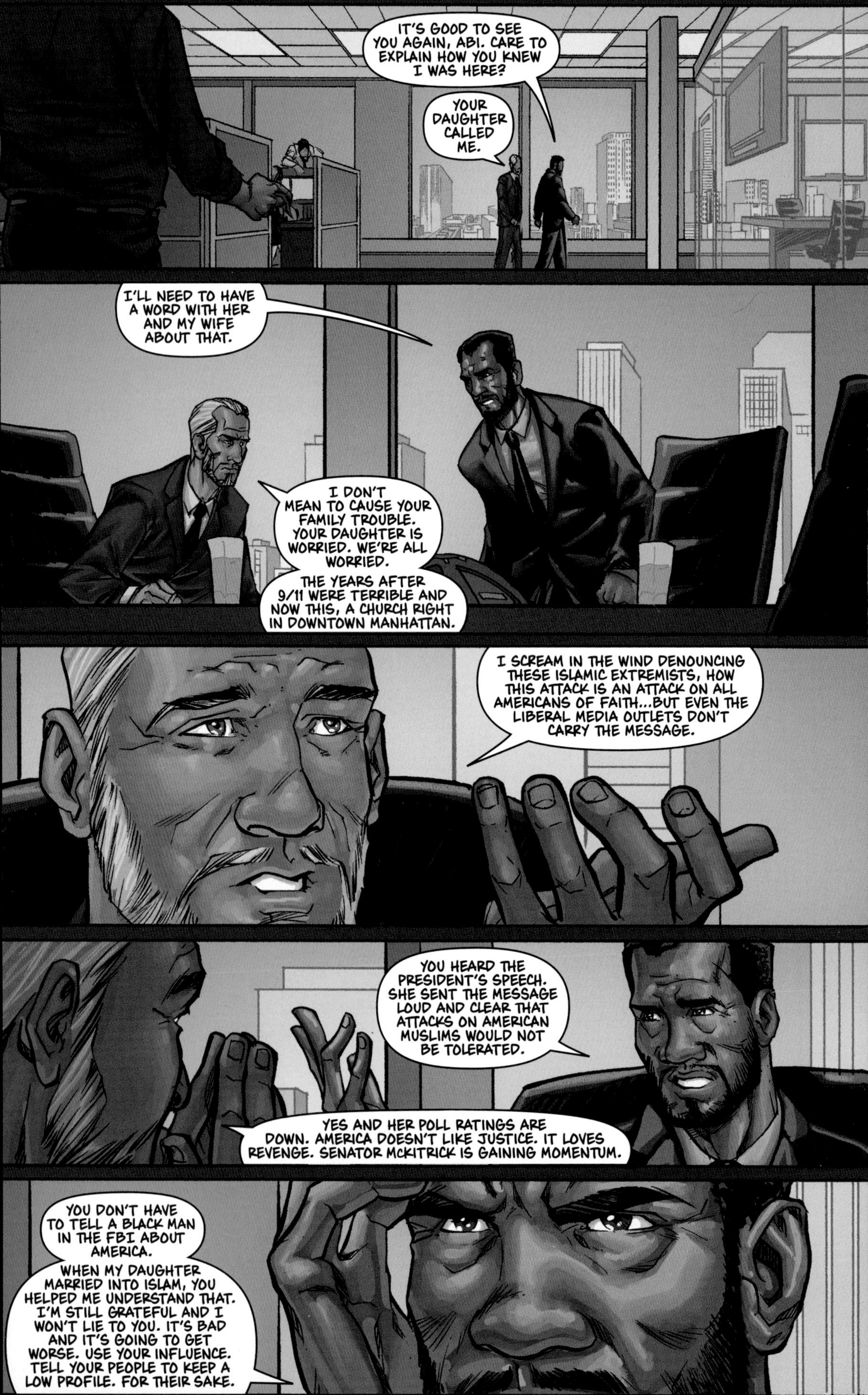
IT'S GOOD TO SEE YOU AGAIN, ABI. CARE TO EXPLAIN HOW YOU KNEW I WAS HERE?
YOUR DAUGHTER CALLED ME.
I'LL NEED TO HAVE A WORD WITH HER AND MY WIFE ABOUT THAT.
I DON'T MEAN TO CAUSE YOUR FAMILY TROUBLE. YOUR DAUGHTER IS WORRIED. WE'RE ALL WORRIED.
THE YEARS AFTER 9/11 WERE TERRIBLE AND NOW THIS, A CHURCH RIGHT IN DOWNTOWN MANHATTAN.
I SCREAM IN THE WIND DENOUNCING THESE ISLAMIC EXTREMISTS, HOW THIS ATTACK IS AN ATTACK ON ALL AMERICANS OF FAITH...BUT EVEN THE LIBERAL MEDIA OUTLETS DON'T CARRY THE MESSAGE.
YOU HEARD THE PRESIDENT'S SPEECH. SHE SENT THE MESSAGE LOUD AND CLEAR THAT ATTACKS ON AMERICAN MUSLIMS WOULD NOT BE TOLERATED.
YES AND HER POLL RATINGS ARE DOWN. AMERICA DOESN'T LIKE JUSTICE. IT LOVES REVENGE. SENATOR McKITRICK IS GAINING MOMENTUM.
YOU DON'T HAVE TO TELL A BLACK MAN IN THE FBI ABOUT AMERICA.
WHEN MY DAUGHTER MARRIED INTO ISLAM, YOU HELPED ME UNDERSTAND THAT. I'M STILL GRATEFUL AND I WON'T LIE TO YOU. IT'S BAD AND IT'S GOING TO GET WORSE. USE YOUR INFLUENCE. TELL YOUR PEOPLE TO KEEP A LOW PROFILE. FOR THEIR SAKE.

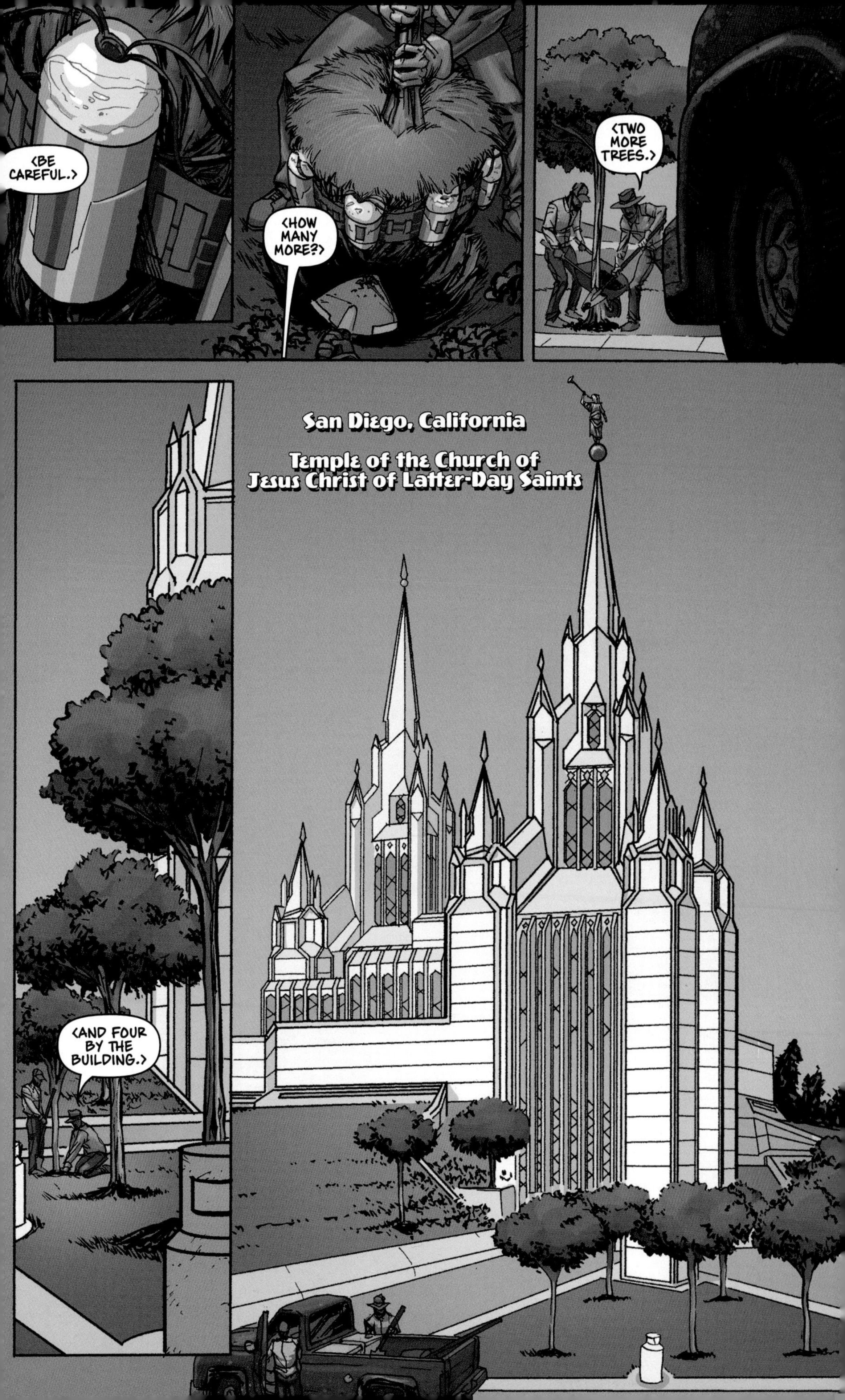
<BE CAREFUL.>
<HOW MANY MORE?>
<TWO MORE TREES.>
San Diego, California
Temple of the Church of Jesus Christ of Latter-Day Saints
<AND FOUR BY THE BUILDING.>

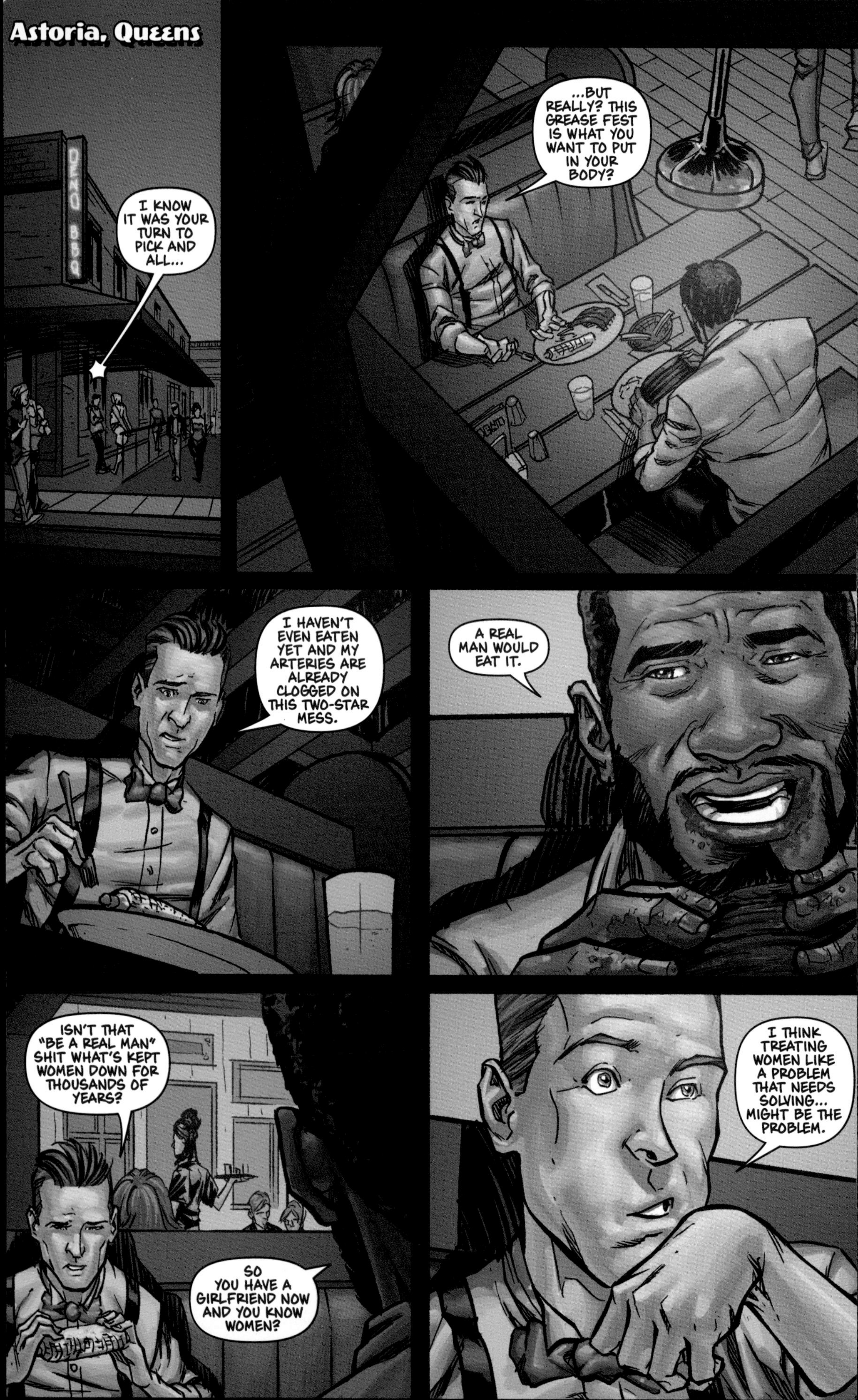
Astoria, Queens
DENO BBQ
I KNOW IT WAS YOUR TURN TO PICK AND ALL...
...BUT REALLY? THIS GREASE FEST IS WHAT YOU WANT TO PUT IN YOUR BODY?
I HAVEN'T EVEN EATEN YET AND MY ARTERIES ARE ALREADY CLOGGED ON THIS TWO-STAR MESS.
A REAL MAN WOULD EAT IT.
ISN'T THAT "BE A REAL MAN" SHIT WHAT'S KEPT WOMEN DOWN FOR THOUSANDS OF YEARS?
SO YOU HAVE A GIRLFRIEND NOW AND YOU KNOW WOMEN?
I THINK TREATING WOMEN LIKE A PROBLEM THAT NEEDS SOLVING... MIGHT BE THE PROBLEM.

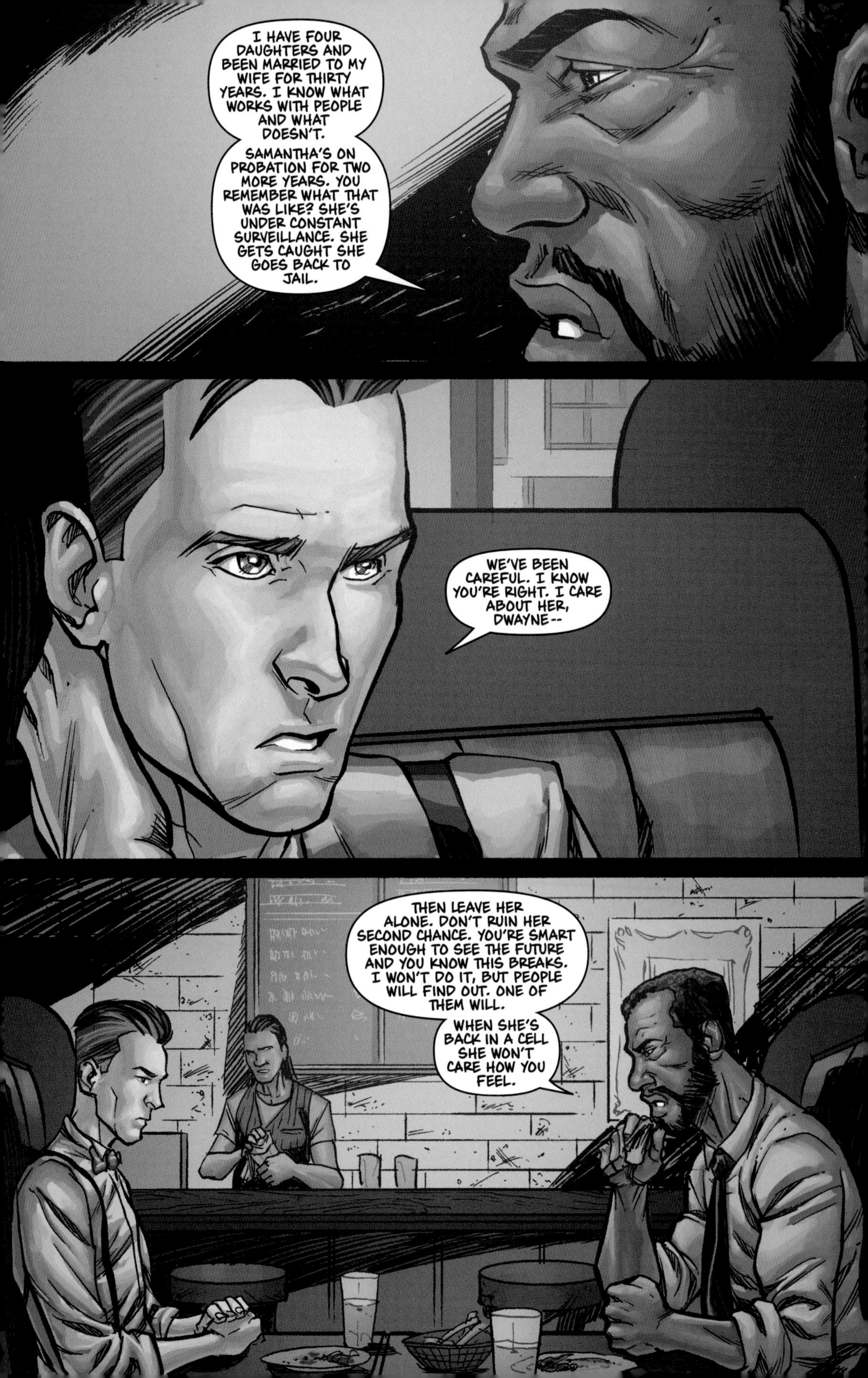
I HAVE FOUR DAUGHTERS AND BEEN MARRIED TO MY WIFE FOR THIRTY YEARS. I KNOW WHAT WORKS WITH PEOPLE AND WHAT DOESN'T.
SAMANTHA'S ON PROBATION FOR TWO MORE YEARS. YOU REMEMBER WHAT THAT WAS LIKE? SHE'S UNDER CONSTANT SURVEILLANCE. SHE GETS CAUGHT SHE GOES BACK TO JAIL.
WE'VE BEEN CAREFUL. I KNOW YOU'RE RIGHT. I CARE ABOUT HER, DWAYNE--
THEN LEAVE HER ALONE. DON'T RUIN HER SECOND CHANCE. YOU'RE SMART ENOUGH TO SEE THE FUTURE AND YOU KNOW THIS BREAKS. I WON'T DO IT, BUT PEOPLE WILL FIND OUT. ONE OF THEM WILL.
WHEN SHE'S BACK IN A CELL SHE WON'T CARE HOW YOU FEEL.

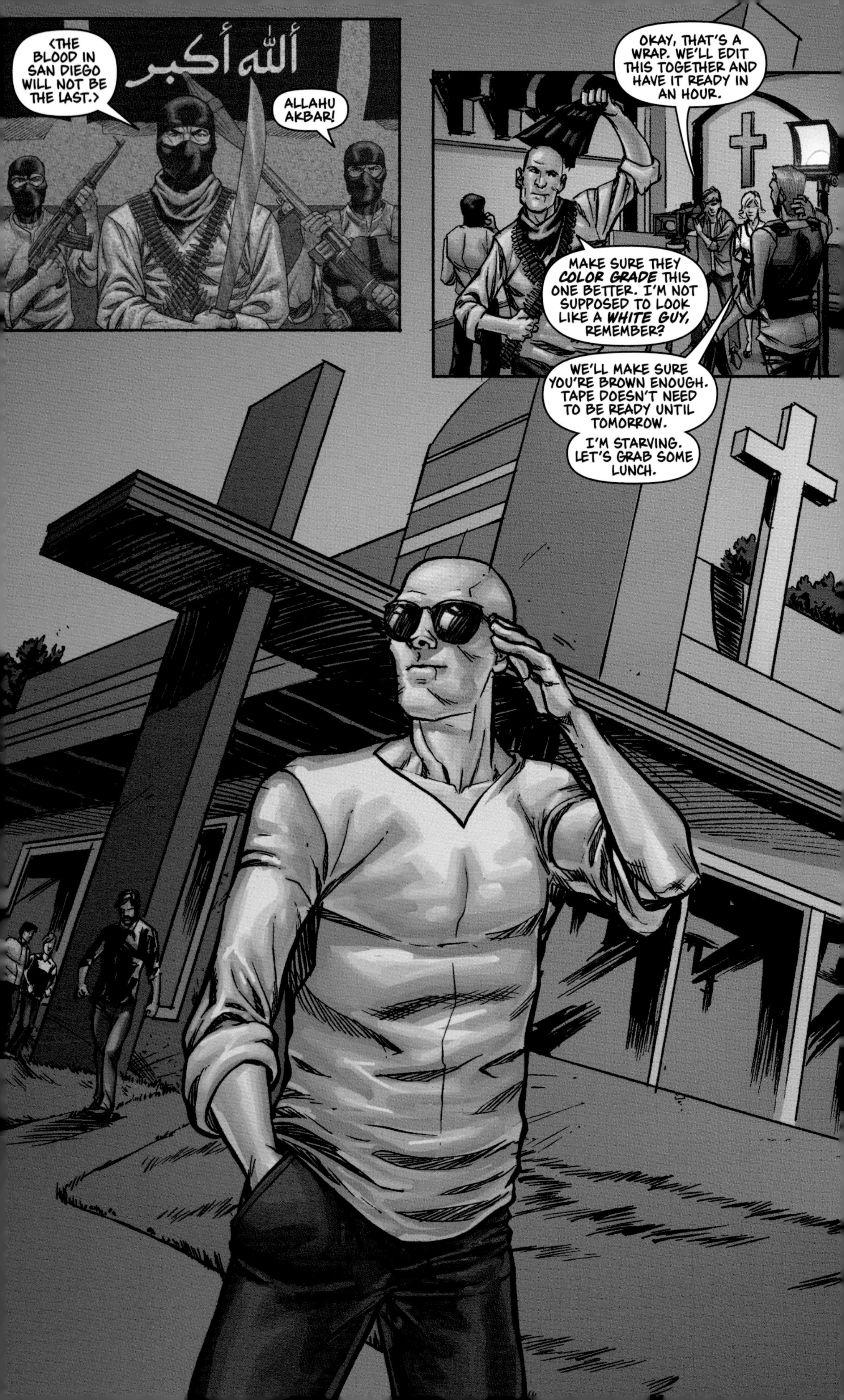

الله أكبر
<THE BLOOD IN SAN DIEGO WILL NOT BE THE LAST.>
ALLAHU AKBAR!
OKAY, THAT'S A WRAP. WE'LL EDIT THIS TOGETHER AND HAVE IT READY IN AN HOUR.
MAKE SURE THEY **COLOR GRADE** THIS ONE BETTER. I'M NOT SUPPOSED TO LOOK LIKE A ***WHITE GUY***, REMEMBER?
WE'LL MAKE SURE YOU'RE BROWN ENOUGH. TAPE DOESN'T NEED TO BE READY UNTIL TOMORROW.
I'M STARVING. LET'S GRAB SOME LUNCH.

IN RELIGION AND POLITICS, PEOPLE'S BELIEFS AND
CONVICTIONS ARE IN ALMOST EVERY CASE GOTTEN AT
SECOND-HAND, AND WITHOUT EXAMINATION.

-MARK TWAIN

Islamophobia: Chapter 2

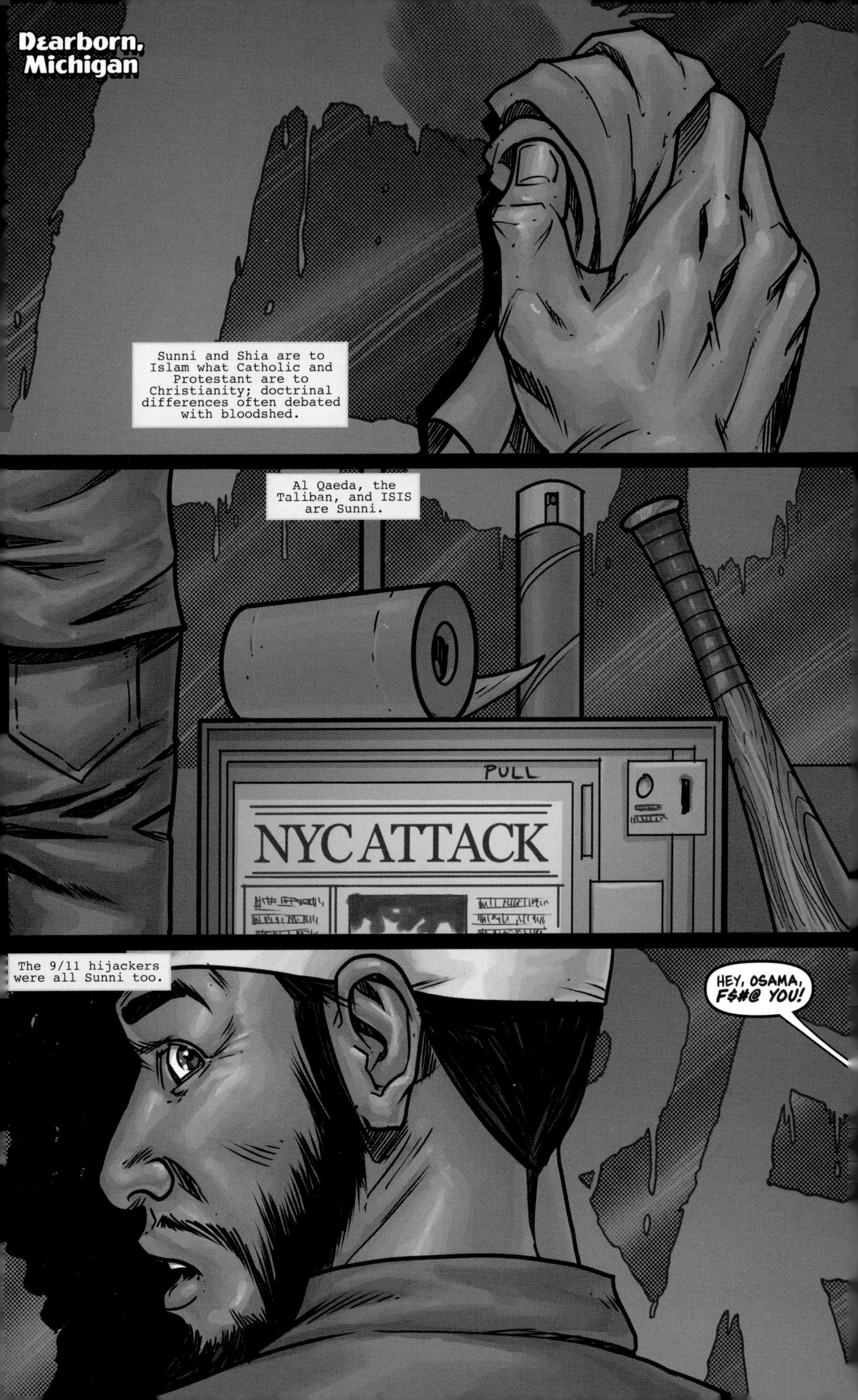
Dearborn, Michigan
Sunni and Shia are to Islam what Catholic and Protestant are to Christianity; doctrinal differences often debated with bloodshed.
Al Qaeda, the Taliban, and ISIS are Sunni.
PULL
NYC ATTACK
The 9/11 hijackers were all Sunni too.
HEY, OSAMA, F$#@ YOU!

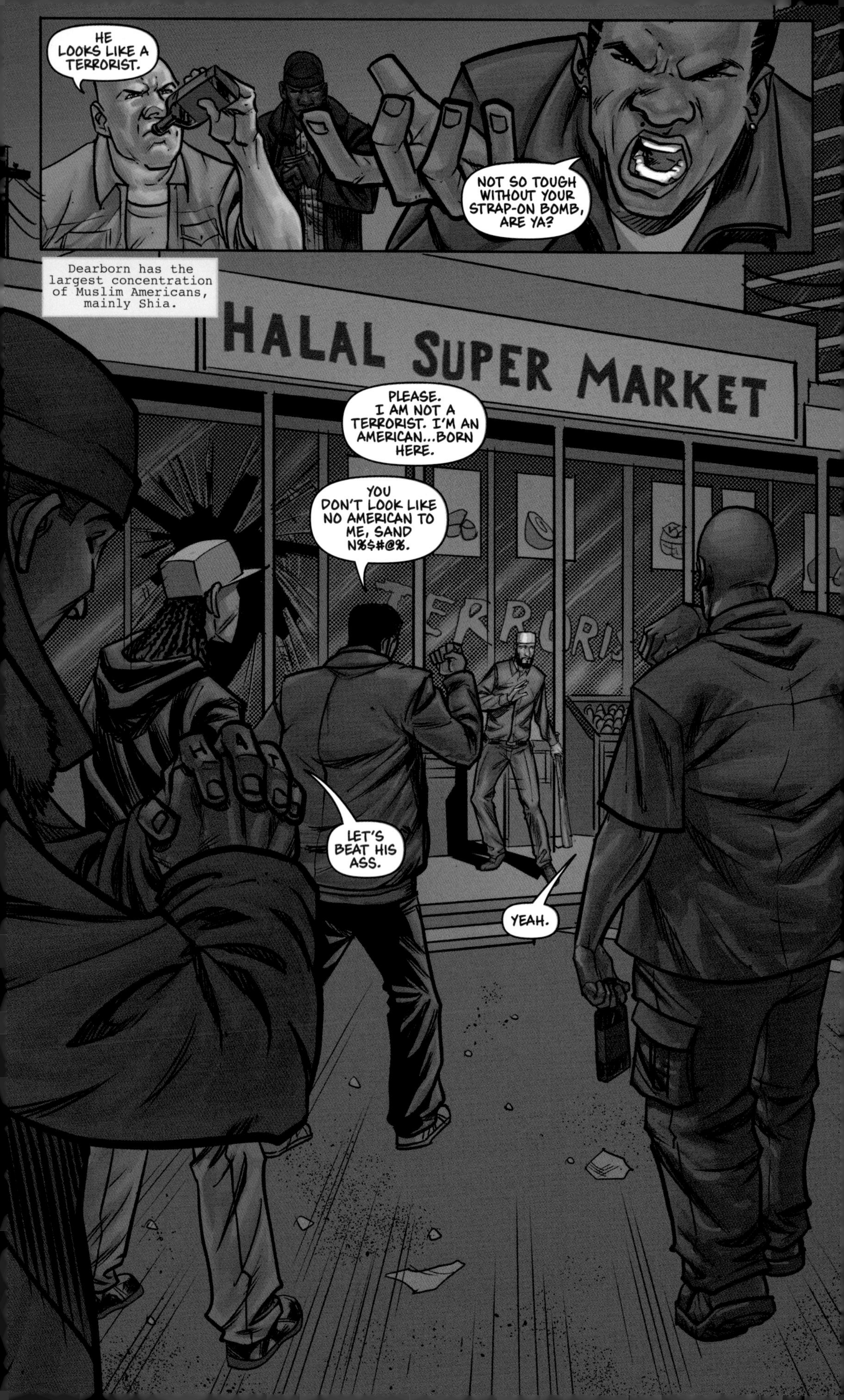
HE LOOKS LIKE A TERRORIST.
NOT SO TOUGH WITHOUT YOUR STRAP-ON BOMB, ARE YA?
Dearborn has the largest concentration of Muslim Americans, mainly Shia.
HALAL SUPER MARKET
PLEASE. I AM NOT A TERRORIST. I'M AN AMERICAN...BORN HERE.
YOU DON'T LOOK LIKE NO AMERICAN TO ME, SAND N%$#@%.
TERRORIS
HATE
LET'S BEAT HIS ASS.
YEAH.

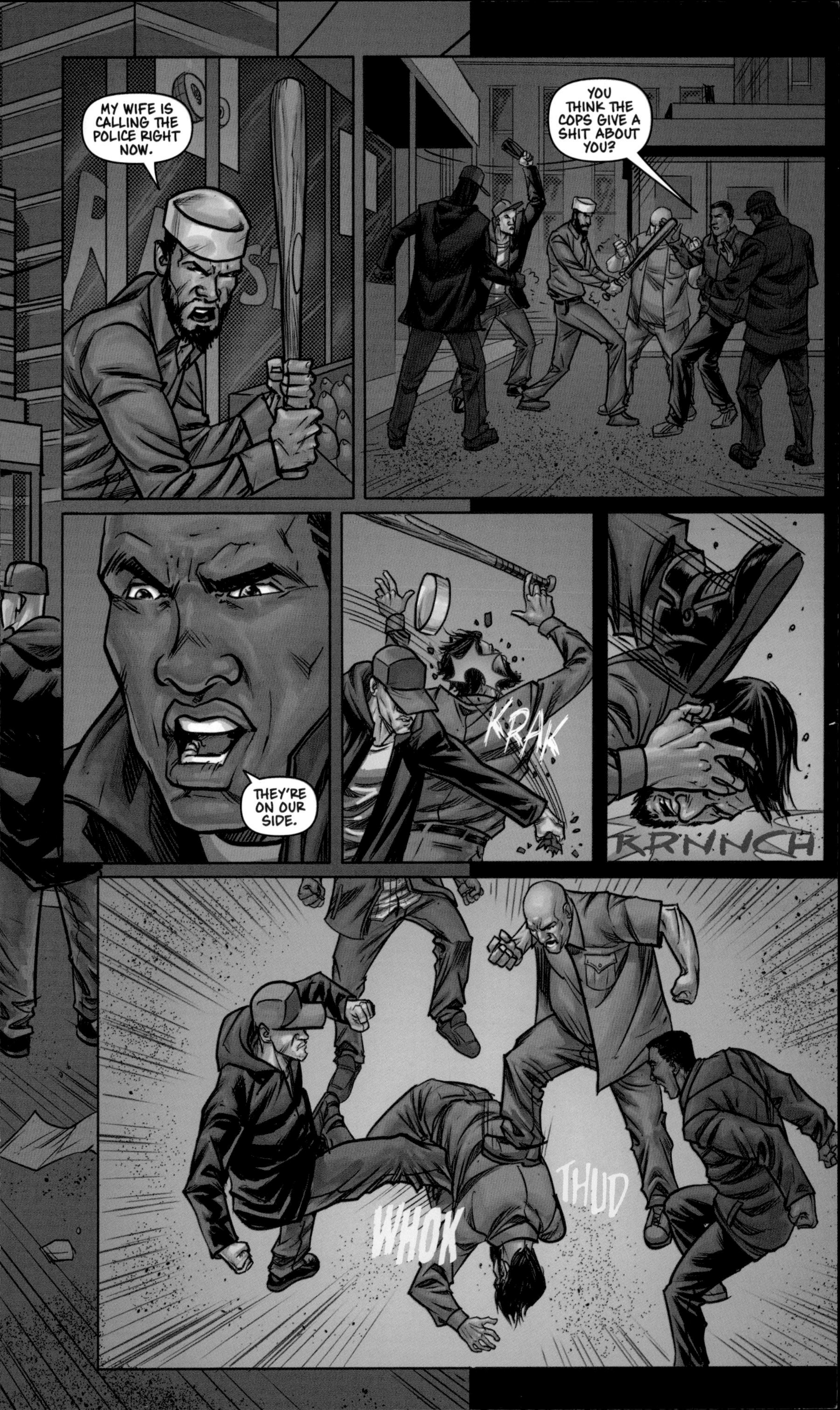
MY WIFE IS CALLING THE POLICE RIGHT NOW.
YOU THINK THE COPS GIVE A SHIT ABOUT YOU?
THEY'RE ON OUR SIDE.
KRAK
KRNNCH
THUD
WHOK

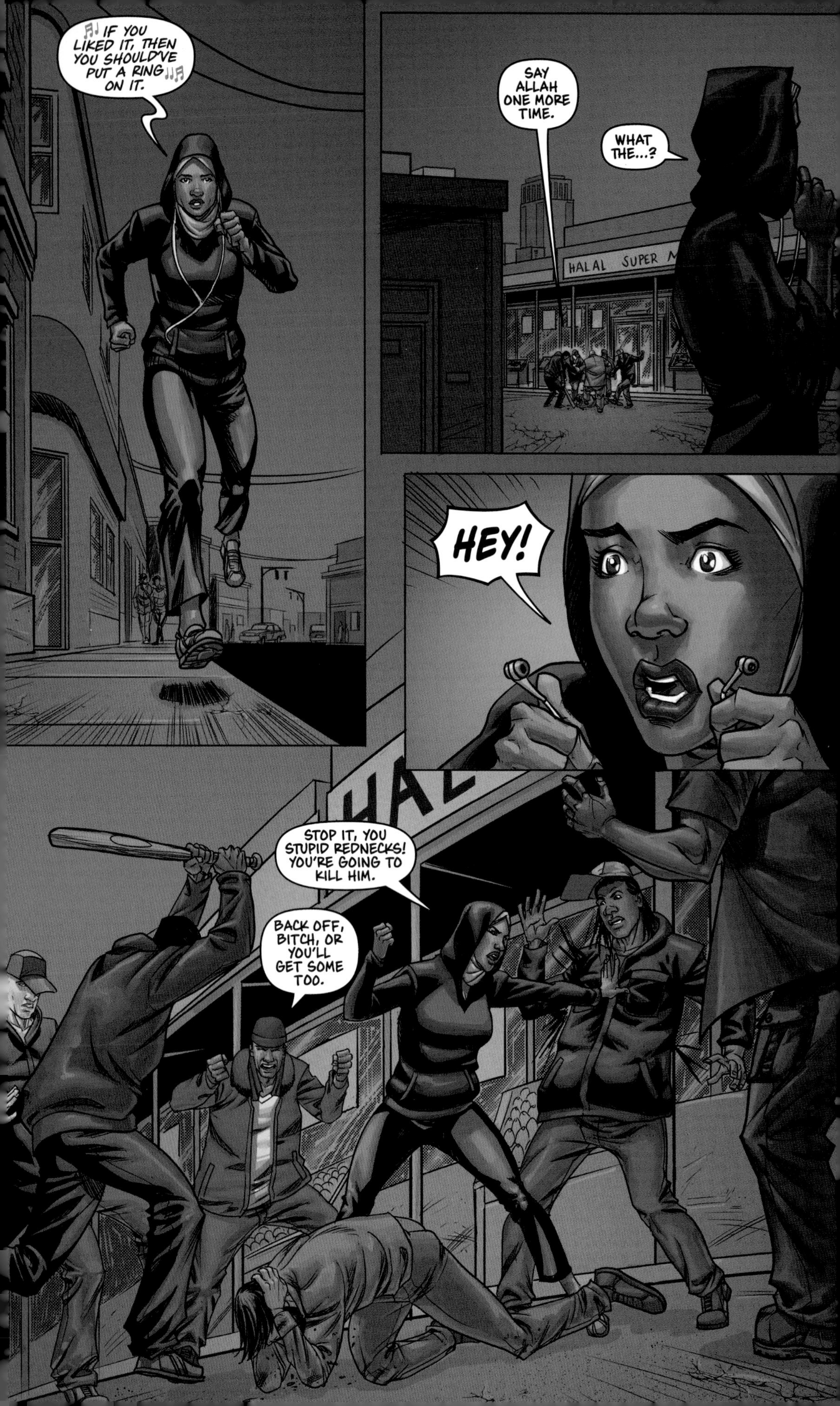
IF YOU LIKED IT, THEN YOU SHOULD'VE PUT A RING ON IT.
SAY ALLAH ONE MORE TIME.
WHAT THE...?
HALAL SUPER M
HEY!
STOP IT, YOU STUPID REDNECKS! YOU'RE GOING TO KILL HIM.
BACK OFF, BITCH, OR YOU'LL GET SOME TOO.

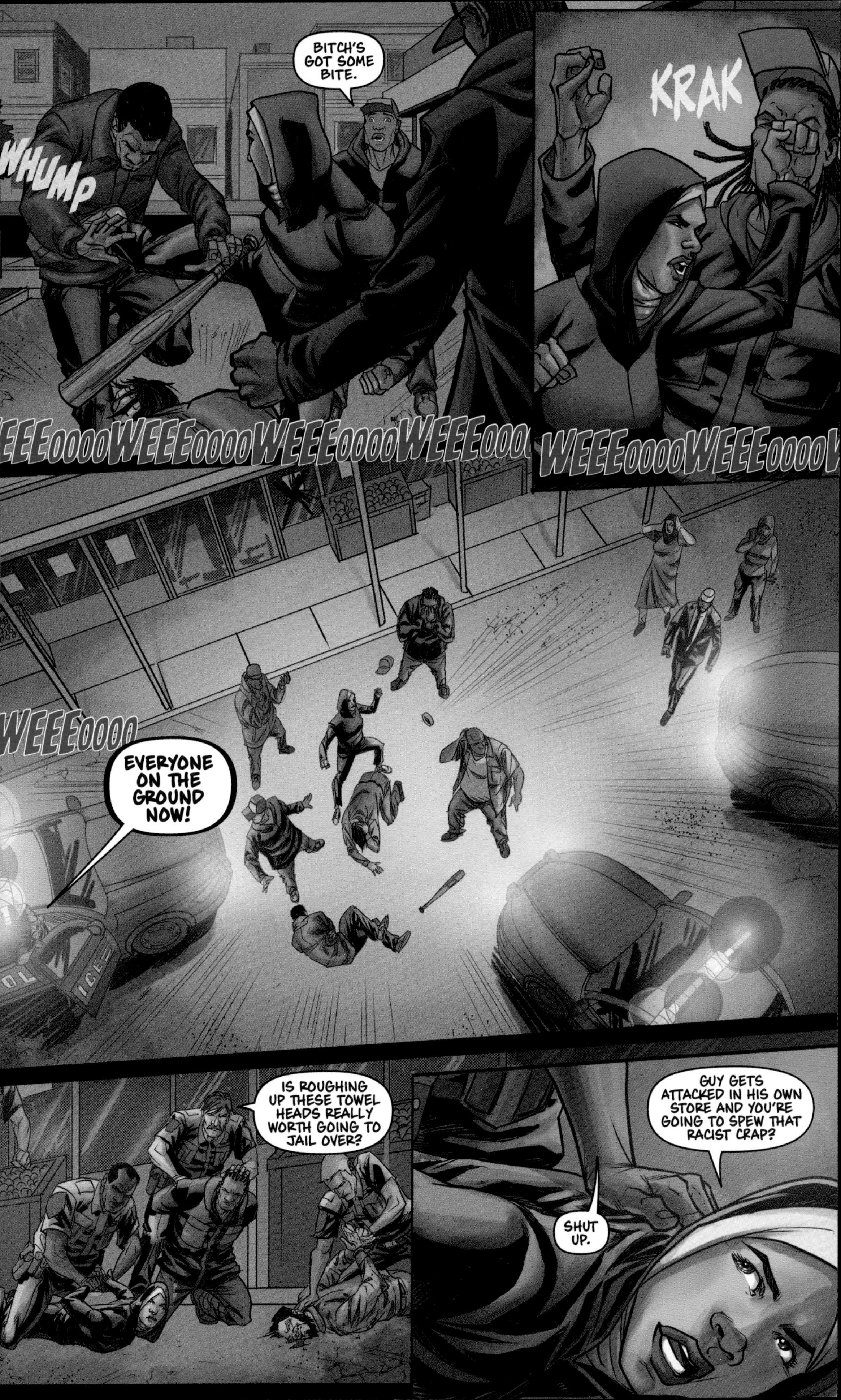
BITCH'S GOT SOME BITE.
WHUMP
KRAK
WEEEooooWEEEooooWEEEooooWEEEoooo
WEEEooooWEEEooooW
WEEEoooo
EVERYONE ON THE GROUND NOW!
IS ROUGHING UP THESE TOWEL HEADS REALLY WORTH GOING TO JAIL OVER?
GUY GETS ATTACKED IN HIS OWN STORE AND YOU'RE GOING TO SPEW THAT RACIST CRAP?
SHUT UP.

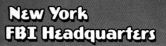

New York
FBI Headquarters
SAM FOUND A TOR BROWSER ON ADNAN'S COMPUTER AND WAS ABLE TO ACCESS A DARK WEB CHAT ROOM WITH A LOGIN HE HAD ON A POST-IT. HANDWRITING'S BEEN CONFIRMED AS HIS.
THE WHOLE THING IS WONKY BECAUSE THE POINT OF THE TOR CLIENT AND THE DARK WEB IS ANONYMITY...BUT THEY EXCHANGED PICTURES AND SHE FOUND SOCIAL MEDIA LINKS THAT LED US TO FOURTEEN OTHER ARAB AMERICAN TEENAGERS, EACH IN A DIFFERENT STATE.
HE ALSO HAD SEVERAL SCREEN CAPS OF CHATS TALKING ABOUT ST. PATRICK'S CATHEDRAL AND OTHER TARGETS IN SEATTLE AND PHILADELPHIA.
THE LAST ENTRY WAS THE MORNING OF THE SUICIDE BOMBING. HE SIGNED OFF WITH, "SEE YOU IN PARADISE."
I DON'T BUY IT.
LEAVING THAT EVIDENCE WOULD BE REALLY STUPID... PROFILE SAYS HE'S INTELLIGENT.
HE IS...BUT IF HE WANTED TO TAKE CREDIT FOR THE ATTACK IT PLAYS.
LOCAL FRIENDS, SCHOOL?
WELL LIKED, PLAYED ON THE SOCCER TEAM. NEIGHBORS SAY HE SEEMED MORE WITHDRAWN IN THE LAST FEW WEEKS BUT THAT HE WAS "SUCH A NICE, QUIET BOY."
HIS ADOPTED PARENTS WERE SENDING HIM TO A SHRINK, I READ HER NOTES; SYMPTOMS OF PTSD FROM ABUSE IN SYRIA. KID HAD IT ROUGH.
THE CONFOUNDING THING IS, I CAN'T FIND ANY CONNECTION BETWEEN ANY OF THESE KIDS AND THE KID IN SAUDI ARABIA WHO UPLOADED THE VIDEO OR THE BROTHERHOOD OF THE ISLAMIC CRESCENT IN THE VIDEO.
HMM. MAYBE SOMEONE WITH MORE LEET HACKING SKILLS SHOULD TAKE ANOTHER LOOK.

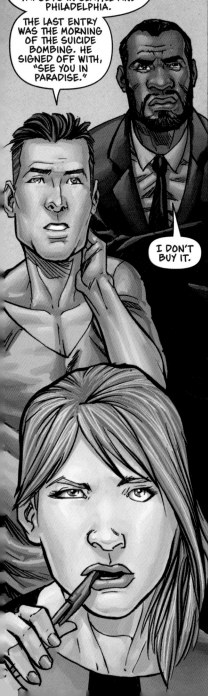

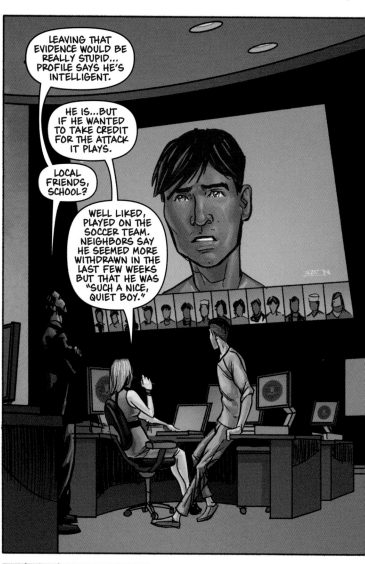

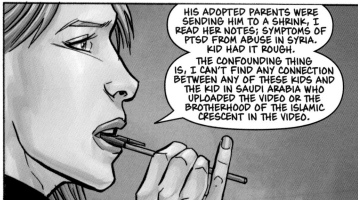

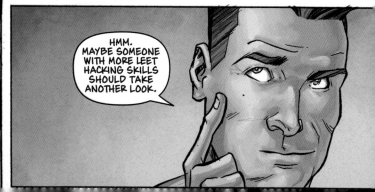

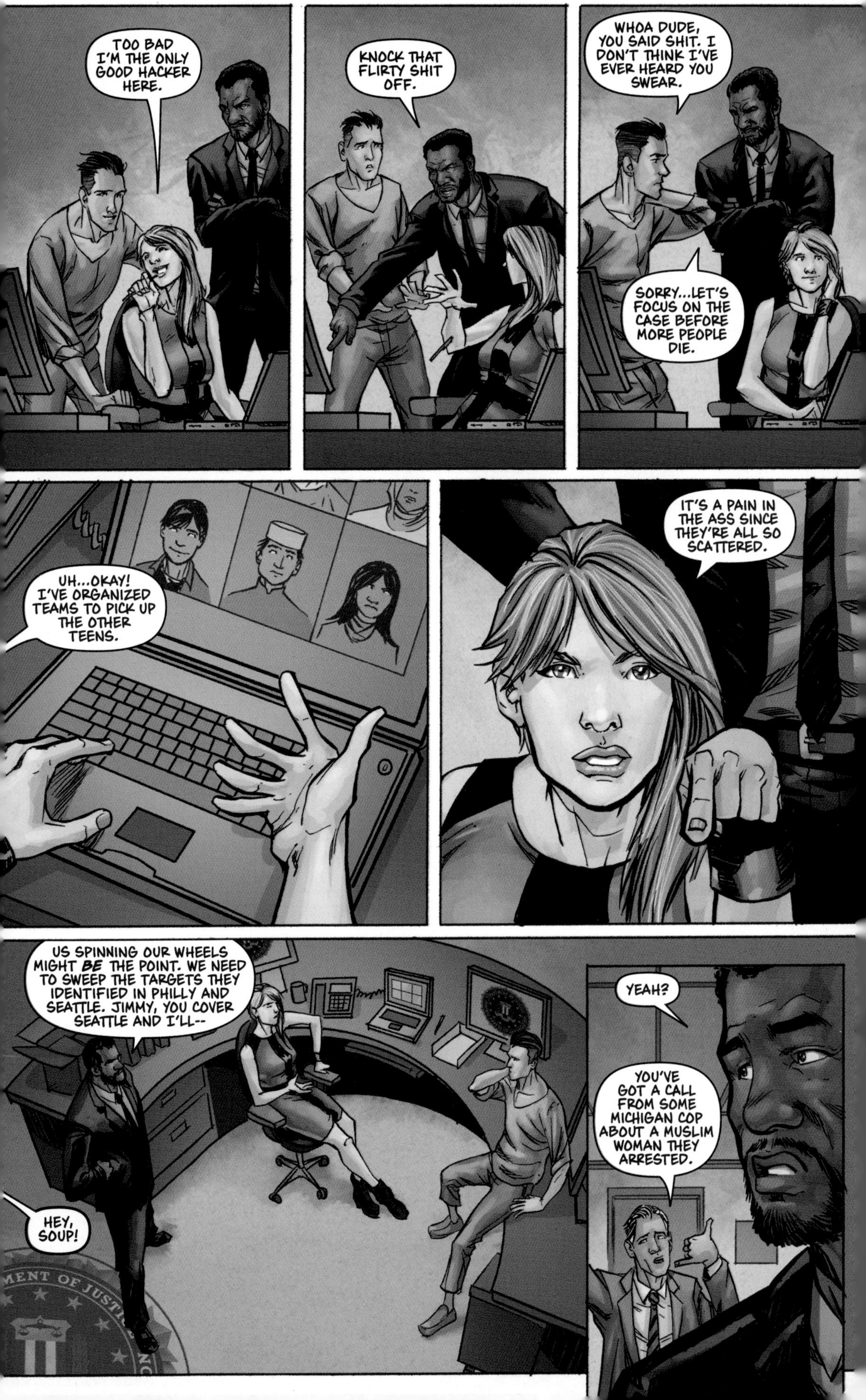
TOO BAD I'M THE ONLY GOOD HACKER HERE.
KNOCK THAT FLIRTY SHIT OFF.
WHOA DUDE, YOU SAID SHIT. I DON'T THINK I'VE EVER HEARD YOU SWEAR.
SORRY...LET'S FOCUS ON THE CASE BEFORE MORE PEOPLE DIE.
UH...OKAY! I'VE ORGANIZED TEAMS TO PICK UP THE OTHER TEENS.
IT'S A PAIN IN THE ASS SINCE THEY'RE ALL SO SCATTERED.
US SPINNING OUR WHEELS MIGHT *BE* THE POINT. WE NEED TO SWEEP THE TARGETS THEY IDENTIFIED IN PHILLY AND SEATTLE. JIMMY, YOU COVER SEATTLE AND I'LL--
HEY, SOUP!
YEAH?
YOU'VE GOT A CALL FROM SOME MICHIGAN COP ABOUT A MUSLIM WOMAN THEY ARRESTED.

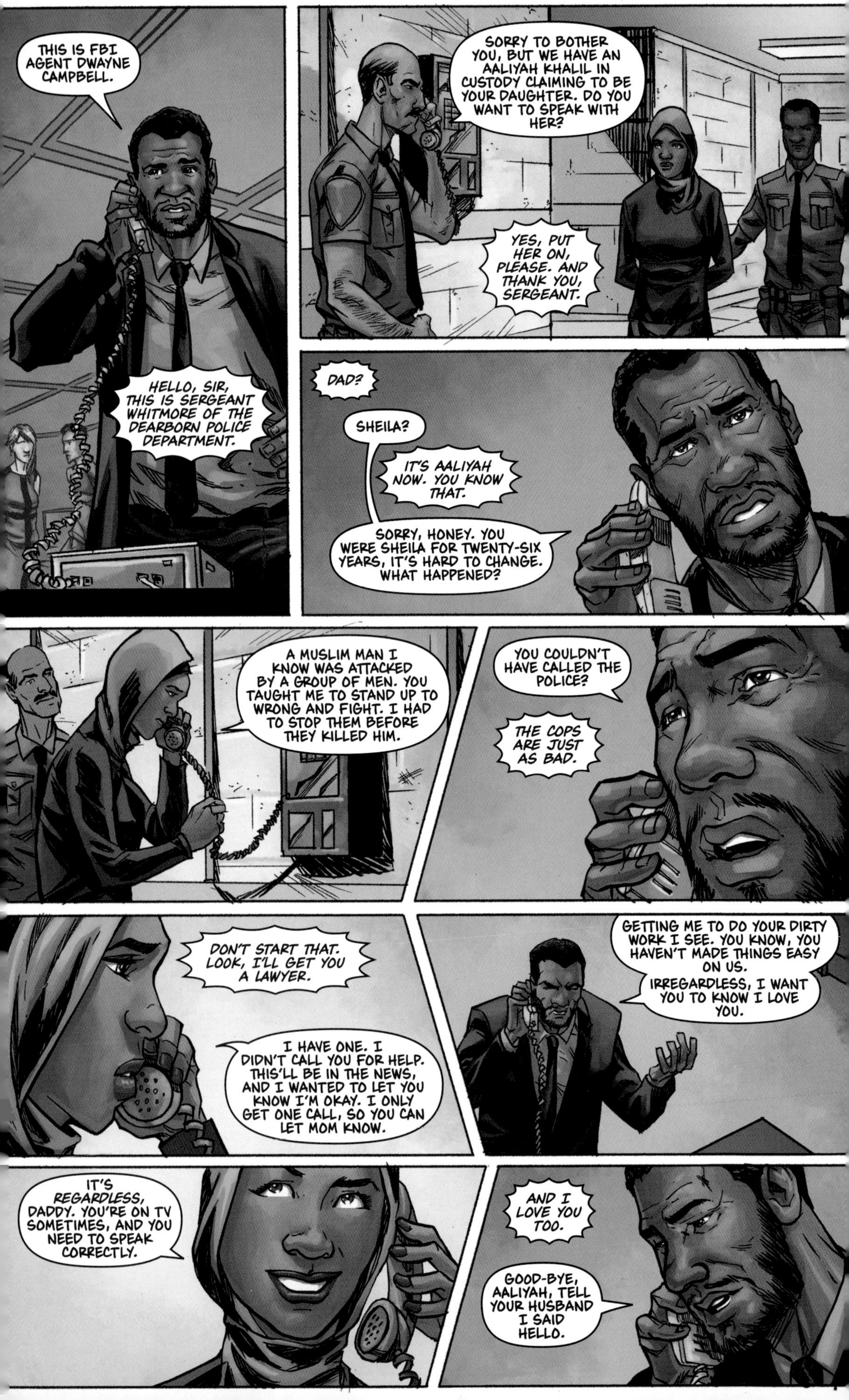
THIS IS FBI AGENT DWAYNE CAMPBELL.
HELLO, SIR, THIS IS SERGEANT WHITMORE OF THE DEARBORN POLICE DEPARTMENT.
SORRY TO BOTHER YOU, BUT WE HAVE AN AALIYAH KHALIL IN CUSTODY CLAIMING TO BE YOUR DAUGHTER. DO YOU WANT TO SPEAK WITH HER?
YES, PUT HER ON, PLEASE. AND THANK YOU, SERGEANT.
DAD?
SHEILA?
IT'S AALIYAH NOW. YOU KNOW THAT.
SORRY, HONEY. YOU WERE SHEILA FOR TWENTY-SIX YEARS, IT'S HARD TO CHANGE. WHAT HAPPENED?
A MUSLIM MAN I KNOW WAS ATTACKED BY A GROUP OF MEN. YOU TAUGHT ME TO STAND UP TO WRONG AND FIGHT. I HAD TO STOP THEM BEFORE THEY KILLED HIM.
YOU COULDN'T HAVE CALLED THE POLICE?
THE COPS ARE JUST AS BAD.
DON'T START THAT. LOOK, I'LL GET YOU A LAWYER.
I HAVE ONE. I DIDN'T CALL YOU FOR HELP. THIS'LL BE IN THE NEWS, AND I WANTED TO LET YOU KNOW I'M OKAY. I ONLY GET ONE CALL, SO YOU CAN LET MOM KNOW.
GETTING ME TO DO YOUR DIRTY WORK I SEE. YOU KNOW, YOU HAVEN'T MADE THINGS EASY ON US.
IRREGARDLESS, I WANT YOU TO KNOW I LOVE YOU.
IT'S REGARDLESS, DADDY. YOU'RE ON TV SOMETIMES, AND YOU NEED TO SPEAK CORRECTLY.
AND I LOVE YOU TOO.
GOOD-BYE, AALIYAH, TELL YOUR HUSBAND I SAID HELLO.

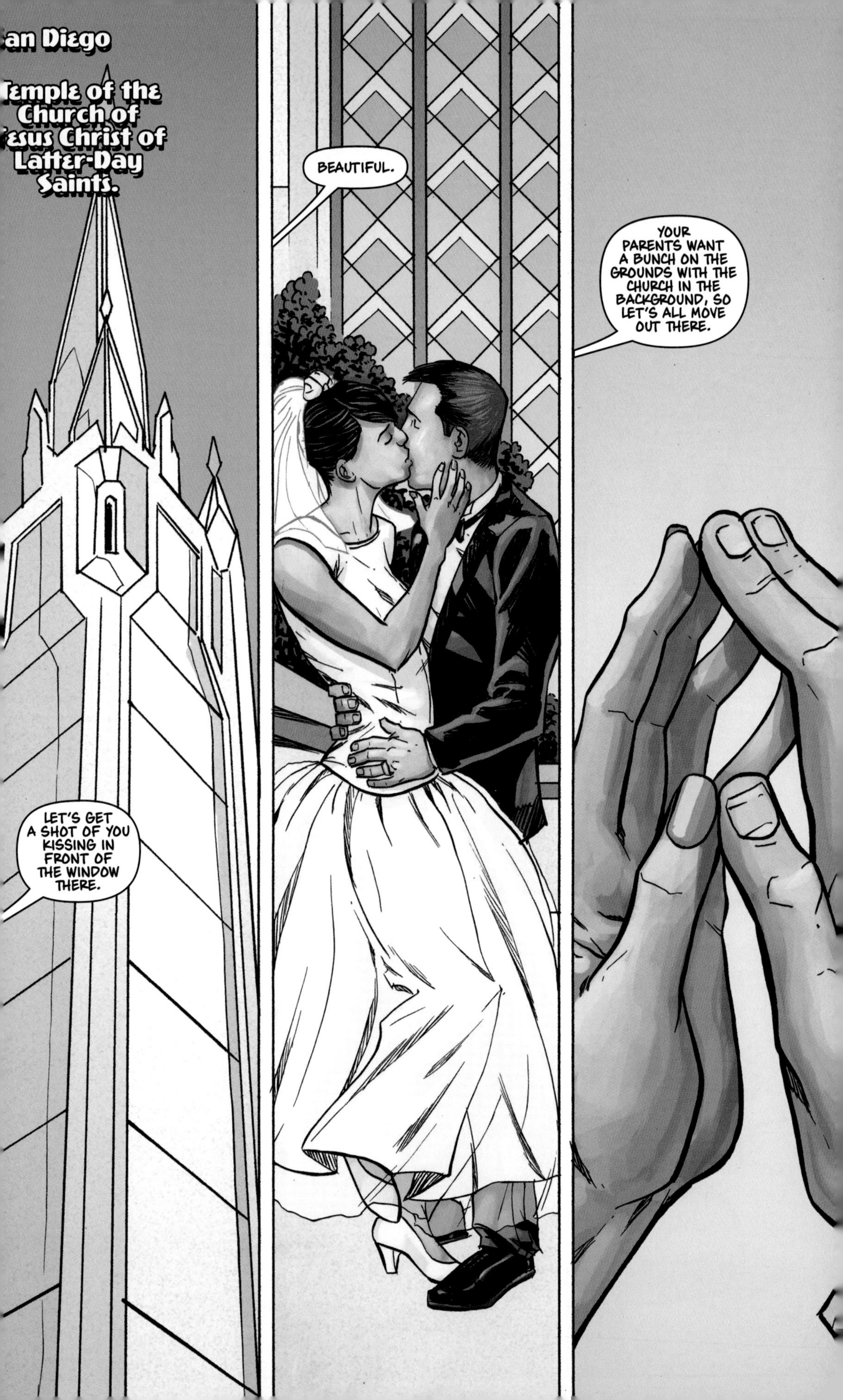

an Diego
Temple of the Church of Jesus Christ of Latter-Day Saints.
LET'S GET A SHOT OF YOU KISSING IN FRONT OF THE WINDOW THERE.
BEAUTIFUL.
YOUR PARENTS WANT A BUNCH ON THE GROUNDS WITH THE CHURCH IN THE BACKGROUND, SO LET'S ALL MOVE OUT THERE.

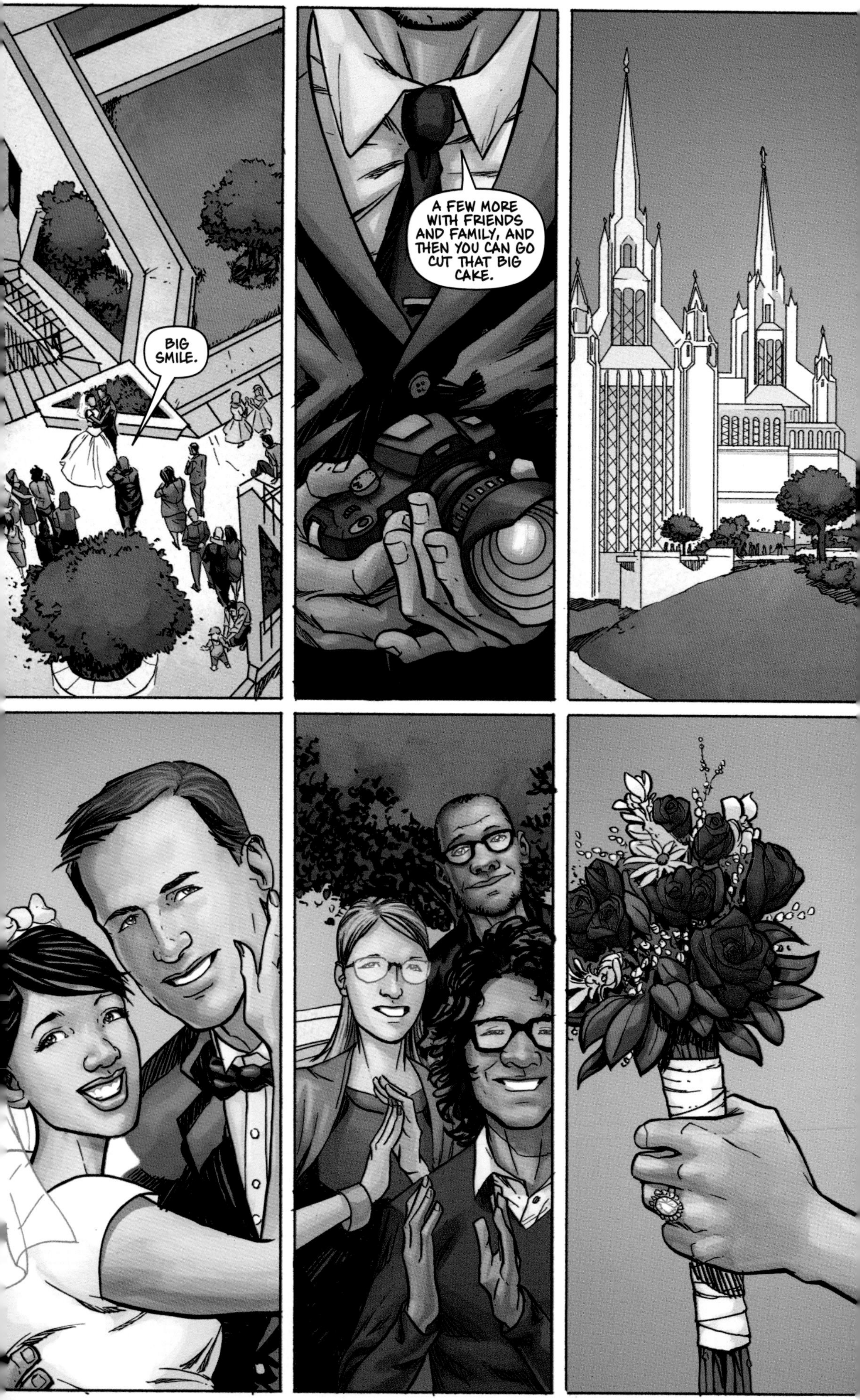
BIG SMILE.
A FEW MORE WITH FRIENDS AND FAMILY, AND THEN YOU CAN GO CUT THAT BIG CAKE.

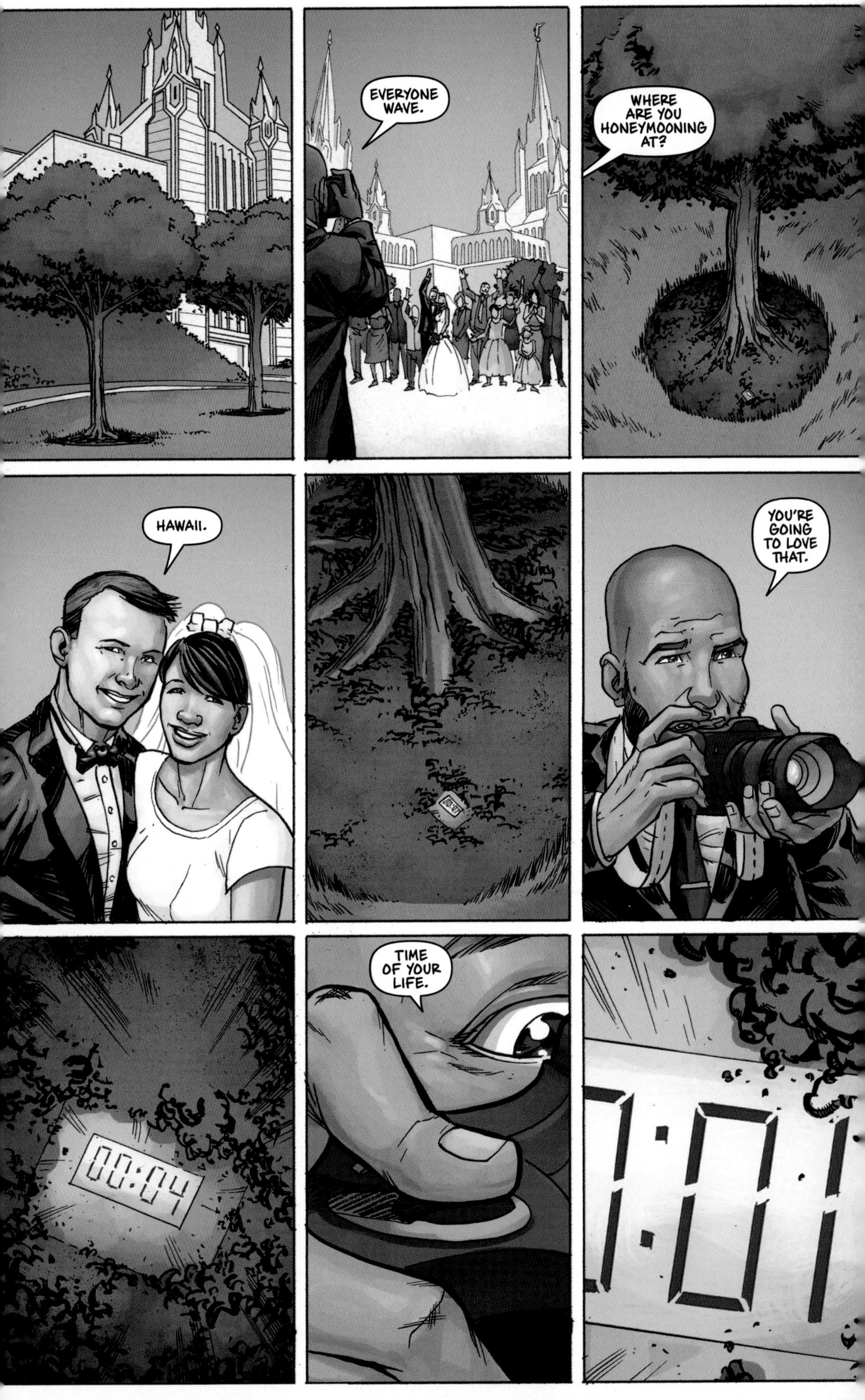
EVERYONE WAVE.
WHERE ARE YOU HONEYMOONING AT?
HAWAII.
YOU'RE GOING TO LOVE THAT.
00:04
TIME OF YOUR LIFE.

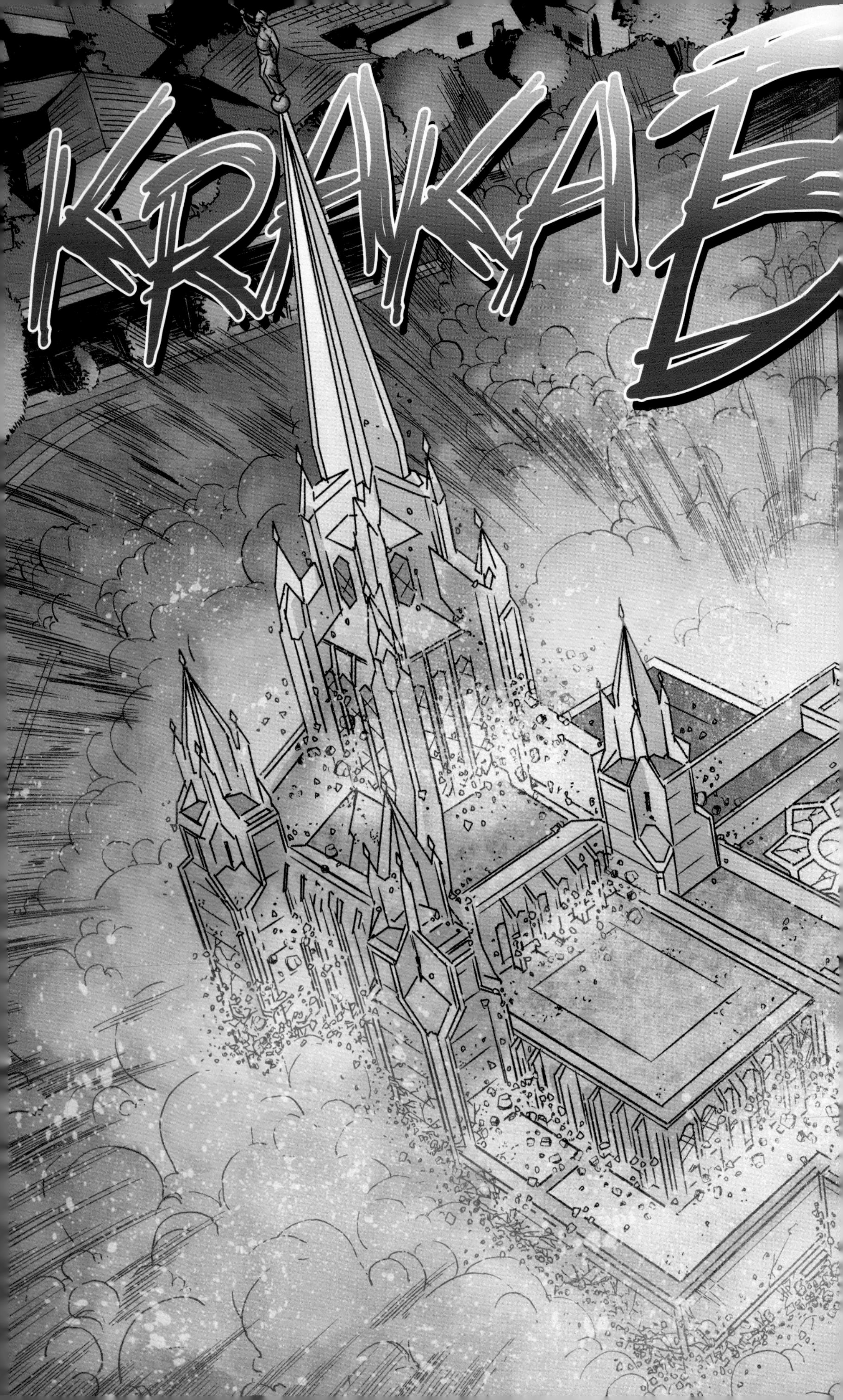
KRAKAB

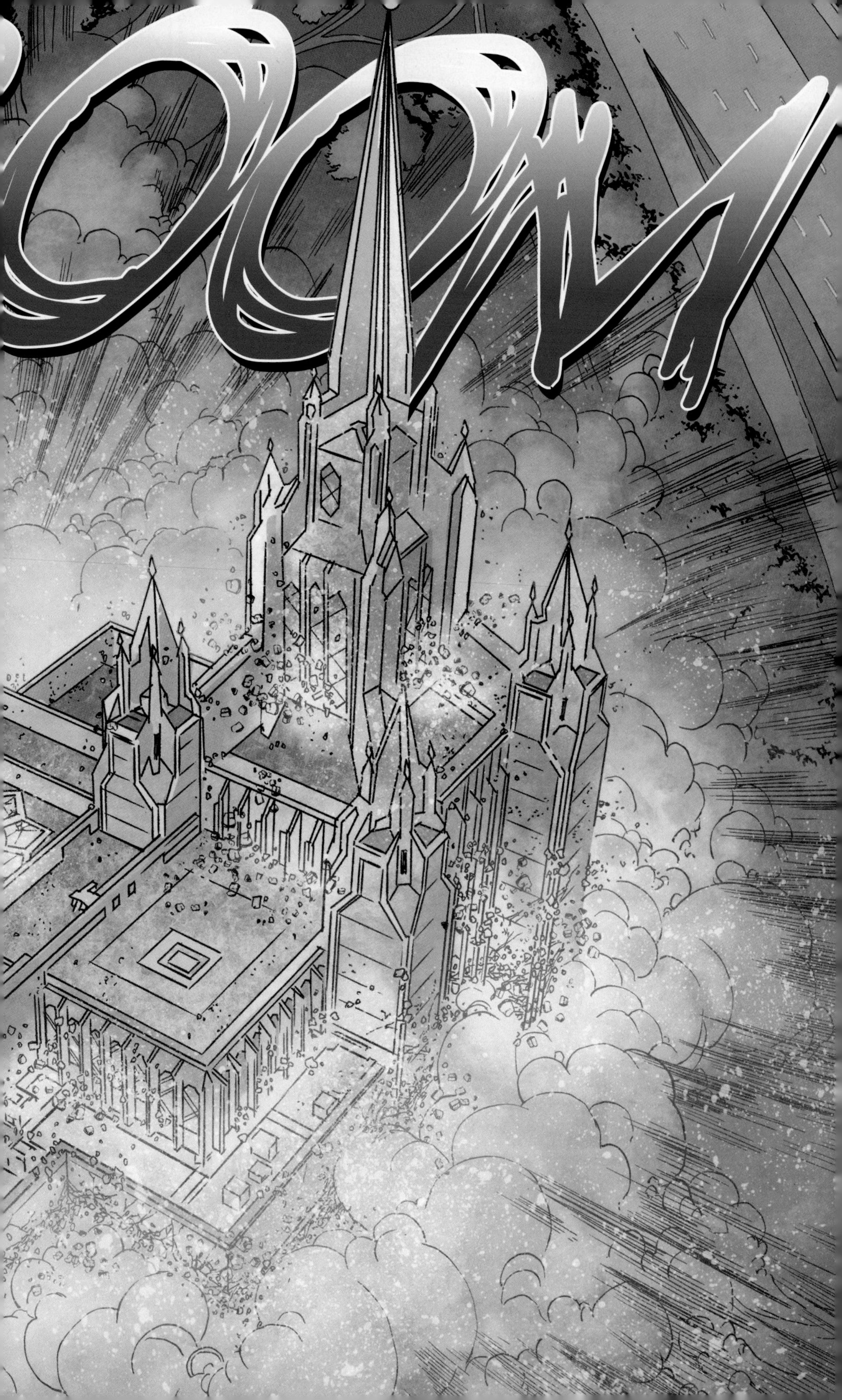

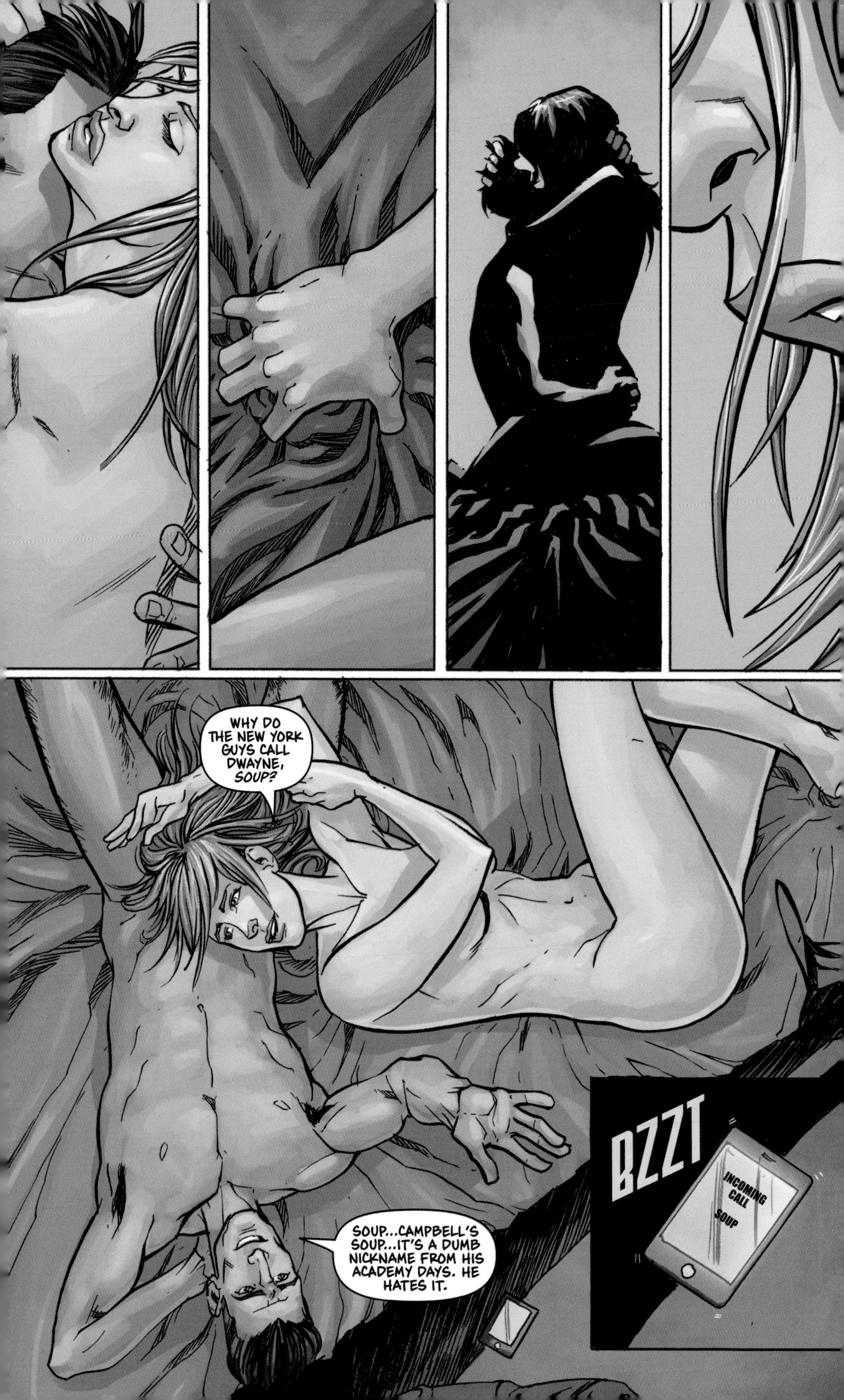
WHY DO THE NEW YORK GUYS CALL DWAYNE, SOUP?
SOUP...CAMPBELL'S SOUP...IT'S A DUMB NICKNAME FROM HIS ACADEMY DAYS. HE HATES IT.
BZZT
INCOMING CALL
SOUP

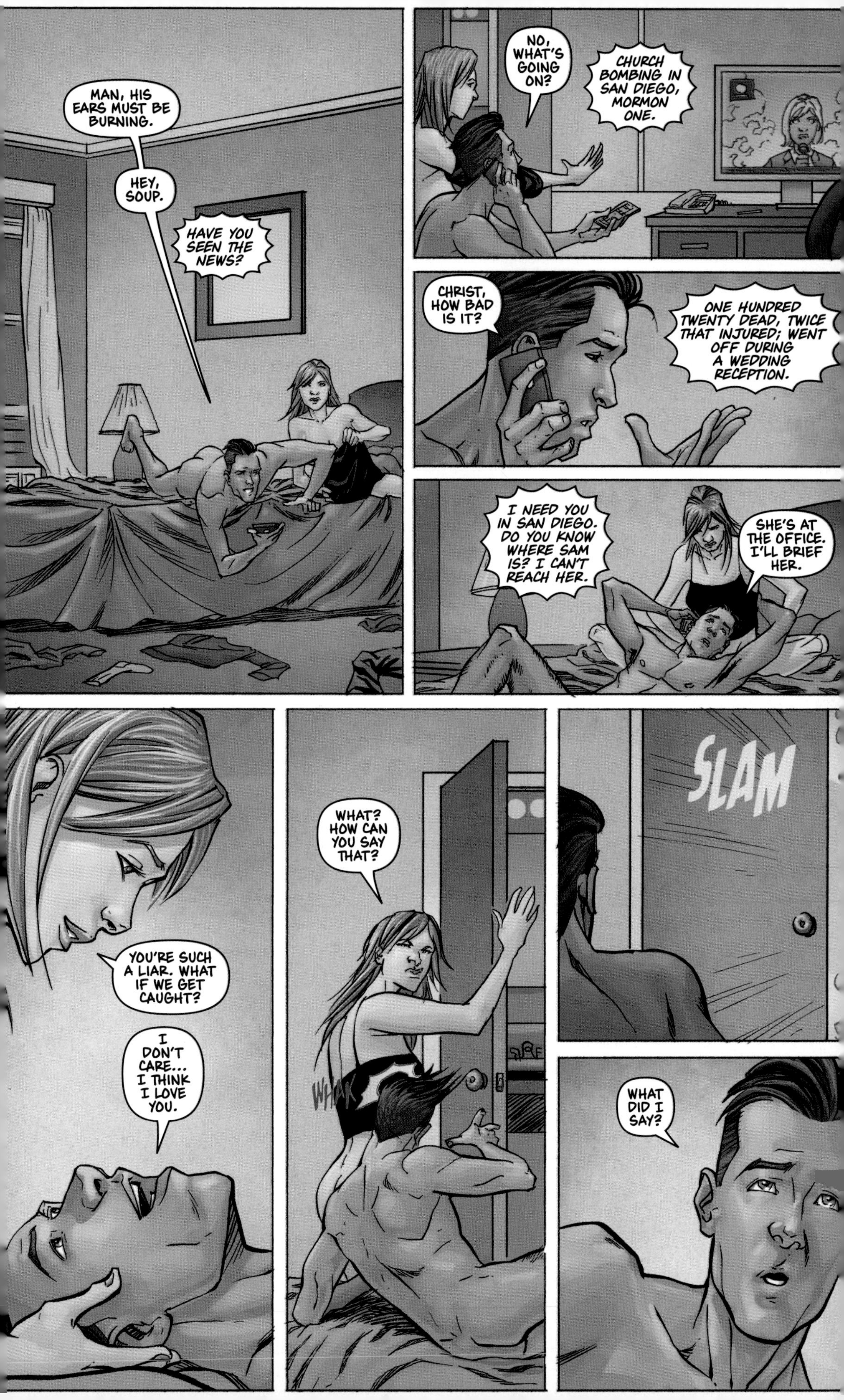

MAN, HIS EARS MUST BE BURNING.
HEY, SOUP.
HAVE YOU SEEN THE NEWS?
NO, WHAT'S GOING ON?
CHURCH BOMBING IN SAN DIEGO, MORMON ONE.
CHRIST, HOW BAD IS IT?
ONE HUNDRED TWENTY DEAD, TWICE THAT INJURED; WENT OFF DURING A WEDDING RECEPTION.
I NEED YOU IN SAN DIEGO. DO YOU KNOW WHERE SAM IS? I CAN'T REACH HER.
SHE'S AT THE OFFICE. I'LL BRIEF HER.
YOU'RE SUCH A LIAR. WHAT IF WE GET CAUGHT?
I DON'T CARE... I THINK I LOVE YOU.
WHAT? HOW CAN YOU SAY THAT?
WHAK
SLAM
WHAT DID I SAY?

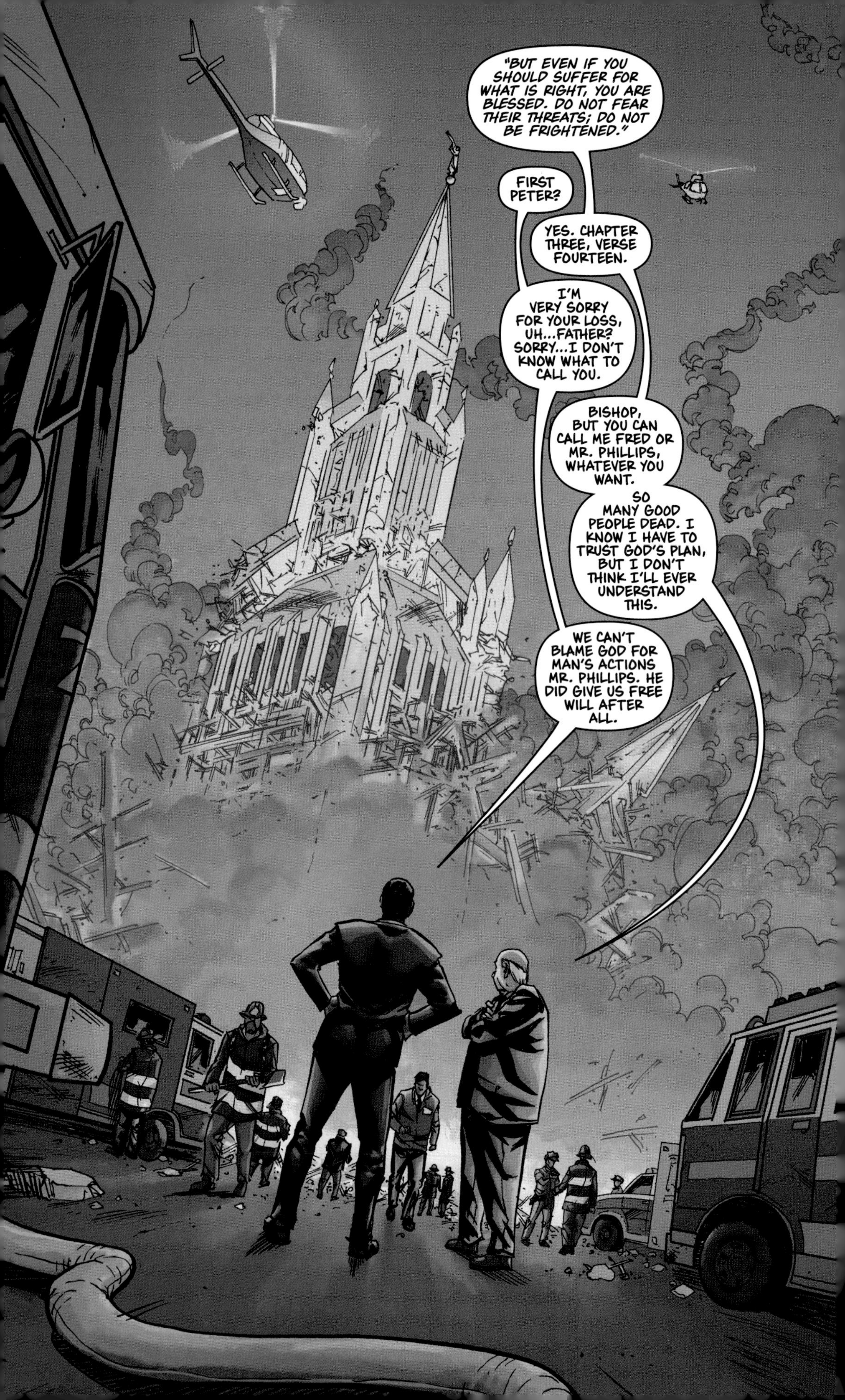
"BUT EVEN IF YOU SHOULD SUFFER FOR WHAT IS RIGHT, YOU ARE BLESSED. DO NOT FEAR THEIR THREATS; DO NOT BE FRIGHTENED."
FIRST PETER?
YES. CHAPTER THREE, VERSE FOURTEEN.
I'M VERY SORRY FOR YOUR LOSS, UH...FATHER? SORRY...I DON'T KNOW WHAT TO CALL YOU.
BISHOP, BUT YOU CAN CALL ME FRED OR MR. PHILLIPS, WHATEVER YOU WANT.
SO MANY GOOD PEOPLE DEAD. I KNOW I HAVE TO TRUST GOD'S PLAN, BUT I DON'T THINK I'LL EVER UNDERSTAND THIS.
WE CAN'T BLAME GOD FOR MAN'S ACTIONS MR. PHILLIPS. HE DID GIVE US FREE WILL AFTER ALL.

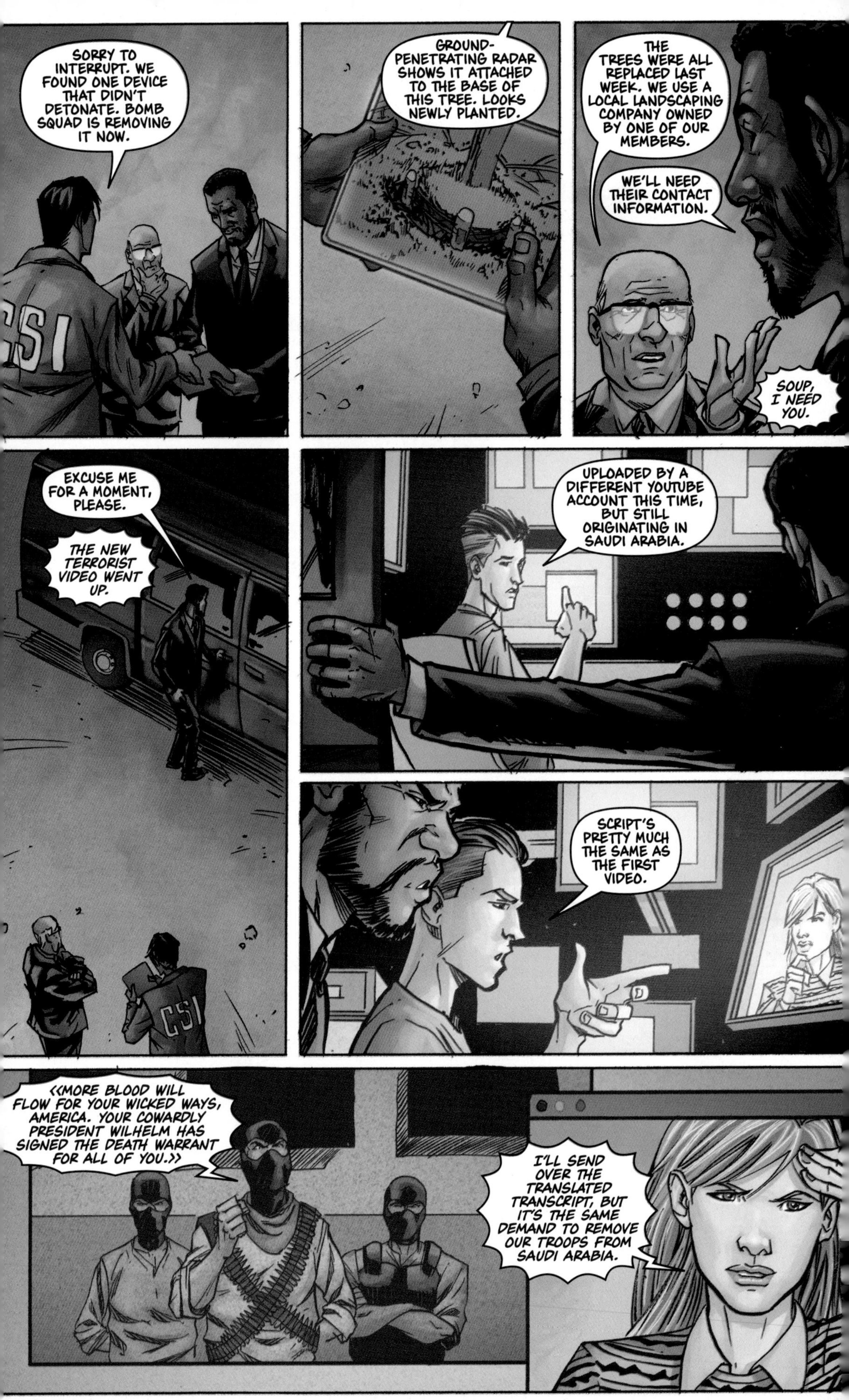
SORRY TO INTERRUPT. WE FOUND ONE DEVICE THAT DIDN'T DETONATE. BOMB SQUAD IS REMOVING IT NOW.
GROUND-PENETRATING RADAR SHOWS IT ATTACHED TO THE BASE OF THIS TREE. LOOKS NEWLY PLANTED.
THE TREES WERE ALL REPLACED LAST WEEK. WE USE A LOCAL LANDSCAPING COMPANY OWNED BY ONE OF OUR MEMBERS.
WE'LL NEED THEIR CONTACT INFORMATION.
SOUP, I NEED YOU.
EXCUSE ME FOR A MOMENT, PLEASE.
THE NEW TERRORIST VIDEO WENT UP.
UPLOADED BY A DIFFERENT YOUTUBE ACCOUNT THIS TIME, BUT STILL ORIGINATING IN SAUDI ARABIA.
SCRIPT'S PRETTY MUCH THE SAME AS THE FIRST VIDEO.
<<MORE BLOOD WILL FLOW FOR YOUR WICKED WAYS, AMERICA. YOUR COWARDLY PRESIDENT WILHELM HAS SIGNED THE DEATH WARRANT FOR ALL OF YOU.>>
I'LL SEND OVER THE TRANSLATED TRANSCRIPT, BUT IT'S THE SAME DEMAND TO REMOVE OUR TROOPS FROM SAUDI ARABIA.

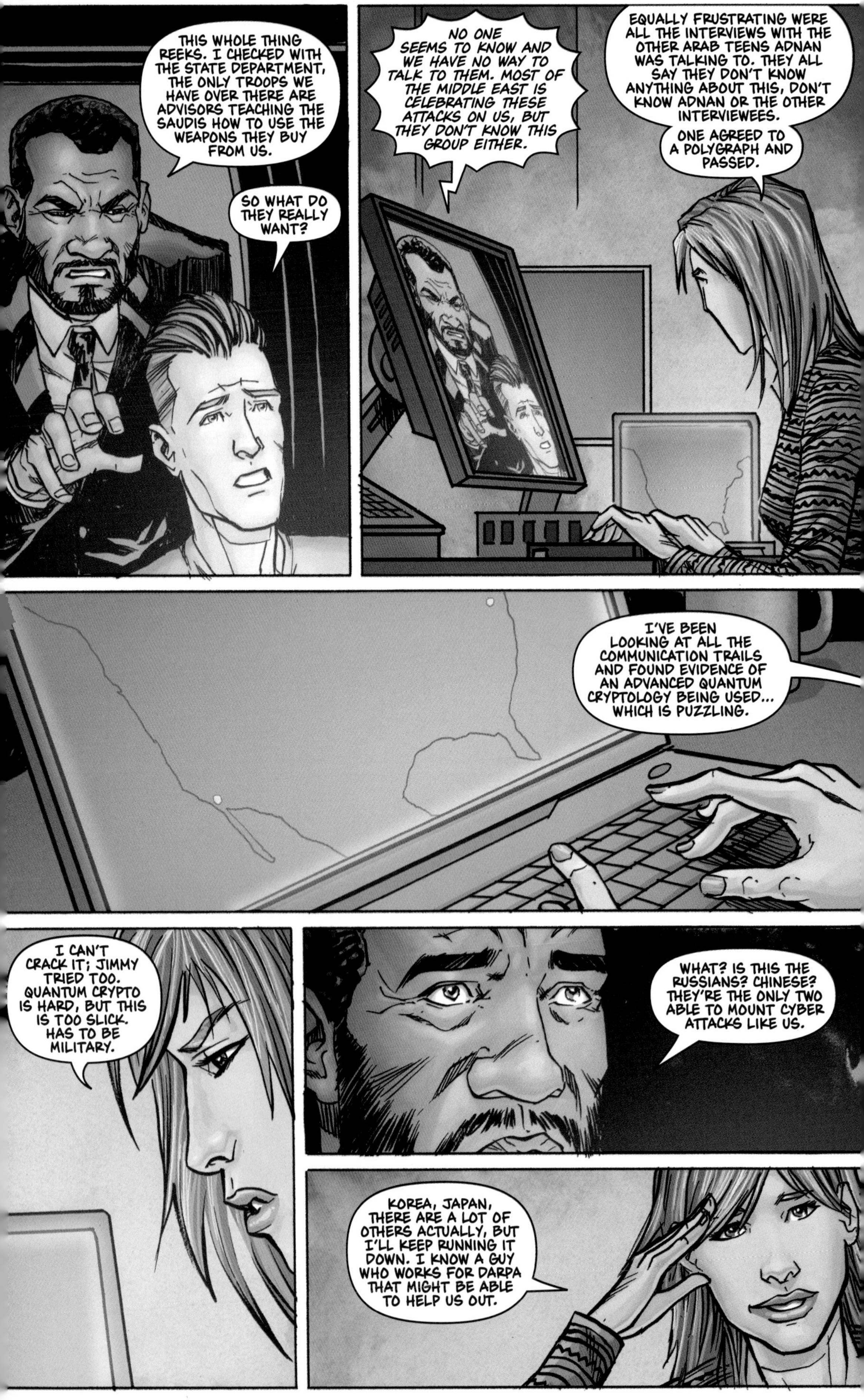
THIS WHOLE THING REEKS. I CHECKED WITH THE STATE DEPARTMENT, THE ONLY TROOPS WE HAVE OVER THERE ARE ADVISORS TEACHING THE SAUDIS HOW TO USE THE WEAPONS THEY BUY FROM US.
SO WHAT DO THEY REALLY WANT?
NO ONE SEEMS TO KNOW AND WE HAVE NO WAY TO TALK TO THEM. MOST OF THE MIDDLE EAST IS CELEBRATING THESE ATTACKS ON US, BUT THEY DON'T KNOW THIS GROUP EITHER.
EQUALLY FRUSTRATING WERE ALL THE INTERVIEWS WITH THE OTHER ARAB TEENS ADNAN WAS TALKING TO. THEY ALL SAY THEY DON'T KNOW ANYTHING ABOUT THIS, DON'T KNOW ADNAN OR THE OTHER INTERVIEWEES.
ONE AGREED TO A POLYGRAPH AND PASSED.
I'VE BEEN LOOKING AT ALL THE COMMUNICATION TRAILS AND FOUND EVIDENCE OF AN ADVANCED QUANTUM CRYPTOLOGY BEING USED... WHICH IS PUZZLING.
I CAN'T CRACK IT; JIMMY TRIED TOO. QUANTUM CRYPTO IS HARD, BUT THIS IS TOO SLICK. HAS TO BE MILITARY.
WHAT? IS THIS THE RUSSIANS? CHINESE? THEY'RE THE ONLY TWO ABLE TO MOUNT CYBER ATTACKS LIKE US.
KOREA, JAPAN, THERE ARE A LOT OF OTHERS ACTUALLY, BUT I'LL KEEP RUNNING IT DOWN. I KNOW A GUY WHO WORKS FOR DARPA THAT MIGHT BE ABLE TO HELP US OUT.

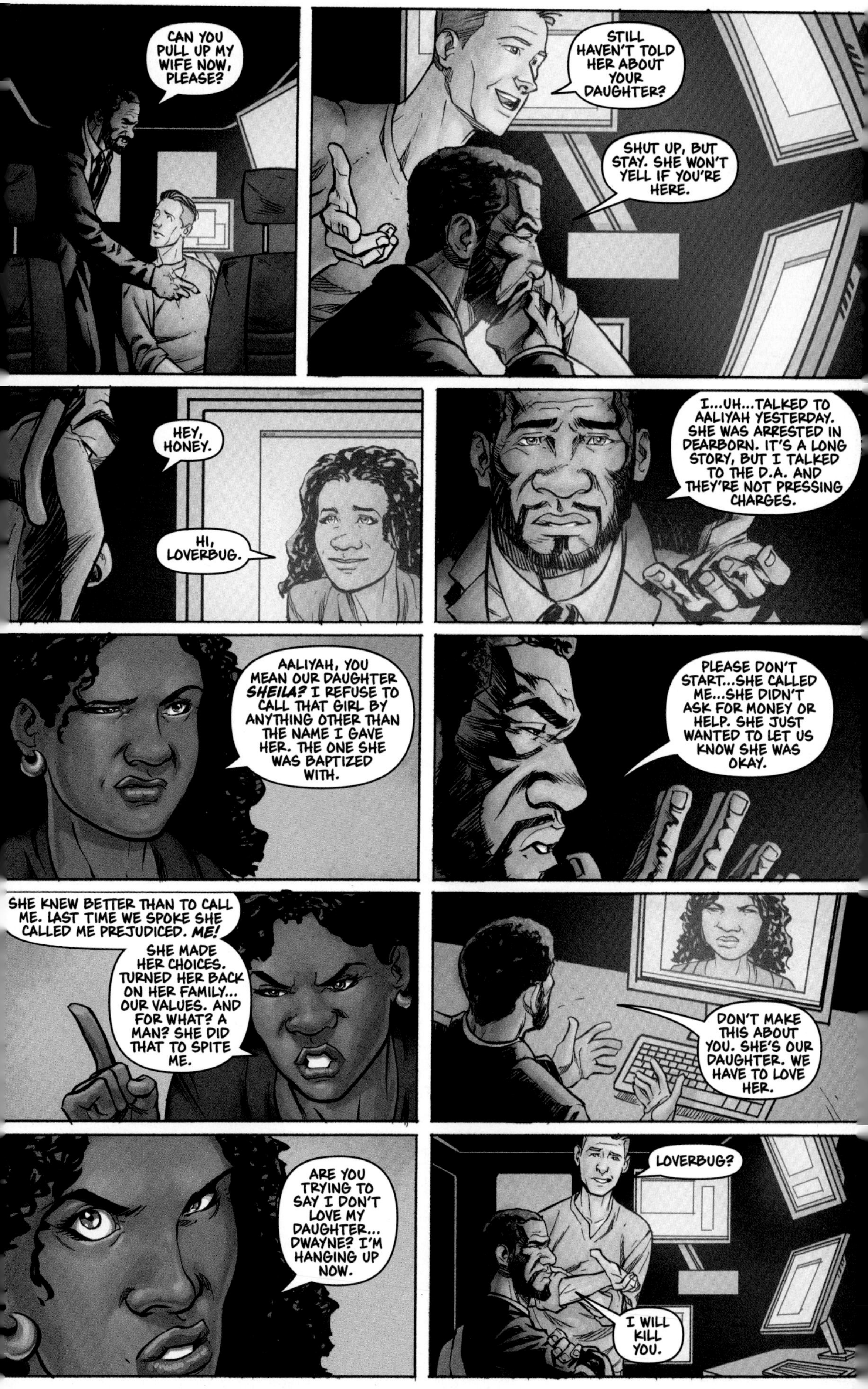
CAN YOU PULL UP MY WIFE NOW, PLEASE?
STILL HAVEN'T TOLD HER ABOUT YOUR DAUGHTER?
SHUT UP, BUT STAY. SHE WON'T YELL IF YOU'RE HERE.
HEY, HONEY.
HI, LOVERBUG.
I...UH...TALKED TO AALIYAH YESTERDAY. SHE WAS ARRESTED IN DEARBORN. IT'S A LONG STORY, BUT I TALKED TO THE D.A. AND THEY'RE NOT PRESSING CHARGES.
AALIYAH, YOU MEAN OUR DAUGHTER *SHEILA?* I REFUSE TO CALL THAT GIRL BY ANYTHING OTHER THAN THE NAME I GAVE HER. THE ONE SHE WAS BAPTIZED WITH.
PLEASE DON'T START...SHE CALLED ME...SHE DIDN'T ASK FOR MONEY OR HELP. SHE JUST WANTED TO LET US KNOW SHE WAS OKAY.
SHE KNEW BETTER THAN TO CALL ME. LAST TIME WE SPOKE SHE CALLED ME PREJUDICED. *ME!*
SHE MADE HER CHOICES. TURNED HER BACK ON HER FAMILY... OUR VALUES. AND FOR WHAT? A MAN? SHE DID THAT TO SPITE ME.
DON'T MAKE THIS ABOUT YOU. SHE'S OUR DAUGHTER. WE HAVE TO LOVE HER.
ARE YOU TRYING TO SAY I DON'T LOVE MY DAUGHTER... DWAYNE? I'M HANGING UP NOW.
LOVERBUG?
I WILL KILL YOU.

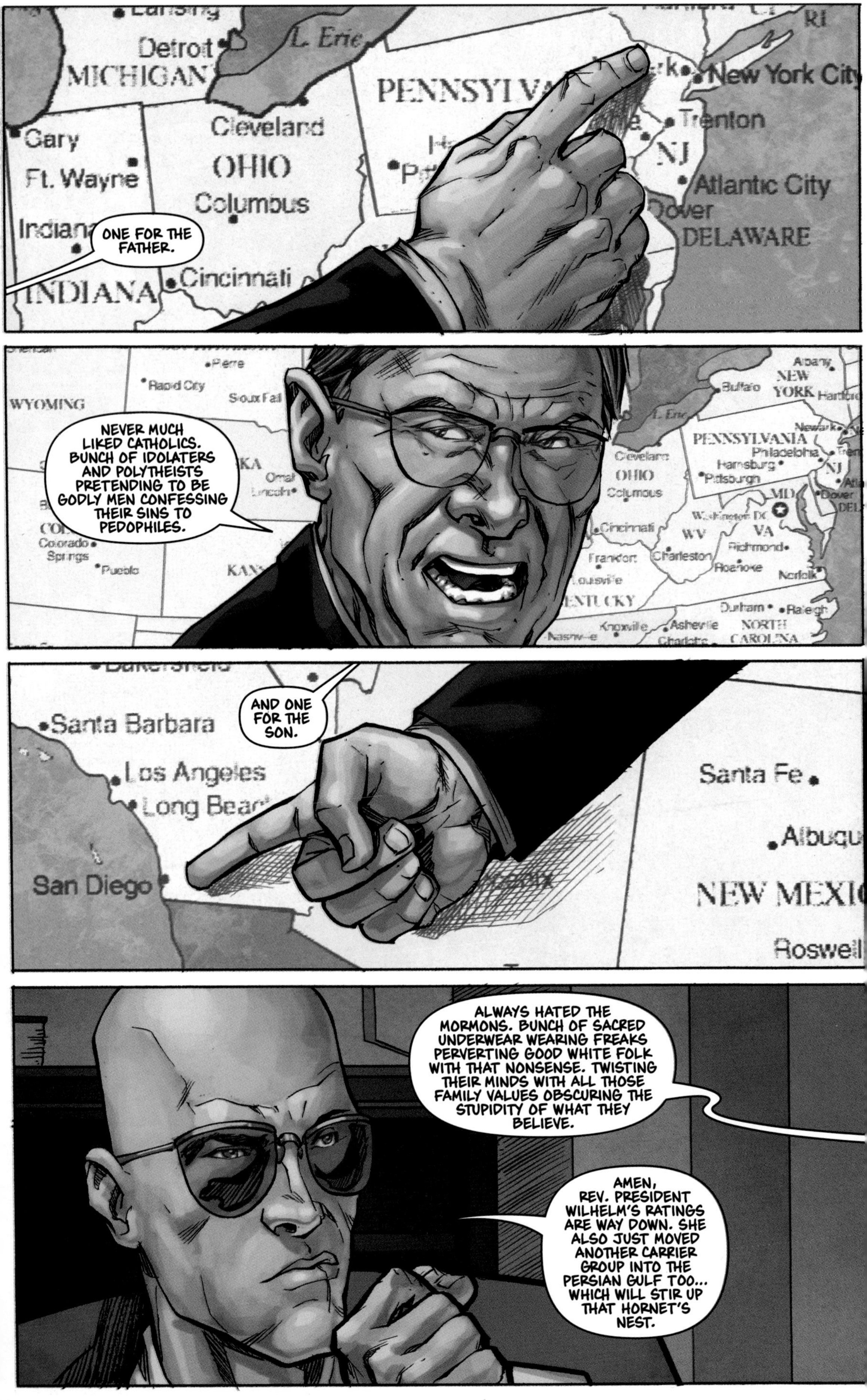
ONE FOR THE FATHER.
NEVER MUCH LIKED CATHOLICS. BUNCH OF IDOLATERS AND POLYTHEISTS PRETENDING TO BE GODLY MEN CONFESSING THEIR SINS TO PEDOPHILES.
AND ONE FOR THE SON.
ALWAYS HATED THE MORMONS. BUNCH OF SACRED UNDERWEAR WEARING FREAKS PERVERTING GOOD WHITE FOLK WITH THAT NONSENSE. TWISTING THEIR MINDS WITH ALL THOSE FAMILY VALUES OBSCURING THE STUPIDITY OF WHAT THEY BELIEVE.
AMEN, REV. PRESIDENT WILHELM'S RATINGS ARE WAY DOWN. SHE ALSO JUST MOVED ANOTHER CARRIER GROUP INTO THE PERSIAN GULF TOO... WHICH WILL STIR UP THAT HORNET'S NEST.

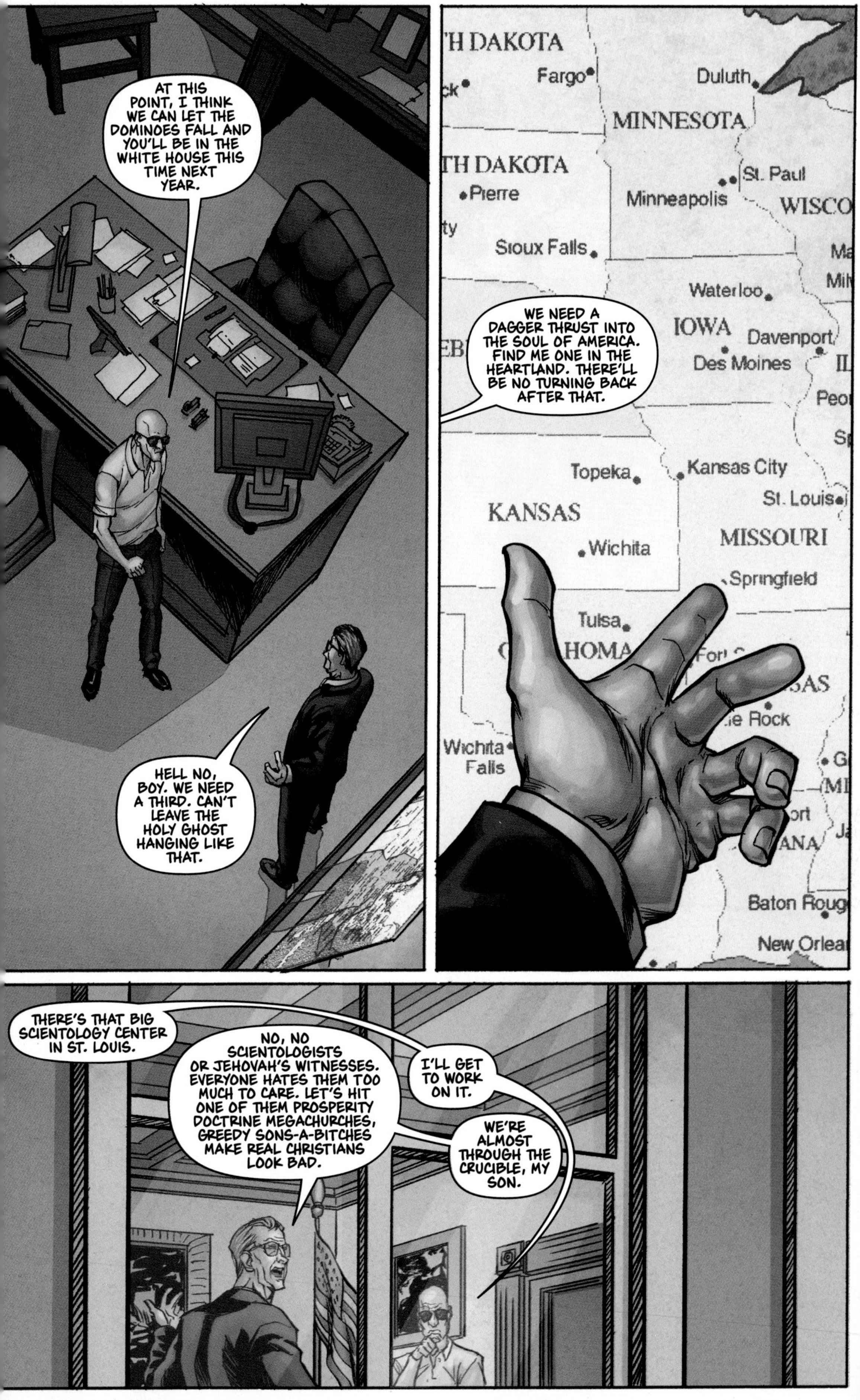
AT THIS POINT, I THINK WE CAN LET THE DOMINOES FALL AND YOU'LL BE IN THE WHITE HOUSE THIS TIME NEXT YEAR.
HELL NO, BOY. WE NEED A THIRD. CAN'T LEAVE THE HOLY GHOST HANGING LIKE THAT.
Fargo
Duluth
MINNESOTA
Pierre
St. Paul
Minneapolis
Sioux Falls
Waterloo
IOWA
Davenport
Des Moines
WE NEED A DAGGER THRUST INTO THE SOUL OF AMERICA. FIND ME ONE IN THE HEARTLAND. THERE'LL BE NO TURNING BACK AFTER THAT.
Topeka
Kansas City
St. Louis
KANSAS
Wichita
MISSOURI
Springfield
Tulsa
Wichita Falls
Baton Roug
New Orlea
THERE'S THAT BIG SCIENTOLOGY CENTER IN ST. LOUIS.
NO, NO SCIENTOLOGISTS OR JEHOVAH'S WITNESSES. EVERYONE HATES THEM TOO MUCH TO CARE. LET'S HIT ONE OF THEM PROSPERITY DOCTRINE MEGACHURCHES, GREEDY SONS-A-BITCHES MAKE REAL CHRISTIANS LOOK BAD.
I'LL GET TO WORK ON IT.
WE'RE ALMOST THROUGH THE CRUCIBLE, MY SON.

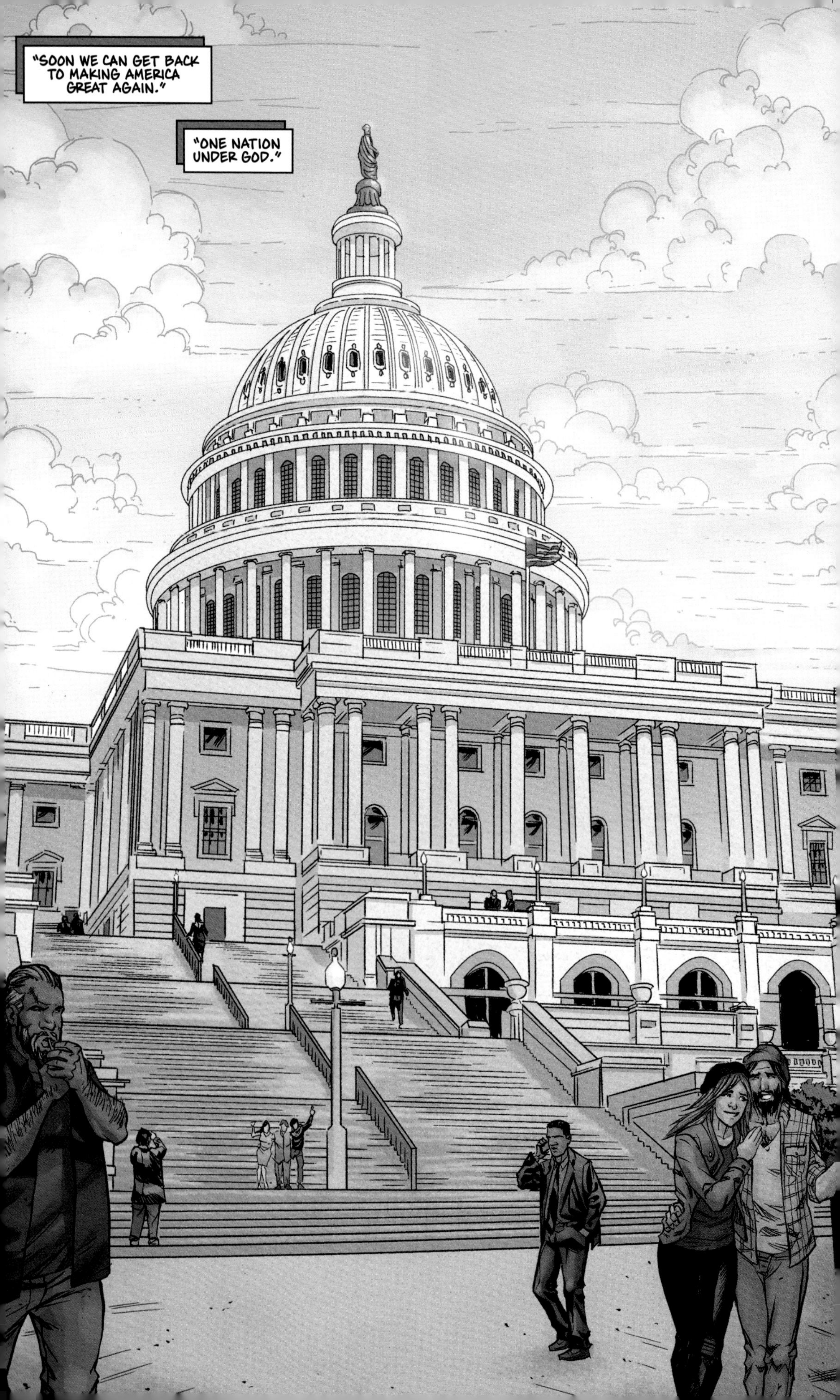
"SOON WE CAN GET BACK TO MAKING AMERICA GREAT AGAIN."
"ONE NATION UNDER GOD."

FOR THE WAGES OF SIN IS DEATH: BUT THE GIFT OF GOD
IS ETERNAL LIFE THROUGH JESUS CHRIST OUR LORD.
-ROMANS 6:23
KING JAMES VERSION (KJV)

ISLAMOPHOBIA: CHAPTER 3

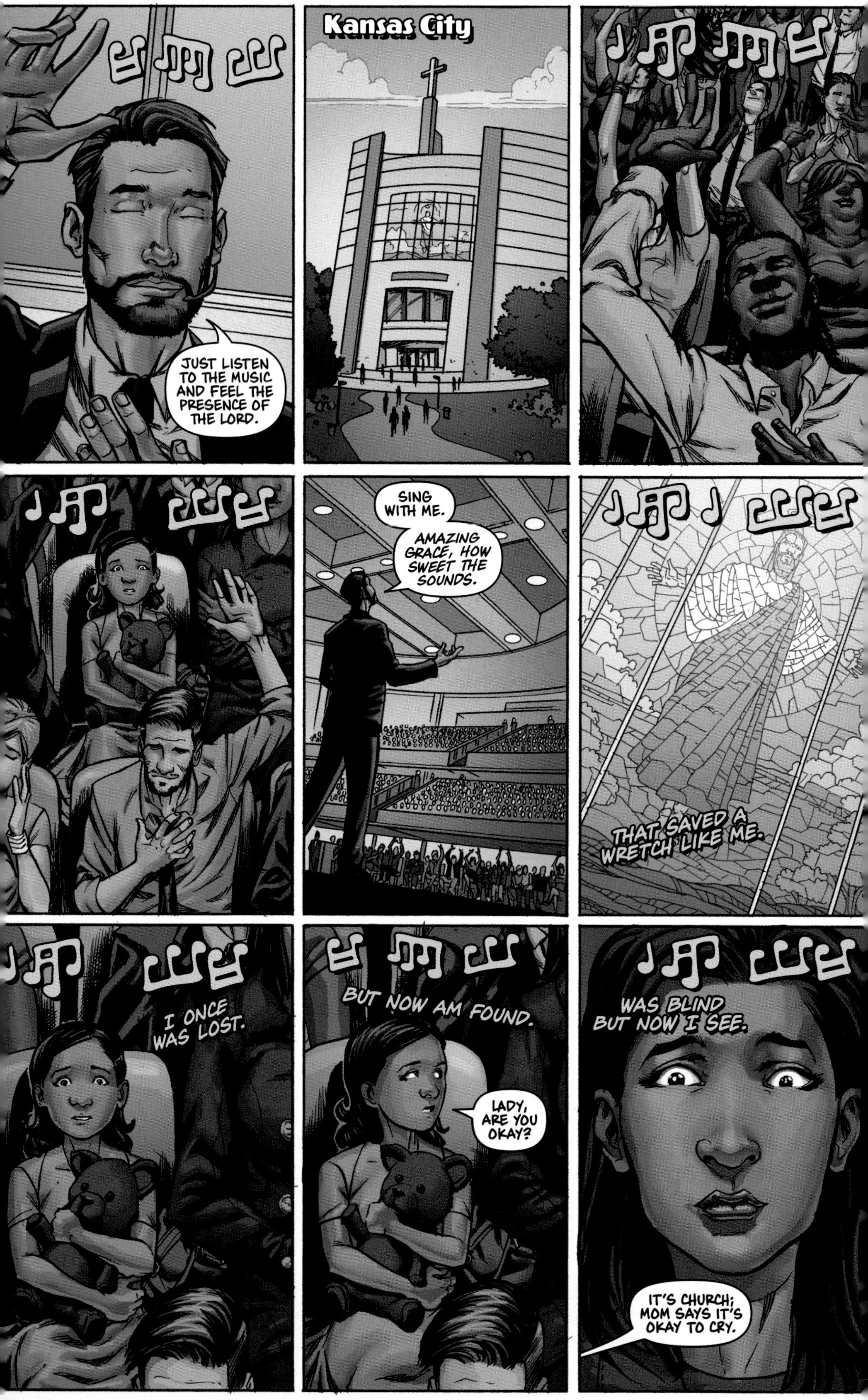
JUST LISTEN TO THE MUSIC AND FEEL THE PRESENCE OF THE LORD.
Kansas City
SING WITH ME.
AMAZING GRACE, HOW SWEET THE SOUNDS.
THAT SAVED A WRETCH LIKE ME.
I ONCE WAS LOST.
BUT NOW AM FOUND.
LADY, ARE YOU OKAY?
WAS BLIND BUT NOW I SEE.
IT'S CHURCH; MOM SAYS IT'S OKAY TO CRY.

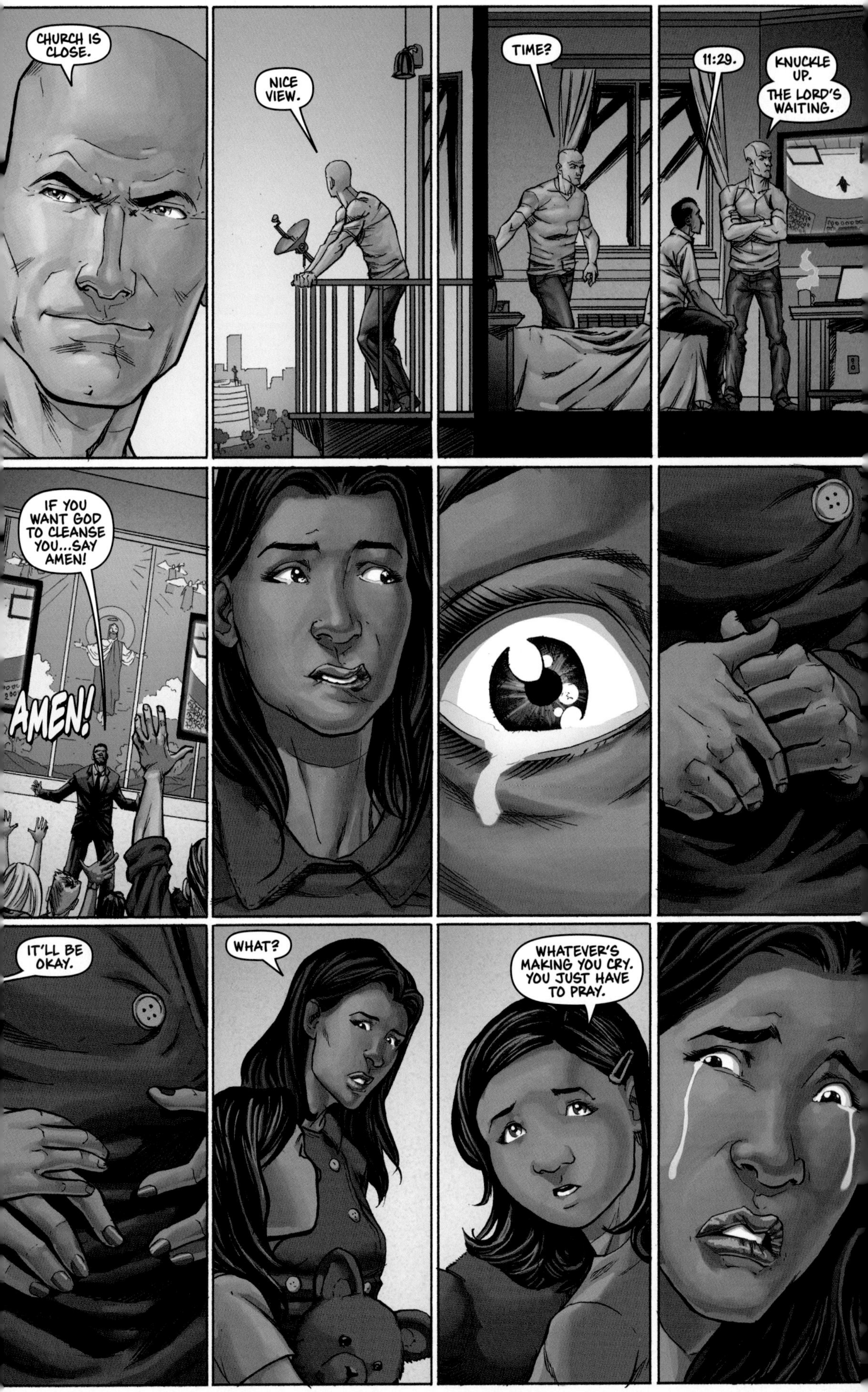
CHURCH IS CLOSE.
NICE VIEW.
TIME?
11:29.
KNUCKLE UP. THE LORD'S WAITING.
IF YOU WANT GOD TO CLEANSE YOU...SAY AMEN!
AMEN!
IT'LL BE OKAY.
WHAT?
WHATEVER'S MAKING YOU CRY. YOU JUST HAVE TO PRAY.

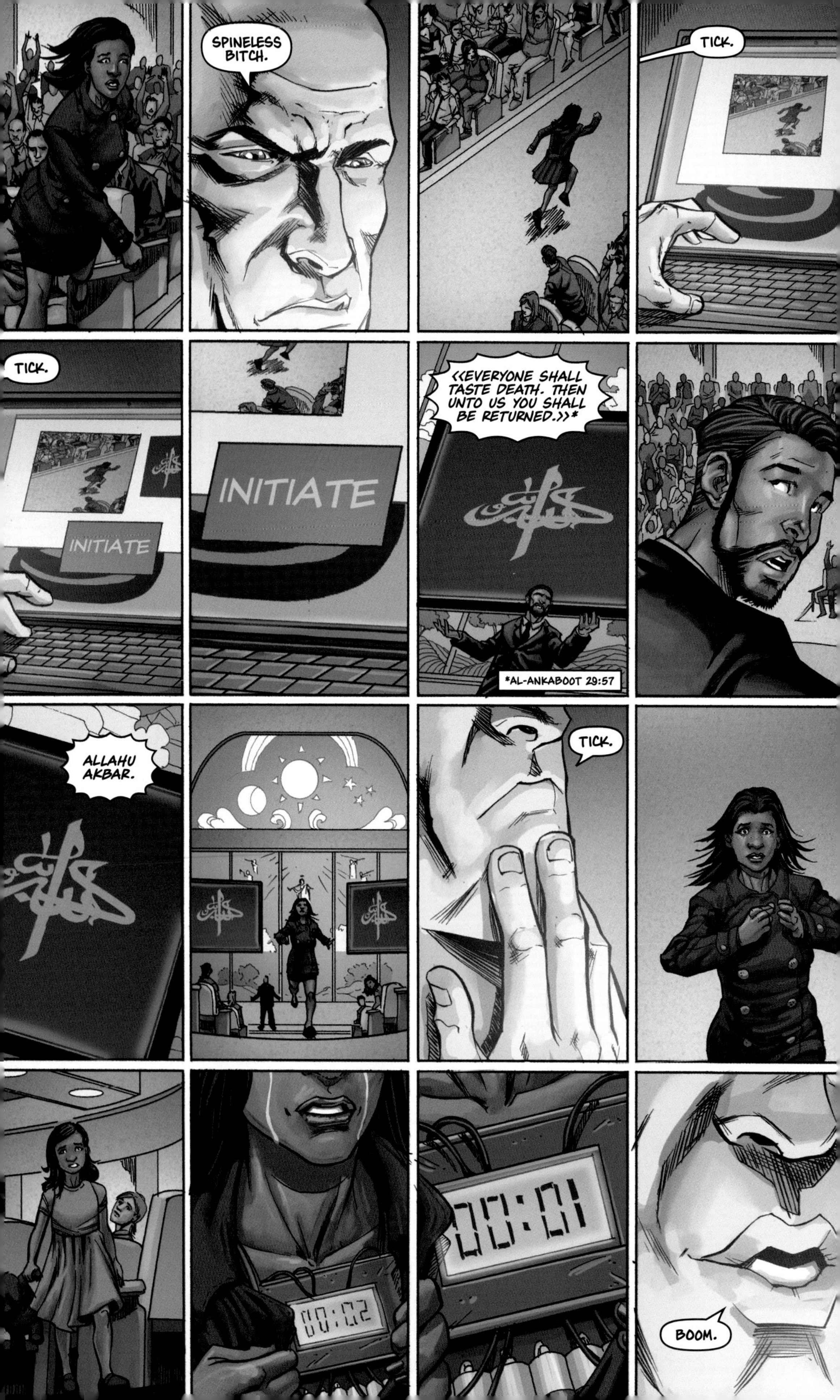
SPINELESS BITCH.
TICK.
TICK.
INITIATE
INITIATE
<<EVERYONE SHALL TASTE DEATH. THEN UNTO US YOU SHALL BE RETURNED.>>*
*AL-ANKABOOT 29:57
ALLAHU AKBAR.
TICK.
00:02
00:01
BOOM.

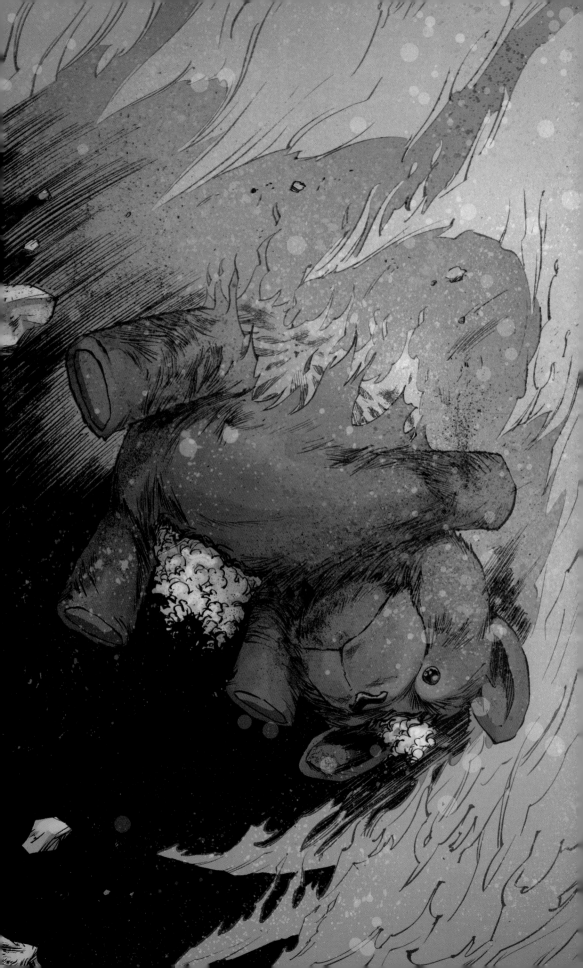

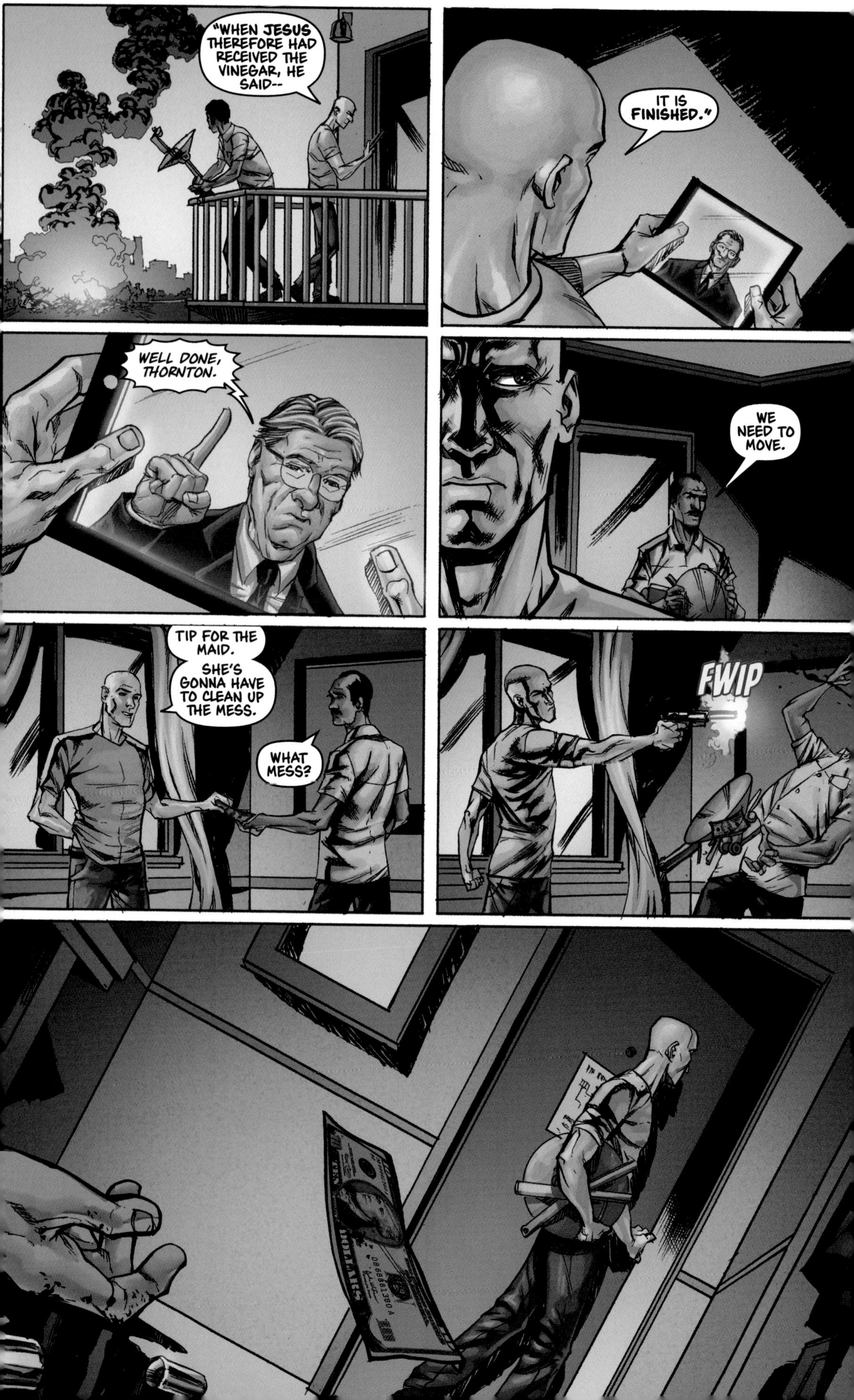
"WHEN JESUS THEREFORE HAD RECEIVED THE VINEGAR, HE SAID--
IT IS FINISHED."
WELL DONE, THORNTON.
WE NEED TO MOVE.
TIP FOR THE MAID.
SHE'S GONNA HAVE TO CLEAN UP THE MESS.
WHAT MESS?
FWIP

ROOM WAS RENTED TO A LIBYAN BUSINESSMAN NAMED HARUN ASAFI -- WHO'S ALIVE AND WELL IN SOUTH AFRICA. NO ID ON THE STIFF...DEFINITELY OF MEDITERRANEAN DESCENT, BUT NO KNOWN CONNECTION TO ASAFI.

NOT MANY ARABS HERE. HOTEL STAFF REMEMBERS THIS GUY. HE WAS HERE FOR TWO NIGHTS WITH THE WOMAN WE'VE IDENTIFIED AS THE SUICIDE BOMBER.

DID THEY SEE EITHER OF THEM WITH ANYONE ELSE?

NOT THAT ANYONE CAN REMEMBER.

NO SURVEILLANCE CAMERAS IN THE HOTEL. RUNNING DOWN ANY IN THE AREA, BUT SO FAR NOTHING.

MORE PAWNS WHOSE VALUE CAME TO AN END.

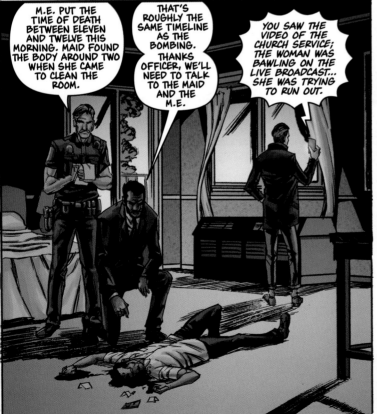

M.E. PUT THE TIME OF DEATH BETWEEN ELEVEN AND TWELVE THIS MORNING. MAID FOUND THE BODY AROUND TWO WHEN SHE CAME TO CLEAN THE ROOM.

THAT'S ROUGHLY THE SAME TIMELINE AS THE BOMBING. THANKS OFFICER, WE'LL NEED TO TALK TO THE MAID AND THE M.E.

YOU SAW THE VIDEO OF THE CHURCH SERVICE; THE WOMAN WAS BAWLING ON THE LIVE BROADCAST... SHE WAS TRYING TO RUN OUT.

NO JIHAD VIDEO POSTED YET, BUT NEWS HAS ALREADY CONNECTED IT TO NEW YORK AND SAN DIEGO. PEOPLE ARE SCARED.

SIX THOUSAND DEAD THIS TIME, CAN YOU BLAME THEM? AND IT IS CONNECTED, I'VE ALREADY FOUND EVIDENCE OF THE SAME QUANTUM CRYPTO USED TO COVER UP THE OTHER TWO BOMBINGS.

WHEN ARE WE TALKING TO THE DARPA GUY?

TOMORROW MORNING, I'VE ALREADY SET YOU UP AT THE LOCAL OFFICE TO USE THEIR TELECONFERENCING ROOM.

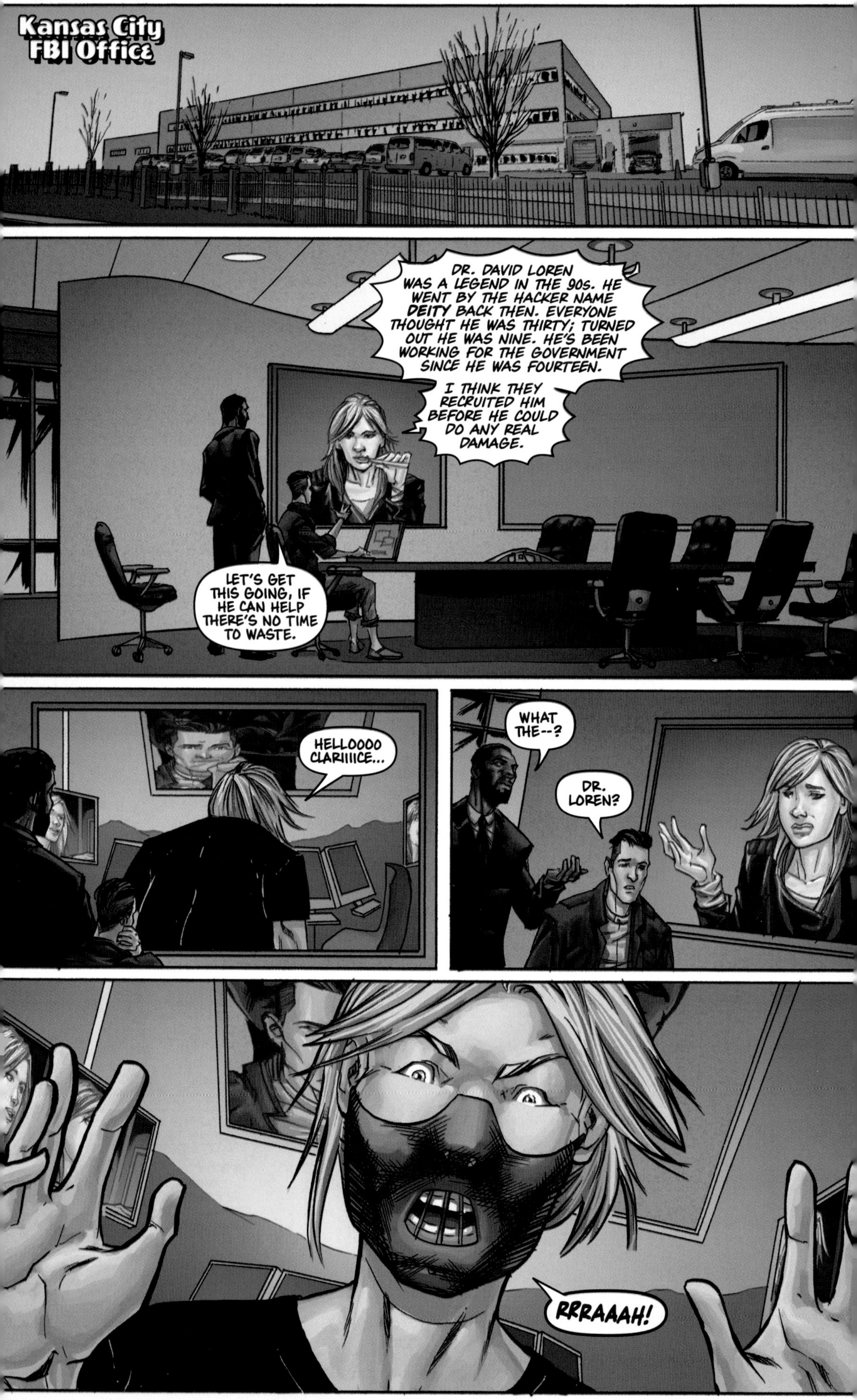
Kansas City FBI Office
DR. DAVID LOREN WAS A LEGEND IN THE 90S. HE WENT BY THE HACKER NAME DEITY BACK THEN. EVERYONE THOUGHT HE WAS THIRTY; TURNED OUT HE WAS NINE. HE'S BEEN WORKING FOR THE GOVERNMENT SINCE HE WAS FOURTEEN.
I THINK THEY RECRUITED HIM BEFORE HE COULD DO ANY REAL DAMAGE.
LET'S GET THIS GOING, IF HE CAN HELP THERE'S NO TIME TO WASTE.
HELLOOOO CLARIIIICE...
WHAT THE--?
DR. LOREN?
RRRAAAH!

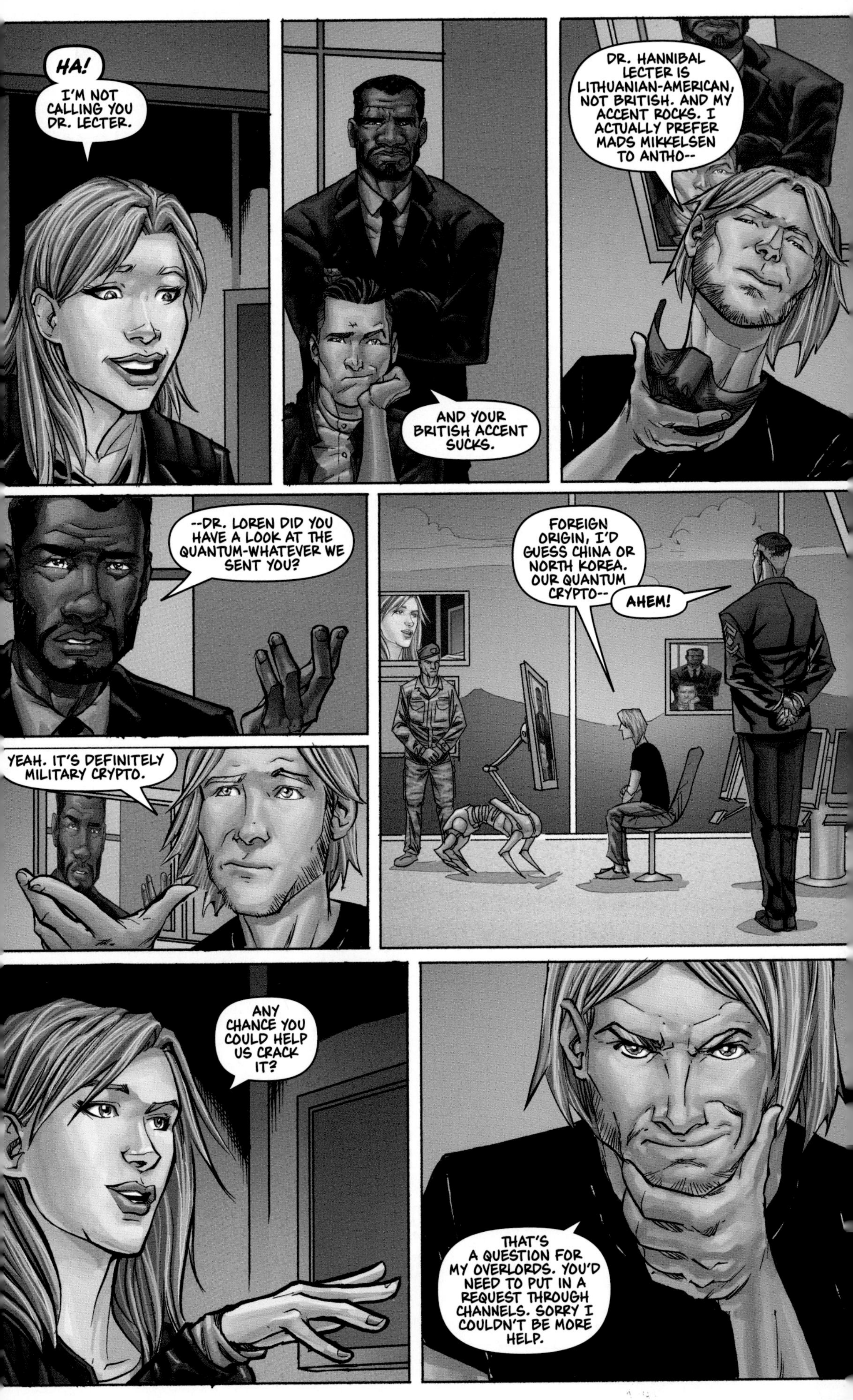
HA!
I'M NOT CALLING YOU DR. LECTER.
AND YOUR BRITISH ACCENT SUCKS.
DR. HANNIBAL LECTER IS LITHUANIAN-AMERICAN, NOT BRITISH. AND MY ACCENT ROCKS. I ACTUALLY PREFER MADS MIKKELSEN TO ANTHO--
--DR. LOREN DID YOU HAVE A LOOK AT THE QUANTUM-WHATEVER WE SENT YOU?
YEAH. IT'S DEFINITELY MILITARY CRYPTO.
FOREIGN ORIGIN, I'D GUESS CHINA OR NORTH KOREA. OUR QUANTUM CRYPTO--
AHEM!
ANY CHANCE YOU COULD HELP US CRACK IT?
THAT'S A QUESTION FOR MY OVERLORDS. YOU'D NEED TO PUT IN A REQUEST THROUGH CHANNELS. SORRY I COULDN'T BE MORE HELP.

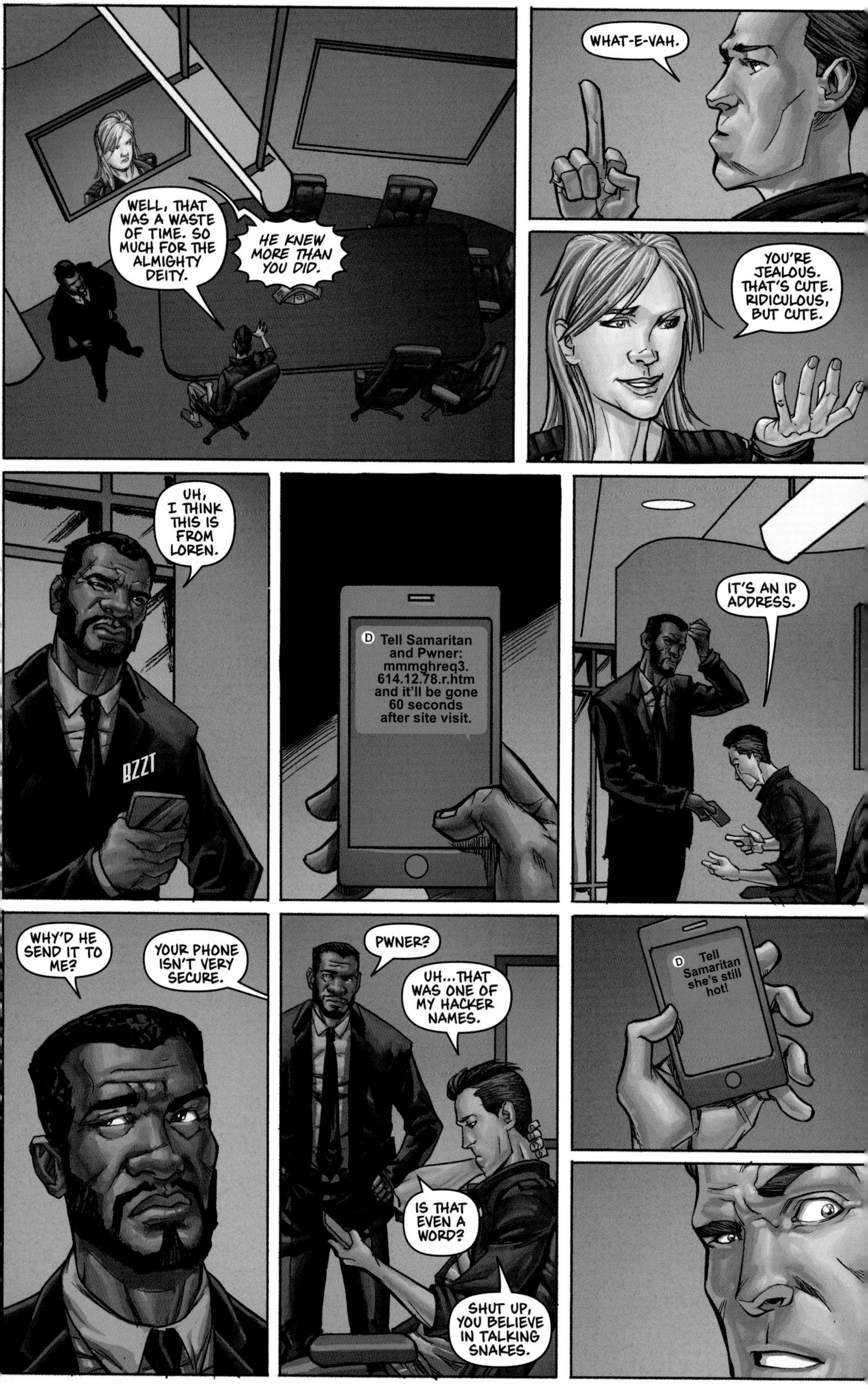
WELL, THAT WAS A WASTE OF TIME. SO MUCH FOR THE ALMIGHTY DEITY.
HE KNEW MORE THAN YOU DID.
WHAT-E-VAH.
YOU'RE JEALOUS. THAT'S CUTE. RIDICULOUS, BUT CUTE.
UH, I THINK THIS IS FROM LOREN.
BZZT
Tell Samaritan and Pwner: mmmghreq3. 614.12.78.r.htm and it'll be gone 60 seconds after site visit.
IT'S AN IP ADDRESS.
WHY'D HE SEND IT TO ME?
YOUR PHONE ISN'T VERY SECURE.
PWNER?
UH...THAT WAS ONE OF MY HACKER NAMES.
IS THAT EVEN A WORD?
SHUT UP, YOU BELIEVE IN TALKING SNAKES.
Tell Samaritan she's still hot!

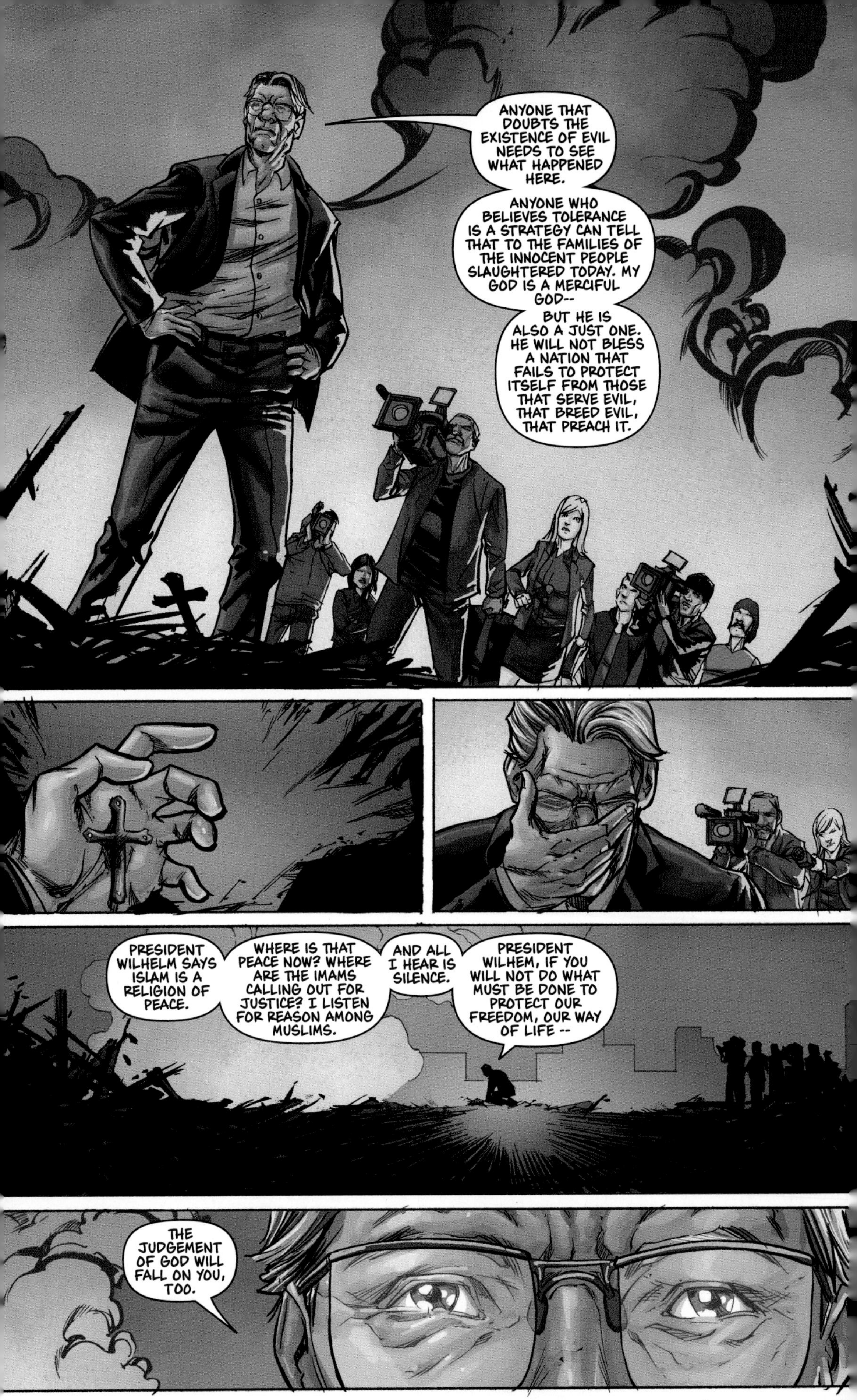
ANYONE THAT DOUBTS THE EXISTENCE OF EVIL NEEDS TO SEE WHAT HAPPENED HERE.
ANYONE WHO BELIEVES TOLERANCE IS A STRATEGY CAN TELL THAT TO THE FAMILIES OF THE INNOCENT PEOPLE SLAUGHTERED TODAY. MY GOD IS A MERCIFUL GOD--
BUT HE IS ALSO A JUST ONE. HE WILL NOT BLESS A NATION THAT FAILS TO PROTECT ITSELF FROM THOSE THAT SERVE EVIL, THAT BREED EVIL, THAT PREACH IT.
PRESIDENT WILHELM SAYS ISLAM IS A RELIGION OF PEACE.
WHERE IS THAT PEACE NOW? WHERE ARE THE IMAMS CALLING OUT FOR JUSTICE? I LISTEN FOR REASON AMONG MUSLIMS.
AND ALL I HEAR IS SILENCE.
PRESIDENT WILHEM, IF YOU WILL NOT DO WHAT MUST BE DONE TO PROTECT OUR FREEDOM, OUR WAY OF LIFE --
THE JUDGEMENT OF GOD WILL FALL ON YOU, TOO.

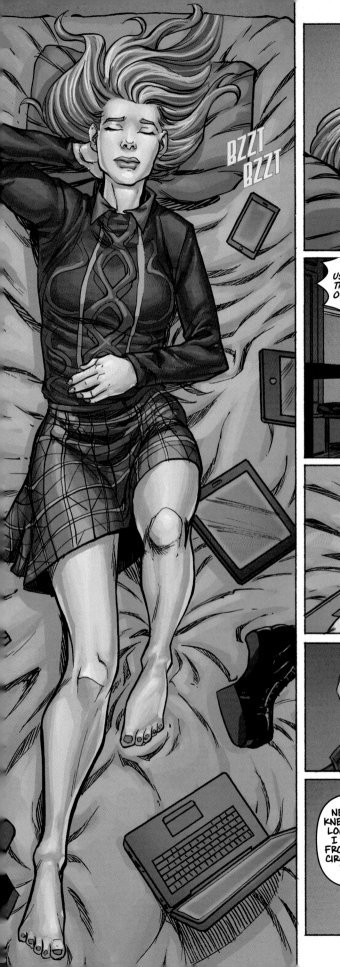

BZZT
BZZT

HEY, SORRY... DOZED OFF FOR A BIT.

SWITCH TO THE SECURE LINE ON YOUR LAPTOP.

K, GIVE ME A SECOND.

I DECRYPTED THE DATA PACKETS LOREN LEFT US, IT'S ALL ON OUR SECURE SERVER. HE CLAIMS THAT QUANTUM CRYPTO PROGRAM BEING USED IS OURS...ONE HE HELPED WRITE. EITHER SOMEONE STOLE IT OR THIS IS SOME KIND OF INSIDE JOB. IT DOESN'T MAKE ANY SENSE.

DWAYNE WANTS TO KEEP THIS JUST BETWEEN THE THREE OF US FOR NOW.

THAT WAS IT FROM LOREN? HE SAY HE'D HELP?

HE DID NOT, BUT INCLUDED SOME XBOX MESSAGE HANDLE...HE DID SAY YOU LOOKED HOT. DID YOU USED TO HOOK UP WITH THIS GUY?

NO, NEVER EVEN KNEW WHAT HE LOOKED LIKE. I KNEW HIM FROM HACKING CIRCLES, SAME WAY YOU DID.

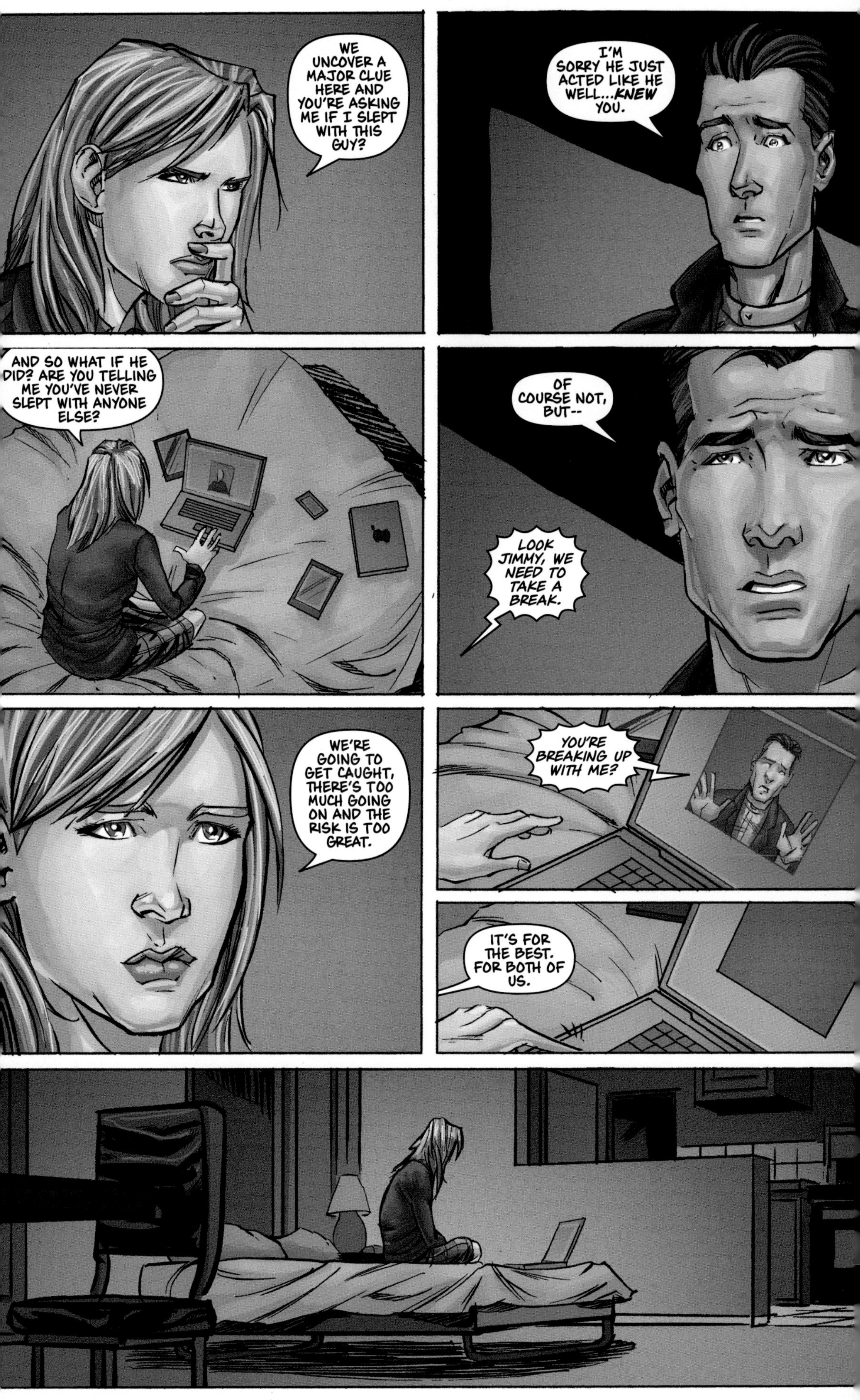
WE UNCOVER A MAJOR CLUE HERE AND YOU'RE ASKING ME IF I SLEPT WITH THIS GUY?
I'M SORRY HE JUST ACTED LIKE HE WELL...KNEW YOU.
AND SO WHAT IF HE DID? ARE YOU TELLING ME YOU'VE NEVER SLEPT WITH ANYONE ELSE?
OF COURSE NOT, BUT--
LOOK JIMMY, WE NEED TO TAKE A BREAK.
WE'RE GOING TO GET CAUGHT, THERE'S TOO MUCH GOING ON AND THE RISK IS TOO GREAT.
YOU'RE BREAKING UP WITH ME?
IT'S FOR THE BEST. FOR BOTH OF US.

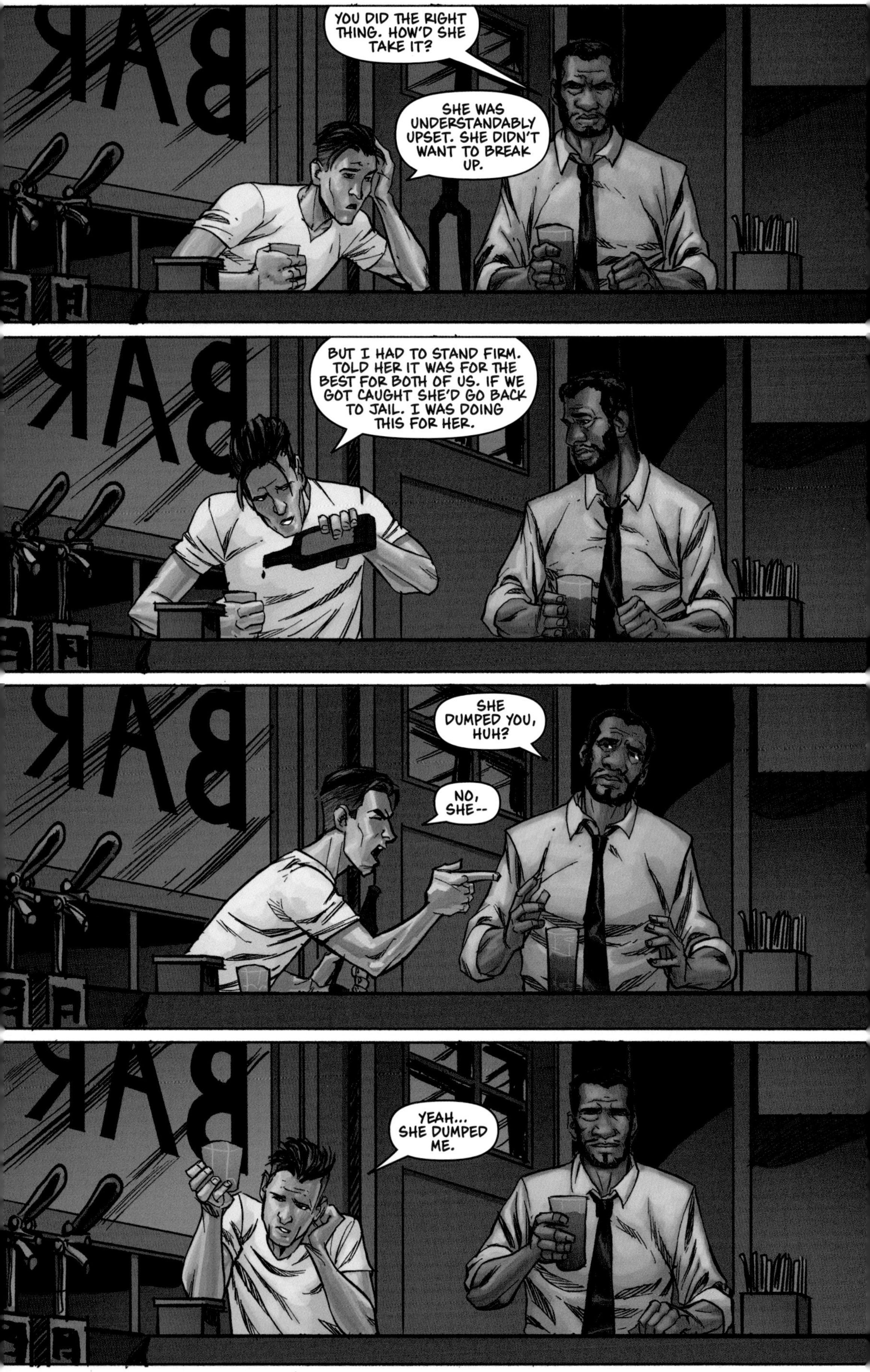
YOU DID THE RIGHT THING. HOW'D SHE TAKE IT?
SHE WAS UNDERSTANDABLY UPSET. SHE DIDN'T WANT TO BREAK UP.
BUT I HAD TO STAND FIRM. TOLD HER IT WAS FOR THE BEST FOR BOTH OF US. IF WE GOT CAUGHT SHE'D GO BACK TO JAIL. I WAS DOING THIS FOR HER.
SHE DUMPED YOU, HUH?
NO, SHE--
YEAH... SHE DUMPED ME.

SAM: First false originator 95.108.142.138 Russia.

SAM: Second is 212.138.92.10 Saudi Arabia.

SAM: You wrote this crypto program?

DEITY: Part of it. Hundreds of people on it, but I always leave me some access.

SAM: You sent me hundreds of .exe files. Which one?

DEITY: It's NMMDHB.

SAM: What's that stand for?

DEITY: Newton and Mirra make David a happy boy.

SAM: That a polyamorous thing?

DEITY: LOL no. Newton's a dog. Mirra's my babe. She wouldn't stand for that shit.

DEITY: You love this Jimmy guy?

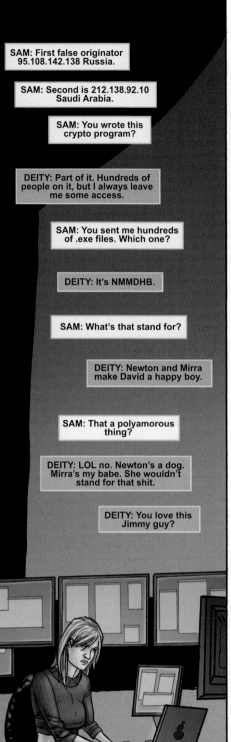

SAM: I don't want to talk about it.

SAM: Running your program.

HOLY SHIT, THAT WAS FAST.

GOT YOU, ASSHOLE. LET'S HAVE A LOOK THROUGH YOUR CAM.

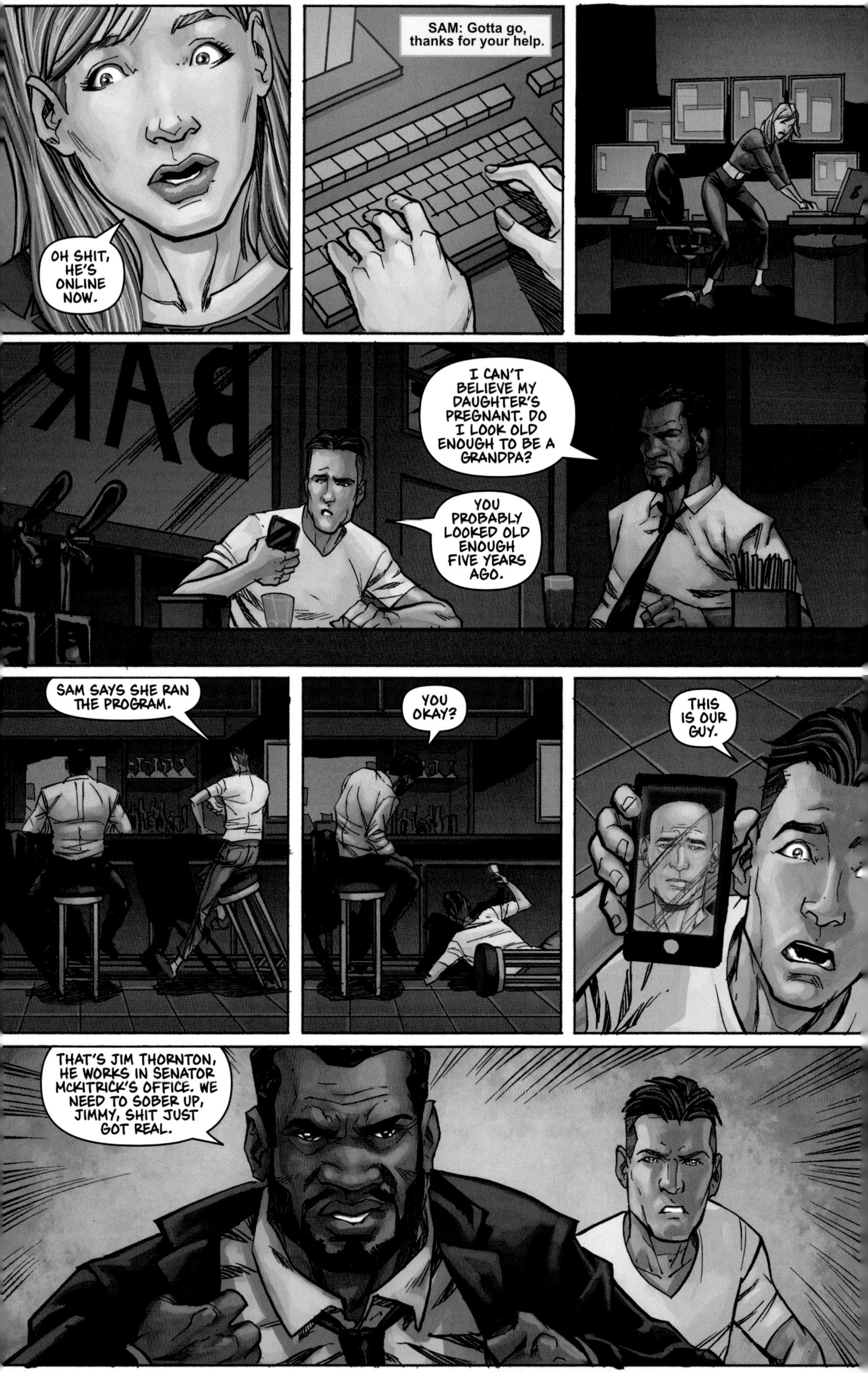
OH SHIT, HE'S ONLINE NOW.
SAM: Gotta go, thanks for your help.
BAR
I CAN'T BELIEVE MY DAUGHTER'S PREGNANT. DO I LOOK OLD ENOUGH TO BE A GRANDPA?
YOU PROBABLY LOOKED OLD ENOUGH FIVE YEARS AGO.
SAM SAYS SHE RAN THE PROGRAM.
YOU OKAY?
THIS IS OUR GUY.
THAT'S JIM THORNTON, HE WORKS IN SENATOR McKITRICK'S OFFICE. WE NEED TO SOBER UP, JIMMY, SHIT JUST GOT REAL.

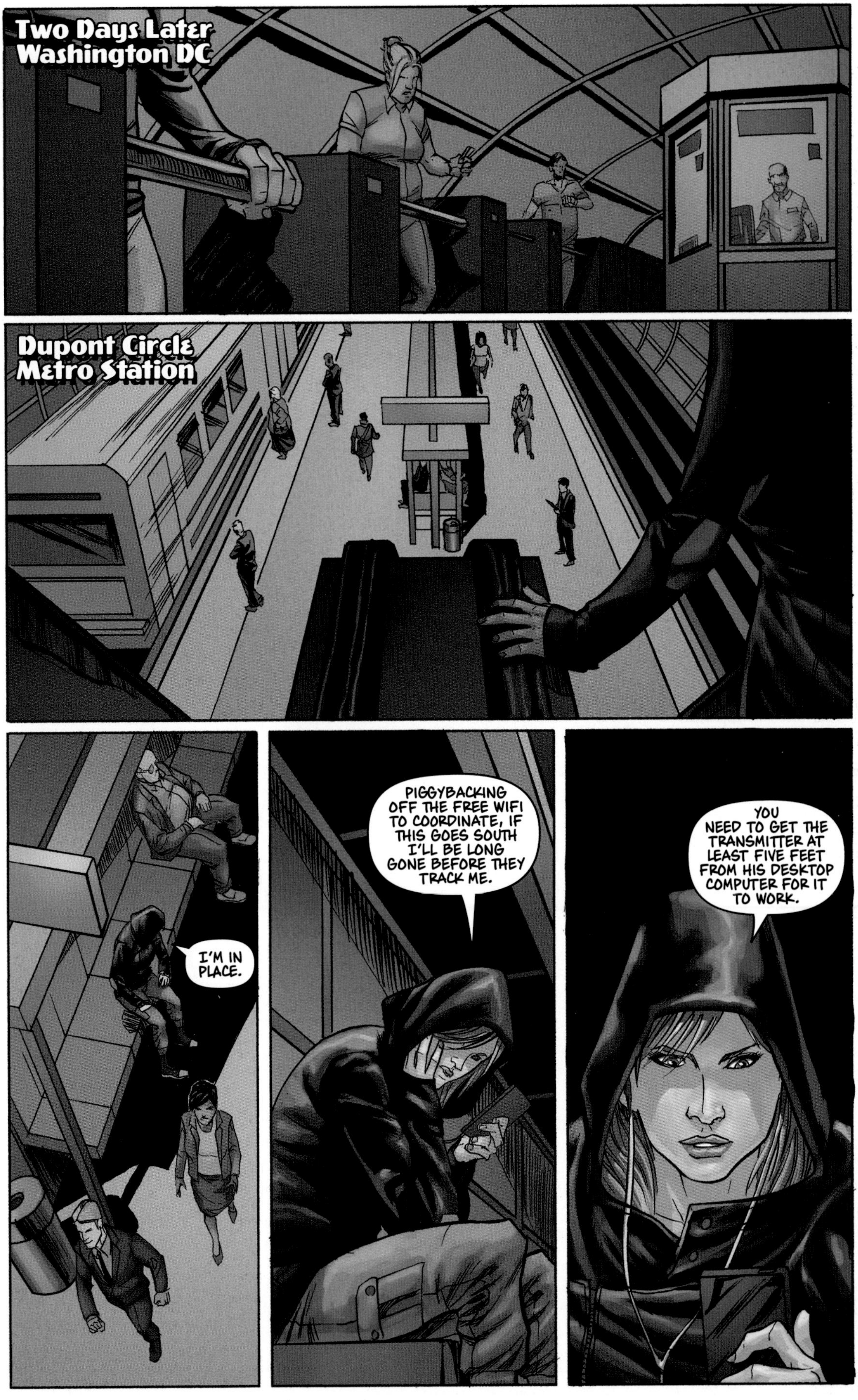
Two Days Later
Washington DC
Dupont Circle
Metro Station
I'M IN PLACE.
PIGGYBACKING OFF THE FREE WIFI TO COORDINATE, IF THIS GOES SOUTH I'LL BE LONG GONE BEFORE THEY TRACK ME.
YOU NEED TO GET THE TRANSMITTER AT LEAST FIVE FEET FROM HIS DESKTOP COMPUTER FOR IT TO WORK.

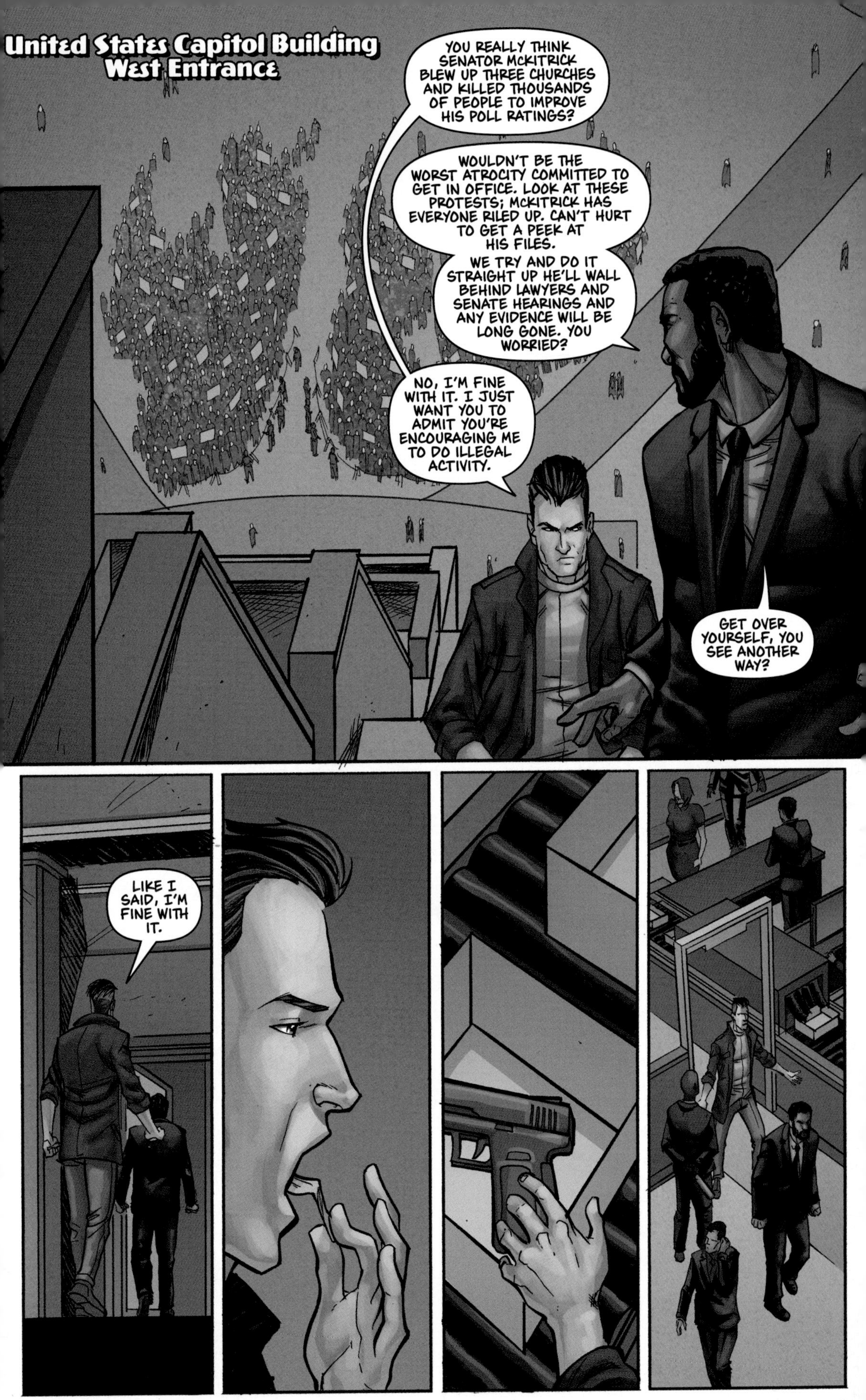
United States Capitol Building
West Entrance
YOU REALLY THINK SENATOR MCKITRICK BLEW UP THREE CHURCHES AND KILLED THOUSANDS OF PEOPLE TO IMPROVE HIS POLL RATINGS?
WOULDN'T BE THE WORST ATROCITY COMMITTED TO GET IN OFFICE. LOOK AT THESE PROTESTS; MCKITRICK HAS EVERYONE RILED UP. CAN'T HURT TO GET A PEEK AT HIS FILES.
WE TRY AND DO IT STRAIGHT UP HE'LL WALL BEHIND LAWYERS AND SENATE HEARINGS AND ANY EVIDENCE WILL BE LONG GONE. YOU WORRIED?
NO, I'M FINE WITH IT. I JUST WANT YOU TO ADMIT YOU'RE ENCOURAGING ME TO DO ILLEGAL ACTIVITY.
GET OVER YOURSELF, YOU SEE ANOTHER WAY?
LIKE I SAID, I'M FINE WITH IT.

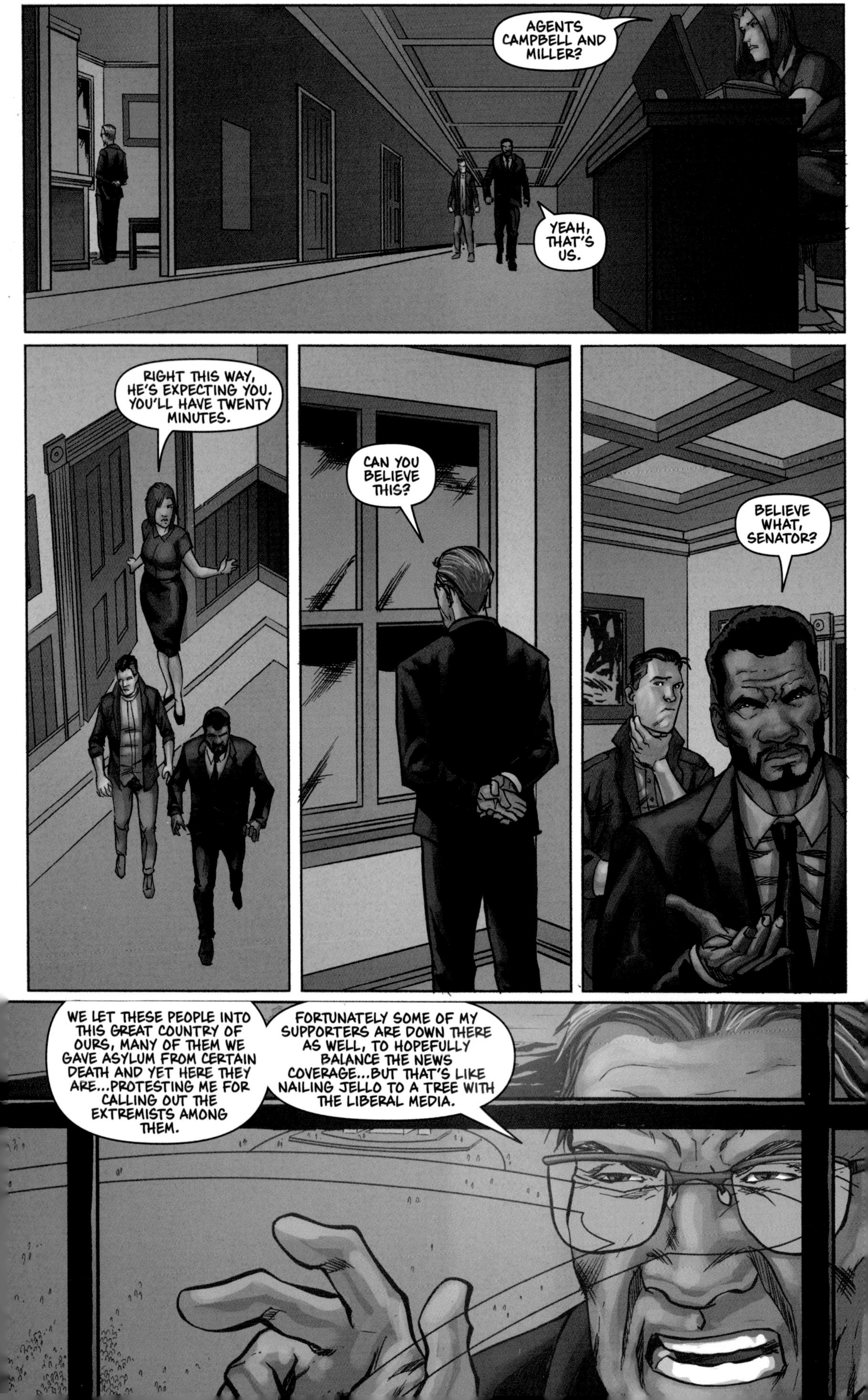
AGENTS CAMPBELL AND MILLER?
YEAH, THAT'S US.
RIGHT THIS WAY, HE'S EXPECTING YOU. YOU'LL HAVE TWENTY MINUTES.
CAN YOU BELIEVE THIS?
BELIEVE WHAT, SENATOR?
WE LET THESE PEOPLE INTO THIS GREAT COUNTRY OF OURS, MANY OF THEM WE GAVE ASYLUM FROM CERTAIN DEATH AND YET HERE THEY ARE...PROTESTING ME FOR CALLING OUT THE EXTREMISTS AMONG THEM.
FORTUNATELY SOME OF MY SUPPORTERS ARE DOWN THERE AS WELL, TO HOPEFULLY BALANCE THE NEWS COVERAGE...BUT THAT'S LIKE NAILING JELLO TO A TREE WITH THE LIBERAL MEDIA.

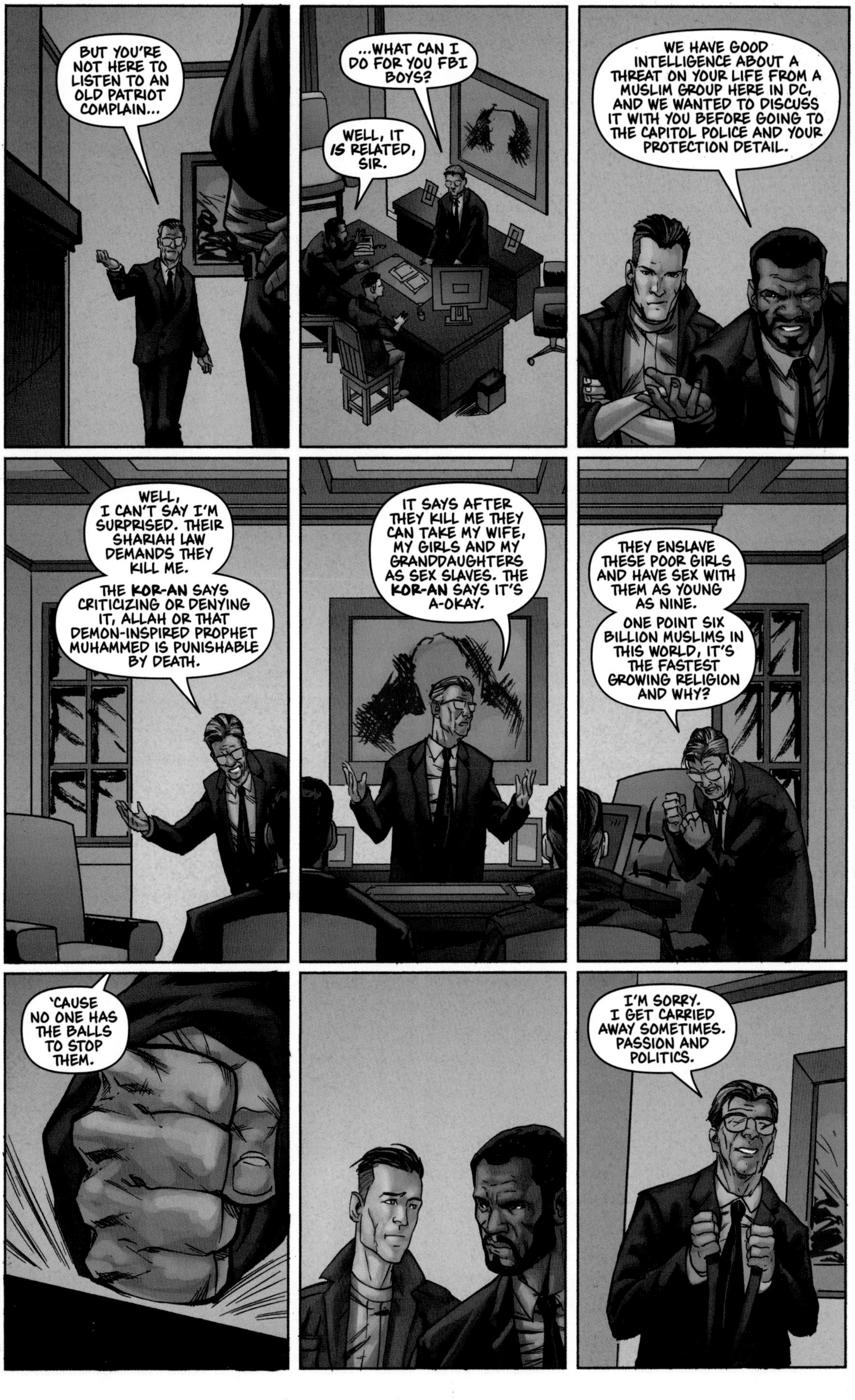
BUT YOU'RE NOT HERE TO LISTEN TO AN OLD PATRIOT COMPLAIN...
...WHAT CAN I DO FOR YOU FBI BOYS?
WELL, IT IS RELATED, SIR.
WE HAVE GOOD INTELLIGENCE ABOUT A THREAT ON YOUR LIFE FROM A MUSLIM GROUP HERE IN DC, AND WE WANTED TO DISCUSS IT WITH YOU BEFORE GOING TO THE CAPITOL POLICE AND YOUR PROTECTION DETAIL.
WELL, I CAN'T SAY I'M SURPRISED. THEIR SHARIAH LAW DEMANDS THEY KILL ME.
THE KOR-AN SAYS CRITICIZING OR DENYING IT, ALLAH OR THAT DEMON-INSPIRED PROPHET MUHAMMED IS PUNISHABLE BY DEATH.
IT SAYS AFTER THEY KILL ME THEY CAN TAKE MY WIFE, MY GIRLS AND MY GRANDDAUGHTERS AS SEX SLAVES. THE KOR-AN SAYS IT'S A-OKAY.
THEY ENSLAVE THESE POOR GIRLS AND HAVE SEX WITH THEM AS YOUNG AS NINE.
ONE POINT SIX BILLION MUSLIMS IN THIS WORLD, IT'S THE FASTEST GROWING RELIGION AND WHY?
'CAUSE NO ONE HAS THE BALLS TO STOP THEM.
I'M SORRY. I GET CARRIED AWAY SOMETIMES. PASSION AND POLITICS.

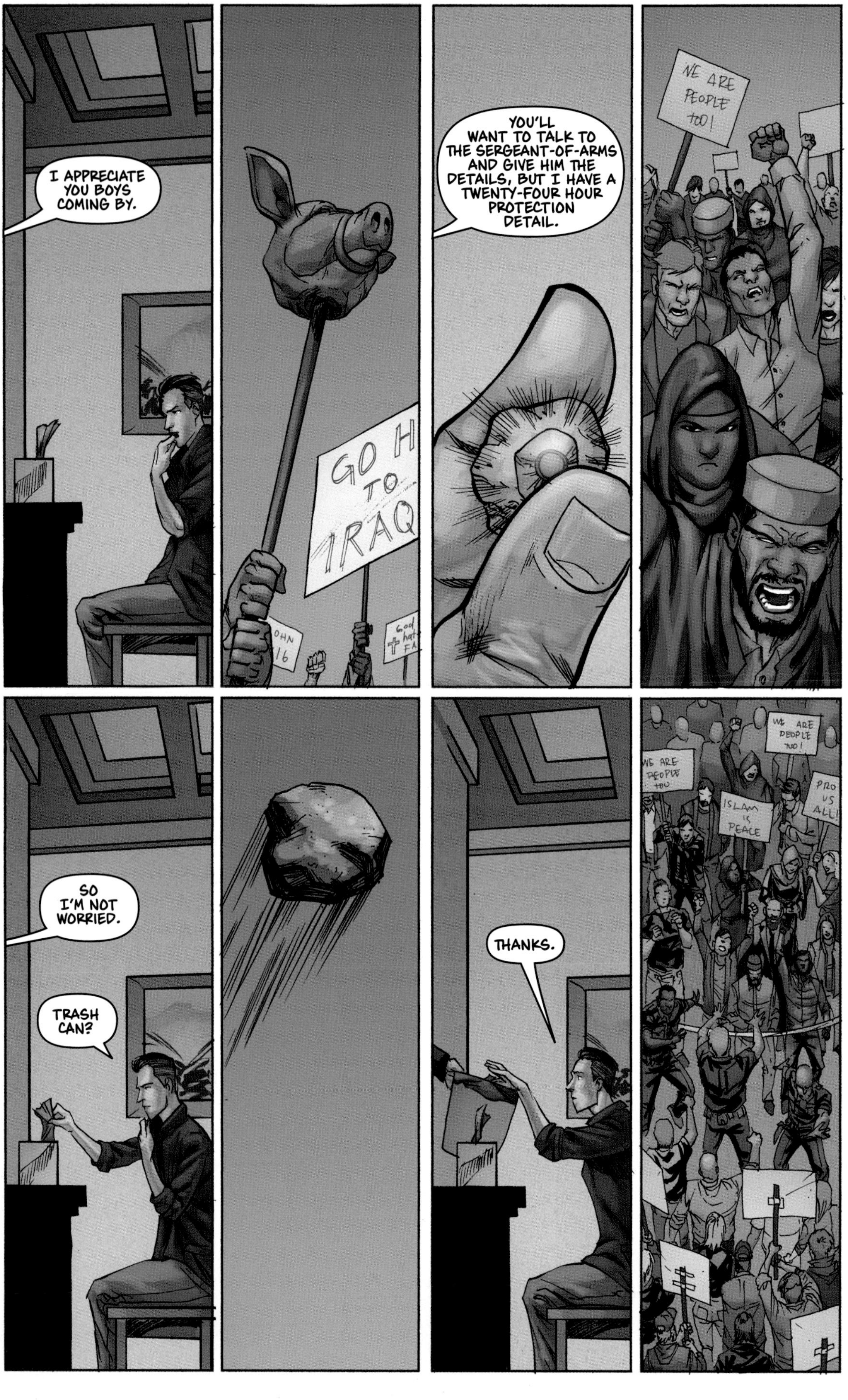
I APPRECIATE YOU BOYS COMING BY.
TO IRAQ
YOU'LL WANT TO TALK TO THE SERGEANT-OF-ARMS AND GIVE HIM THE DETAILS, BUT I HAVE A TWENTY-FOUR HOUR PROTECTION DETAIL.
WE ARE PEOPLE TOO!
SO I'M NOT WORRIED.
TRASH CAN?
THANKS.
WE ARE PEOPLE TOO!
WE ARE PEOPLE TOO
ISLAM IS PEACE

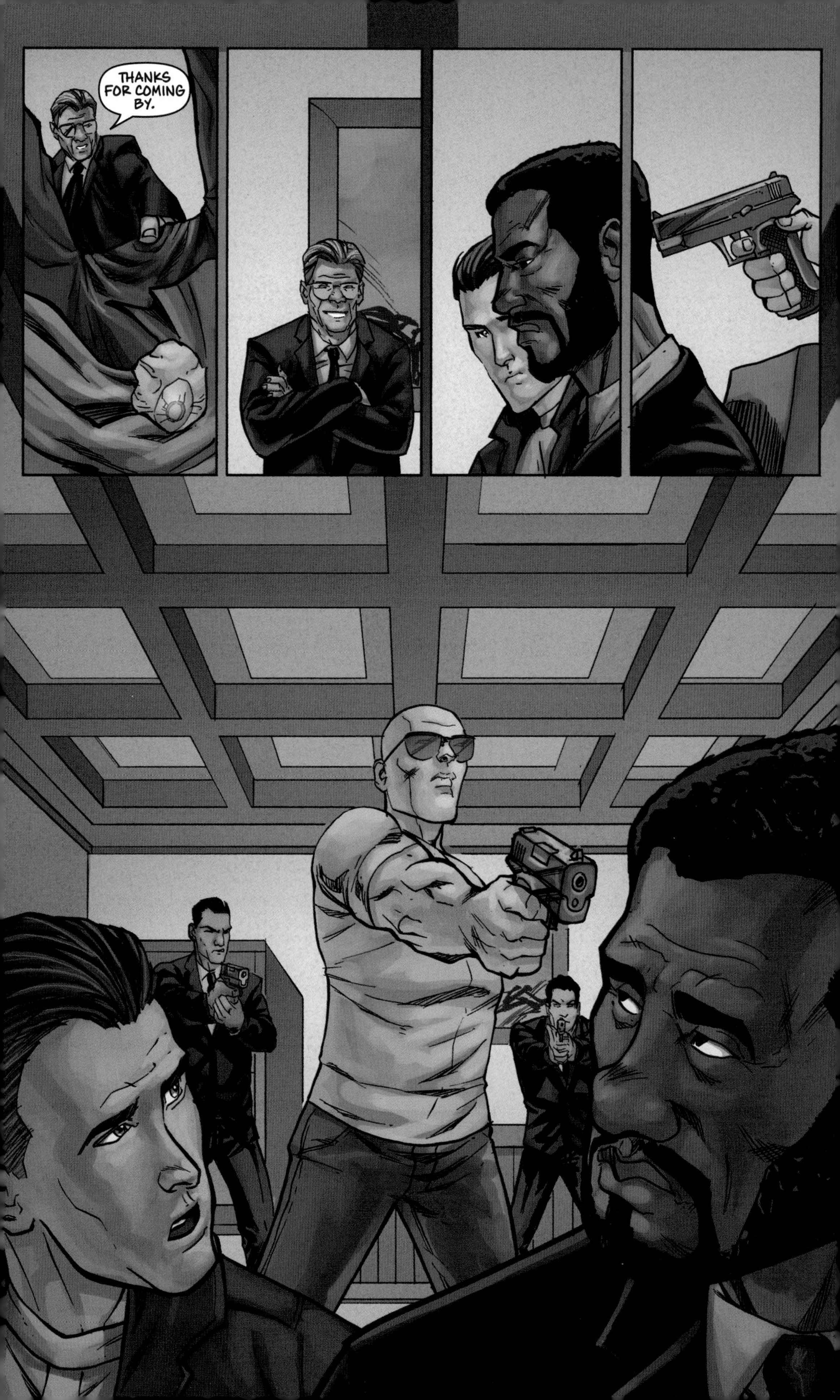
THANKS FOR COMING BY.

FIRST OF ALL, THEN, I URGE THAT SUPPLICATIONS, PRAYERS, INTERCESSIONS, AND THANKSGIVINGS BE MADE FOR ALL PEOPLE, FOR KINGS AND ALL WHO ARE IN HIGH POSITIONS, THAT WE MAY LEAD A PEACEFUL AND QUIET LIFE, GODLY AND DIGNIFIED IN EVERY WAY.

I TIMOTHY 2:1-2

ISLAMOPHOBIA: CHAPTER 4

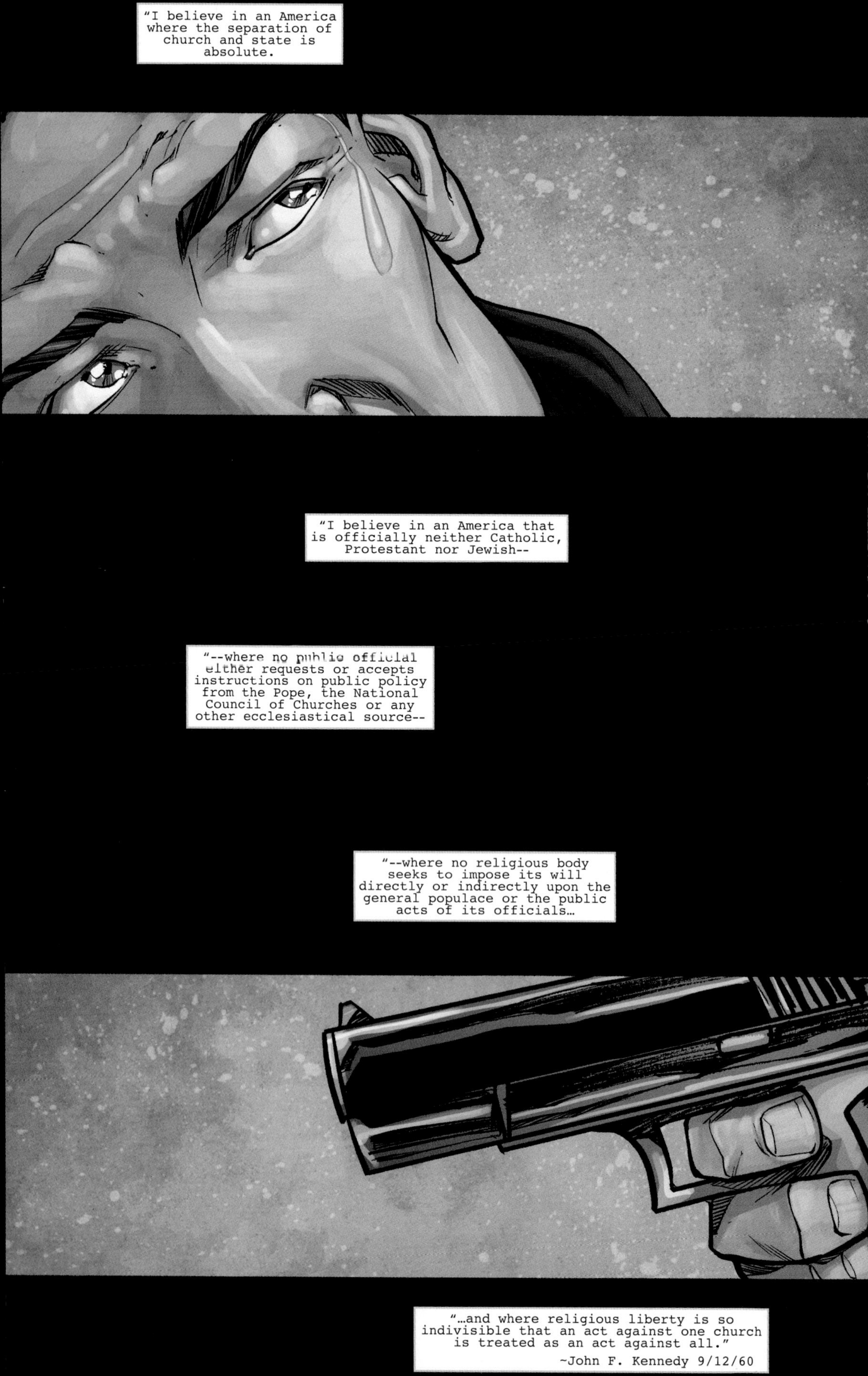
"I believe in an America where the separation of church and state is absolute.
"I believe in an America that is officially neither Catholic, Protestant nor Jewish--
"--where no public official either requests or accepts instructions on public policy from the Pope, the National Council of Churches or any other ecclesiastical source--
"--where no religious body seeks to impose its will directly or indirectly upon the general populace or the public acts of its officials…
"…and where religious liberty is so indivisible that an act against one church is treated as an act against all."
~John F. Kennedy 9/12/60

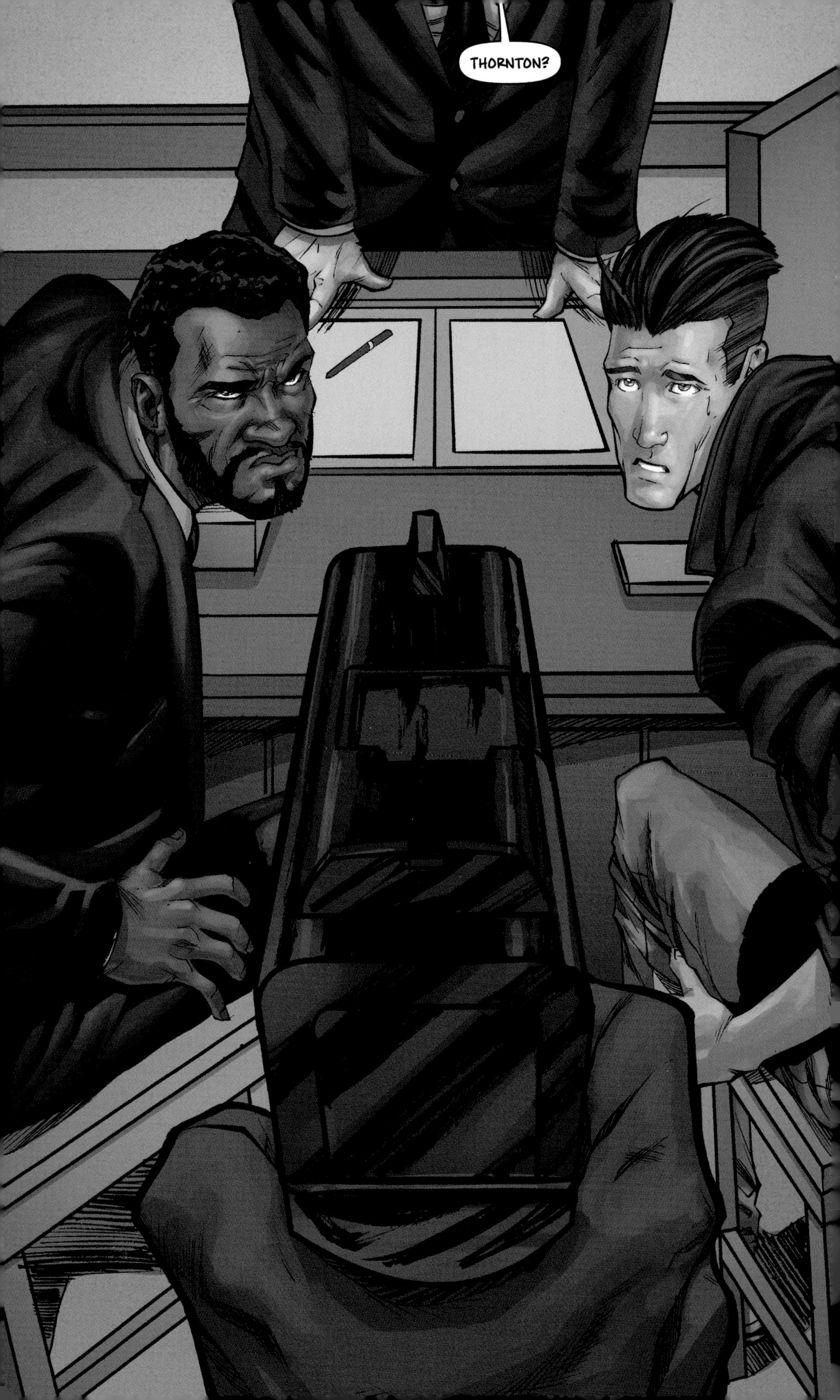
THORNTON?

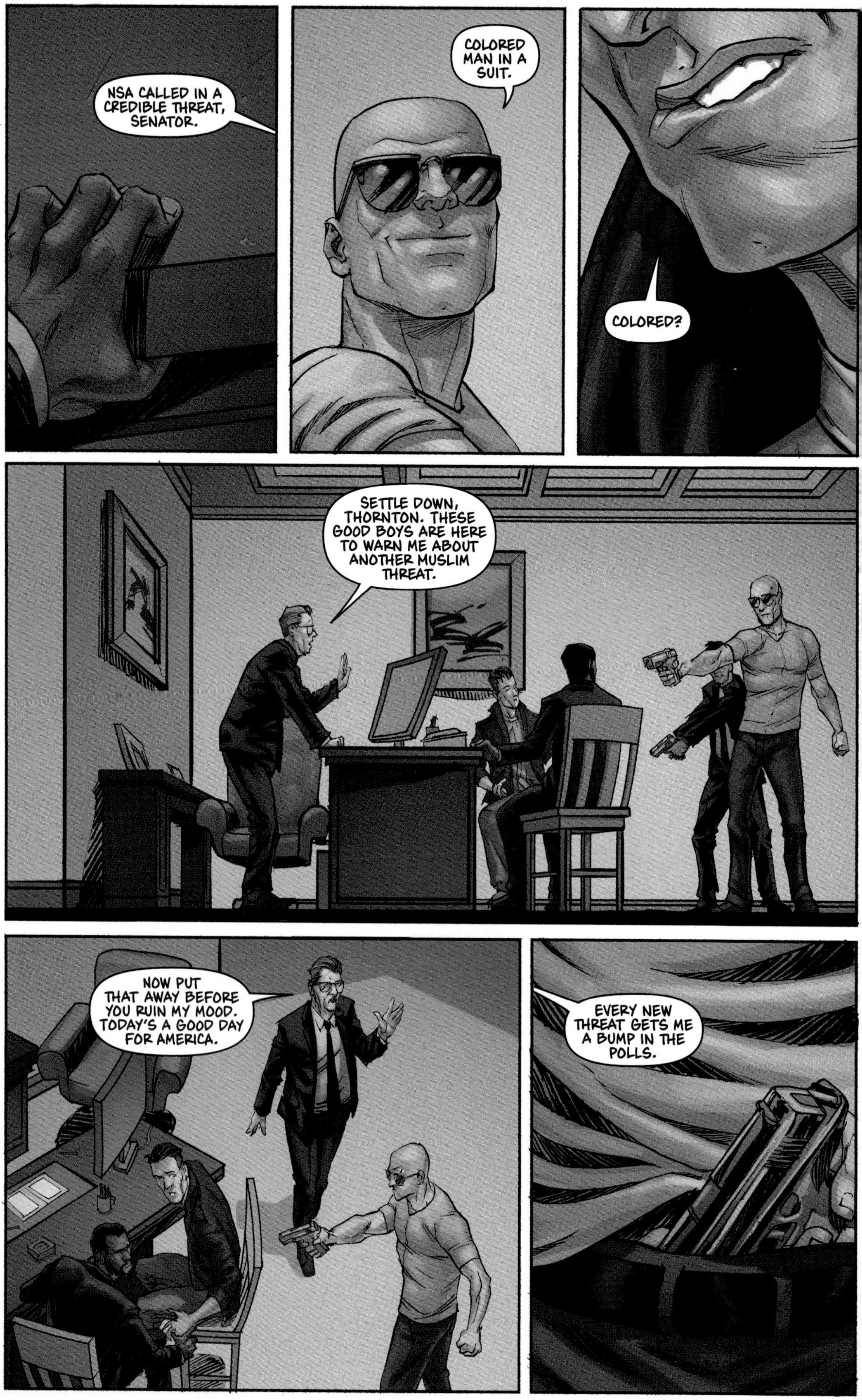
NSA CALLED IN A CREDIBLE THREAT, SENATOR.
COLORED MAN IN A SUIT.
COLORED?
SETTLE DOWN, THORNTON. THESE GOOD BOYS ARE HERE TO WARN ME ABOUT ANOTHER MUSLIM THREAT.
NOW PUT THAT AWAY BEFORE YOU RUIN MY MOOD. TODAY'S A GOOD DAY FOR AMERICA.
EVERY NEW THREAT GETS ME A BUMP IN THE POLLS.

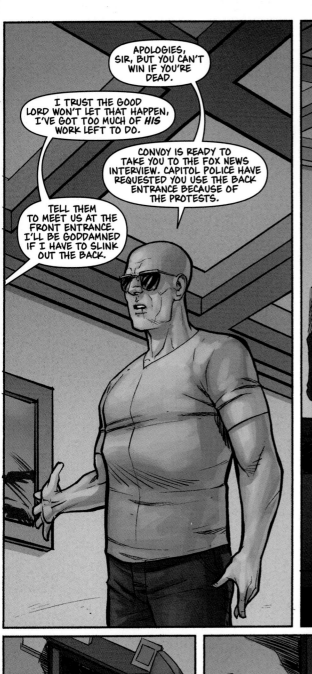

APOLOGIES, SIR, BUT YOU CAN'T WIN IF YOU'RE DEAD.

I TRUST THE GOOD LORD WON'T LET THAT HAPPEN, I'VE GOT TOO MUCH OF *HIS* WORK LEFT TO DO.

CONVOY IS READY TO TAKE YOU TO THE FOX NEWS INTERVIEW. CAPITOL POLICE HAVE REQUESTED YOU USE THE BACK ENTRANCE BECAUSE OF THE PROTESTS.

TELL THEM TO MEET US AT THE FRONT ENTRANCE. I'LL BE GODDAMNED IF I HAVE TO SLINK OUT THE BACK.

WHEN I'M PRESIDENT, I'LL USE SOME *HARD DIPLOMACY* TO TURN ISLAM FROM A RELIGION OF PEACE INTO A RELIGION OF PIECES.

AGENTS, THANK YOU FOR STOPPING BY. I APOLOGIZE FOR THORNTON. WHAT HE LACKS IN PERSONALITY HE MORE THAN MAKES UP FOR IN PROFESSIONALISM. TELL QUANTICO I'M SAFE AS A CHURCH.

THANKS FOR SEEING US, SENATOR.

WHAT TIME ARE YOU HEADING FOR NEW YORK?

RIGHT AFTER THE INTERVIEW.

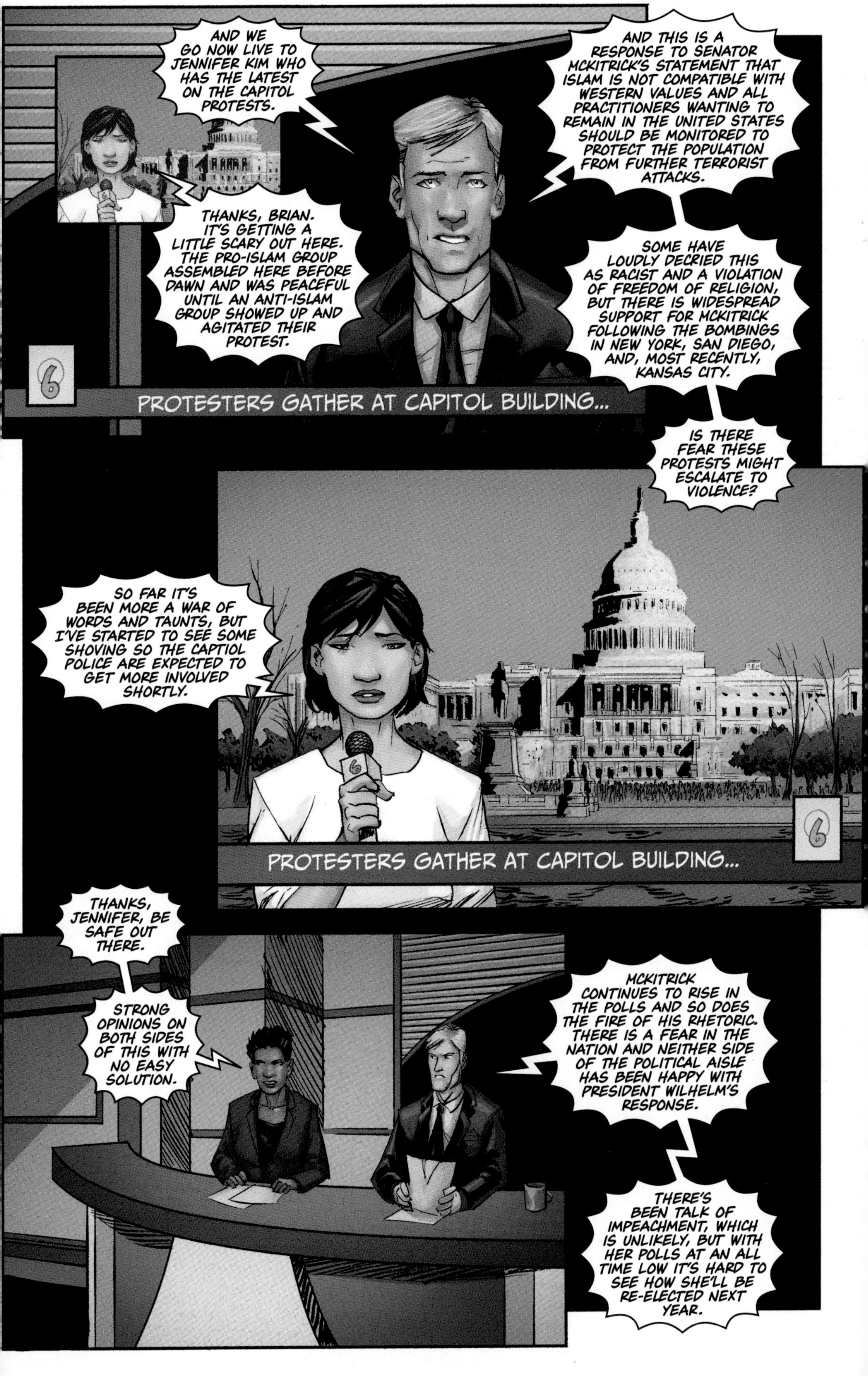
AND WE GO NOW LIVE TO JENNIFER KIM WHO HAS THE LATEST ON THE CAPITOL PROTESTS.
THANKS, BRIAN. IT'S GETTING A LITTLE SCARY OUT HERE. THE PRO-ISLAM GROUP ASSEMBLED HERE BEFORE DAWN AND WAS PEACEFUL UNTIL AN ANTI-ISLAM GROUP SHOWED UP AND AGITATED THEIR PROTEST.
AND THIS IS A RESPONSE TO SENATOR MCKITRICK'S STATEMENT THAT ISLAM IS NOT COMPATIBLE WITH WESTERN VALUES AND ALL PRACTITIONERS WANTING TO REMAIN IN THE UNITED STATES SHOULD BE MONITORED TO PROTECT THE POPULATION FROM FURTHER TERRORIST ATTACKS.
SOME HAVE LOUDLY DECRIED THIS AS RACIST AND A VIOLATION OF FREEDOM OF RELIGION, BUT THERE IS WIDESPREAD SUPPORT FOR MCKITRICK FOLLOWING THE BOMBINGS IN NEW YORK, SAN DIEGO, AND, MOST RECENTLY, KANSAS CITY.
6
PROTESTERS GATHER AT CAPITOL BUILDING...
IS THERE FEAR THESE PROTESTS MIGHT ESCALATE TO VIOLENCE?
SO FAR IT'S BEEN MORE A WAR OF WORDS AND TAUNTS, BUT I'VE STARTED TO SEE SOME SHOVING SO THE CAPTIOL POLICE ARE EXPECTED TO GET MORE INVOLVED SHORTLY.
6
PROTESTERS GATHER AT CAPITOL BUILDING...
THANKS, JENNIFER, BE SAFE OUT THERE.
STRONG OPINIONS ON BOTH SIDES OF THIS WITH NO EASY SOLUTION.
MCKITRICK CONTINUES TO RISE IN THE POLLS AND SO DOES THE FIRE OF HIS RHETORIC. THERE IS A FEAR IN THE NATION AND NEITHER SIDE OF THE POLITICAL AISLE HAS BEEN HAPPY WITH PRESIDENT WILHELM'S RESPONSE.
THERE'S BEEN TALK OF IMPEACHMENT, WHICH IS UNLIKELY, BUT WITH HER POLLS AT AN ALL TIME LOW IT'S HARD TO SEE HOW SHE'LL BE RE-ELECTED NEXT YEAR.

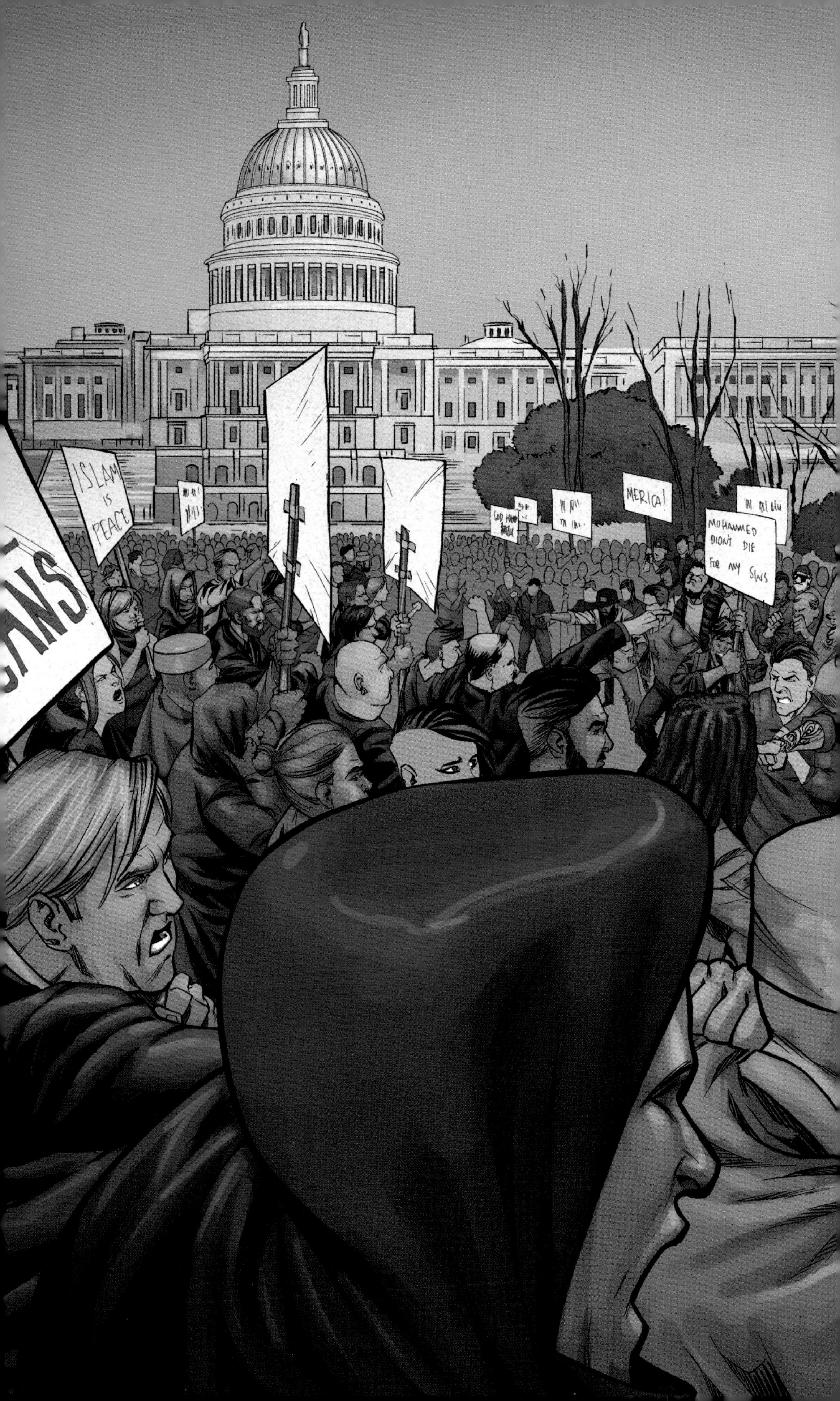
ISLAM IS PEACE
MERICA!
MOHAMMED DIDN'T DIE FOR MY SINS

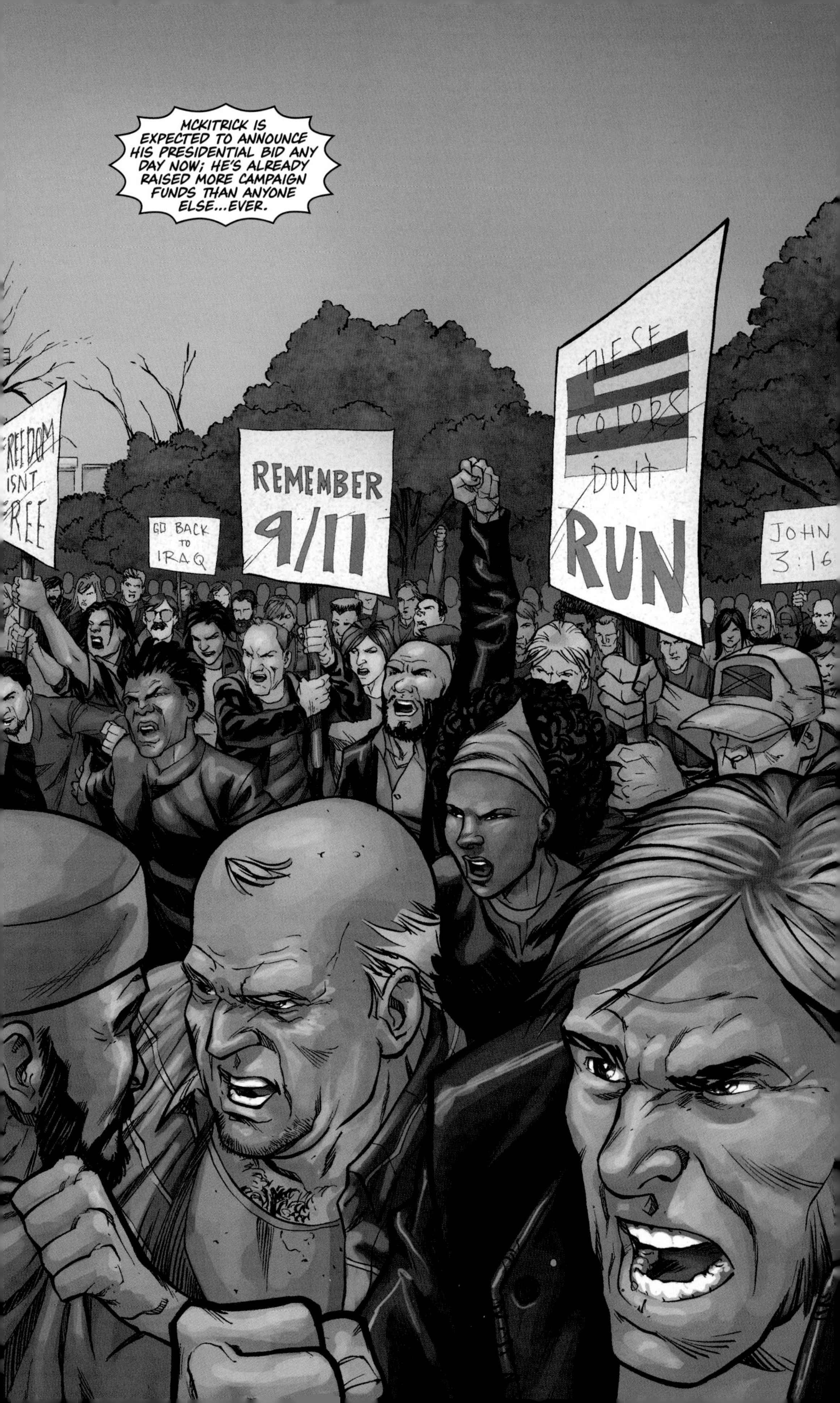
MCKITRICK IS EXPECTED TO ANNOUNCE HIS PRESIDENTIAL BID ANY DAY NOW; HE'S ALREADY RAISED MORE CAMPAIGN FUNDS THAN ANYONE ELSE...EVER.
GO BACK TO IRAQ
REMEMBER 9/11
THESE COLORS DON'T RUN
JOHN 3:16

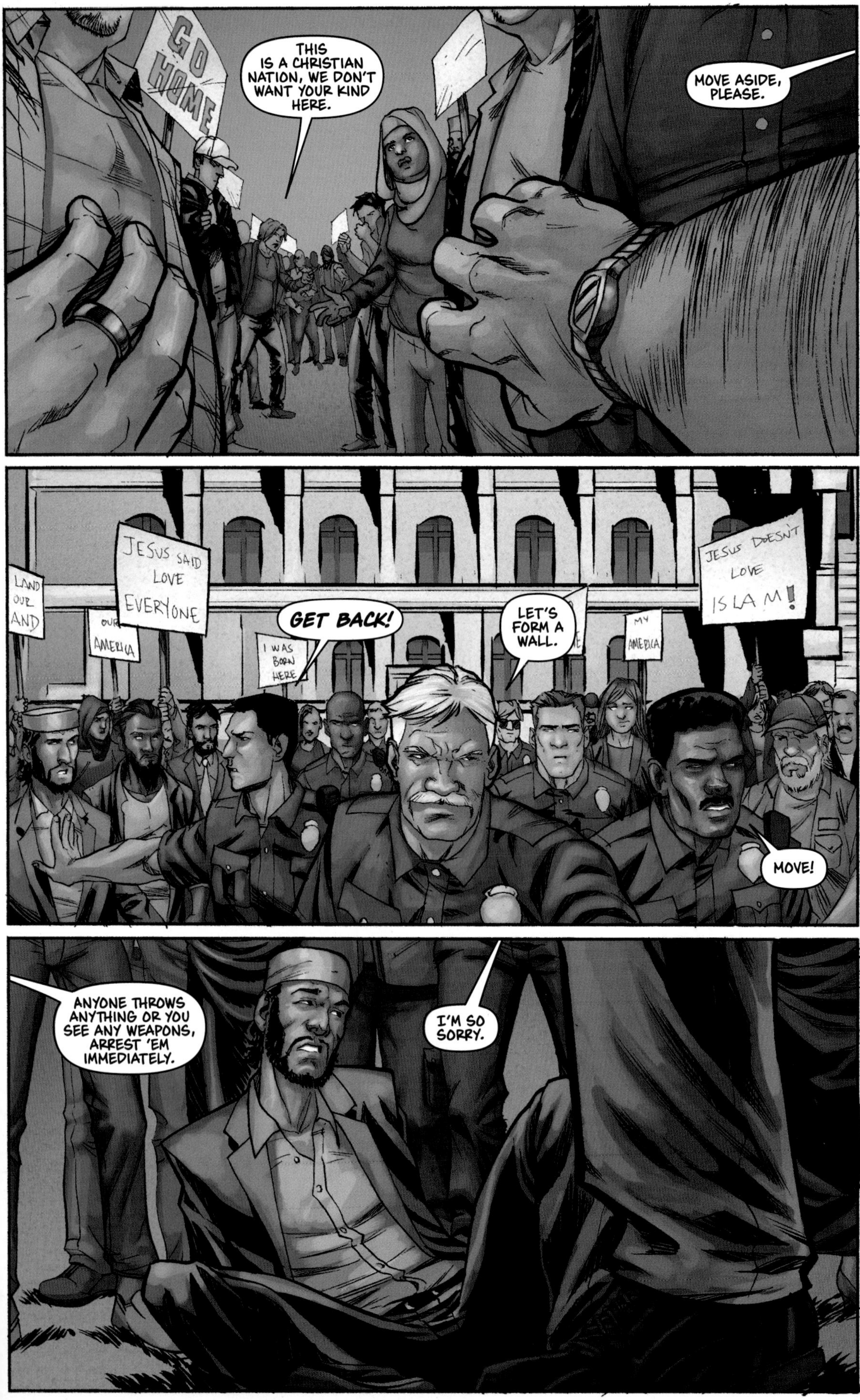
GO HOME
THIS IS A CHRISTIAN NATION, WE DON'T WANT YOUR KIND HERE.
MOVE ASIDE, PLEASE.
JESUS SAID LOVE EVERYONE
OUR AMERICA
I WAS BORN HERE
GET BACK!
LET'S FORM A WALL.
MY AMERICA
JESUS DOESN'T LOVE ISLAM!
MOVE!
ANYONE THROWS ANYTHING OR YOU SEE ANY WEAPONS, ARREST 'EM IMMEDIATELY.
I'M SO SORRY.

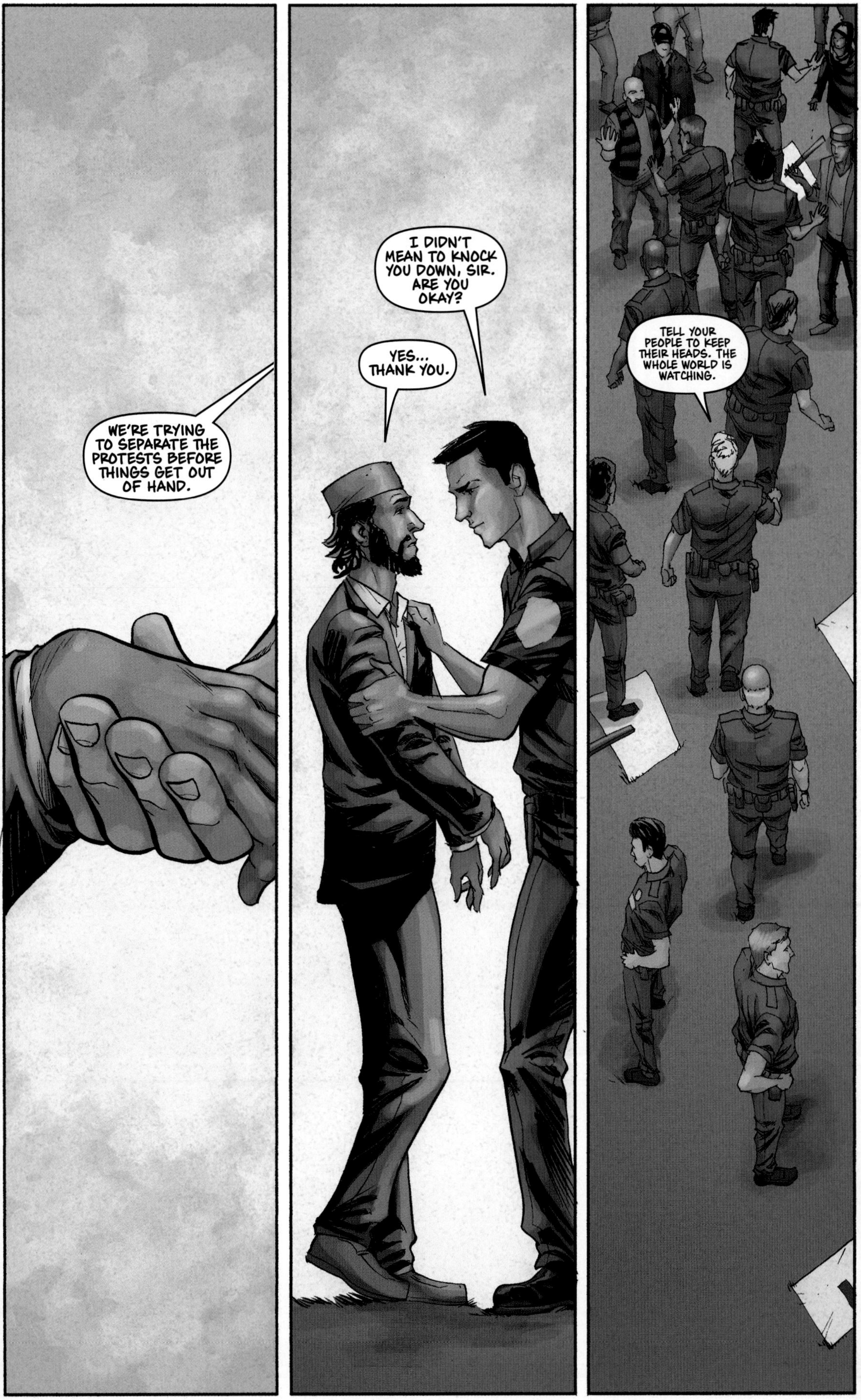
WE'RE TRYING TO SEPARATE THE PROTESTS BEFORE THINGS GET OUT OF HAND.
I DIDN'T MEAN TO KNOCK YOU DOWN, SIR. ARE YOU OKAY?
YES... THANK YOU.
TELL YOUR PEOPLE TO KEEP THEIR HEADS. THE WHOLE WORLD IS WATCHING.

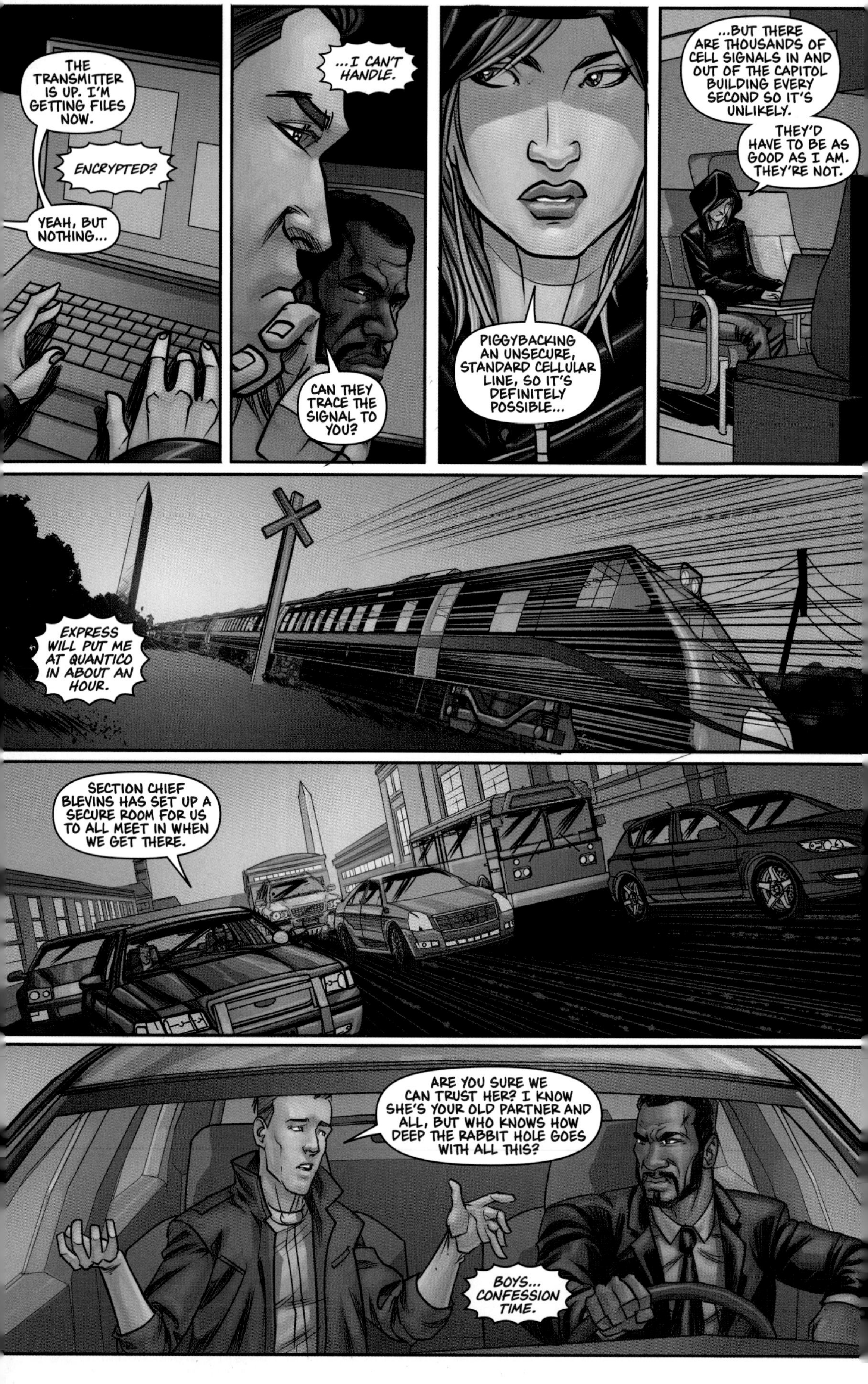
THE TRANSMITTER IS UP. I'M GETTING FILES NOW.
ENCRYPTED?
YEAH, BUT NOTHING...
...I CAN'T HANDLE.
CAN THEY TRACE THE SIGNAL TO YOU?
PIGGYBACKING AN UNSECURE, STANDARD CELLULAR LINE, SO IT'S DEFINITELY POSSIBLE...
...BUT THERE ARE THOUSANDS OF CELL SIGNALS IN AND OUT OF THE CAPITOL BUILDING EVERY SECOND SO IT'S UNLIKELY.
THEY'D HAVE TO BE AS GOOD AS I AM. THEY'RE NOT.
EXPRESS WILL PUT ME AT QUANTICO IN ABOUT AN HOUR.
SECTION CHIEF BLEVINS HAS SET UP A SECURE ROOM FOR US TO ALL MEET IN WHEN WE GET THERE.
ARE YOU SURE WE CAN TRUST HER? I KNOW SHE'S YOUR OLD PARTNER AND ALL, BUT WHO KNOWS HOW DEEP THE RABBIT HOLE GOES WITH ALL THIS?
BOYS... CONFESSION TIME.

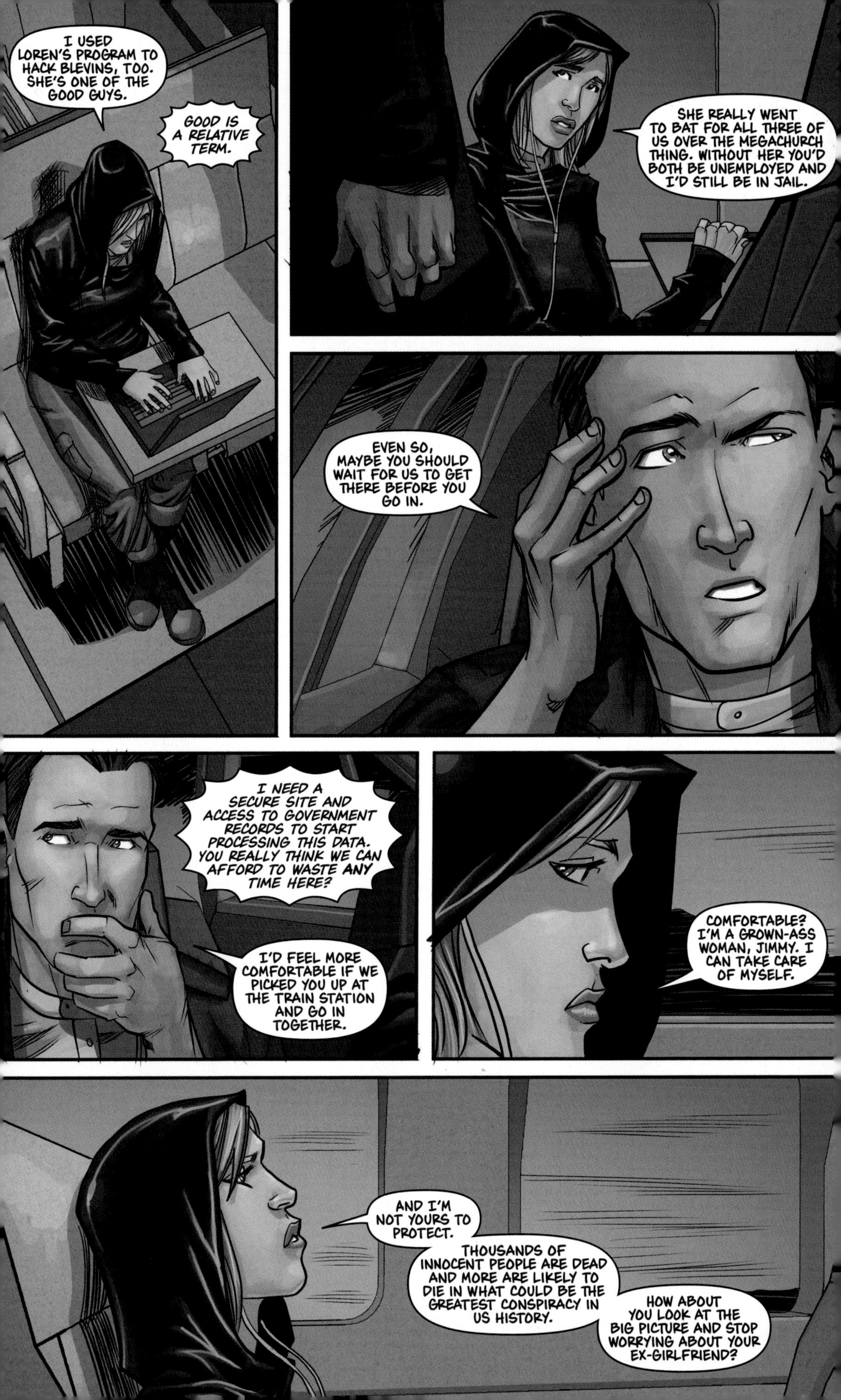
I USED LOREN'S PROGRAM TO HACK BLEVINS, TOO. SHE'S ONE OF THE GOOD GUYS.
GOOD IS A RELATIVE TERM.
SHE REALLY WENT TO BAT FOR ALL THREE OF US OVER THE MEGACHURCH THING. WITHOUT HER YOU'D BOTH BE UNEMPLOYED AND I'D STILL BE IN JAIL.
EVEN SO, MAYBE YOU SHOULD WAIT FOR US TO GET THERE BEFORE YOU GO IN.
I NEED A SECURE SITE AND ACCESS TO GOVERNMENT RECORDS TO START PROCESSING THIS DATA. YOU REALLY THINK WE CAN AFFORD TO WASTE ANY TIME HERE?
I'D FEEL MORE COMFORTABLE IF WE PICKED YOU UP AT THE TRAIN STATION AND GO IN TOGETHER.
COMFORTABLE? I'M A GROWN-ASS WOMAN, JIMMY. I CAN TAKE CARE OF MYSELF.
AND I'M NOT YOURS TO PROTECT.
THOUSANDS OF INNOCENT PEOPLE ARE DEAD AND MORE ARE LIKELY TO DIE IN WHAT COULD BE THE GREATEST CONSPIRACY IN US HISTORY.
HOW ABOUT YOU LOOK AT THE BIG PICTURE AND STOP WORRYING ABOUT YOUR EX-GIRLFRIEND?

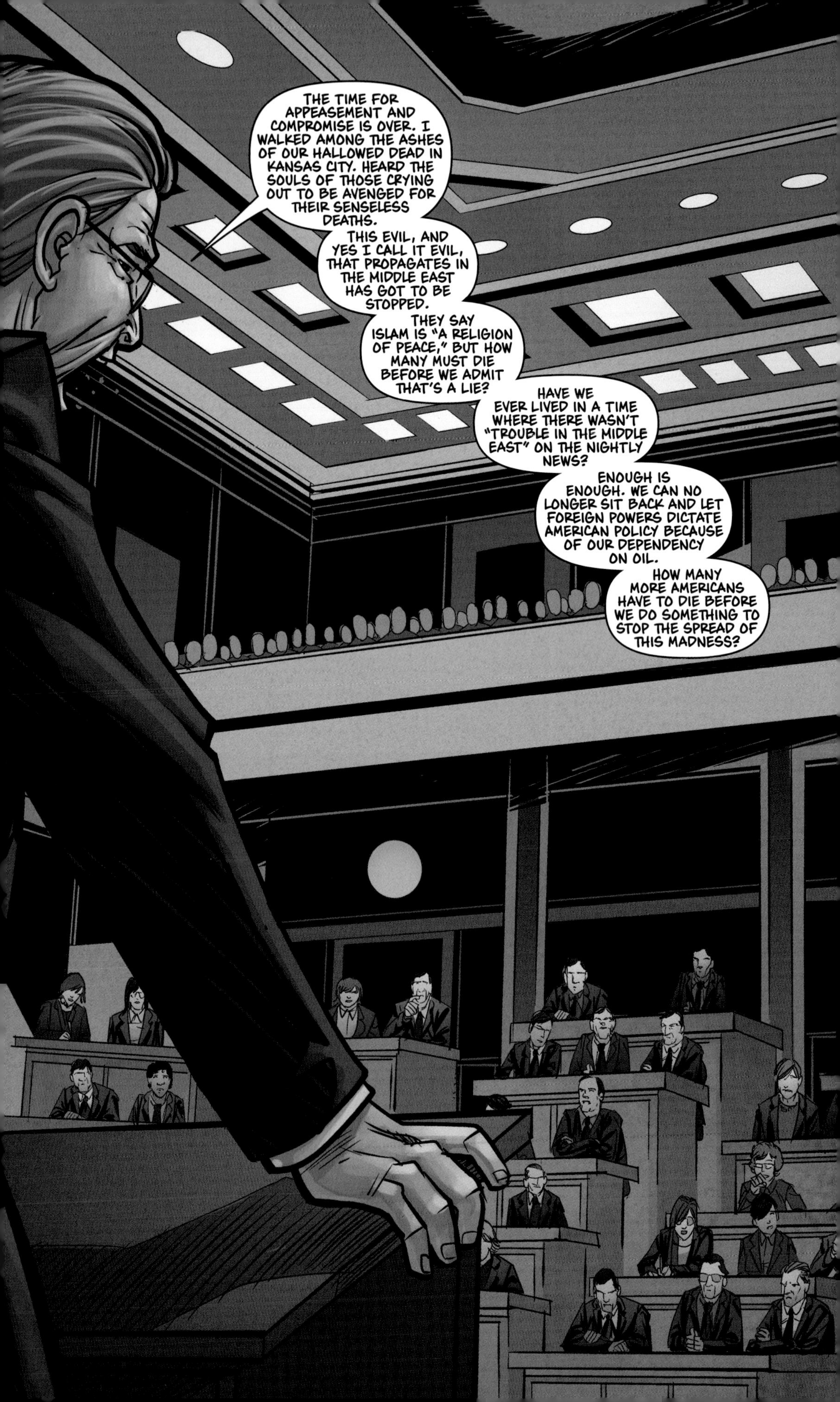
THE TIME FOR APPEASEMENT AND COMPROMISE IS OVER. I WALKED AMONG THE ASHES OF OUR HALLOWED DEAD IN KANSAS CITY. HEARD THE SOULS OF THOSE CRYING OUT TO BE AVENGED FOR THEIR SENSELESS DEATHS.
THIS EVIL, AND YES I CALL IT EVIL, THAT PROPAGATES IN THE MIDDLE EAST HAS GOT TO BE STOPPED.
THEY SAY ISLAM IS "A RELIGION OF PEACE," BUT HOW MANY MUST DIE BEFORE WE ADMIT THAT'S A LIE?
HAVE WE EVER LIVED IN A TIME WHERE THERE WASN'T "TROUBLE IN THE MIDDLE EAST" ON THE NIGHTLY NEWS?
ENOUGH IS ENOUGH. WE CAN NO LONGER SIT BACK AND LET FOREIGN POWERS DICTATE AMERICAN POLICY BECAUSE OF OUR DEPENDENCY ON OIL.
HOW MANY MORE AMERICANS HAVE TO DIE BEFORE WE DO SOMETHING TO STOP THE SPREAD OF THIS MADNESS?

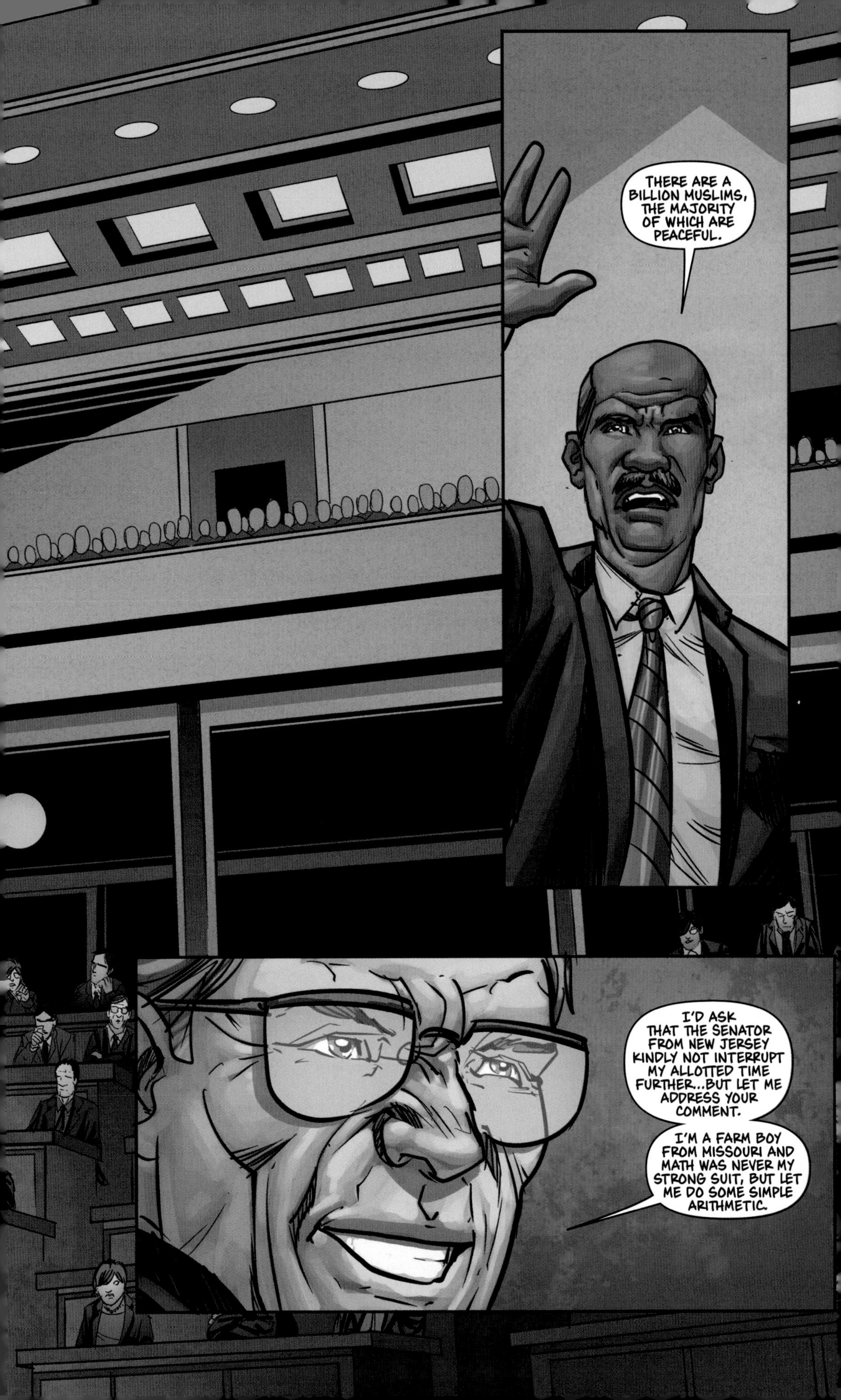
THERE ARE A BILLION MUSLIMS, THE MAJORITY OF WHICH ARE PEACEFUL.
I'D ASK THAT THE SENATOR FROM NEW JERSEY KINDLY NOT INTERRUPT MY ALLOTTED TIME FURTHER...BUT LET ME ADDRESS YOUR COMMENT.
I'M A FARM BOY FROM MISSOURI AND MATH WAS NEVER MY STRONG SUIT, BUT LET ME DO SOME SIMPLE ARITHMETIC.

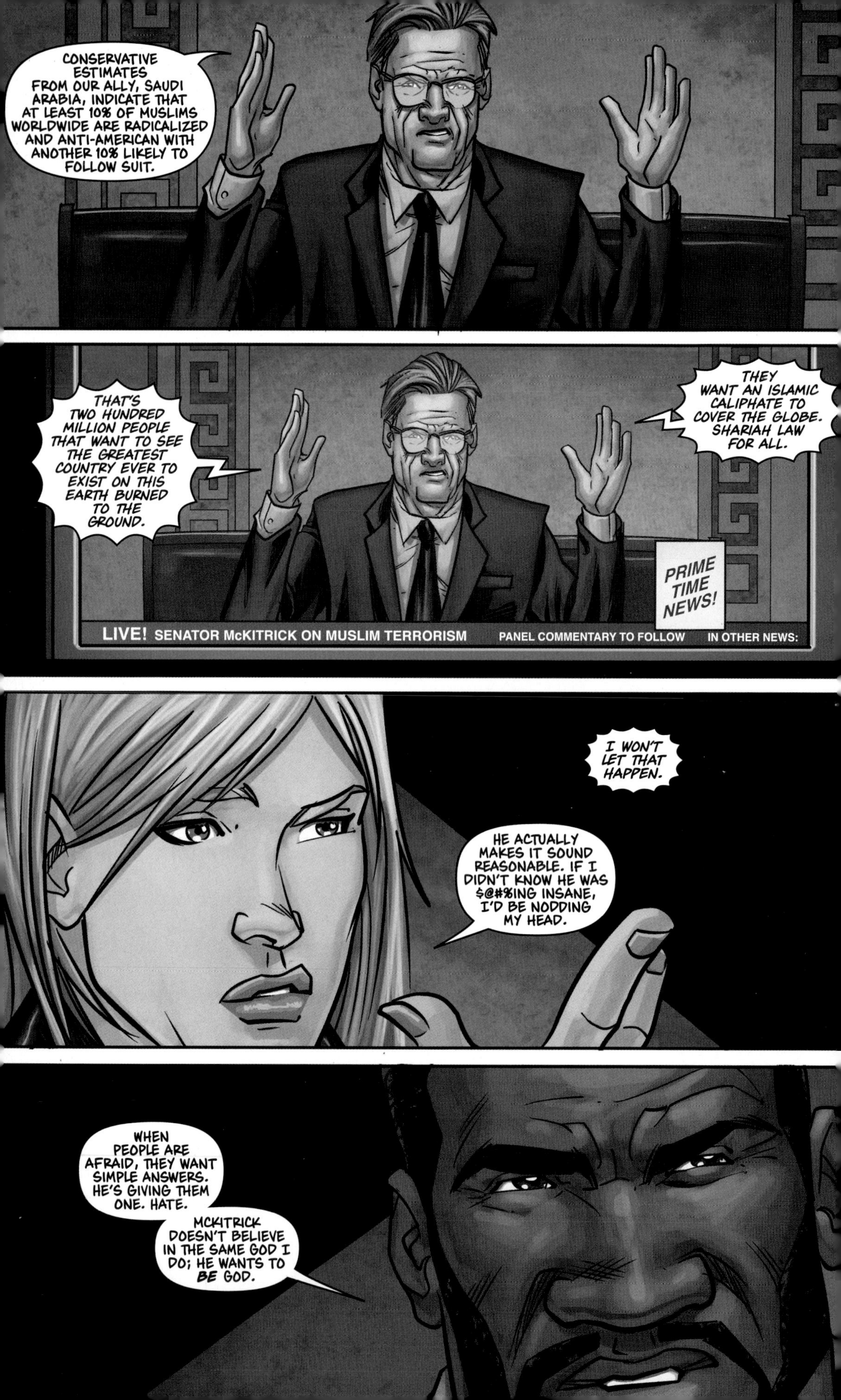
CONSERVATIVE ESTIMATES FROM OUR ALLY, SAUDI ARABIA, INDICATE THAT AT LEAST 10% OF MUSLIMS WORLDWIDE ARE RADICALIZED AND ANTI-AMERICAN WITH ANOTHER 10% LIKELY TO FOLLOW SUIT.
THAT'S TWO HUNDRED MILLION PEOPLE THAT WANT TO SEE THE GREATEST COUNTRY EVER TO EXIST ON THIS EARTH BURNED TO THE GROUND.
THEY WANT AN ISLAMIC CALIPHATE TO COVER THE GLOBE. SHARIAH LAW FOR ALL.
PRIME TIME NEWS!
LIVE! SENATOR McKITRICK ON MUSLIM TERRORISM
PANEL COMMENTARY TO FOLLOW
IN OTHER NEWS:
I WON'T LET THAT HAPPEN.
HE ACTUALLY MAKES IT SOUND REASONABLE. IF I DIDN'T KNOW HE WAS $@#%ING INSANE, I'D BE NODDING MY HEAD.
WHEN PEOPLE ARE AFRAID, THEY WANT SIMPLE ANSWERS. HE'S GIVING THEM ONE. HATE.
MCKITRICK DOESN'T BELIEVE IN THE SAME GOD I DO; HE WANTS TO *BE* GOD.

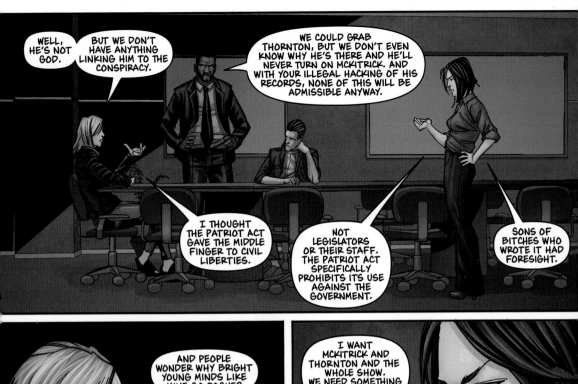

WELL, HE'S NOT GOD.

BUT WE DON'T HAVE ANYTHING LINKING HIM TO THE CONSPIRACY.

WE COULD GRAB THORNTON, BUT WE DON'T EVEN KNOW WHY HE'S THERE AND HE'LL NEVER TURN ON MCKITRICK. AND WITH YOUR ILLEGAL HACKING OF HIS RECORDS, NONE OF THIS WILL BE ADMISSIBLE ANYWAY.

I THOUGHT THE PATRIOT ACT GAVE THE MIDDLE FINGER TO CIVIL LIBERTIES.

NOT LEGISLATORS OR THEIR STAFF. THE PATRIOT ACT SPECIFICALLY PROHIBITS ITS USE AGAINST THE GOVERNMENT.

SONS OF BITCHES WHO WROTE IT HAD FORESIGHT.

AND PEOPLE WONDER WHY BRIGHT YOUNG MINDS LIKE MINE GO ROGUE?

I WANT MCKITRICK AND THORNTON AND THE WHOLE SHOW. WE NEED SOMETHING IRONCLAD. PHYSICAL EVIDENCE.

OBTAINED LEGALLY.

A CONFESSION. GET THE BASTARD ON TAPE.

WE'LL WAIT A YEAR TO GET SURVEILLANCE AUTHORIZATION. THORNTON'S THE KEY. WE TRACKED HIM TO SOME KIND OF COMPOUND, NEARLY OFF THE GRID.

IF WE GO THERE FAST AND HARD -- NO OVERSIGHT, NO ONE TO TIP THEM OFF -- WE'LL FIND SOMETHING.

YOU WILLING TO BET YOUR CAREER ON THAT?

THORNTON. TELL ME THE LINK.

I COMPARED THE CAMPAIGN DONOR LISTS ON MCKITRICK'S COMPUTER TO ADDRESSES ON THORNTON'S LAPTOP AND RAN THOSE AGAINST WHAT WAS PUBLICLY FILED.

MOST WERE FUGAZI, BUT ONE OF THEM CORRESPONDED TO A NAVIGATION SEARCH THORNTON HAD PULLED UP ON HIS PHONE SEVERAL TIMES IN THE LAST YEAR.

IF YOU DO SOMETHING ON YOUR PHONE, THE WORLD CAN FIND IT.

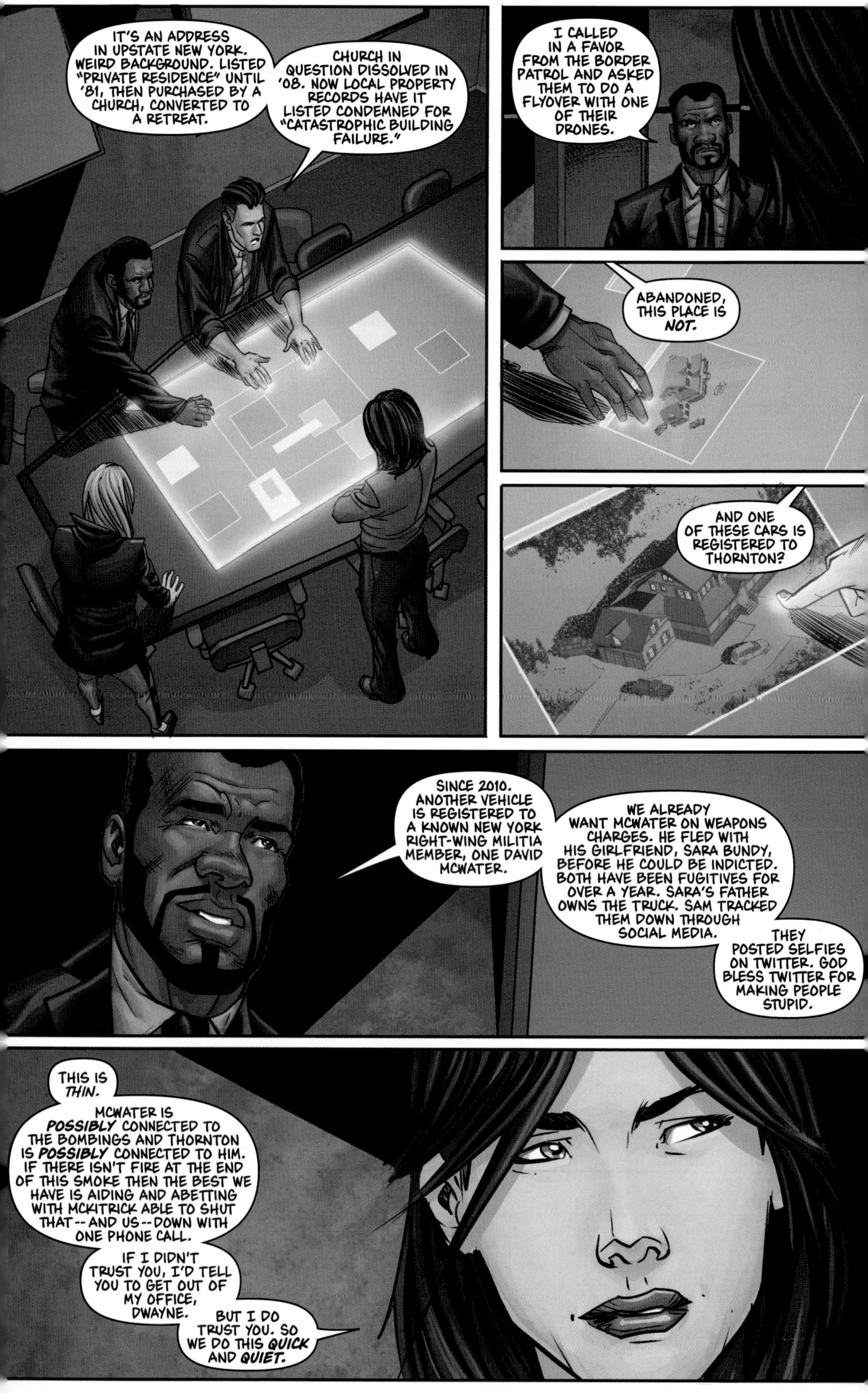

IT'S AN ADDRESS IN UPSTATE NEW YORK. WEIRD BACKGROUND. LISTED "PRIVATE RESIDENCE" UNTIL '81, THEN PURCHASED BY A CHURCH, CONVERTED TO A RETREAT.
CHURCH IN QUESTION DISSOLVED IN '08. NOW LOCAL PROPERTY RECORDS HAVE IT LISTED CONDEMNED FOR "CATASTROPHIC BUILDING FAILURE."
I CALLED IN A FAVOR FROM THE BORDER PATROL AND ASKED THEM TO DO A FLYOVER WITH ONE OF THEIR DRONES.
ABANDONED, THIS PLACE IS *NOT.*
AND ONE OF THESE CARS IS REGISTERED TO THORNTON?
SINCE 2010. ANOTHER VEHICLE IS REGISTERED TO A KNOWN NEW YORK RIGHT-WING MILITIA MEMBER, ONE DAVID MCWATER.
WE ALREADY WANT MCWATER ON WEAPONS CHARGES. HE FLED WITH HIS GIRLFRIEND, SARA BUNDY, BEFORE HE COULD BE INDICTED. BOTH HAVE BEEN FUGITIVES FOR OVER A YEAR. SARA'S FATHER OWNS THE TRUCK. SAM TRACKED THEM DOWN THROUGH SOCIAL MEDIA.
THEY POSTED SELFIES ON TWITTER. GOD BLESS TWITTER FOR MAKING PEOPLE STUPID.
THIS IS *THIN.*
MCWATER IS ***POSSIBLY*** CONNECTED TO THE BOMBINGS AND THORNTON IS ***POSSIBLY*** CONNECTED TO HIM. IF THERE ISN'T FIRE AT THE END OF THIS SMOKE THEN THE BEST WE HAVE IS AIDING AND ABETTING WITH MCKITRICK ABLE TO SHUT THAT -- AND US -- DOWN WITH ONE PHONE CALL.
IF I DIDN'T TRUST YOU, I'D TELL YOU TO GET OUT OF MY OFFICE, DWAYNE.
BUT I DO TRUST YOU. SO WE DO THIS ***QUICK*** AND ***QUIET.***

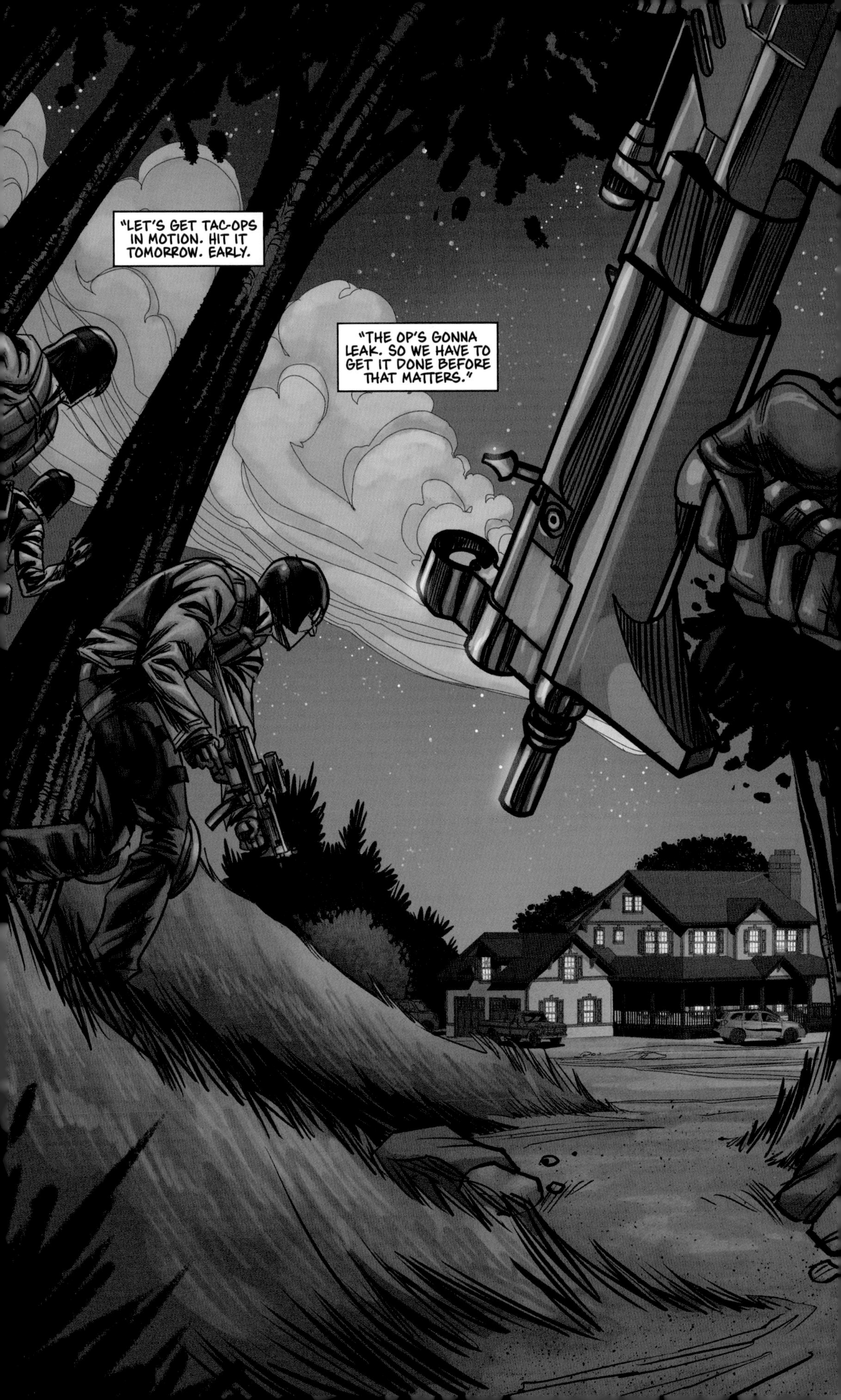
"LET'S GET TAC-OPS IN MOTION. HIT IT TOMORROW. EARLY.
"THE OP'S GONNA LEAK. SO WE HAVE TO GET IT DONE BEFORE THAT MATTERS."

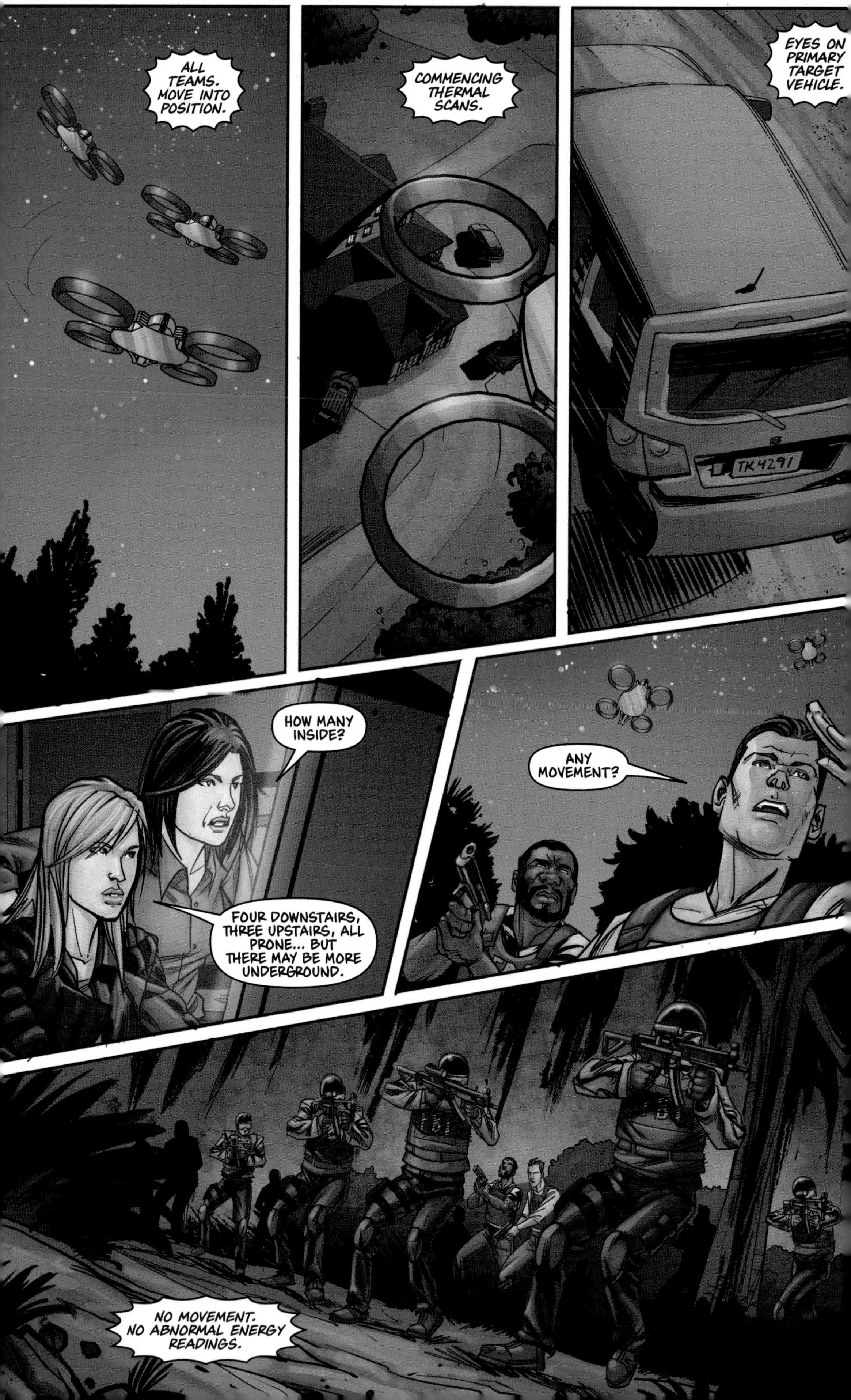
ALL TEAMS. MOVE INTO POSITION.
COMMENCING THERMAL SCANS.
EYES ON PRIMARY TARGET VEHICLE.
TK4291
HOW MANY INSIDE?
FOUR DOWNSTAIRS, THREE UPSTAIRS, ALL PRONE... BUT THERE MAY BE MORE UNDERGROUND.
ANY MOVEMENT?
NO MOVEMENT. NO ABNORMAL ENERGY READINGS.

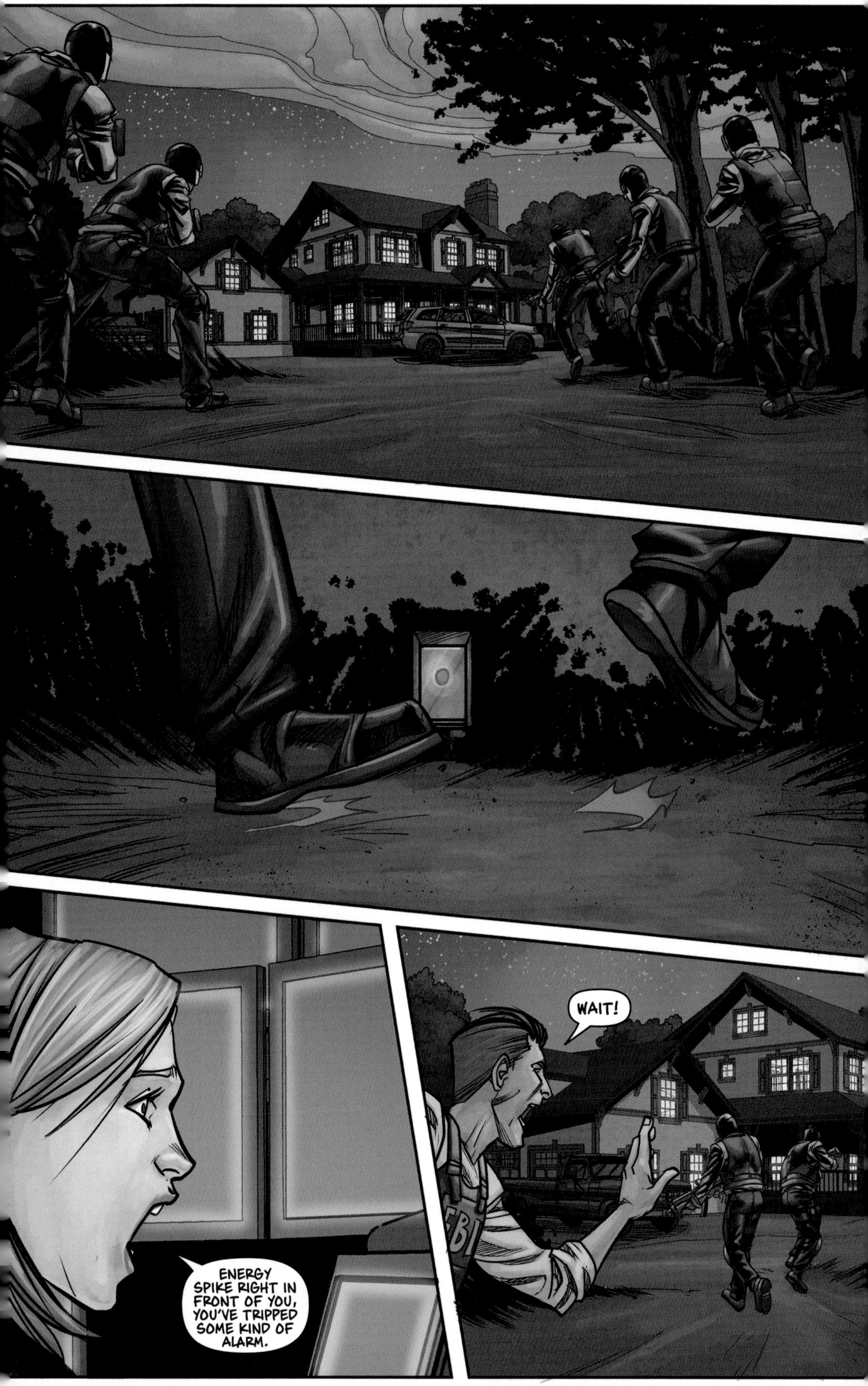
ENERGY SPIKE RIGHT IN FRONT OF YOU, YOU'VE TRIPPED SOME KIND OF ALARM.
WAIT!

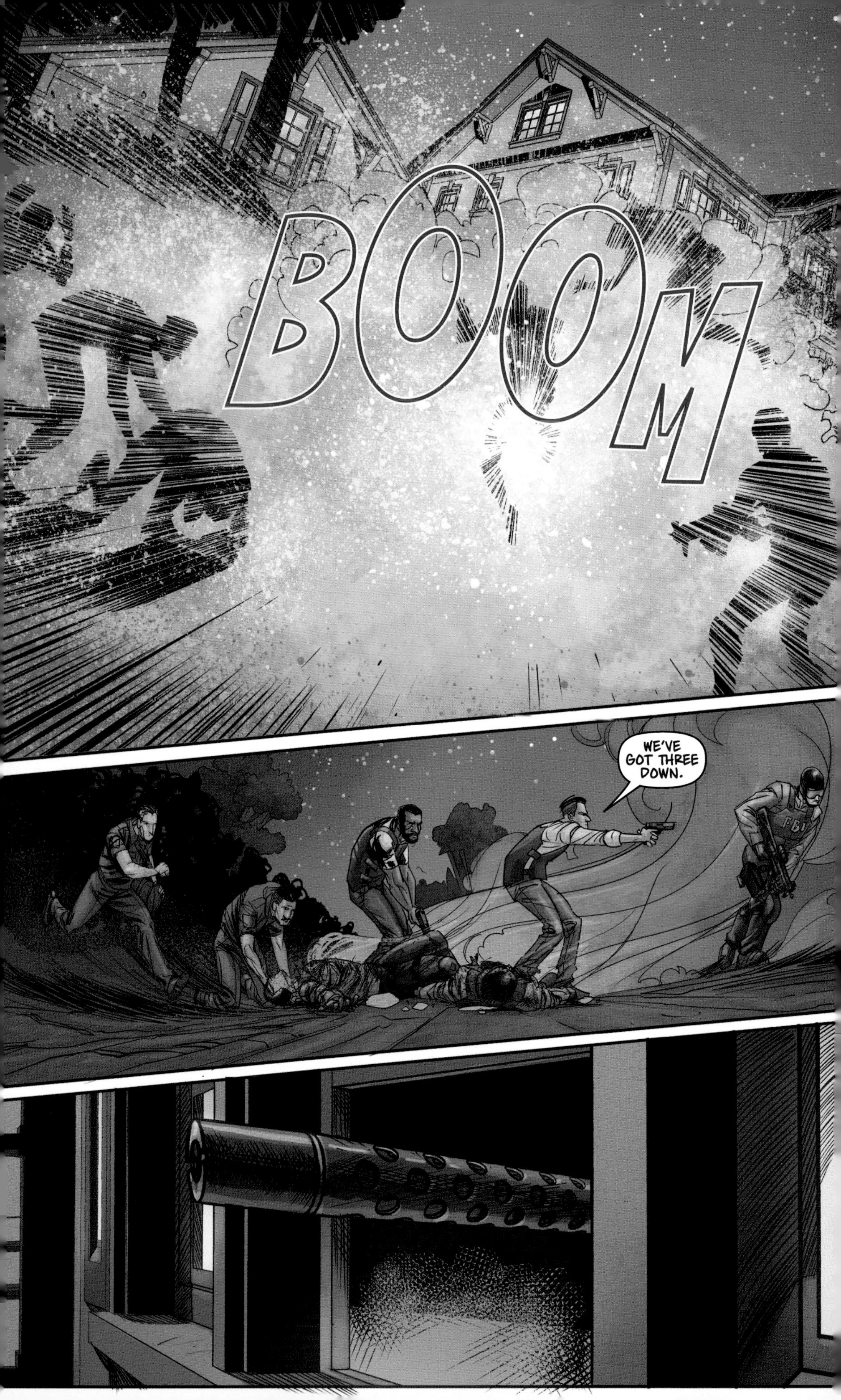
BOOM
WE'VE GOT THREE DOWN.
FBI

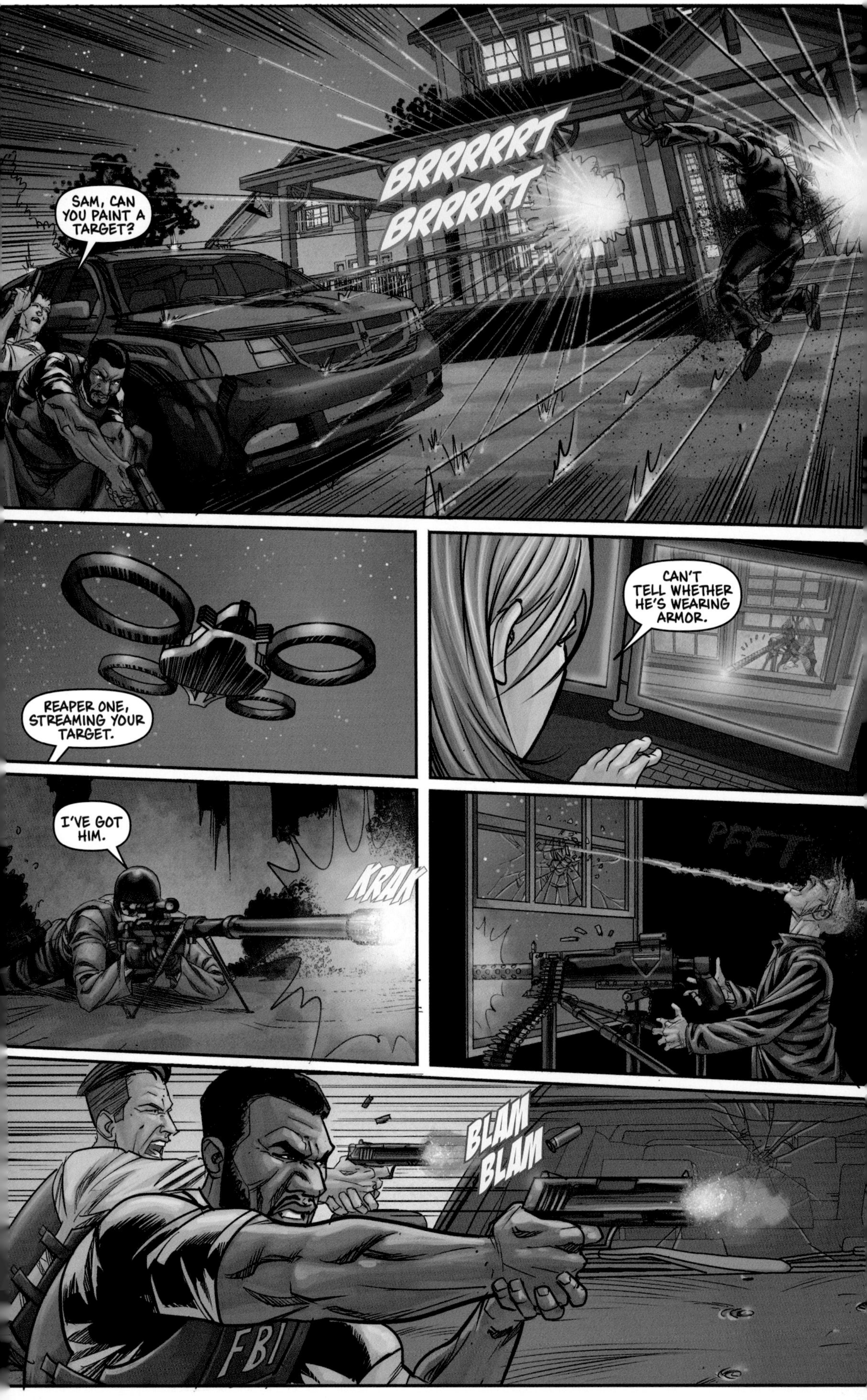
BRRRRRT
BRRRRT
SAM, CAN YOU PAINT A TARGET?
REAPER ONE, STREAMING YOUR TARGET.
CAN'T TELL WHETHER HE'S WEARING ARMOR.
I'VE GOT HIM.
KRAK
PFFT
BLAM
BLAM
FBI

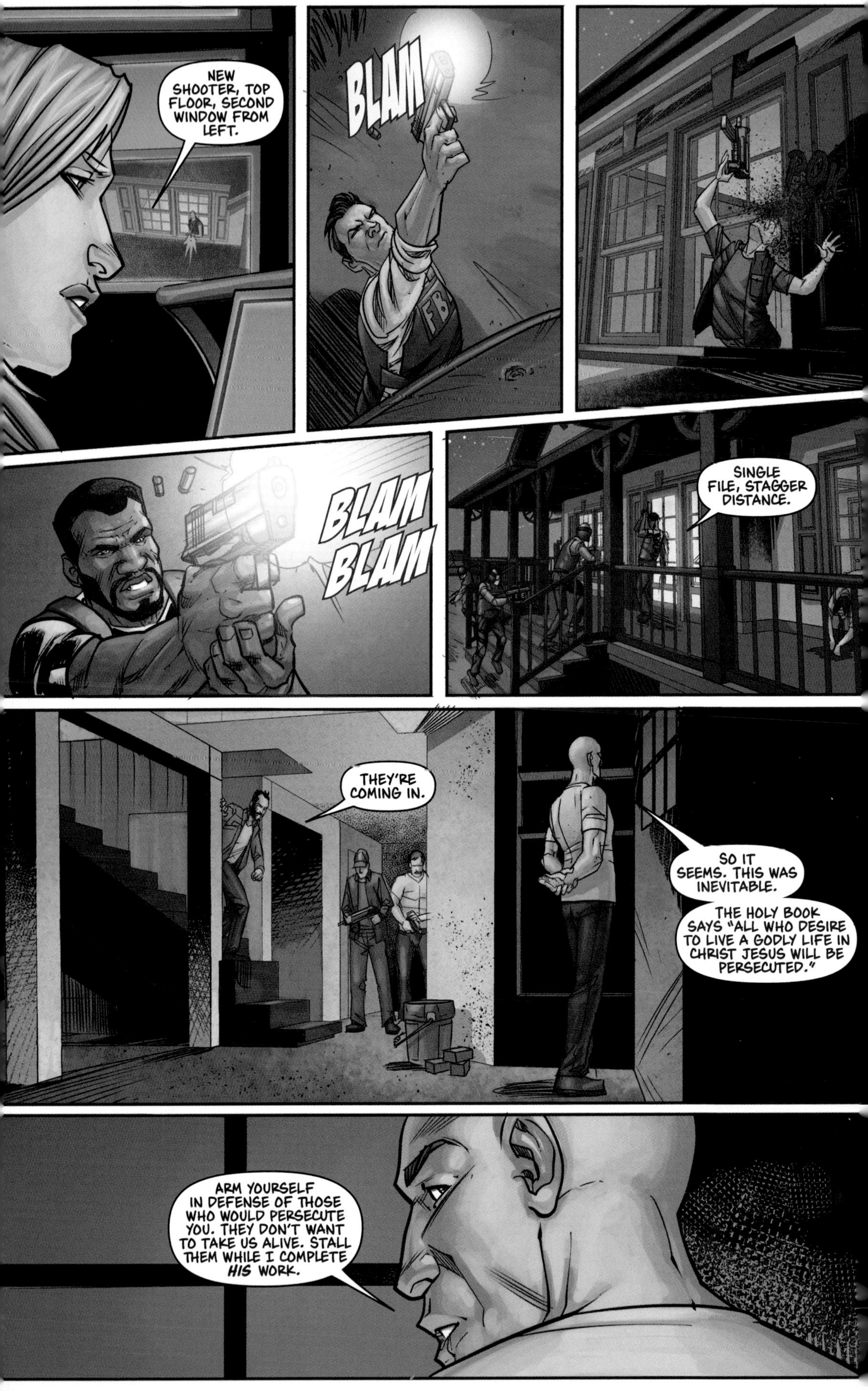

NEW SHOOTER, TOP FLOOR, SECOND WINDOW FROM LEFT.
BLAM
BLAM BLAM
SINGLE FILE, STAGGER DISTANCE.
THEY'RE COMING IN.
SO IT SEEMS. THIS WAS INEVITABLE.
THE HOLY BOOK SAYS "ALL WHO DESIRE TO LIVE A GODLY LIFE IN CHRIST JESUS WILL BE PERSECUTED."
ARM YOURSELF IN DEFENSE OF THOSE WHO WOULD PERSECUTE YOU. THEY DON'T WANT TO TAKE US ALIVE. STALL THEM WHILE I COMPLETE *HIS* WORK.

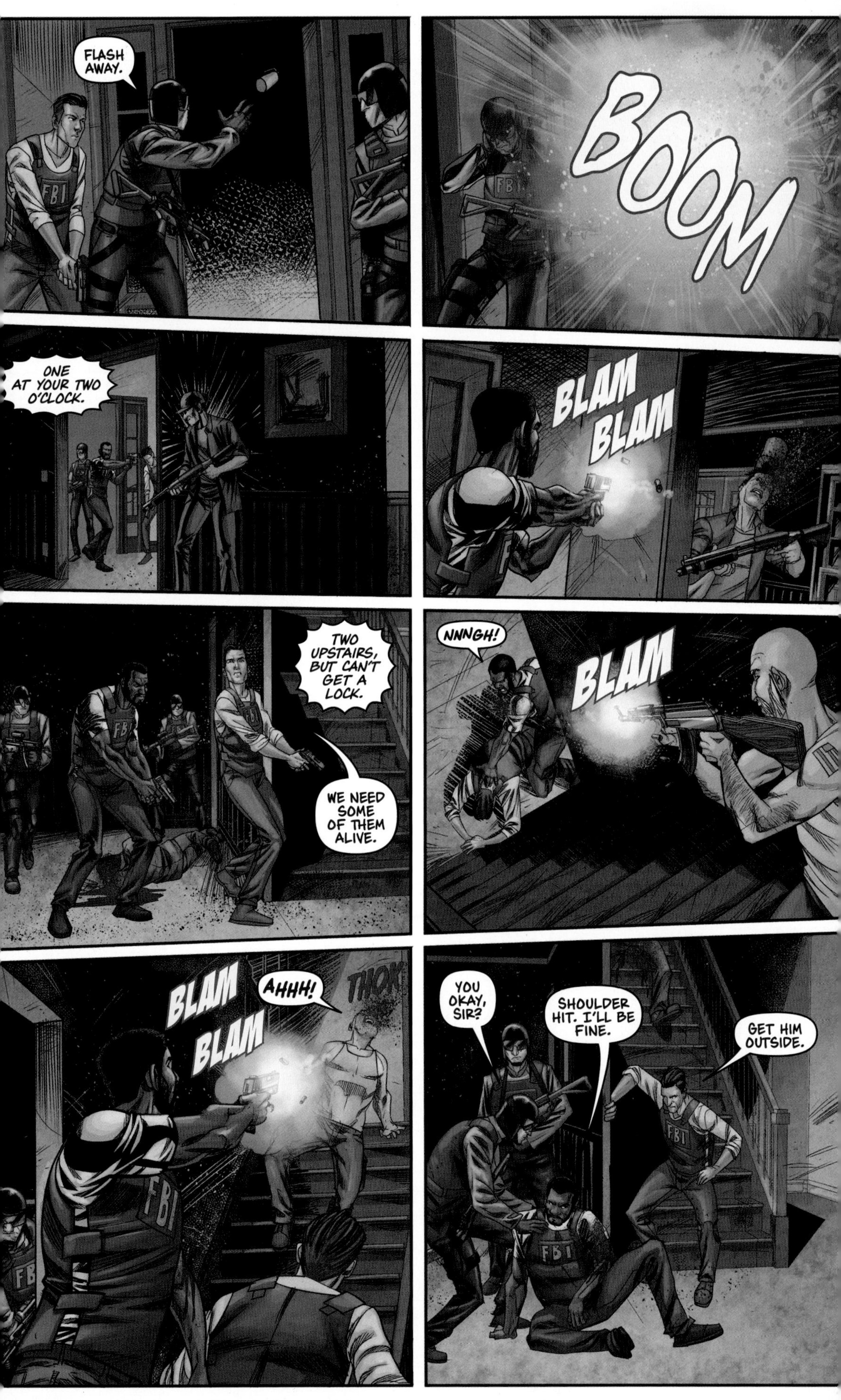
FLASH AWAY.
BOOM
ONE AT YOUR TWO O'CLOCK.
BLAM BLAM
TWO UPSTAIRS, BUT CAN'T GET A LOCK.
WE NEED SOME OF THEM ALIVE.
NNNGH!
BLAM
BLAM BLAM
AHHH!
THOK
YOU OKAY, SIR?
SHOULDER HIT. I'LL BE FINE.
GET HIM OUTSIDE.

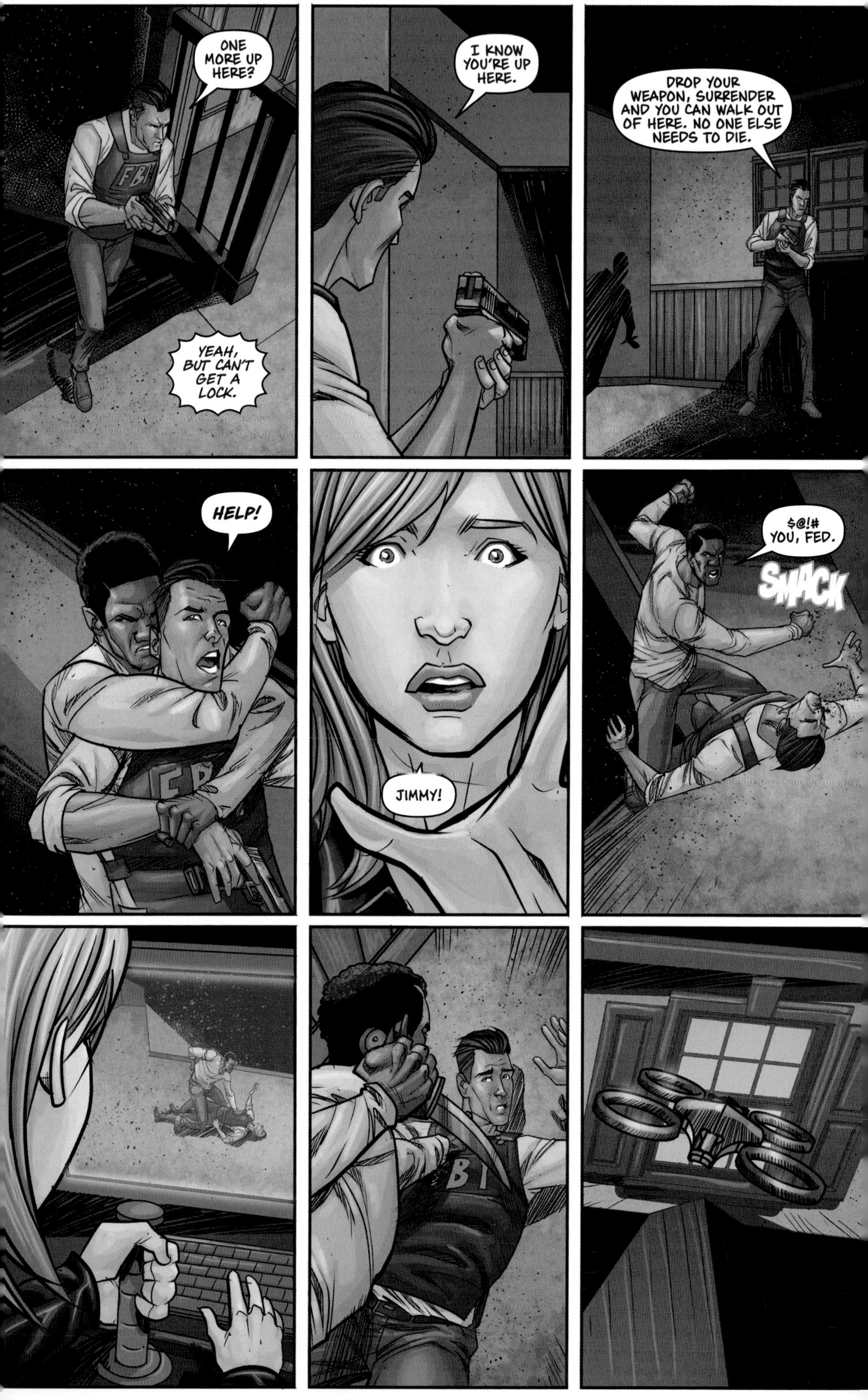
ONE MORE UP HERE?
YEAH, BUT CAN'T GET A LOCK.
I KNOW YOU'RE UP HERE.
DROP YOUR WEAPON, SURRENDER AND YOU CAN WALK OUT OF HERE. NO ONE ELSE NEEDS TO DIE.
HELP!
JIMMY!
$@!# YOU, FED.
SMACK

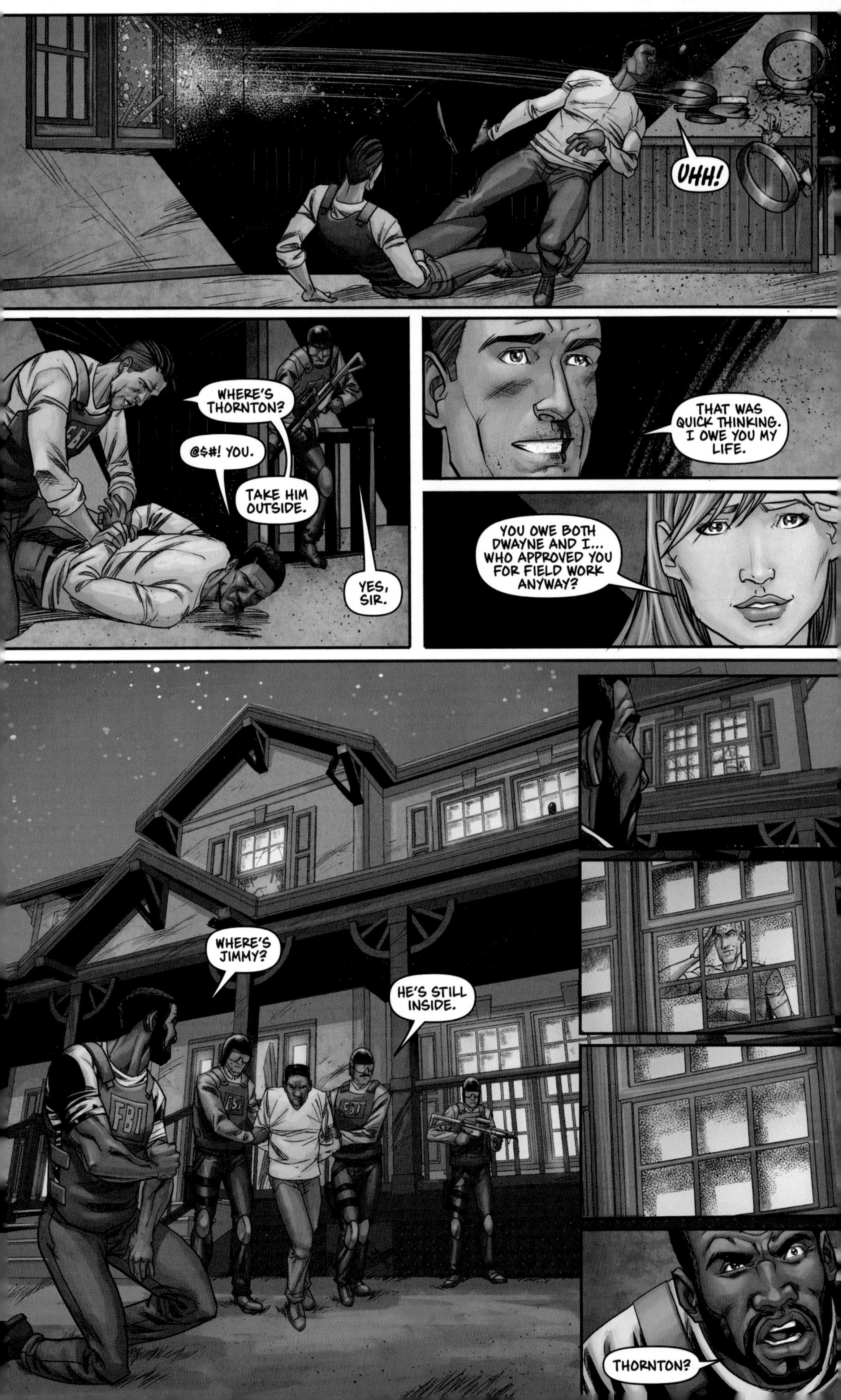
UHH!
WHERE'S THORNTON?
@$#! YOU.
TAKE HIM OUTSIDE.
YES, SIR.
THAT WAS QUICK THINKING. I OWE YOU MY LIFE.
YOU OWE BOTH DWAYNE AND I... WHO APPROVED YOU FOR FIELD WORK ANYWAY?
WHERE'S JIMMY?
HE'S STILL INSIDE.
THORNTON?

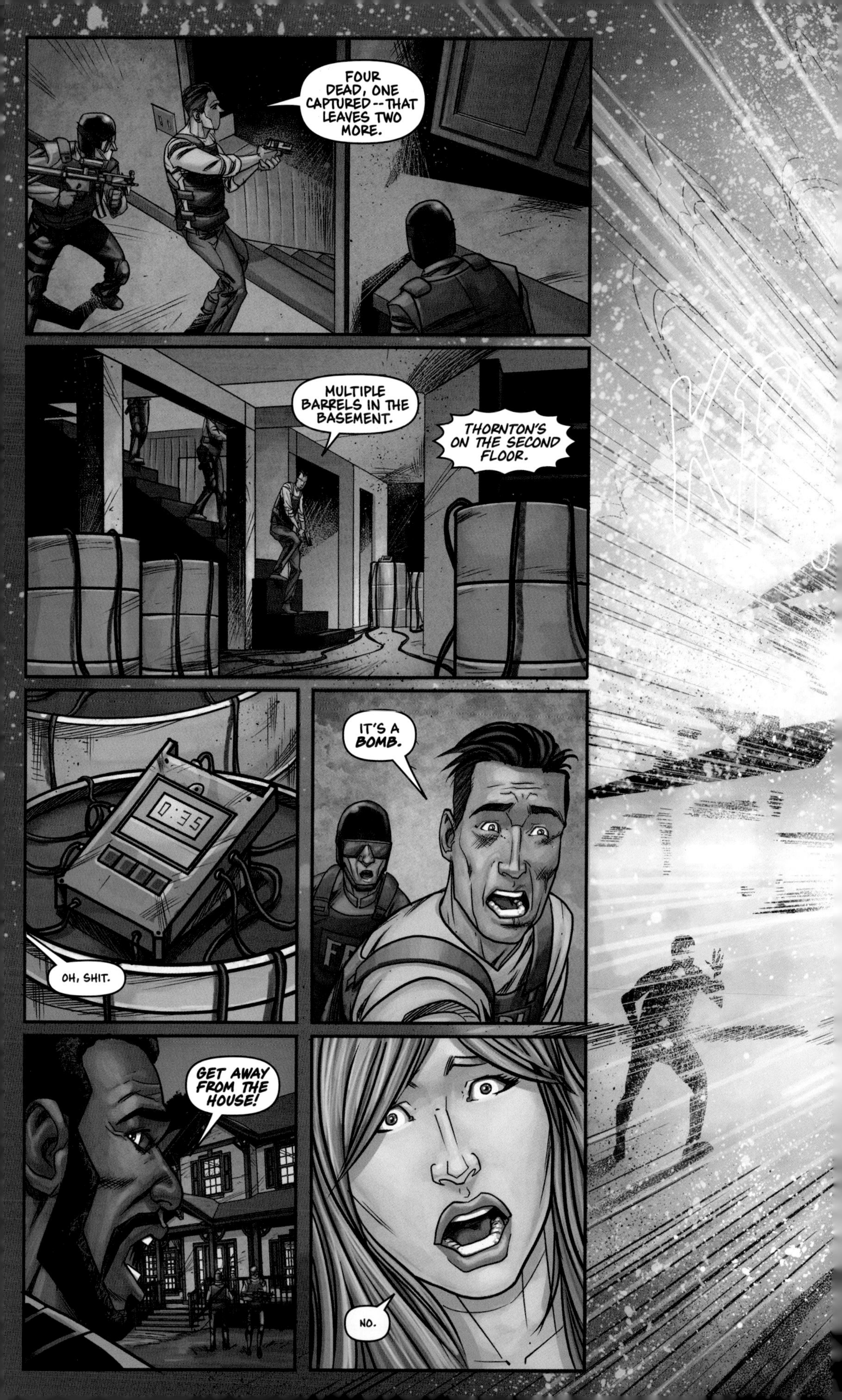
FOUR DEAD, ONE CAPTURED--THAT LEAVES TWO MORE.
MULTIPLE BARRELS IN THE BASEMENT.
THORNTON'S ON THE SECOND FLOOR.
0:35
OH, SHIT.
IT'S A BOMB.
GET AWAY FROM THE HOUSE!
NO.

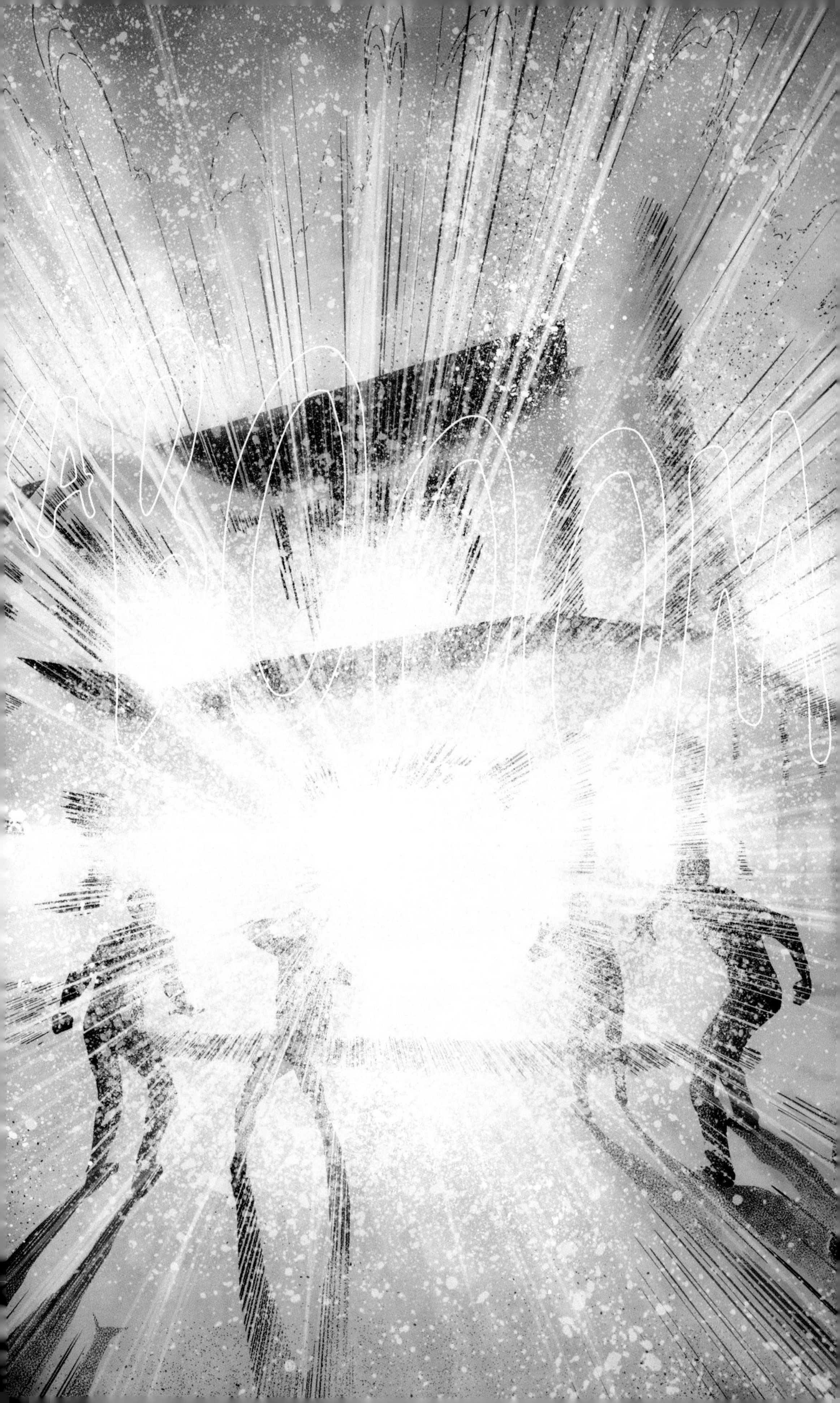

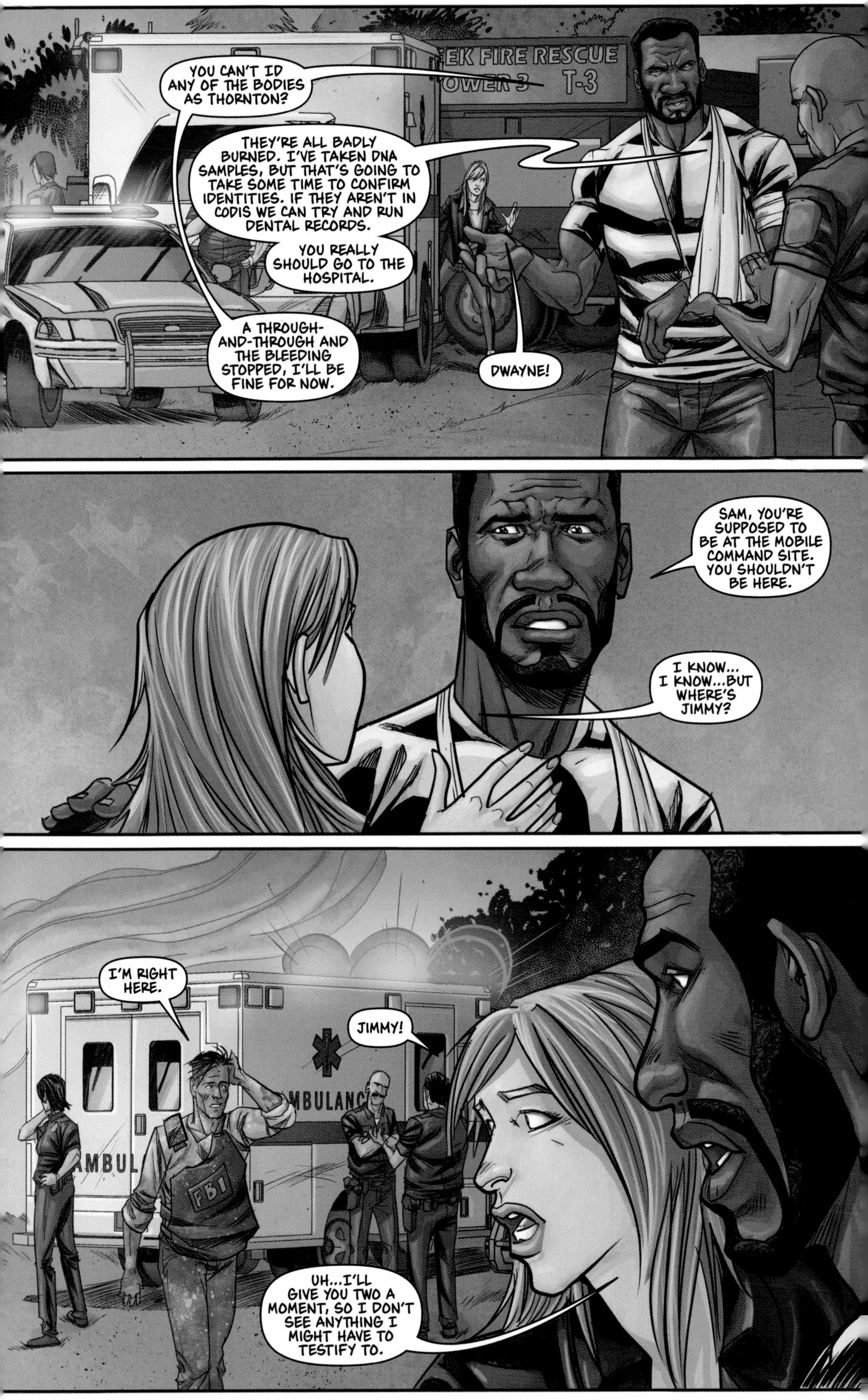
EK FIRE RESCUE
OWER 3 T-3
YOU CAN'T ID ANY OF THE BODIES AS THORNTON?
THEY'RE ALL BADLY BURNED. I'VE TAKEN DNA SAMPLES, BUT THAT'S GOING TO TAKE SOME TIME TO CONFIRM IDENTITIES. IF THEY AREN'T IN CODIS WE CAN TRY AND RUN DENTAL RECORDS.
YOU REALLY SHOULD GO TO THE HOSPITAL.
A THROUGH-AND-THROUGH AND THE BLEEDING STOPPED, I'LL BE FINE FOR NOW.
DWAYNE!
SAM, YOU'RE SUPPOSED TO BE AT THE MOBILE COMMAND SITE. YOU SHOULDN'T BE HERE.
I KNOW... I KNOW...BUT WHERE'S JIMMY?
I'M RIGHT HERE.
JIMMY!
AMBULANC
AMBUL
FBI
UH...I'LL GIVE YOU TWO A MOMENT, SO I DON'T SEE ANYTHING I MIGHT HAVE TO TESTIFY TO.

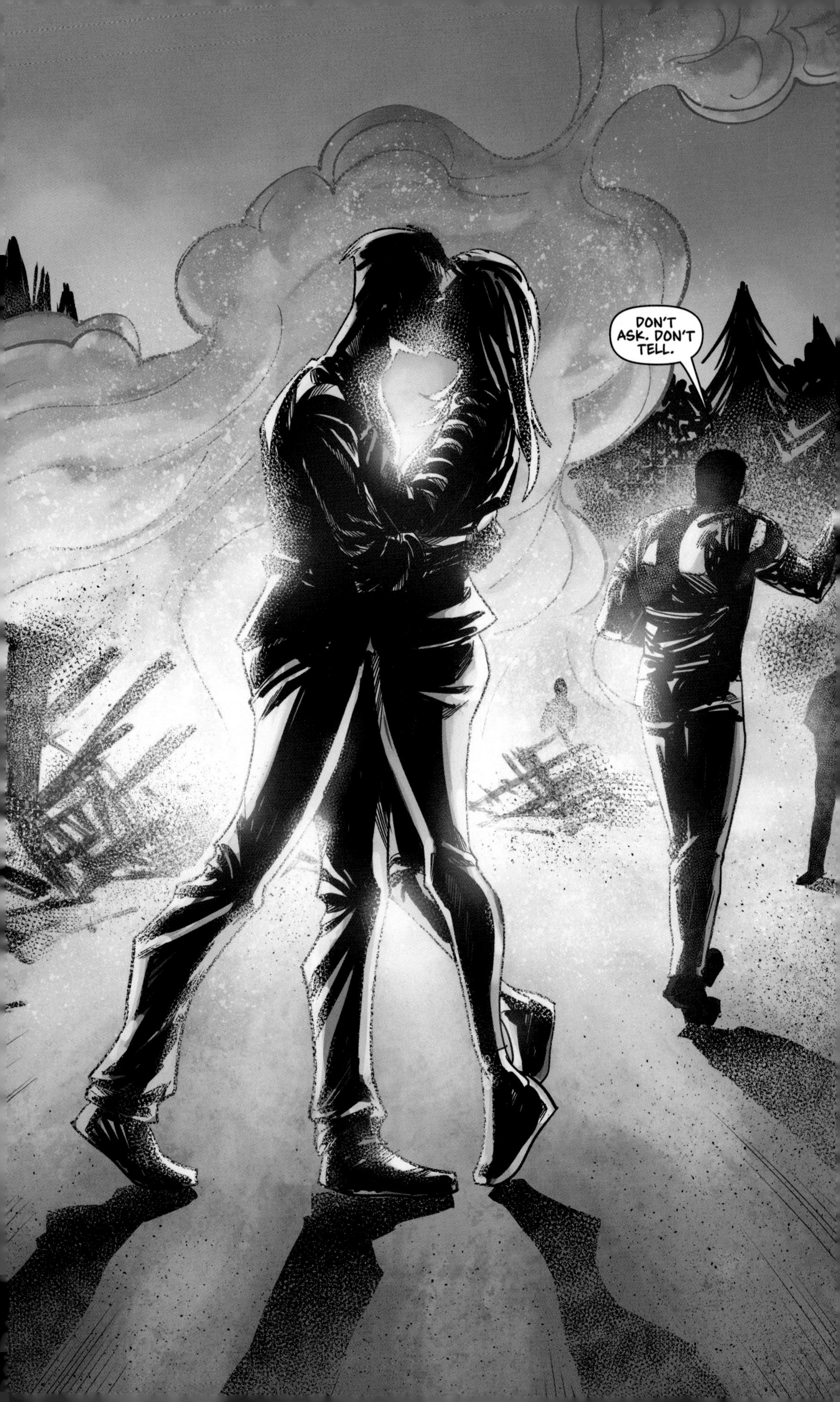
DON'T ASK. DON'T TELL.

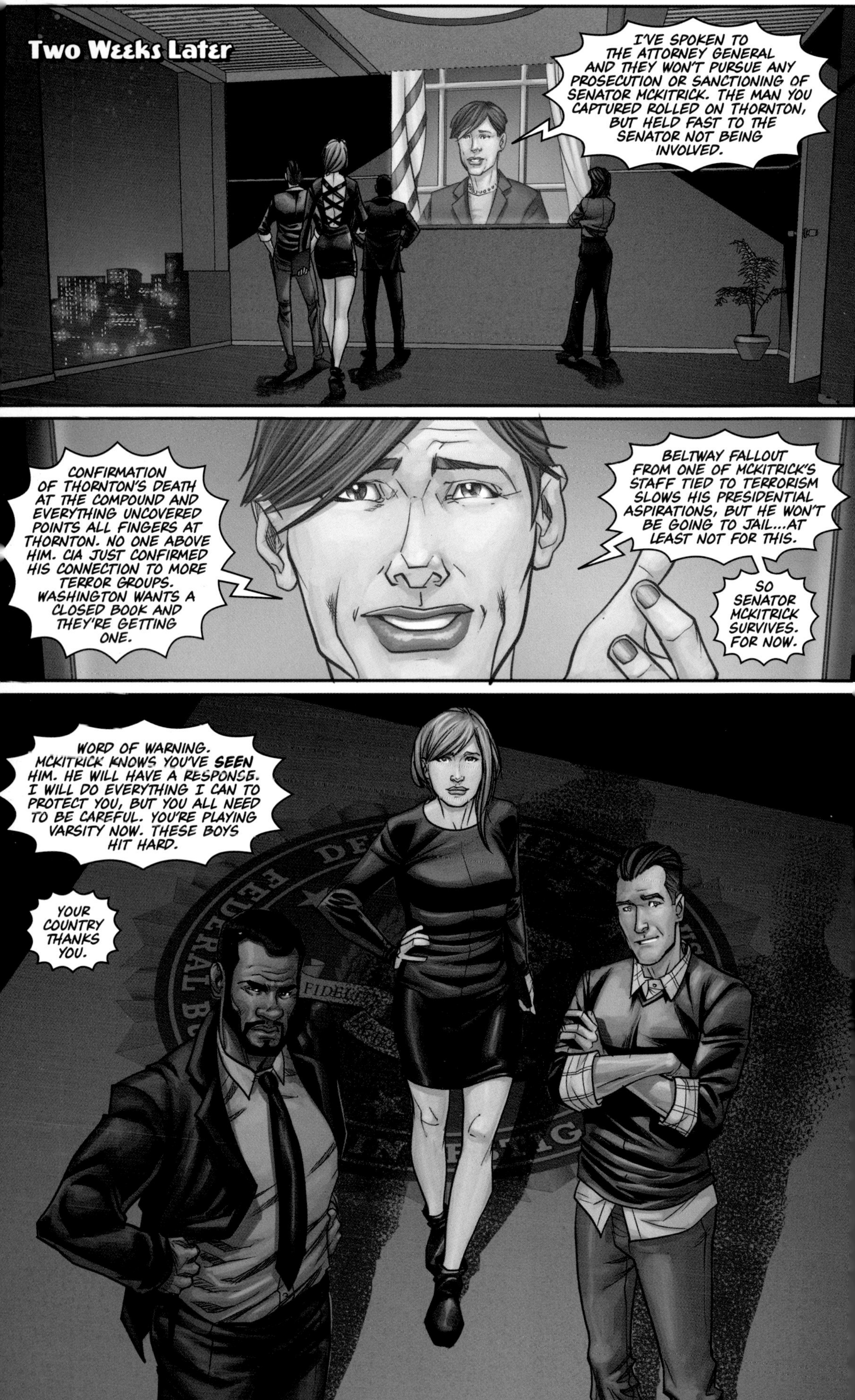
Two Weeks Later
I'VE SPOKEN TO THE ATTORNEY GENERAL AND THEY WON'T PURSUE ANY PROSECUTION OR SANCTIONING OF SENATOR MCKITRICK. THE MAN YOU CAPTURED ROLLED ON THORNTON, BUT HELD FAST TO THE SENATOR NOT BEING INVOLVED.
CONFIRMATION OF THORNTON'S DEATH AT THE COMPOUND AND EVERYTHING UNCOVERED POINTS ALL FINGERS AT THORNTON. NO ONE ABOVE HIM. CIA JUST CONFIRMED HIS CONNECTION TO MORE TERROR GROUPS. WASHINGTON WANTS A CLOSED BOOK AND THEY'RE GETTING ONE.
BELTWAY FALLOUT FROM ONE OF MCKITRICK'S STAFF TIED TO TERRORISM SLOWS HIS PRESIDENTIAL ASPIRATIONS, BUT HE WON'T BE GOING TO JAIL...AT LEAST NOT FOR THIS.
SO SENATOR MCKITRICK SURVIVES. FOR NOW.
WORD OF WARNING. MCKITRICK KNOWS YOU'VE SEEN HIM. HE WILL HAVE A RESPONSE. I WILL DO EVERYTHING I CAN TO PROTECT YOU, BUT YOU ALL NEED TO BE CAREFUL. YOU'RE PLAYING VARSITY NOW. THESE BOYS HIT HARD.
YOUR COUNTRY THANKS YOU.

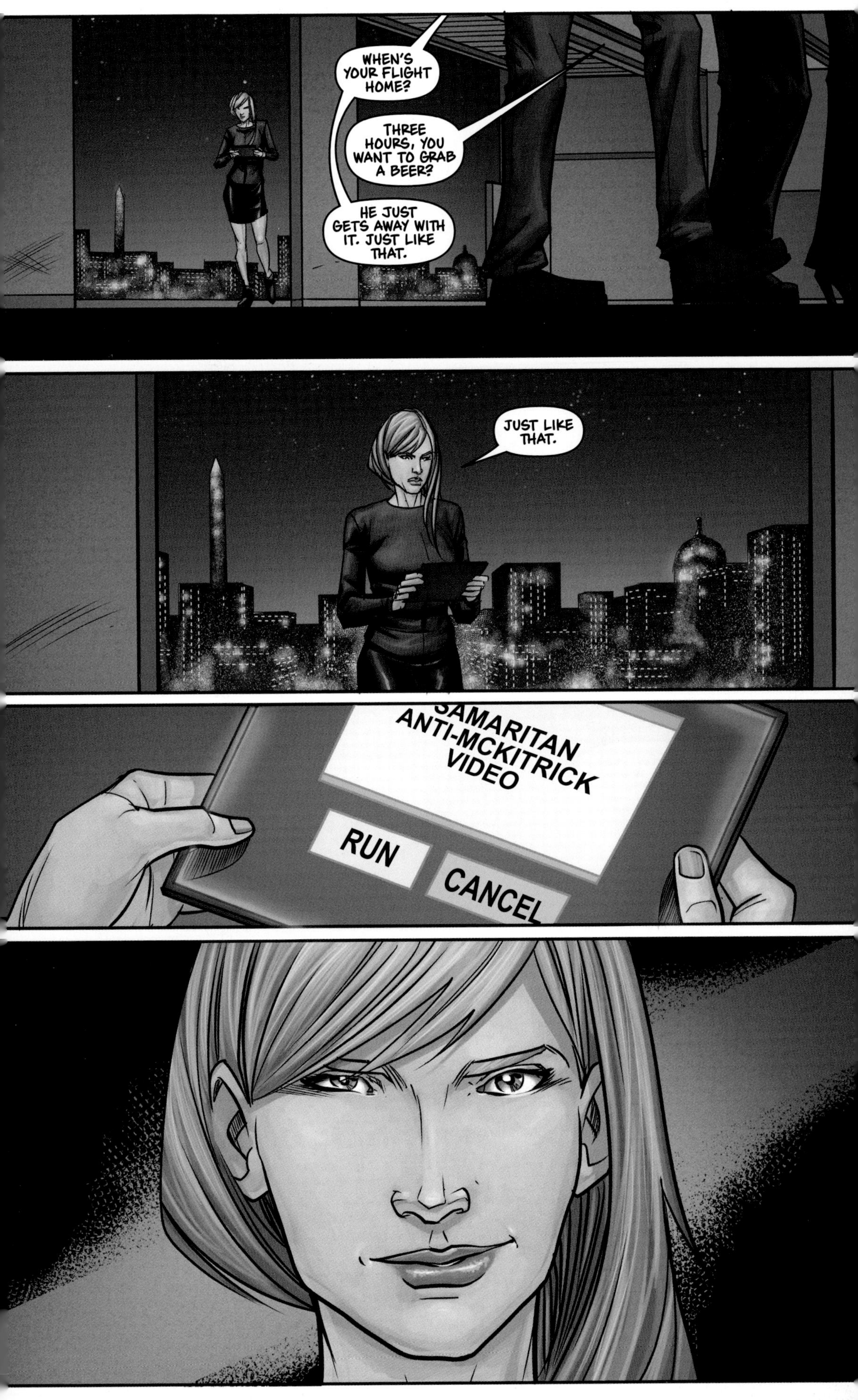
WHEN'S YOUR FLIGHT HOME?
THREE HOURS, YOU WANT TO GRAB A BEER?
HE JUST GETS AWAY WITH IT. JUST LIKE THAT.
JUST LIKE THAT.
SAMARITAN ANTI-MCKITRICK VIDEO
RUN
CANCEL

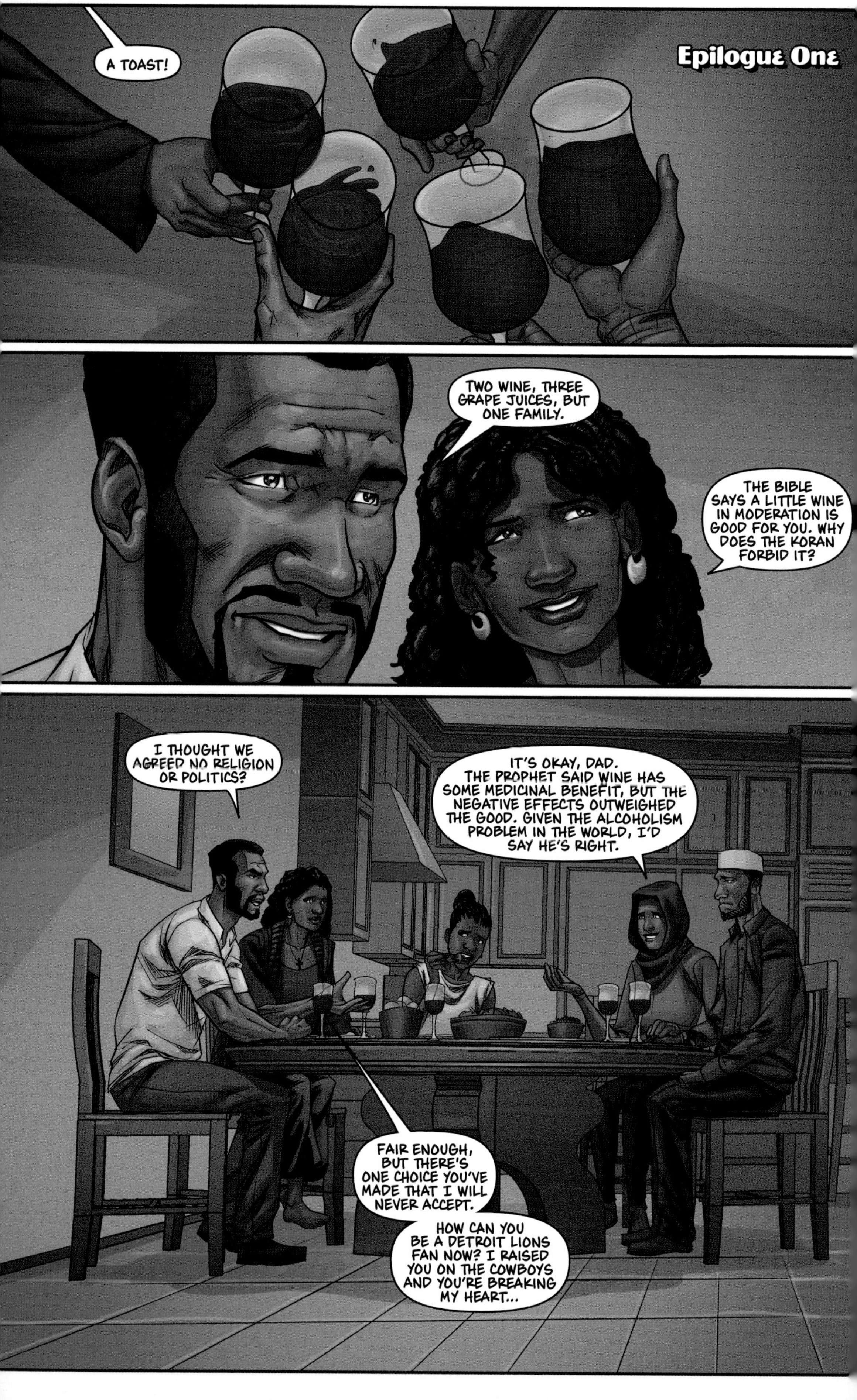
Epilogue One
A TOAST!
TWO WINE, THREE GRAPE JUICES, BUT ONE FAMILY.
THE BIBLE SAYS A LITTLE WINE IN MODERATION IS GOOD FOR YOU. WHY DOES THE KORAN FORBID IT?
I THOUGHT WE AGREED NO RELIGION OR POLITICS?
IT'S OKAY, DAD. THE PROPHET SAID WINE HAS SOME MEDICINAL BENEFIT, BUT THE NEGATIVE EFFECTS OUTWEIGHED THE GOOD. GIVEN THE ALCOHOLISM PROBLEM IN THE WORLD, I'D SAY HE'S RIGHT.
FAIR ENOUGH, BUT THERE'S ONE CHOICE YOU'VE MADE THAT I WILL NEVER ACCEPT.
HOW CAN YOU BE A DETROIT LIONS FAN NOW? I RAISED YOU ON THE COWBOYS AND YOU'RE BREAKING MY HEART...

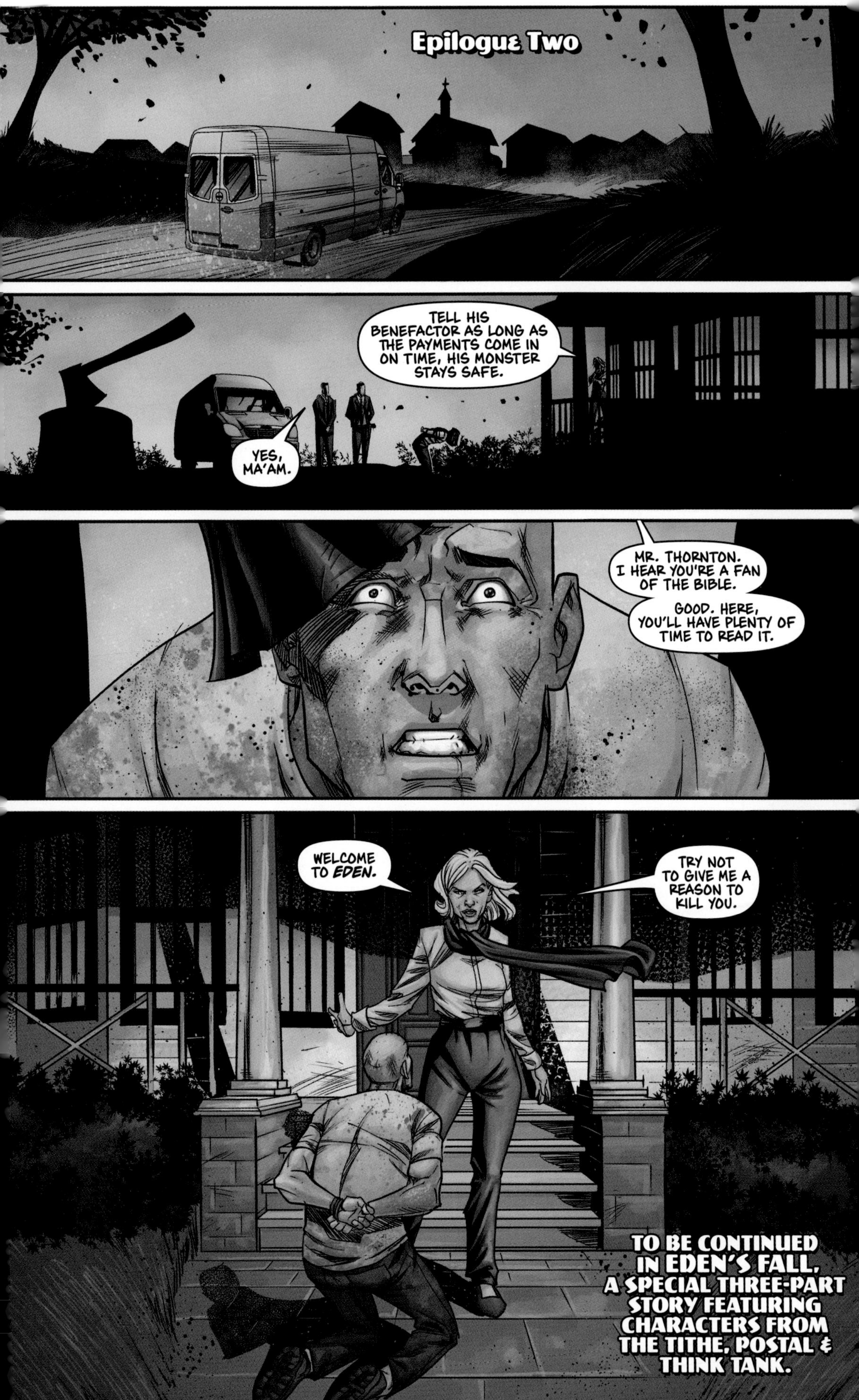
Epilogue Two
TELL HIS BENEFACTOR AS LONG AS THE PAYMENTS COME IN ON TIME, HIS MONSTER STAYS SAFE.
YES, MA'AM.
MR. THORNTON. I HEAR YOU'RE A FAN OF THE BIBLE.
GOOD. HERE, YOU'LL HAVE PLENTY OF TIME TO READ IT.
WELCOME TO *EDEN.*
TRY NOT TO GIVE ME A REASON TO KILL YOU.
TO BE CONTINUED IN EDEN'S FALL, A SPECIAL THREE-PART STORY FEATURING CHARACTERS FROM THE TITHE, POSTAL & THINK TANK.

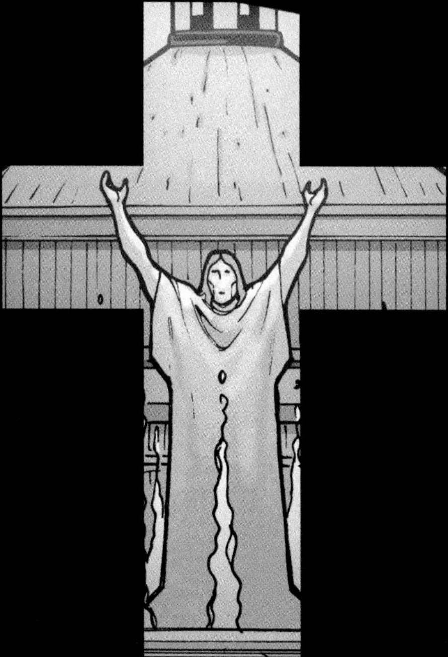

SUNDAY SCHOOL - CHAPTER ONE

Note – spoilers in here, read chapter one first please!

Thanks for reading *The Tithe: Islamophobia Volume 2*! Nothing is better than word of mouth, so I'd ask that if you liked this book please recommend it to a friend. If you hated it, tell someone you don't like to go buy it. Win, win for both of us! By buying and reading the second volume of a book, I can assume you've read the first volume and already know my atheist views on religion, faith, etc. If you have not, that first volume is available in stores now.

ISLAM

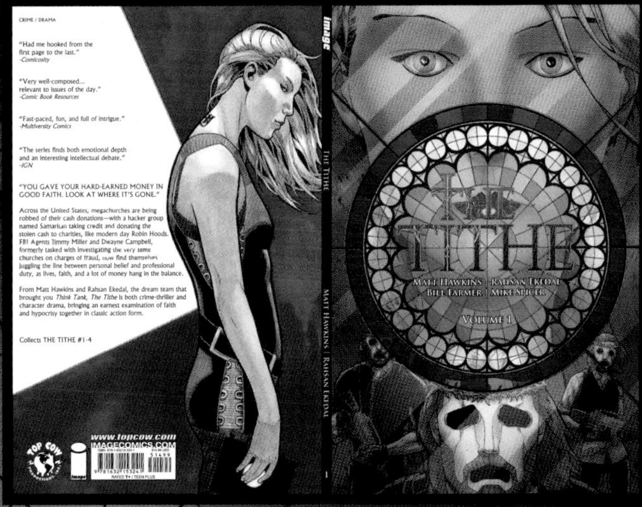

CRIME / DRAMA
"Had me hooked from the first page to the last." -Comicosity
"Very well-composed... relevant to issues of the day." -Comic Book Resources
"Fast-paced, fun, and full of intrigue." -Multiversity Comics
"The series finds both emotional depth and an interesting intellectual debate." -IGN
"YOU GAVE YOUR HARD-EARNED MONEY IN GOOD FAITH. LOOK AT WHERE IT'S GONE."
Across the United States, megachurches are being robbed of their cash donations—with a hacker group named Samaritan taking credit and donating the stolen cash to charities, like modern day Robin Hoods. FBI Agents Jimmy Miller and Dwayne Campbell, formerly tasked with investigating the very same churches on charges of fraud, now find themselves juggling the line between personal belief and professional duty, as lives, faith, and a lot of money hang in the balance.
From Matt Hawkins and Rahsan Ekedal, the dream team that brought you Think Tank, The Tithe is both crime-thriller and character drama, bringing an earnest examination of faith and hypocrisy together in classic action form.
Collects THE TITHE #1-4
www.topcow.com
IMAGECOMICS.COM
image
THE TITHE
MATT HAWKINS | RAHSAN EKEDAL
THE TITHE
MATT HAWKINS | RAHSAN EKEDAL
BILL FARMER | MIKE SPICER
VOLUME 1

I was cautioned against using Islam in the story but rejected that as it needs to be thought about and discussed. Islam is a mystery to most people in the West. We see what's in the news and some lefty politicians tell us it's a religion of peace, which doesn't jive with the constant news images of beheadings and other insane violence. If you're reading this and are Muslim, I have no issue with your religion or you as long as:

1) You don't want to kill me for not believing and/or
2) You don't want to force me to adhere to a pre-8th century morality.

I feel the same way about Christianity as I do about Islam. Unlike most Americans, I actually know Muslims. I've been to the Middle East ComiCon in Dubai twice in the last five years. I met and have stayed in contact with several people from Iran, Palestine, Lebanon, Saudi Arabia, UAE, and one man from Syria that I have actually lost contact with and hope is okay (his last Facebook post was April 2015). I know the difference between Shia and Sunni and that Iranians aren't Arabs. That alone gives me more street cred than the average American when talking to Middle Eastern people. And I've actually read and studied the Qu'ran which you can download and read for free if you want here: http://www.pdfquran.com/en/

Here are a couple pics from the more recent Dubai trip.

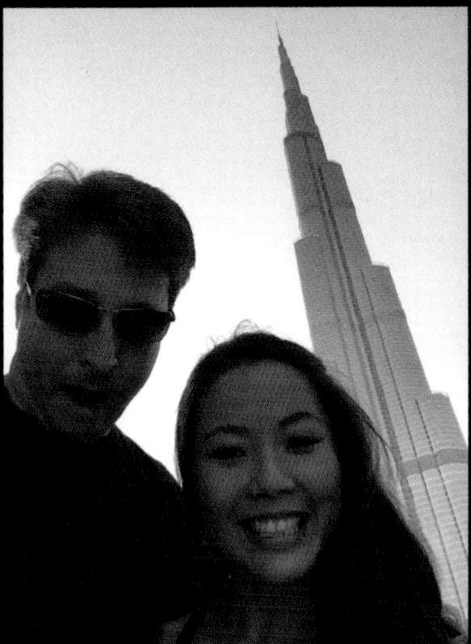

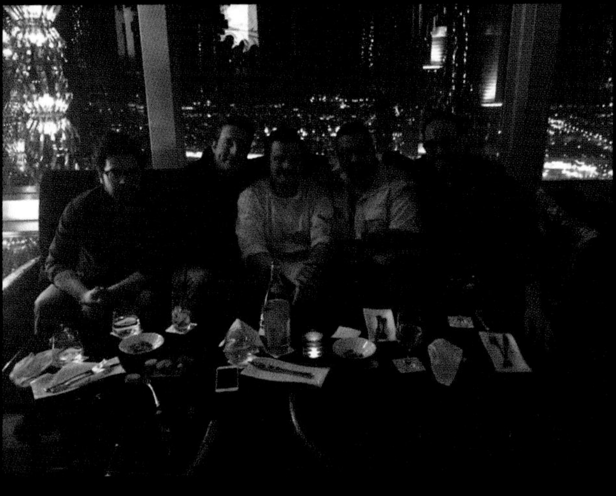

Left to right: Andy Suriano, me, Charles Soule, Ryan Penagos, and Jonah Weiland.

NEW YORK ST. PATRICK'S CATHEDRAL BOMBING

When you get to the end of this chapter, you realize it isn't as simple as Muslim terrorists behind this. The second chapter will reveal the machinations behind the attacks, who is doing them and why. You can glean some of it from the final page. Any of you who've read my work before, you'll know that one of my goals is to get YOU to think about things. Nothing is ever as simple as what we think it is. Why does a kid strap a bomb to his chest and blow himself up, and usually a bunch of non-militants with him? There's a fantastic free documentary on YouTube about women suicide bombers here:

https://www.youtube.com/watch?v=zBLH8YyIfZ8

Why children are used as bombers is tackled in a documentary called Children of the Taliban. It's discussed here:

https://www.ctc.usma.edu/posts/indoctrinating-children-the-making-of-pakistan%E2%80%99s-suicide-bombers

Suicide bombers are typically poor, uneducated people with nothing to lose, often victims of war themselves with family members killed or severely injured. They are offered money for their families and promised a glorious afterlife. I'm not justifying it, but when you have nothing to lose and your death can improve the lives of those you love AND you believe that you'll be rewarded after death…you begin to understand the mindset. Watch the linked free documentary above, the parents and family members of the suicide bombers revere the "sacrifice" of the martyr as heroes. It's hard for us in the West to wrap our minds around it, but most of us have never known real poverty either.

ST. PATRICK'S CATHEDRAL

This is a real church in Manhattan. I've been there once. I'm Irish, so had to stop by.

http://www.irishcentral.com/culture/entertainment/top-ten-facts-about-st-patricks-cathedral-in-new-york-city-video-188402891-237561151.html

https://www.youtube.com/watch?v=8YlnG6qtCEA

CATHOLIC RITES

Growing up in Baptist and Protestant churches, the Catholics and their rituals fascinate me. Lots of pageantry and symbolism involved in everything they do. I've been to a lot of Catholic masses and it's so different to Protestant ones that if you've never been, I'd encourage you to go check it out just for the experience.

I took the Priest's words directly from a video of a Mass I saw. I had to cut it short for space reasons in the dialogue. but you can read all of it here:

"Truly, truly, I say to you, unless you eat the flesh of the Son of man and drink his blood, you have no life in you; he who eats my flesh and drinks my blood has eternal life, and I will raise him up at the last day. For my flesh is real food, and my blood is real drink. He who eats my flesh and drinks my blood abides in me, and I in him. As the living Father sent me, and I live because of the Father, so he who eats me will live because of me. This is the bread which came down from heaven, not such as the fathers ate and died; he who eats this bread will live forever" (John 6:53–58).

https://www.youtube.com/watch?v=lpOVsFtZ1hM

https://www.youtube.com/watch?v=MwXJBm6nahM

CHRISTIAN HATE GROUPS

Seems an oxymoron, and they wouldn't identify themselves this way, but there are Christian groups that advocate violence as well.

http://thehumanist.com/news/religion/5-dangerous-christian-hate-groups

CHRISTIAN VIEW OF ISLAM

This is from a Baptist preacher: "It was Satan himself who delivered those delusions to those people to lead people by the millions away from God. Islam is a false religion that will lead you to hell. It is based on a false book that is based on a fraud. It was founded by a false prophet who was leading people away instead of to the one true God."

http://www.firstdallas.org/media/sermon-worship-library/

Man, I ran out of space fast, there's so much to discuss. Email us at fanmail@topcow.com and ask specific questions you want discussed. You can also hit me up on my social media feeds below. I talk about this stuff on Facebook every day.

This Sunday School will be posted to my blog site http://matttalks.com/ by the time this is in stores. Point being, you can go to that link and it will have hyperlinks to all the referenced stuff in the body above.

Thanks to Rahsan Ekedal, Phillip Sevy, and Jeremy Colwell for the art on this issue. Fantastic job, gents! And as always, thanks to Bryan Hill and Betsy Gonia for making me sound smarter than I am.

Carpe Diem

Matt Hawkins
@topcowmatt
facebook.com/selfloathingnarcissist

SUNDAY SCHOOL - CHAPTER TWO

Thanks for buying this book! If you like it, I'd appreciate it if you could tell a friend. I'd like to do a third volume of *The Tithe*, but that's really up to you. Vote with your dollar and share the love if you want to see it!

ISLAM

It's hard to have a good opinion of Islam if you live in the United States. Our news is filled with terrorist bombings, beheadings, and generally negative news about Islam. It transcends left/right as there are plenty on both side of the political aisle who see Islam as a negative. I admit I too had a lot of false assumptions when I started doing my research. There are roughly 5-6 million Muslim Americans in a nation of 300 million. That's about 1.7% of the U.S. population.

UNITED STATES A CHRISTIAN NATION?

Is the U.S. a Christian nation? We hear this all the time but is it true? Eighty-three percent of U.S citizens identify as Christian (see first link). Less than 20% actually attend church (see second link). How many of those are Christian in name only, who knows, but I'm not sure that matters. For political reasons even those fair-weather or fake Christians will support the actual ones. So based on that, I would say objectively that yes, the United States is a Christian nation.

http://abcnews.go.com/US/story?id=90356&page=1

http://www.churchleaders.com/pastors/pastor-articles/139575-7-startling-facts-an-up-close-look-at-church-attendance-in-america.html

FOUNDED A CHRISTIAN NATION?

The First Amendment says:

> "Congress shall make no law respecting an establishment of religion, or prohibiting the free exercise thereof; or abridging the freedom of speech, or of the press; or the right of the people peaceably to assemble, and to petition the government for a redress of grievances."

The "under god" on our currency and in the pledge of allegiance was added in 1954 in response to the atheist Communist threat.

http://www.ushistory.org/documents/pledge.htm

I've often wondered why red states are "red" when that color was associated with Communism. Seems the right wing would pick a different color to represent them. Turns out it was the media that dubbed it so in 2000, not that long ago.

http://www.baruch.cuny.edu/library/alumni/online_exhibits/pres_election_08map/page2.htm

The founding fathers went out of their way to say the United States was NOT a Christian nation.

> "The government of the United States is not, in any sense, founded on the Christian religion."
> -John Adams

http://www.huffingtonpost.com/jeff-schweitzer/founding-fathers-we-are-n_b_6761840.html

Christianity neither is, nor ever was a part of the common law.
-Thomas Jefferson

http://www.nobeliefs.com/jefferson.htm

> "The Government of the United States of America is not, in any sense, founded on the Christian religion."
> -President Adams, in Barbary Pirate Treaty 1797

http://www.forbes.com/sites/billflax/2012/09/25/was-america-founded-as-a-christian-nation/

> "The Founding Fathers did not create a secular government because they disliked religion. Many were believers themselves. Yet they were well aware of the dangers of church-state union. They had studied and even seen first-hand the difficulties that church-state partnerships spawned in Europe. During the American colonial period, alliances between religion and government produced oppression and tyranny on our own shores."

https://www.au.org/resources/publications/is-america-a-christian-nation

http://www.wallbuilders.com/libissuesarticles.asp?id=8755

DEARBORN, MICHIGAN

This suburb of Detroit has the largest concentration of Muslims in the United States. Researching this it seems this is because of auto factory jobs and Henry Ford recruiting cheap labor. Community started there in the early 20th century and expanded as people fled the Middle East during the Gulf, Iraq, and Afghanistan wars.

https://en.wikipedia.org/wiki/History_of_the_Middle_Eastern_people_in_Metro_Detroit

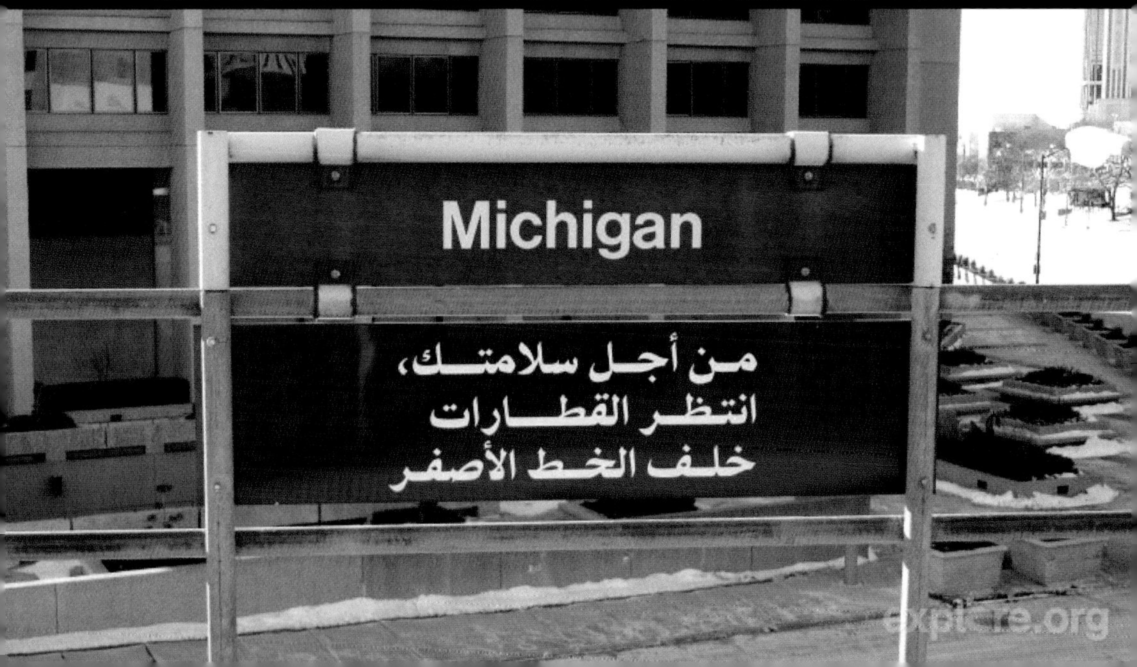
Michigan
من أجل سلامتك،
انتظر القطارات
خلف الخط الأصفر
explore.org

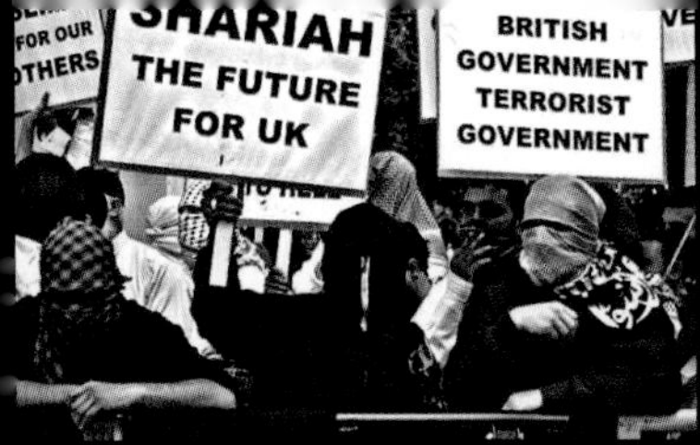
SHARIAH
THE FUTURE
FOR UK
BRITISH
GOVERNMENT
TERRORIST
GOVERNMENT

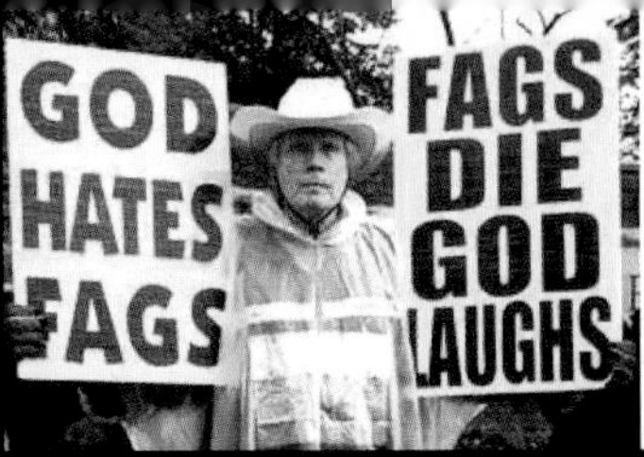
GOD
HATES
FAGS
FAGS
DIE
GOD
LAUGHS

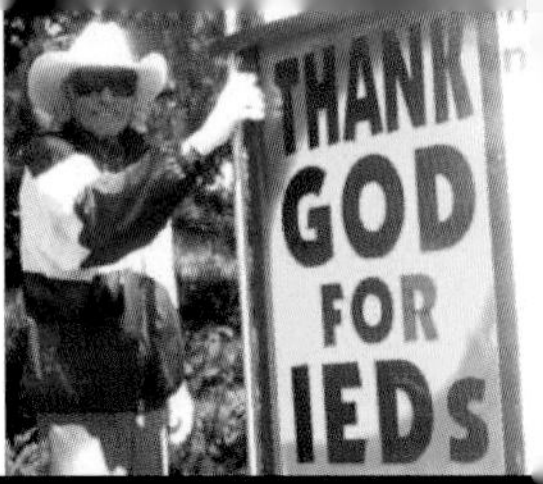
THANK
GOD
FOR
IEDs

MY PERSONAL OPINION

I'm not a Christian, despite being raised as one. Having lost that faith and spending so much time thinking about Christianity, when I look at Islam I see it as the same thing. They don't believe the same and the books and prophets are different, but they both make supernatural and divine claims that are not provable and require faith to buy in.

ISLAMOPHOBIA IN THE U.S.

There's always been mild anti-Islam sentiment in the U.S. Seems natural since there are so many "Christians" in the U.S. and they see Islam as false. I've read many sermons from pastors talking about how Satan talked to Mohammed. This has elevated to national pastime post-9/11. Despite the rhetoric spoken by lefty politicians and some celebrities, the average person on the street does not like Islam. Bill Maher is a liberal, let that sink in.

http://www.huffingtonpost.com/entry/david-salha-michigan-muslim-camp-islamophobia_55a7a1d3e4b0896514d060e3

http://www.gallup.com/poll/157082/islamophobia-understanding-anti-muslim-sentiment-west.aspx

http://fusion.net/story/171442/the-everyday-terror-of-islamophobia-in-america/

MADE UP STORIES

Islam has enough of its own PR problems from legitimate things, but it bothers me that right-wingers make shit up. The Shariah Law thing in Dearborn, Christians stoned there, American Muslim men having four wives all on welfare, etc. have all been stories widely circulated and proven to be not true. They're targeting white, right-wingers and others who read this stuff and believe it…despite it being completely fabricated.

http://www.clarionproject.org/news/american-muslims-stone-christians-dearborn-michigan

http://shoebat.com/2015/06/23/dearbornistan-muslim-police-chief-to-enforce-sharia-compliant-curfew-during-month-of-ramadaneven-on-christians/

http://www.snopes.com/politics/immigration/4wives.asp

Next Sunday School chapter I'm going to get into the differences between Sunni and Shia, Shariah Law, and its similarities to the Old Testament. Thanks again for reading.

Carpe Diem

Matt Hawkins - @topcowmatt - facebook.com/selfloathingnarcissist

Thanks, as always, for buying and reading this book! If you enjoy it, I'd ask that you share tha ike/love with a friend so we can keep putting this book out.

promised last Sunday School to dive into some of the differences in Islam, Shariah Law and compare it to the Old Testament so let's get started.

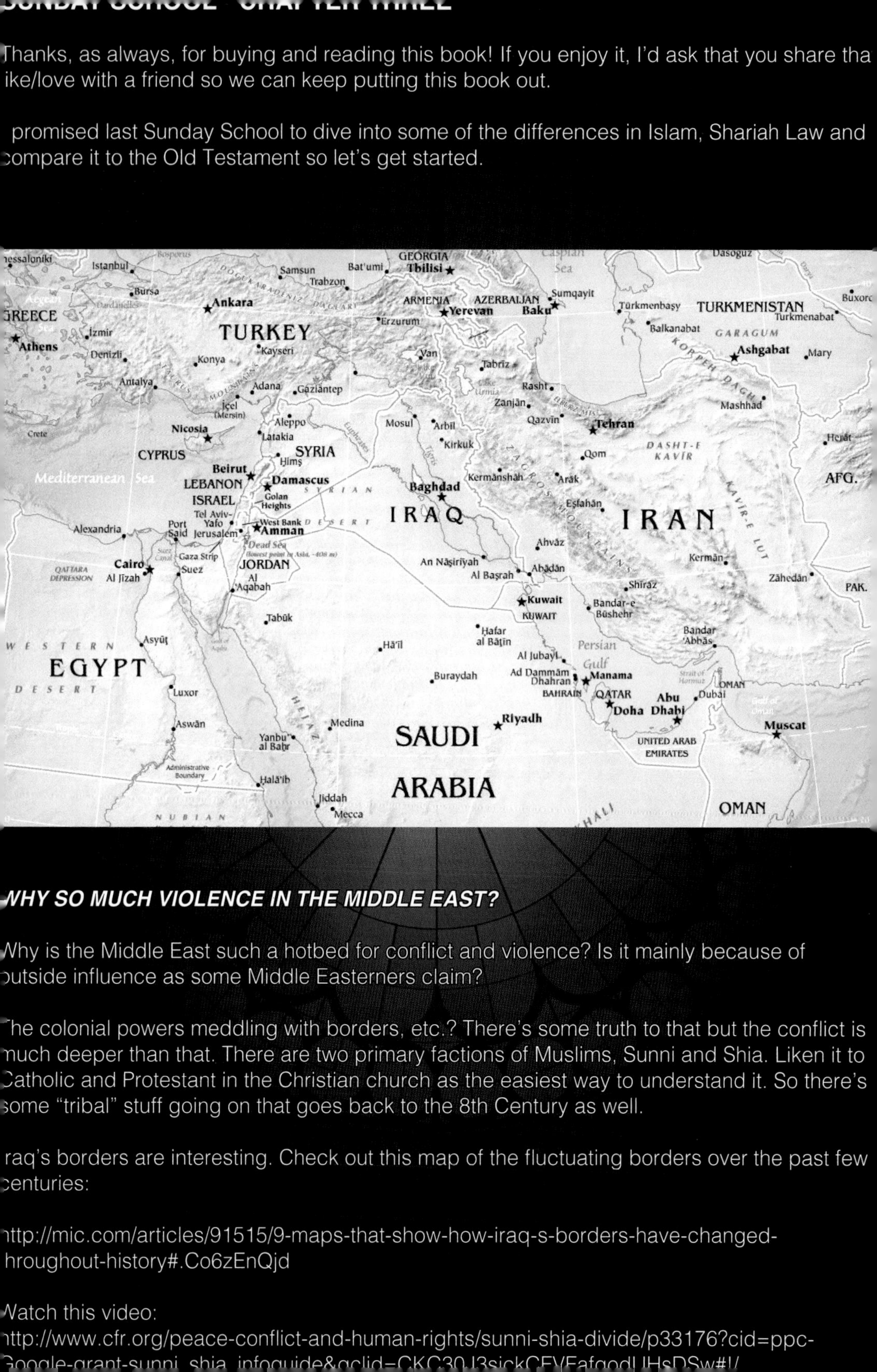
GEORGIA
Tbilisi
ARMENIA
Yerevan
AZERBAIJAN
Baku
TURKEY
Ankara
Istanbul
Bursa
Samsun
Trabzon
Erzurum
Kayseri
Konya
Denizli
Izmir
Antalya
Adana
Gaziantep
Içel (Mersin)
Van
GREECE
Athens
Crete
Nicosia
CYPRUS
Mediterranean Sea
SYRIA
Aleppo
Latakia
Hims
Damascus
Beirut
LEBANON
Golan Heights
ISRAEL
Tel Aviv-Yafo
Jerusalem
West Bank
Amman
Dead Sea
JORDAN
Gaza Strip
Port Said
Alexandria
Cairo
Al Jīzah
Suez
Al 'Aqabah
Tabūk
EGYPT
WESTERN DESERT
Asyūt
Luxor
Aswān
Ḥalā'ib
Mosul
Arbil
Kirkuk
IRAQ
Baghdad
An Nāṣirīyah
Al Baṣrah
Kuwait
KUWAIT
IRAN
Tabrīz
Rasht
Zanjān
Qazvīn
Tehran
Qom
Kermānshāh
Arāk
Eṣfahān
Ahvāz
Abādān
Shīrāz
Kermān
Zāhedān
Bandar-e Būshehr
Bandar 'Abbās
Mashhad
TURKMENISTAN
Türkmenbaşy
Turkmenabat
Balkanabat
Ashgabat
Mary
Buxoro
Dasoguz
Caspian Sea
Herāt
AFG.
PAK.
SAUDI ARABIA
Riyadh
Ḥā'il
Buraydah
Ḥafar al Bāṭin
Al Jubayl
Ad Dammām
Dhahran
Medina
Yanbu' al Baḥr
Jiddah
Mecca
Persian Gulf
Manama
BAHRAIN
QATAR
Doha
Abu Dhabi
UNITED ARAB EMIRATES
Dubai
OMAN
Muscat

WHY SO MUCH VIOLENCE IN THE MIDDLE EAST?

Why is the Middle East such a hotbed for conflict and violence? Is it mainly because of outside influence as some Middle Easterners claim?

The colonial powers meddling with borders, etc.? There's some truth to that but the conflict is much deeper than that. There are two primary factions of Muslims, Sunni and Shia. Liken it to Catholic and Protestant in the Christian church as the easiest way to understand it. So there's some "tribal" stuff going on that goes back to the 8th Century as well.

Iraq's borders are interesting. Check out this map of the fluctuating borders over the past few centuries:

http://mic.com/articles/91515/9-maps-that-show-how-iraq-s-borders-have-changed-throughout-history#.Co6zEnQjd

Watch this video:
http://www.cfr.org/peace-conflict-and-human-rights/sunni-shia-divide/p33176?cid=ppc-Google-grant-sunni_shia_infoguide&gclid=CKC30J3sickCFVFafgodUHsDSw#!/

SUNNI AND SHIA DIVIDE

"Muslims are split into two main branches, the Sunnis and Shia. The split originates in a dispute soon after the death of the Prophet Muhammad over who should lead the Muslim community."

http://www.bbc.com/news/world-middle-east-16047709

So it's a succession issue. Who was to take over after the Prophet died? Would it be based on the Prophet's bloodline or qualified religious leaders.

"A group of prominent early followers of Islam elected Abu Bakr, a companion of Mohammed, to be the first caliph, or leader of the Islamic community, over the objections of those who favored Ali ibn Abi Talib, Mohammed's cousin and son-in-law. The opposing camps in the succession debate eventually evolved into Islam's two main sects. Shias, a term that stems from shi'atu Ali, Arabic for "partisans of Ali," believe that Ali and his descendants are part of a divine order. Sunnis, meaning followers of the sunna, or 'way' in Arabic, of Mohammed, are opposed to political succession based on Mohammed's bloodline." From that CFR.ORG piece posted on the previous page.

So Shia and Sunni for the most part believe the same things, but there are subtle differences that I personally associate more as cultural than spiritual but that's debatable. The two power players actually from the region are Iran (Shia) and Saudi Arabia (Sunni). There are other smaller offshoots of Islam and divisions within Shia and Sunni as well…just like Christianity.

Good article breaking down the various sects of Islam:

http://www.wildolive.co.uk/islam_denominations.htm

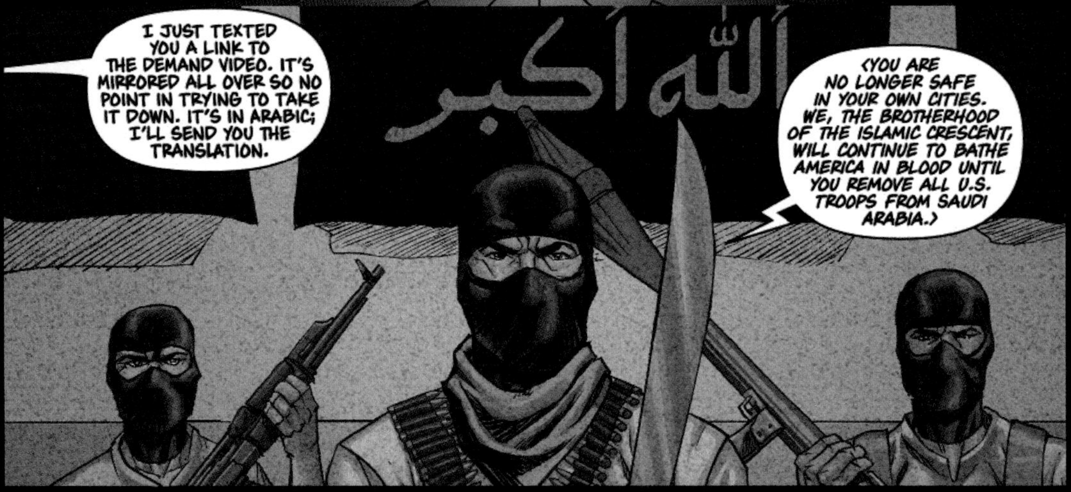
I JUST TEXTED YOU A LINK TO THE DEMAND VIDEO. IT'S MIRRORED ALL OVER SO NO POINT IN TRYING TO TAKE IT DOWN. IT'S IN ARABIC; I'LL SEND YOU THE TRANSLATION.
الله أكبر
<YOU ARE NO LONGER SAFE IN YOUR OWN CITIES. WE, THE BROTHERHOOD OF THE ISLAMIC CRESCENT, WILL CONTINUE TO BATHE AMERICA IN BLOOD UNTIL YOU REMOVE ALL U.S. TROOPS FROM SAUDI ARABIA.>

MUSLIM CONDEMNATION OF TERRORISM

We don't hear much of this in our news because it's not sensational enough, but a lot of Muslims and Muslim leaders condemn terrorism.

"The truth is that killing innocent people is always wrong — and no argument or excuse, no matter how deeply believed, can ever make it right. No religion on earth condones the killing of innocent people, no faith tradition tolerates the random killing of our brothers and sisters on this earth. ... Islamic law is clearly against terrorism, against any kind of deliberate killing of civilians or similar 'collateral damage.'" -Imam Feisal Abdul Rauf

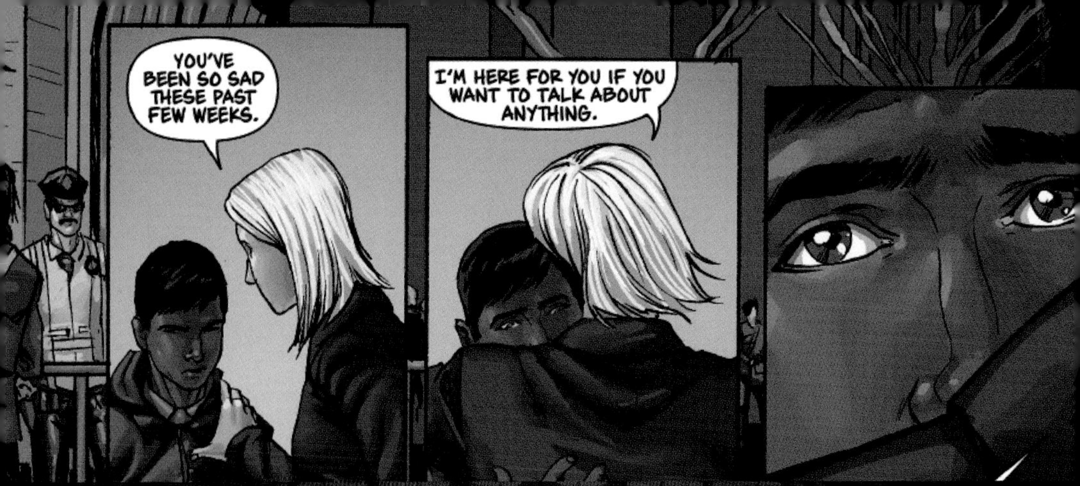
YOU'VE BEEN SO SAD THESE PAST FEW WEEKS.
I'M HERE FOR YOU IF YOU WANT TO TALK ABOUT ANYTHING.

WHAT IS SHARIAH LAW?

"Shariah law is the body of Islamic law. The term means "way" or "path"; it is the legal framework within which the public and some private aspects of life are regulated for those living in a legal system based on Islam.

Sharia deals with all aspects of day-to-day life, including politics, economics, banking, business law, contract law, sexuality, and social issues." From Wikipedia.

Most of Shariah law is not all that controversial and deals with day-to-day matters, but there are some that are wild throwbacks to a darker time in world history.

Examples:

Theft is punishable by amputation of the right hand.
Criticizing or denying any part of the Quran is punishable by death.
Criticizing or denying Muhammad is a prophet is punishable by death.
A Muslim who becomes a non-Muslim is punishable by death.
A non-Muslim who leads a Muslim away from Islam is punishable by death.
A non-Muslim man who marries a Muslim woman is punishable by death.
A man can marry an infant girl and consummate the marriage when she is 9 years old.

The list goes on, these are just some extreme examples.

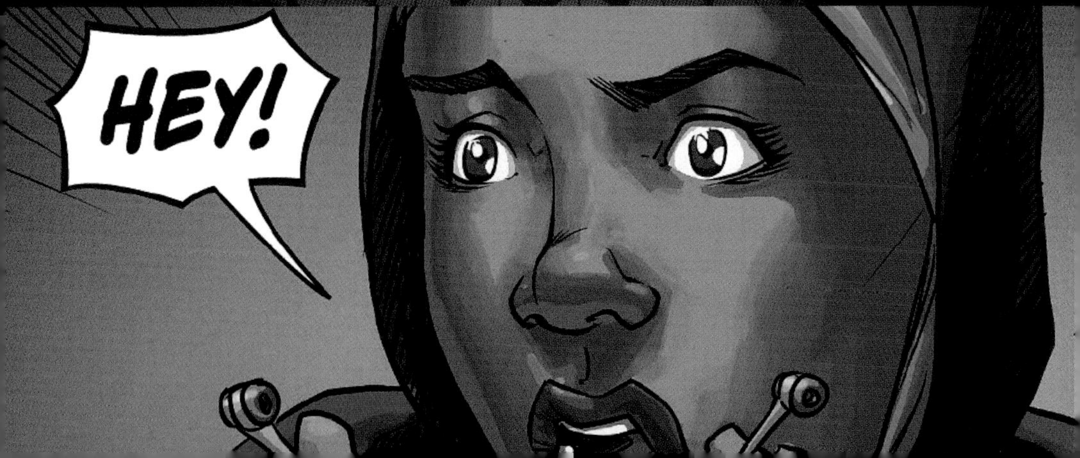
HEY!

OLD TESTAMENT SIMILARITY

Christians reading about Shariah Law tend to freak out and I'm not comparing Shariah Law to Levitical Law...okay yes I am...they both have equally heinous things in them to our modern minds. The difference is no one takes the Westboro Church and other Christian extremists seriously and we do take the Muslim extremists very seriously.

Leviticus 20:13 says we have to kill the gays.
Leviticus 20:10 says kill the adulterers.
Leviticus 25:44-46 approves of slavery as long as its slaves from other nations.

http://www.swapmeetdave.com/Bible/Christianity-Islam-chart.htm

KORAN VERSE USED IN TITHE CHAPTER THREE: ISLAMOPHOBIA

<<Everyone shall taste death. Then unto us you shall be returned.>> al-Ankaboot 29:57

This is from the Koran. I picked it solely because it sounds cool.

FINGERPRINTS

I spent about four hours trying to validate or come up with why they wouldn't get Thornton's prints off of that $10 and finally gave up when I realized even if they found a print they found out his identity shortly thereafter anyway. Found some interesting things out about fingerprints from an ME who chimed in on quora:

https://www.quora.com/From-what-can-fingerprints-be-lifted-and-from-what-cant-they-be-lifted

Carpe Diem!

Matt Hawkins - @topcowmatt - facebook.com/selfloathingnarcissist

SUNDAY SCHOOL - CHAPTER FOUR

Remember – spoilers in here, read the chapter first please!

Welcome and thanks for hanging in with me through eight issues of *The Tithe*! In hindsight, I wish I'd titled this book *Samaritan*. It seems a lot of people don't know what a Tithe is or how to say the word. It's tie-the (like tie fighter followed by a the), two syllables. You can call it whatever the hell you want though as long as you keep reading! I appreciate you =)

Getting a lot of questions about whether this is the end of the series or not. The answer is, unfortunately, I don't know. Of all the books I write this one sells the lowest number of copies. Might be because people are afraid of what it's about (I've pissed off a fair amount of religious people it seems). Honestly, I don't know. We're selling almost three times the number of copies for *Symmetry*. I love this book, but I have to bow to the gods of economics. I'll use these characters elsewhere, including the *Eden's Fall* storyline (see below) but the volume 2 trade needs to sell decently for a volume 3 to be a reality. So...if you want it, please recommend the book to a friend and thanks!

TITHE VOLUME THREE

I have a distinct third volume story arc in mind, which takes place in Italy, and, you guessed it, the Vatican. Jimmy and Sam are on the run together and stealing something, and Dwayne is reluctantly in pursuit with the CIA. I've always wanted to really get into some Catholic history and mythology. This may not end up being what Volume 3 ends up being, but I like the idea and have set it up somewhat that Jimmy and Sam might take off. We shall see!

EDEN'S FALL

You might have noticed in *The Tithe Volume 1*, I referenced "Eden" when Samantha said to Kyle Araman that she found a place in Wyoming that would take them (at the time, fugitives,) in. I also included in this second volume Dr. David Loren from *Think Tank* and that second epilogue of this issue where Thornton ends up in Eden talking to the mayor is a pretty direct tie-in with *Postal*.

I really, really hate massive forced cross-overs, but we've done a few smaller ones and when they're organic they work well. This one is story driven and the plan is to do a three-issue mini-series called "Eden's Fall" that will be co-written by myself and Bryan Hill and we want Atilio Rojo (artist on *IXth Generation* and the *Postal: Dossier* story) but we haven't actually asked him yet as I write this...so could be someone else.

The story of "Eden's Fall" will feature characters from *The Tithe*, *Postal* and *Think Tank* in a single story. I don't want to give too much away, but it will essentially be about some people that want to take out Jim Thornton from this very arc of *The Tithe*.

RIGHT-WING REVIEWS

I used to be a right-winger, so I find it amusing when right-wingers call me out for being too liberal. This blog site and its reviews of multiple issues of *The Tithe*, I find especially amusing:
http://therorshachrant.blogspot.com/

MY REASONING FOR MAKING THIS ARC A RIGHT-WING CONSPIRACY

Some people have taken me to task for this and let me explain it very simply; I did it because it made for a good story that I wanted to tell. That's it. I really don't have an agenda. I'm a centrist; a semi-conservative fiscal and a semi-liberal social person. I equally loathe both parties in our two-party system. Conspiracy theories always seem to float around, even when things are on video and fairly clear. Our chief antagonist in this story arc was Senator McKitrick who pulled all the strings. I liked the idea that he saw some of these conspiracy theories and thought that was a good idea and formulated his plan after that.

9/11 conspiracy documentary, long, but free:
https://www.youtube.com/watch?v=TpRZiQ_gqJc

Easily debunked:
http://www.popularmechanics.com/military/a49/1227842/

JOHN F. KENNEDY QUOTE

I considered skipping the full text page this issue when I found this JFK quote. I sometimes spend hours scouring for the right "quote" but I found this one quickly. I look for these last, after the story is written so I can try and find a quote that I feel encapsulates the heart of what I'm trying to say. I do try to incorporate social commentary in my stories, I know some of you don't like that, but I grew up with the 50's-80's science fiction authors and learned about many of the social issues in society from them. Star Trek alone boldly takes on so many social problems from the 20th century. First on screen interracial kiss, anyone?

Here is the full JFK quote in his Remarks to the Greater Houston Ministerial Association:

"I believe in an America where the separation of church and state is absolute - where no Catholic prelate would tell the President (should he be Catholic) how to act, and no Protestant minister would tell his parishioners for whom to vote - where no church or church school is granted any public funds or political preference - and where no man is denied public office merely because his religion differs from the President who might appoint him or the people who might elect him.

I believe in an America that is officially neither Catholic, Protestant nor Jewish - where no public official either requests or accepts instructions on public policy from the Pope, the National Council of Churches or any other ecclesiastical source - where no religious body seeks to impose its will directly or indirectly upon the general populace or the public acts of its officials - and where religious liberty is so indivisible that an act against one church is treated as an act against all." JFK September 12, 1960.

This quote seems more applicable today to the Islam/Christianity religious drama in our world today, but back then people were concerned that JFK was a Catholic. He was the first Catholic President, and before he was elected there was some concern that he would listen to the Pope over the USA's own interests.

11/22/63

Given the above quote, wanted to give a plug to Stephen King's book, which I happened to just recently read. Long, but I thoroughly enjoyed it. It's about a guy going back in time to prevent JFK from being assassinated and how that would affect the world.

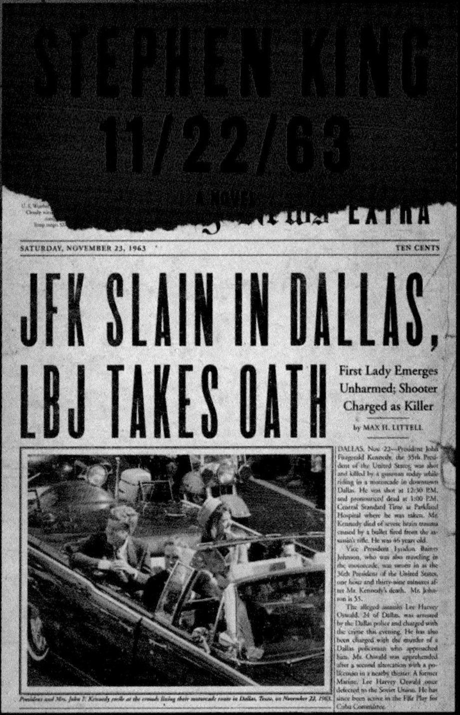
STEPHEN KING
11/22/63
A NOVEL
EXTRA
SATURDAY, NOVEMBER 23, 1963
TEN CENTS
JFK SLAIN IN DALLAS, LBJ TAKES OATH
First Lady Emerges Unharmed; Shooter Charged as Killer
by MAX H. LITTELL

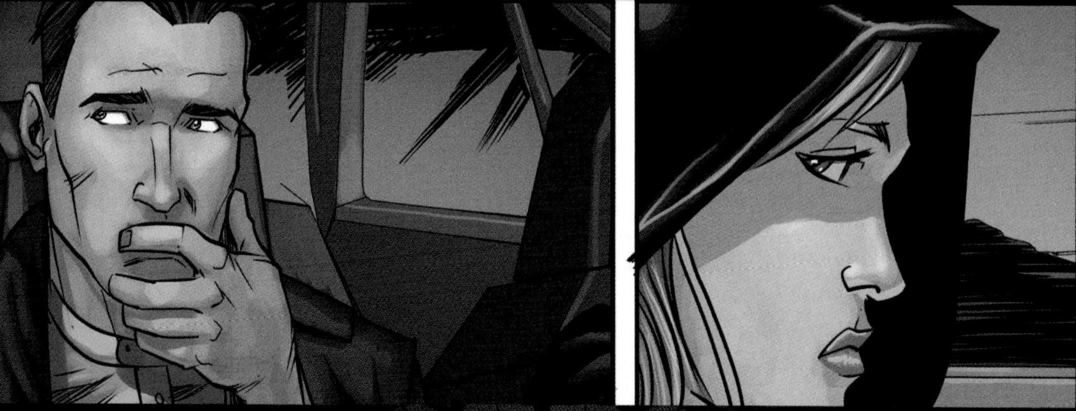

CLOSED NETWORKS NOT ON THE INTERNET

I was interested to discover this is how a lot of large firms protect their data from being hacked…they're not on the internet. China has a closed internet that allows them to more thoroughly control and censor what goes up, but it's still "connected" and hackable. Hackers are pretty smart though, read this first link if you want to be scared shitless.

https://www.hackread.com/hacking-offline-computer-and-phone/
https://www.fbi.gov/scams-safety/computer_protect

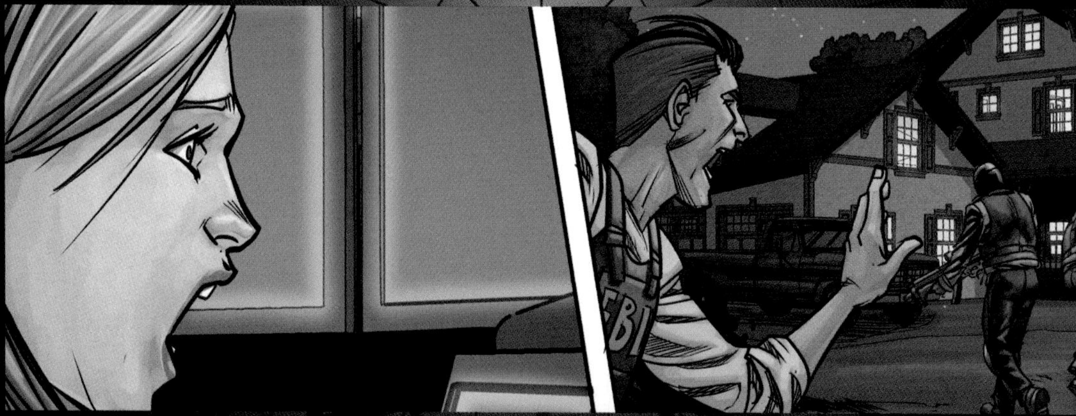

FUTURE CRIME BY MARK GOODMAN

This book is a bit dry but talks about the "internet of things" and how someone can be spying on you from your coffee maker. Scary shit. Worth a read. I used a lot of reference from this book for hacking in *The Tithe* and in *Think Tank.*

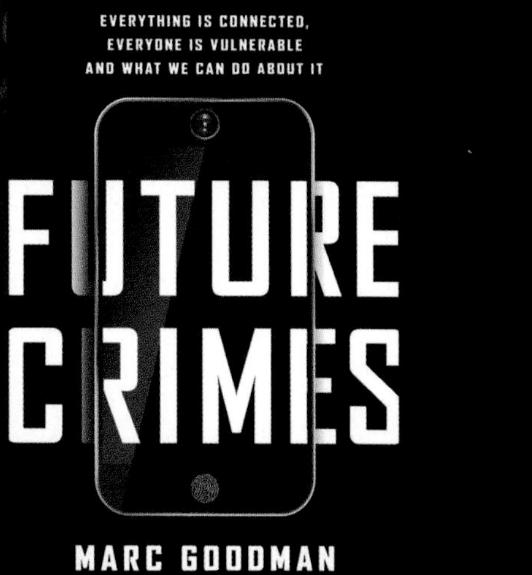
EVERYTHING IS CONNECTED,
EVERYONE IS VULNERABLE
AND WHAT WE CAN DO ABOUT IT
FUTURE
CRIMES
MARC GOODMAN

CELL PHONE HACKING/LISTENING

I'm sure you've seen how phones are clone-able to listen in on calls or read texts in real time, but there are a lot of interesting things you can do remotely with someone else's phone. Bottom line, your phone is not that secure, regardless of model, so don't leave nude pics of your significant other on there.

http://www.physics.utah.edu/spectrum/index.php/demolicious-physics/130-5-tricks-you-did-not-know-you-could-do-with-cell-phones

IMPEACHMENT

Writing this script, I was curious about the process of impeachment. Presidents Andrew Johnson and Bill Clinton were both impeached by the U.S. House of Representatives, but acquitted by the Senate. Richard Nixon resigned before he could be impeached. Interesting stuff.

http://www.senate.gov/reference/resources/pdf/98-806.pdf
https://en.wikipedia.org/wiki/Impeachment_in_the_United_States

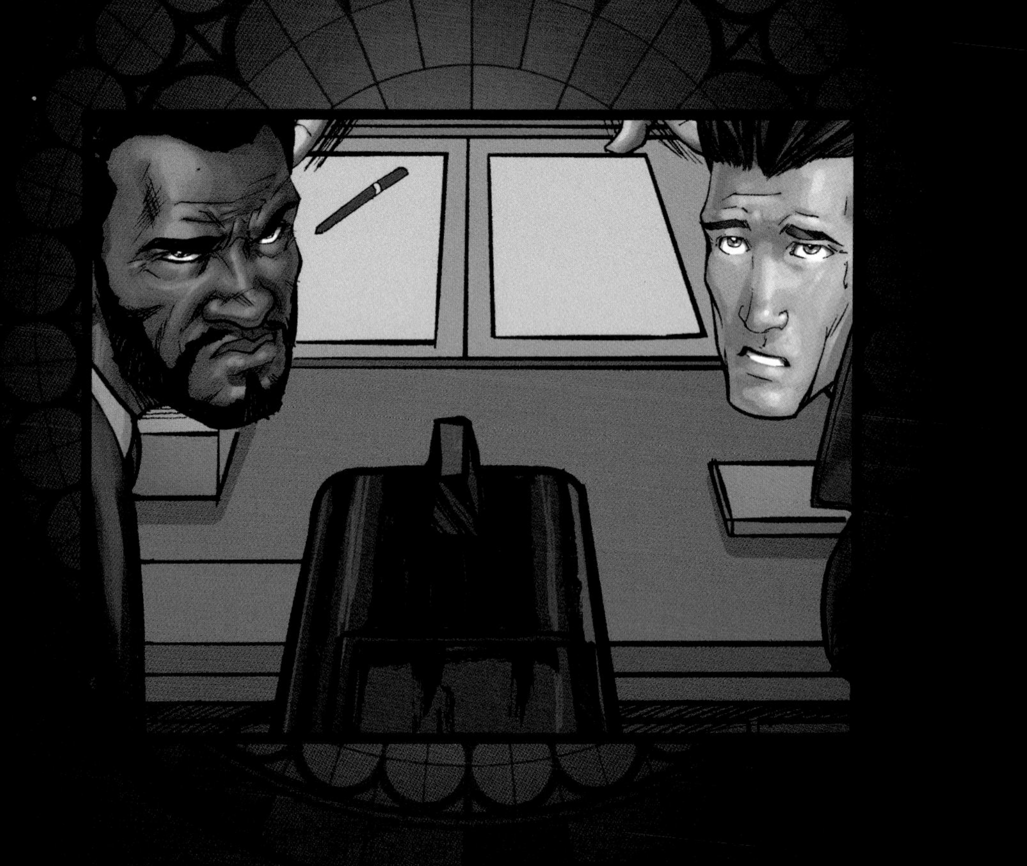

MILITIA GROUPS

Given the recent Oregon militia deal up at that Wildlife Refuge I include this list merely for your amusement and education. Reading this list will add you to some FBI watch lists! Fun, fun.

http://www.darkgovernment.com/news/list-of-u-s-militia-groups/

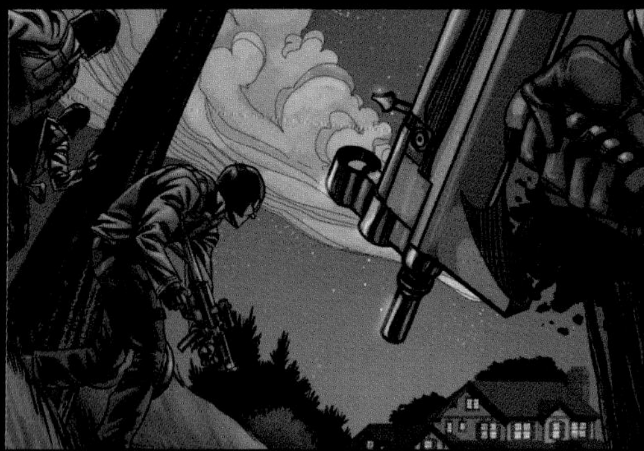

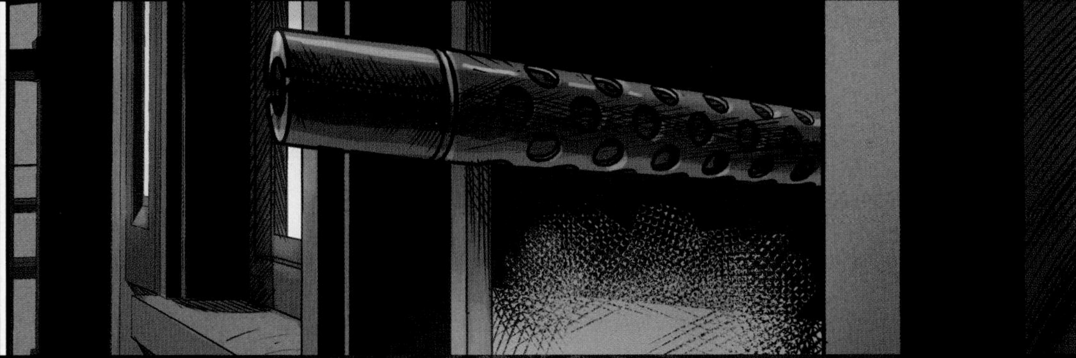

MOTION SENSORS / BOOBY TRAPS

That laser motion detector is legit, I took it from here:

http://www.cpss.net/blog/post/2013/11/13/How-Does-an-Alarm-Motion-Sensor-Work.aspx

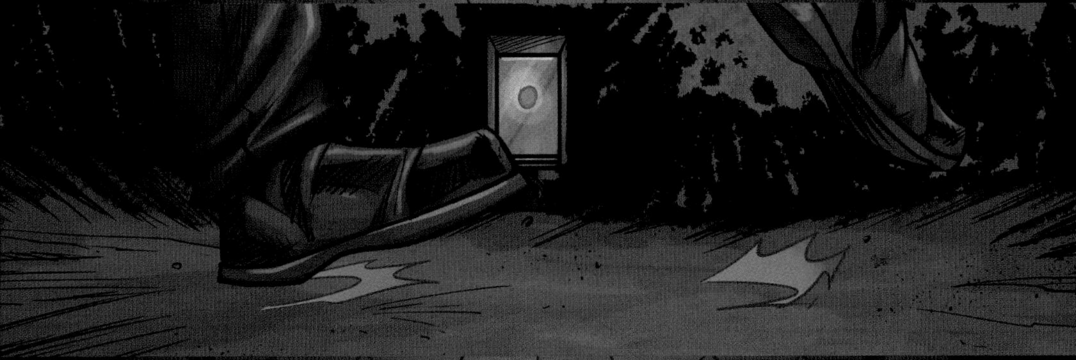

HOW TO THROW A HAND GRENADE

Came across this link when I was sending reference for that page where the FBI Tac-ops guy throws the flash grenade. You never know when you might need to know this (cue the old NBC, "The More you Know" music).

http://www.armystudyguide.com/content/army_board_study_guide_topics/hand_grenades/throwing-of-hand-grenades.shtml

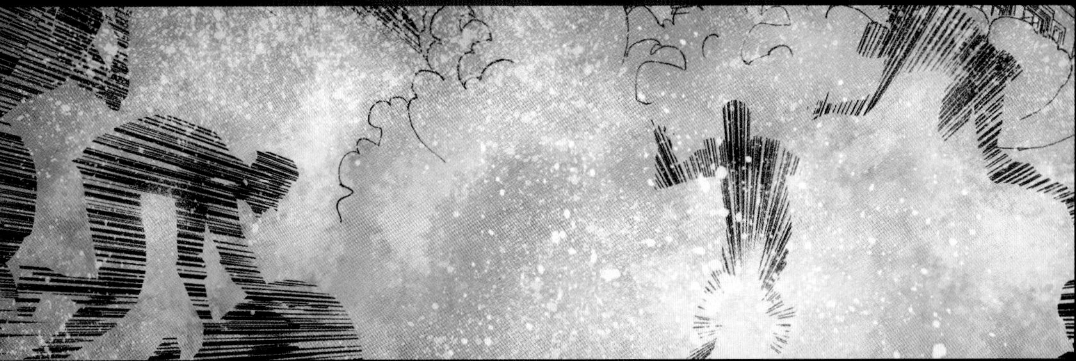

ALCOHOL, CHRISTIANITY AND ISLAM

Slight distinction on alcohol from the two different religions. Christianity takes the "in moderation" it's fine approach, but Islam says alcohol is BAD, m'kay? The Christian explanation is at the first link, the Muslim one the second. If you're too lazy to click and read, the basic view is that Muslims should not have alcohol in their system when they pray and they have to pray five times a day…so no alcohol!

https://www.gci.org/series/alcohol/bible
http://www.greenprophet.com/2011/11/muslims-alcohol-haraam/

That's it for this volume!

Thanks for sticking it out with me, I appreciate you reading this and my other books. Phil Sevy has gone on to take over a new Tomb Raider series coming out from Dark Horse so be sure and check that out. Hopefully I'll get a chance to work with him again.

Carpe Diem

Matt Hawkins
@topcowmatt
facebook.com/selfloathingnarcissist

MATT HAWKINS

A veteran of the initial Image Comics launch, Matt started his career in comic book publishing in 1993 and has been working with Image as a creator, writer, and executive for over twenty years. President/COO of Top Cow since 1998, Matt has created and written over thirty new franchises for Top Cow and Image including *Think Tank*, *The Tithe*, *Necromancer*, *VICE*, *Lady Pendragon*, *Aphrodite IX*, and *Tales of Honor*, as well as handling the company's business affairs.

OTHER TITLES FROM MATT THAT YOU MAY ENJOY:
Think Tank vol. 1 (978-1607066606) | *The Tithe vol. 1* (978-1632153241) | *Aphrodite IX vol. 1* (978-1607068280)

COVER GALLERY

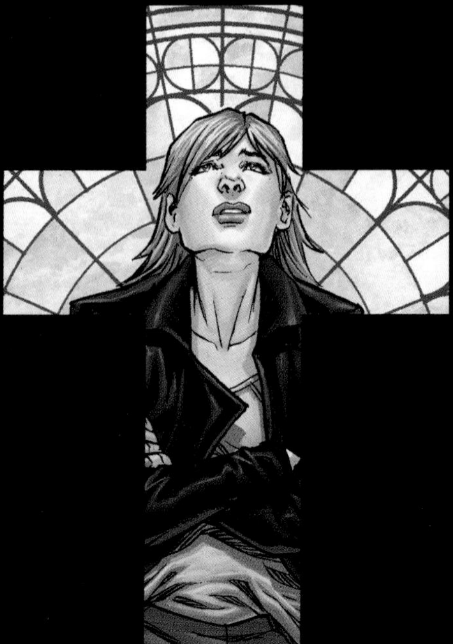

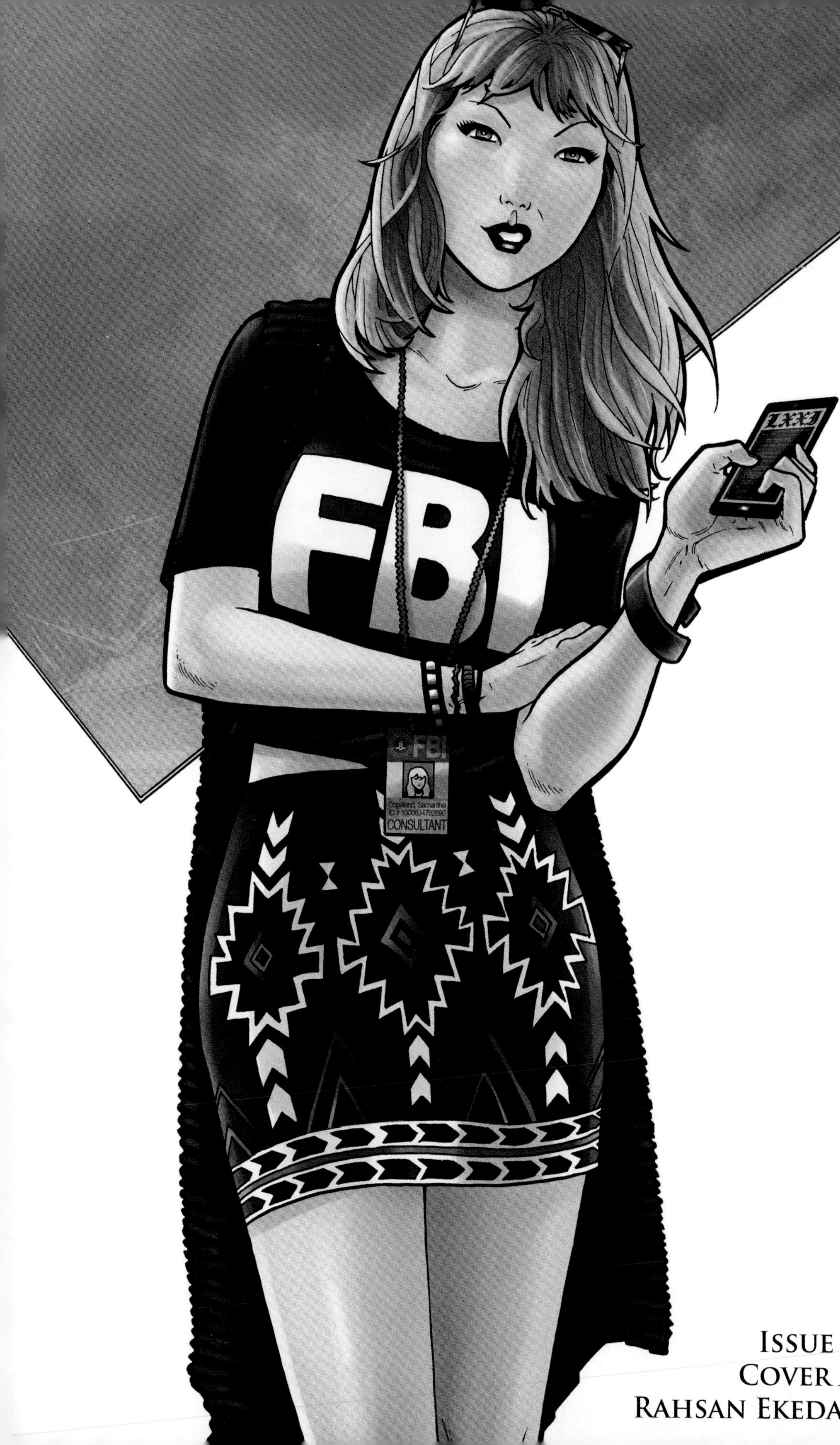
FBI
LXXI
FBI
Copeland, Samantha
CONSULTANT

Issue 5
Cover A
Rahsan Ekedal

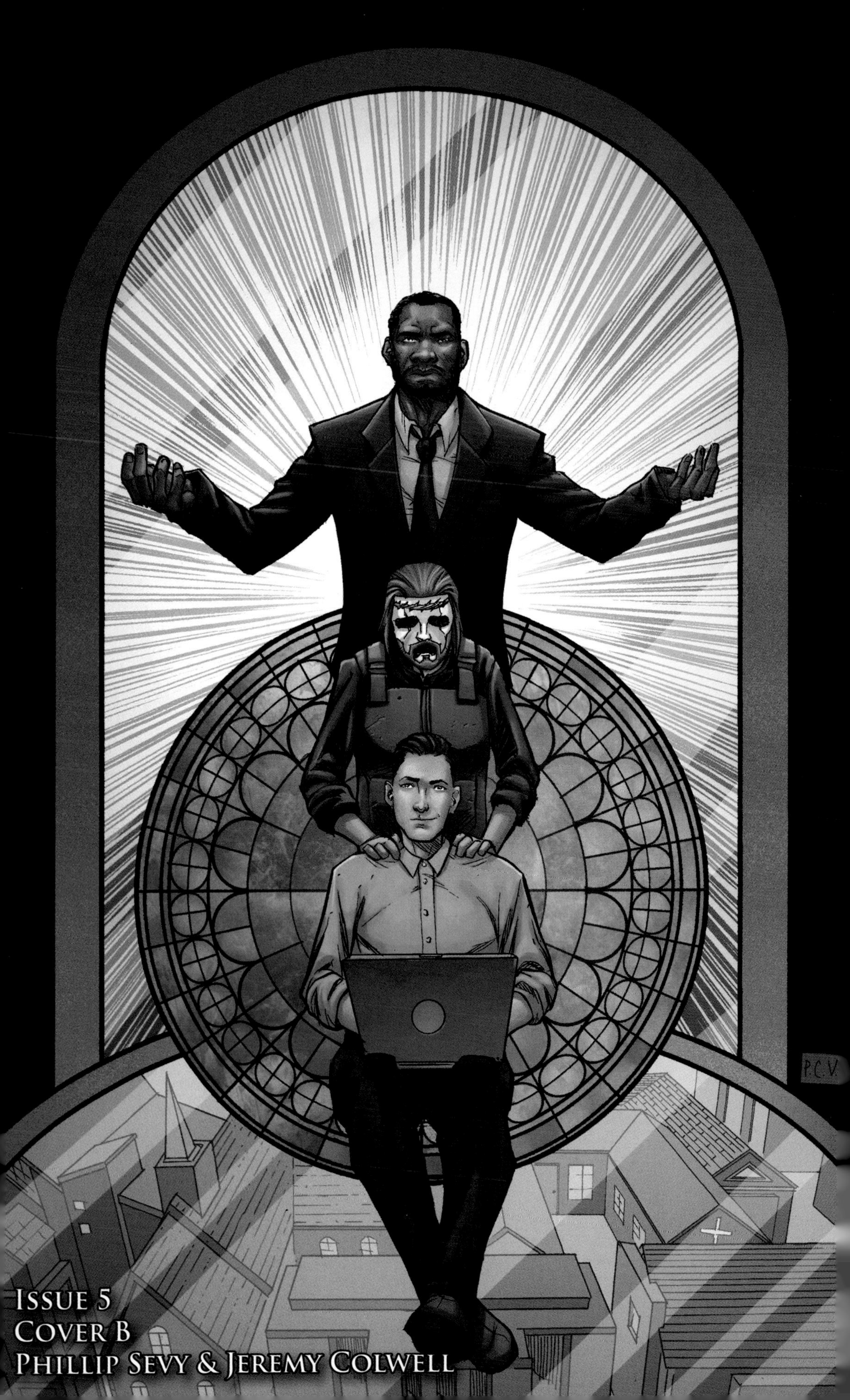
P.C.V.

Issue 5
Cover B
Phillip Sevy & Jeremy Colwell

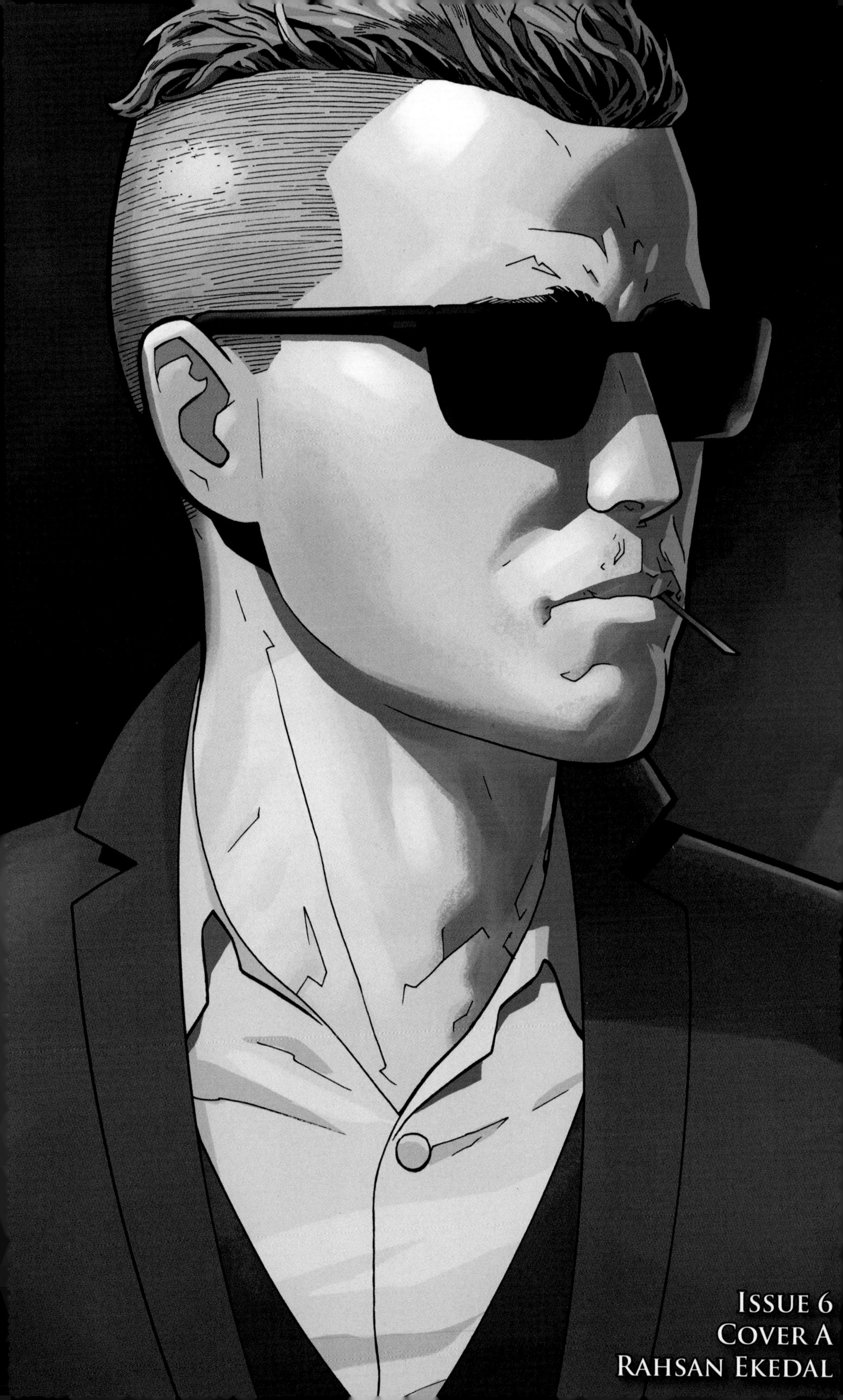

ISSUE 6
COVER A
RAHSAN EKEDAL

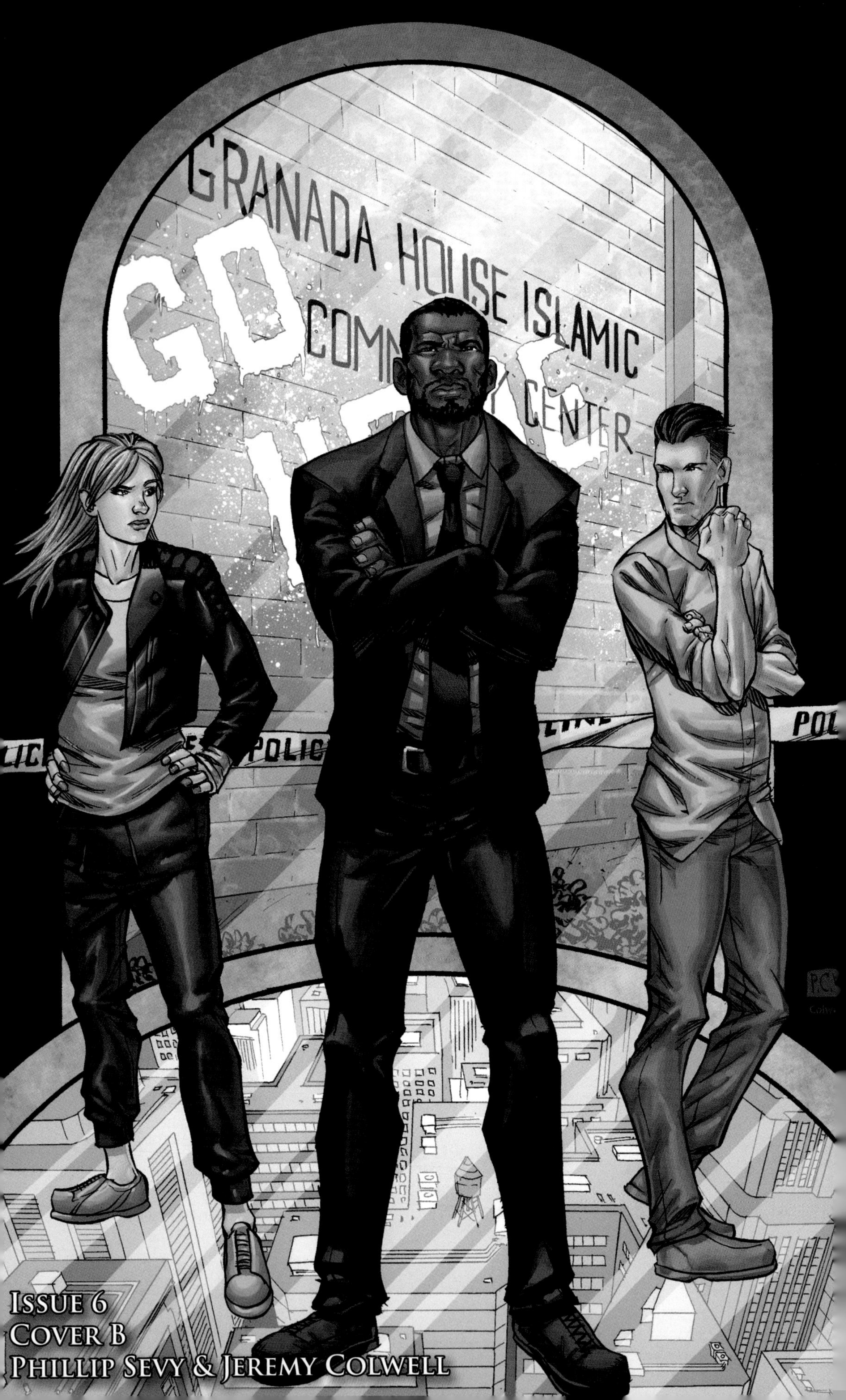
GRANADA HOUSE ISLAMIC
GO
Issue 6
Cover B
Phillip Sevy & Jeremy Colwell

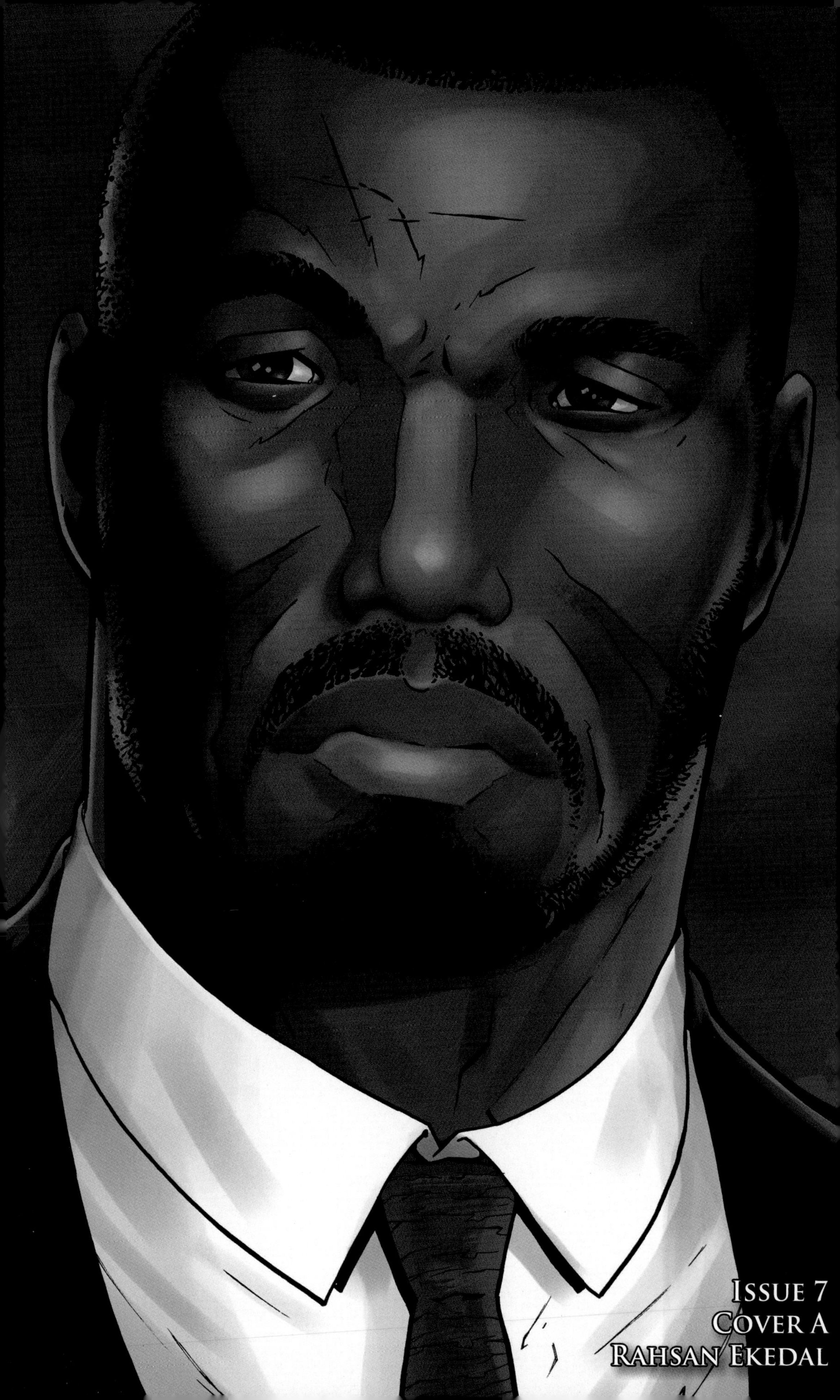
Issue 7
Cover A
Rahsan Ekedal

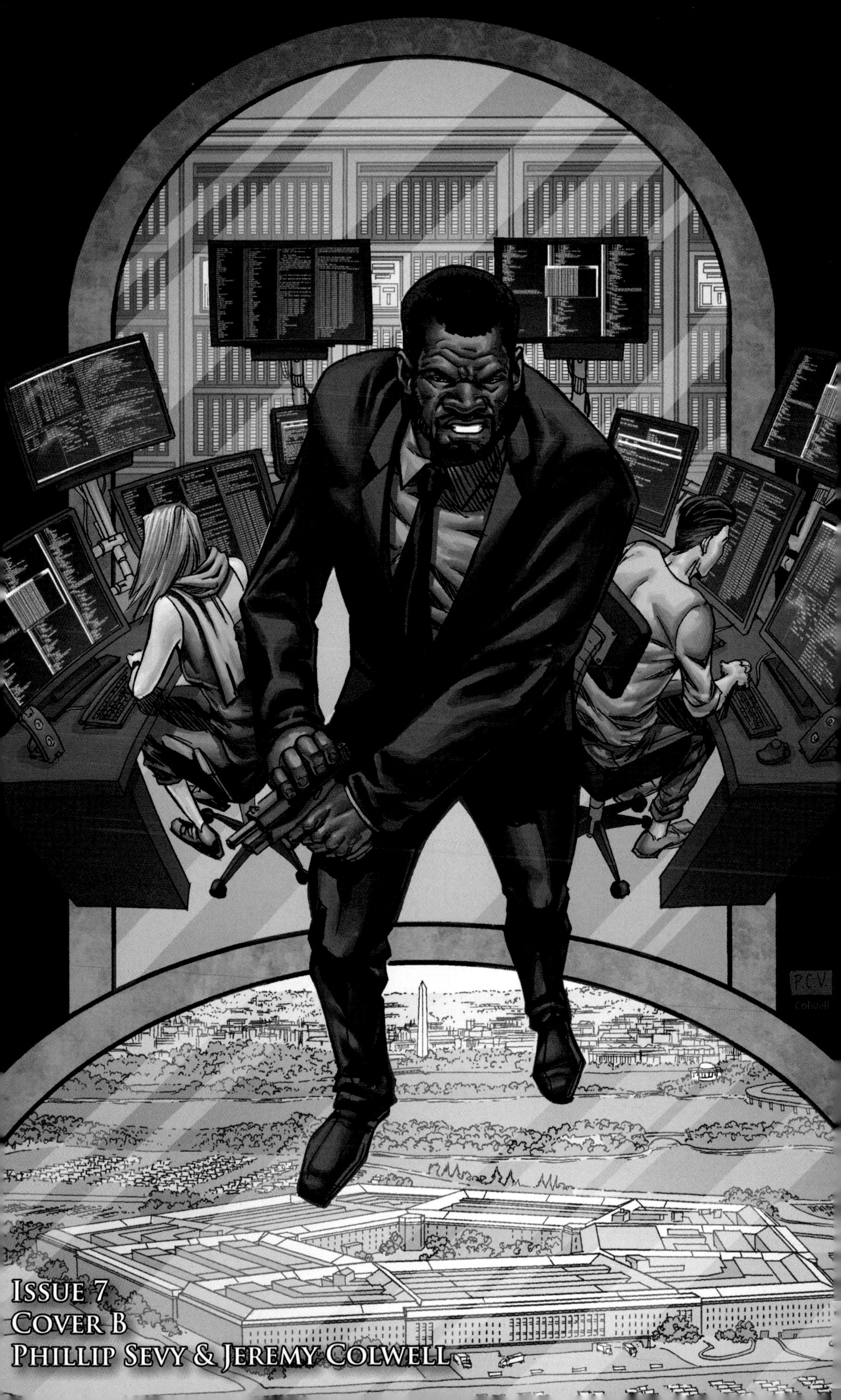
P.C.V.
Colwell

Issue 7
Cover B
Phillip Sevy & Jeremy Colwell

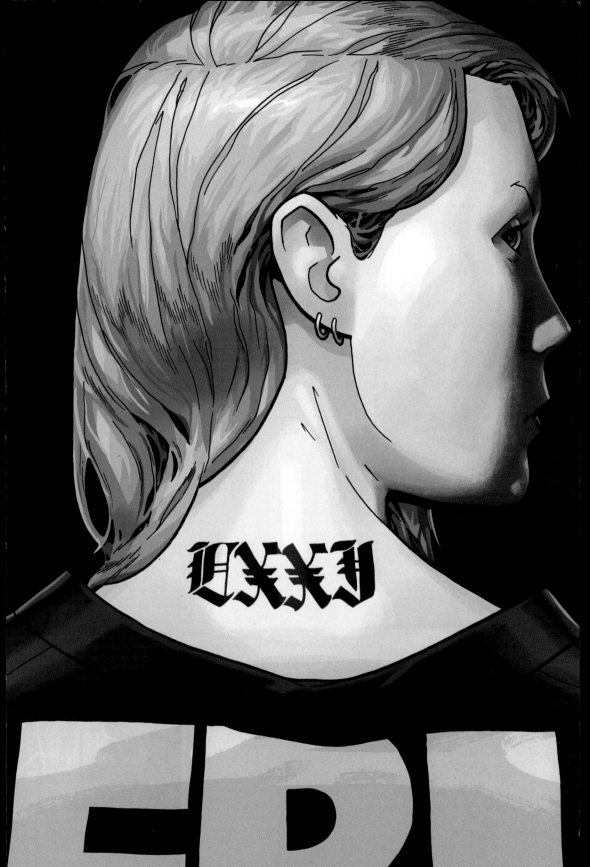

ISSUE 8
COVER A
RAHSAN EKEDAL

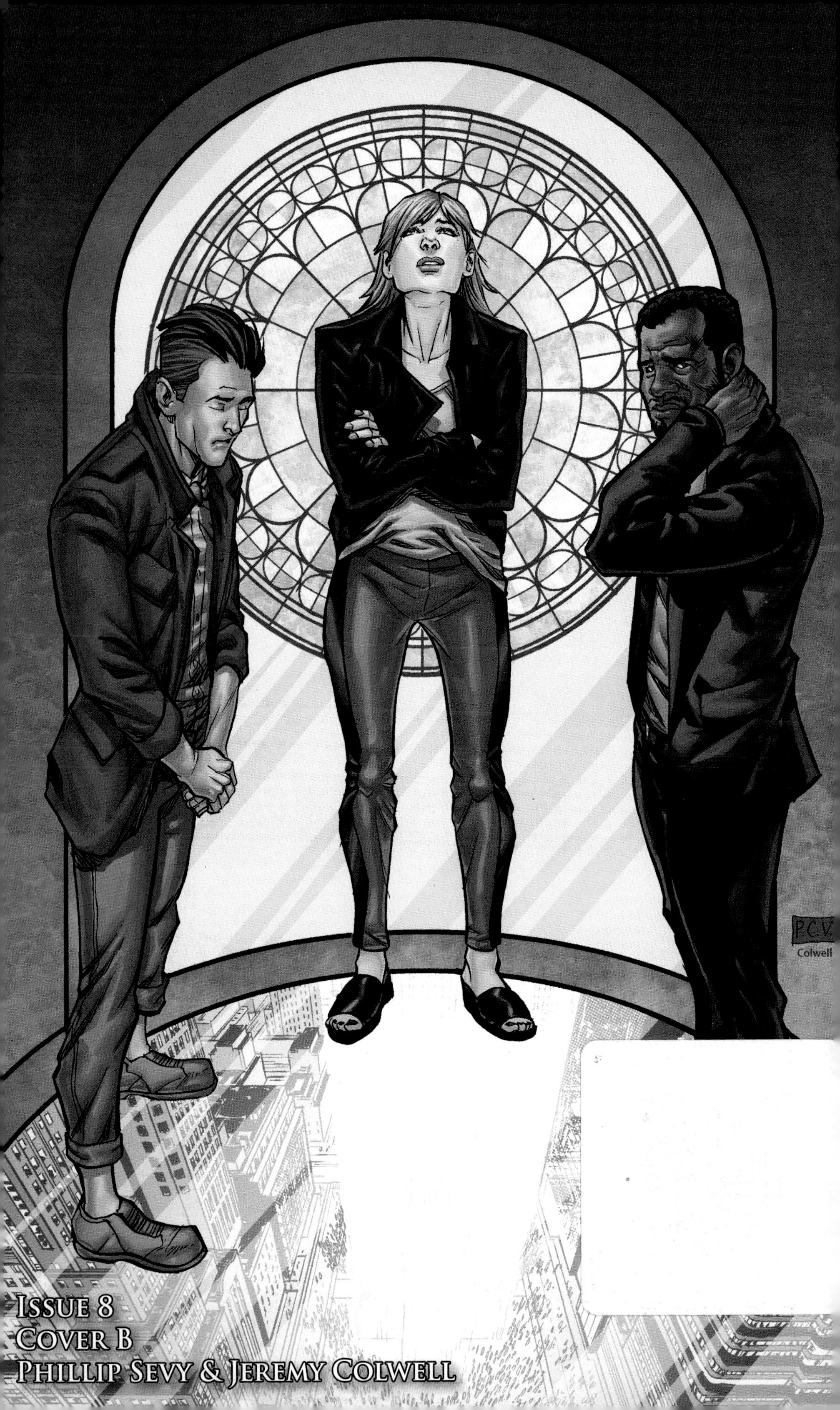
P.C.V.
Colwell

Issue 8
Cover B
Phillip Sevy & Jeremy Colwell